Can't Hide What's Inside

C. J. Heigelmann

COMMON FOLK PRESS

For information contact:

Email: cj@cjheigelmann.com

P.O. Box 801 Lexington, SC 29071-0801

https://www.MustReadCJ.com

ISBN: 978-0-9994898-2-6

First Edition: APRIL 2021

Table of Contents

CHAPTER 1

It was near dawn on a wintry January morning on the outskirts of Minneapolis. A pickup truck rolled through the quiet subdivision, disrupting the stillness and compacting the recent snowfall into the frozen asphalt. Despite being plowed two days before, new flurries now blanketed the road and covered the surrounding landscape.

The truck u-turned just short of a small house and parked with the engine running. A hooded man wearing a winter jacket stepped out and walked toward the driveway, nervously glancing at nearby homes. Feeling reassured that everyone was asleep, he looked at his wristwatch. It was 5:45 am; everyone would be rising soon. He convinced himself that this prank was long overdue and trotted up the steep driveway to the rear of the car.

Kneeling behind the trunk, he peered up at the front windows of the house. After making sure there was no movement, he plunged his hands into the embankment beside the driveway, cupping up handfuls of snow and packing them into the tailpipe. He filled the exhaust, pushing the powdery snow deeper until no more would fit. He patted the end of the exhaust and hastily brushed the area which he had disturbed. He thought it humorous as he trotted down the driveway toward the running truck.

Good luck starting your car. Payback is a bitch. Just like you. Have a late, great Monday morning, compliments of the Pack.

Shivering, he climbed into the warm truck and drove back to the primary road, a dog's bark rippling through the darkness after him.

***

At 7:00 am, the cell phone alarm sounded with Jim Carroll's music as 27-year-old Madison Sanders stretched her arms out beneath her goose-down comforter. She shunned the generic alarms on her phone. They dulled her motivation to start the day and were annoying. As always, she stayed still for five minutes, using the brief period before rising to set her daily intentions for the day, and establish a positive mood. She craved these private moments. She needed them. It was her time and space when no one else had set demands or expectations of her. She reminded herself that she was in control and responsible for her daily goals - and mindset. Her former therapist had drilled this mantra into her during several sessions.

Her current job was going well and, after a rough first three months, things had settled down. Her work life had finally transformed into a delicate routine of normality. She reflected on the day when she had nearly submitted her resignation to Human Resources. It seemed the only way to escape her hostile and sexist work environment. But that chapter was over, and she was relieved that the tumultuous episode had passed. Had it not been for her four-year-old son, Elijah, she wouldn't have given another minute of her life to the company and would have resigned soon after their arrival.

Elijah. The thought of him triggered her smile. He was her first and only child, and the light of her life. She sat on the edge of the bed for a minute and turned on the nightstand lamp, allowing her eyes to adjust to the brightness. After sorting through her emotional inventory and confirming a positive mindset, she energetically began her daily morning routine, despite having a cold.

She walked to Elijah's room and turned on the light. As usual, he didn't budge. So she took a moment to watch him sleep before sitting on the side of the bed and rubbing his back.

"Elijah, it's time to wake up, sweetie," she whispered.

He stirred, frowning with his eyes closed, and stretched his tiny limbs. Madison smiled, cherishing the sight of him rousing from slumber. She kept on tenderly massaging his back.

"Come on, let's go to the bathroom." She helped him down from his bed and led him over to the commode. "Lift the seat, remember?"

He raised the lid and relieved himself, splashing between the water of the outer rim, his indiscriminate overspray dousing outside the commode.

"No, Elijah put it in the water," she said, helping him to control his hand.

Although only four years old, he was doing well with potty training. She lifted him over the sink. There, he turned on the water, fumbling with the soap. After letting him down and giving him a hand towel, she spread toothpaste to his toothbrush and watched as he brushed his teeth. Elijah adapted well to the routine. His height was the only limitation. But he was becoming heavier every day, and she was now straining to hold him.

On the next payday, buy him a step stool. He's wearing you out.

After washing his face, she helped him get dressed, and they both went into the kitchen. She sat him on his booster seat on a kitchen chair and opened a cabinet door.

"What cereal would you like this morning? Honey Nut Cheerios or Captain Crunch?"

He stared at the boxes for a moment. "I want Cappy Crunch," he eventually said, pointing a chubby finger.

"Captain Crunch it is, sir!"

A minute later, she placed a bowl in front of him along with a cup of orange juice.

"Mommy will be right back." She left him eating, hurrying off to fix her hair and put on makeup before returning to the kitchen. She helped him down and he ran into the living room, plopping down in front of the television. She walked over and turned it to his favorite show on the Children's Network, The Funny Farm. She left the room and prepared her breakfast. Then she sat on the couch to eat.

"Ha, ha!" he laughed at the characters' on-screen antics as Madison chuckled at his amusement.

When she'd finished her breakfast, she glanced at the clock.

Get your butt moving!

She rushed into the kitchen to put the dish in the sink. Then, grabbing her jacket and car keys, she opened the front door. Instantly, an icy wind hit her, prickling her red cheeks and blowing her back. She scrunched up her face in disgust. She still hadn't got used to the long Minnesota winters, much preferring the warm drizzle of her hometown, Seattle. Shuffling through the snow, she clambered into her car and turned the key. But today, there was no throaty growl; instead, there was total and utter silence.

"Damn it!" she huffed.

The chill of the seat stung her buttocks, radiating cold through her thin dress. Shivering, her teeth chattering, she shakily turned the key again. The engine cranked over but wouldn't ignite. She repeatedly tried, her anxiety increasing with every passing second. She licked her chapped lips and clenched her teeth.

"You piece of shit car! You carried us across the country. Now start!"

But all her efforts were futile. Stopping, she closed her eyes and hugged the steering wheel. She needed a moment. "God, please don't let me be late to work again. Not today. I'm begging you."

She turned the key.

Rar – rar – rar – rar.

There was a loud pop, followed by intermittent sputtering.

"Yes! Thank you!"

She set the heat to maximum, checked the time, and rushed back inside.

After putting on Elijah's hat, coat and gloves, she carried him to the car and strapped him into his safety seat. The sunrise brightened the neighborhood, giving light to the passing students as they walked toward the school bus stop. She slipped inside the warm interior, instantly noticing the car was vibrating abnormally and didn't sound healthy at all.

That's just great! Now you have to take the car to a mechanic. What else could go wrong?

While backing down the driveway, she felt she'd forgotten something. She stopped and searched for her cell phone.

Where is it?

She fumbled through her handbag and probed her pockets.

Shit! It must be inside.

She drove back to the top of the drive and parked. There, she reset the emergency brake and left the car running, fearing that it might not start again.

She glanced in the rearview mirror. "Mommy will be right back, okay?"

Elijah gazed through the side window, seemingly oblivious to his frantic mother's mutterings. She raced back inside the house. After five minutes of frantic searching, she found her phone in the bathroom.

Why did you leave it in here?

Panting heavily and breathing through her mouth, she blew her stuffy nose and scampered back to the car. She climbed inside and peeked at Elijah, who was now asleep. Then, slowly, she backed down the slippery driveway. She blinked her eyes as they began to water, and then sting.

What's going on?

She couldn't smell anything or inhale through her congested nose, but her lungs were beginning to burn.

Something's wrong. What's happening to me?

Her vision grew cloudy, making it difficult to focus. By the time she reached the bottom of the driveway, her head was drooping and she was beginning to lose consciousness.

Get out of the car. Get Elijah out of this car.

She was confused, disorientated, and steered toward the curb to try to park, but fumbled the gear shift while pressing the brake. With her vision nearly gone, she reached for the key. Her fingers were numb, and she was beginning to panic.

Roll the windows down and get Elijah out!

She grasped at the door panel, haphazardly stabbing at the window switches until she felt a sudden jolt. The car had hit the lip of the curb. Her hand found the gearshift, and she instinctively pushed it forward into Park. She hadn't realized the window locks were engaged and now couldn't locate the switch.

Get out. Get Elijah. The door. Open the door!

Blindly, she felt for the handle.

Please. Plea...

The door flung open and her unconscious body tumbled headfirst onto the frozen asphalt.

A student, standing at the bus stop, yelled, "Hey! Look at that lady!"

"What's wrong with her?" asked another.

Some of the children meandered towards the car, while a passing neighbor who was leaving for work slowed down, saw Madison on the ground, and stopped.

He got out and ran over to the motionless body lying face down in the road. He was about to kneel beside her when he noticed Elijah in the backseat. He reached inside and turned off the car, gagging from the potent smell of the exhaust fumes flowing out. Without hesitation, he opened the rear door, unbuckled Elijah, and pulled him out. Then he called 911.

After speaking with the operator, the military veteran pocketed his phone and resorted to his combat first aid training, checking for breath and pulse. Elijah wasn't breathing, so he began CPR, oblivious to the students gathered around him.

The sirens of the ambulance drew closer as he checked for Elijah's vitals. None were present. The paramedics arrived and continued resuscitation, deploying oxygen and a defibrillator. But Elijah would not revive. He was dead.

"What's wrong with him? Is he sleeping?" a boy asked.

The tearful neighbor stood up. "Yes," he choked. "He's asleep. All you kids, please go back to the bus stop."

They sauntered off, chatting excitedly and peeking back.

The horrific events which transpired would set in motion an unrelenting wave of grief and guilt for Madison. But, unbeknown to her, it would be the catalyst to set her soul on fire, revealing the unknown parts of her inner being and bringing to light the dark secrets of her family. Those unspeakable things withheld from her knowledge had already shaped her future, and would soon reveal what she carried inside. This is her story.

CHAPTER 2

3 Months Earlier

It was 9:05 a.m. on Monday as a car raced into the corporate office parking lot at the Traxtonite Corporation and skidded to a stop. Hoping to go unnoticed, an office staff employee rushed inside. Depending on who you were in the executive staff pecking order and what office clique you associated with, even excessive tardiness was overlooked. That was true on the factory wall's corporate side, where white-collar offices and conference rooms abounded.

The same did not hold true on the other side of the wall at Traxtonite's primary manufacturing facility located outside Minneapolis, Minnesota. As a lead producer of Industrial Mining equipment, the plant operated twenty-four hours a day, shutting down only for Christmas. For the hourly employees, being tardy three times within a calendar year would merit disciplinary action up to and including termination.

Despite the misapplication of equal standards for hourly and salaried employees, the company operated efficiently, and net profits had doubled over the last three years. Plans for rapid expansion into other related markets were being discussed in the boardroom. Additional administrative and project-related employment slots were always opening up and were filled by new personnel or existing tenured employees who opted to transfer to new locations.

Inside his office, Ron Tatum, the Assistant Director of Internal Operations, sat alone at his desk, focusing on his computer screen. In twenty minutes, the middle-aged office manager would conduct the regularly scheduled Monday morning office meeting in front of twenty subordinates, soon to be twenty-one. He looked at his watch and glanced at the office door, expecting the recent transfer from the company's Seattle facility to enter. He hadn't met her in person and, strangely enough, he had no input concerning her re-assignment. This decision came down via the Human Resources Department, with upper-level management approval, further stirring his deviant curiosity.

What could be her story? Maybe she was a sex toy for her former boss, but the affair became volatile, too close for comfort. He could have offered her a bone, hence a transfer. Or maybe she just couldn't get along with the other chicks in her department. She was only 27 years old, and most of those young, idealistic chicks fresh out of college were headstrong and impetuous. They walk around thinking that they are entitled. Like the world owed them something. Especially the beautiful ones, like her. Bitches. I'll break her in correctly, just like the rest.

His unscrupulous and misogynistic thought patterns embodied the unofficial and close-knit office fraternity he had created and named, the Wolf Pack. Established five years earlier, the group's name, along with the objects of their appetites, left little to the imagination for the curious-minded. But if the office walls could speak, they would tell the same repetitive, broken-hearted tales from dozens of current and former female employees, confessing how they were singled out from the herd and devoured by members of the Pack.

"What's up, Ron?" Conor asked, as he walked into the office.

Ron looked up.

Conor was the epitome of tall, dark-haired and handsome. The 30-year old graphic designer who joined the Pack, did so out of boredom and friendly competition more than any other reason. It was something for him to do in between girlfriends. To him, it was all in good fun, and over the years, he'd convinced himself of it. In his mind, he wasn't specifically out to hurt any woman, or make any enemies. All parties involved were mature adults. He believed women should know the apparent outcomes of office dating and, if they didn't, their ignorance wasn't excused.

"Morning Conor. Come check this out."

He walked behind Ron's desk.

"I found some personal photos of the new transfer, Madison Sanders." He enlarged her photo. "This chick barely uses social media, except for LinkedIn. Can you believe that shit? But I did find some great photos of her, my god."

Conor bent forward to get a closer look.

"Wow, she's hot, and definitely has a model's body. Look at those sexy blue eyes."

Just then, Terrance and Luis from the IT department marched in and sat down. Both were in their late twenties, and began working at Traxtonite on the same day, five years prior. They shared many of the same qualities, which was the primary reason they gained membership in the Pack. Ron had spent weeks evaluating the two minority candidates during their probation hiring period, noticing their likability among the female staff.

Terrance was African-American, a baby-faced, good-looking charmer who had a unique sense of style and charisma. To Ron's surprise, the office rumor mill reported Terrance's multiple conquests of the female staff, all within his first 90 days. Rather than have Terrance single-handedly decimate the herd, Ron prudently invited him into the newfound clique. There were rules to be followed, and Terrance needed a leash. Ron's message to the Pack was, "If we organize, there's enough ass in this office for everyone to pass around."

Luis typified the quintessential Latin lover. What he lacked in height, he made up for with seductive swagger and machismo, all the while appearing to be the man who a woman might bring home to meet her parents. Luis's Spanish accent, paired with his soft-spoken tone, gave the Wolf Pack an international and exotic flavor. Luis accepted his invitation with pride. Although married now and not actively hunting with the Pack, he continued to stay current on the group's exploits, providing them information whenever they requested it. To his credit, he consistently warned his comrades of the potential dangers of their escapades. Despite his newfound monogamous lifestyle, they continued to accept him personally, socializing with him after work and validating his place within the group. They considered him retired—a Hall of Fame inductee of sorts.

"What are y'all looking at?" Terrance asked.

Ron grinned. "Fresh meat to eat."

Terrance and Luis glanced at each other; then walked over to see.

Luis covered his mouth.

Terrance's eyes widened. "Dang, she is so fine. She's got that sexy, short French hairstyle and a tight body to match. I've got to get with that."

"Muy bonita!" Luis exclaimed. "She's a real looker."

Ron enlarged another photo.

Ron pointed at the monitor. "Look at that ass. Do you see that? That is primo, grade A butt cheeks. Am I the only one who feels that way? It doesn't matter anyway; I'm going for it. Consider yourselves on notice."

"I'm all in, too," Terrance told them, returning to his seat.

Conor walked over to the door. "I'm game, but you two can try and nail her first. I'm in no hurry. It's best to play the long game. I'll see you guys at the meeting. I got to take a leak."

"Okay uber playboy," Ron said. "Noted. But hold on, that makes three of us in the hunt." He looked at Luis. "Well?"

Luis shook his head. "Na, I'm out. I've told all of you before, I'm married now and can't be doing that shit. You fools keep jeopardizing your relationships for a piece of ass. I don't get it."

Ron postured. "I remember the days when you were always game. In fact, wasn't your wife, Rita, one of the hunted? Yes, I believe so. But even though you broke the cardinal rule and fell in love with her, we're all happy that it worked out for you. How about you keep your criticisms to yourself, boy scout?"

Luis stood up and saluted. "Good luck, guys. Let me know when you'll be appearing on the next episode of Divorce Court."

Terrance shook his head and frowned. "Look man, Conor and I live with our girlfriends, but we aren't married. You keep forgetting, amigo."

"What's the difference? You both live together and play husband and wife. Don't risk it, I'm telling you," Luis warned.

"Luis, take that sentimental bullshit somewhere else," Terrance said. "Go audit the network or something. Make yourself useful."

Luis nodded and walked out, presenting the room with his middle finger as he went.

Ron stood up. "Listen up, guys, the standard rules apply. When hunting Ms. Sanders, no badmouthing any other members. And Terrance, no remote breaking her computer then showing up to fix it. That's considered an unfair IT technician advantage." Ron looked at Conor, who nodded his head and smirked at Terrance.

Terrance frowned. "What about Conor, the guy who does nothing all day and can walk anywhere, anytime, for any reason? That's not fair. Come on, Ron, that's bullshit. He should be banned from this hunt."

Conor laughed. "I told you guys, I'll give you a head start before I move in on her and seal the deal. For the first two weeks, you both can work on her, unless she throws herself at me. Until then, you both have to work out first dibs among yourselves." He walked out, leaving Ron and Terrance alone.

"When is she coming in?" Terrance asked.

"I expected her to report to me already. Still, no word yet. I suppose she'll be here this afternoon."

"Cool. May the best player win."

They bumped fists. Then Ron gathered up his notepad and swaggered off to the conference room to begin the meeting.

***

The noisy conference room was packed as Ron walked in and stood at the podium.

"Good morning! I hope everyone is feeling refreshed from the weekend and ready to get back to work. Just a note, Charles from Purchasing called in sick today and won't be here. Brittany will handle questions concerning his project list, so please direct any inquiries to her."

The next thirty minutes of the meeting comprised a power-point presentation that detailed project status progress, department budget tracking, followed by a discussion of selected memos from corporate headquarters. The information in the meeting was vaguely informative but unnecessary. It was an aspect of the company's communication initiative, and followed a uniform protocol across all administrative and executive departments. Had the lighting in the room been any dimmer, several of the staff would have nodded off to sleep, being lulled by Ron's monotone voice along with boredom. After forty minutes, the meeting ended.

"All right, that concludes our beloved Monday morning get-together. Does anyone have questions, comments or concerns?" Ron asked.

Trina, who worked in finance, raised her hand. "When are you going to fill Margaret's position in marketing? There are several purchase order requisitions in the system that she submitted and already issued. They've been sitting stagnate for over thirty days and will have to be re-issued if they aren't paid this week."

"That is a significant question, Trina! I intended to introduce Margaret's replacement this morning, but she hasn't reported in yet. She's a transfer from the Seattle facility and..." Ron paused as the door opened, and a young woman slipped into the room. He immediately recognized her.

"Excuse me, miss, what's your name?"

Humbled to be the center of attention, she blushed. "Sir, I'm Madison Sanders, from Seattle. I apologize for being late. I got turned around and lost trying to get here. My GPS was wrong, again."

The room filled with chuckles.

"I thought that might be you, Madison. I'm Ron Tatum, your point of contact. Please, come to the front so I can introduce you to the team."

Nervously, she walked through the group and shook his hand. Then, trying her best to look confident, she stood beside him.

"Everyone, Madison is a graduate of Washington State University holding her B.S. in Business Administration and an M.S. in Digital Marketing. She comes to us highly recommended. Please, I want everyone to welcome her."

He began the applause, and everyone stood up. Some clapped and welcomed her to the group, while others cheered the ending of the meeting. The warm response took Madison by surprise, reducing her anxiety. She was a classic introvert who didn't like crowds or being the center of attention. Half of the staff left the conference room, while the remaining employees lined up to introduce themselves.

Ron stood just behind her, smiling, keeping one eye on the unfolding meet and greet and his other eye below her waistline. He put his hand on her shoulder and whispered in her ear. "Madison, I've got to run, but stop by my office later when you get a chance."

She smiled. "Yes, sir. I will."

"You're going to love working here. I can sense significant opportunities coming your way. Huge ones." He winked and strutted away.

The conference room was almost empty when someone tapped Madison on the shoulder.

"Hey, I'm Brittany, from the Purchasing Department. How do you like Minneapolis so far?"

"It's nice to meet you, Brittany. I haven't had a chance to see or do anything yet. I've been super busy moving in and trying to get settled."

"It will take some time. Are you renting or buying?"

"I leased a small two-bedroom house in New Hope for me and my son, Elijah. That's one reason I was late today. I had to fight traffic and drop him off at daycare. Then I got lost. Late on my first day. A great first impression."

"Don't worry about being late; it's understandable. So, you have a baby boy. Aww, I love the name Elijah. How old is he?"

Madison smiled. "He's four years old, going on ten. My little buttercup."

"Bless his heart. I have a fourteen-year-old princess at home, and girl, let me tell you something, if you ever have a daughter, get ready to pull your hair out. Little Miss Ayana is a full-blown diva. Do you hear me?"

Madison laughed. "I can imagine."

"Listen, I won't keep you. I know you have things to do, but if you ever want to eat lunch together or chat, let me know."

"I'd like that. How about lunch today?"

"That sounds good," she answered. "I'll find you around noon." And, with that, she left.

Madison stood there alone, looking around the empty conference room.

This is a fresh beginning, Maddy. Focus on constructive thoughts and positive energy. You can do it. You can make it on your own.

She turned off the lights and left.

***

Ron was sitting at his desk when he heard a knock. "Yes?" he called.

Terrance and Conor walked in, closing the door behind them.

"She looks even better than her photos," Terrance remarked while rubbing his hands together. "She has got to be the sexiest female in the office. We might as well give her that award and I'll be the first to nominate her."

Conor sat down. "You're right, man. Usually, women's online photos look way better than the actual person, but in this case, they don't do her justice."

Ron licked his lips. "I know. It's almost too good to be true. To be honest, I think I can get her within two or three weeks."

"Why is that?" Terrance asked.

Ron smirked. "Let's just say I have a gut feeling about this one. I could sense her tremble when I put my arm around her. Like, a slight shudder, a submissive signal. She kind of reminds me of Margaret in that aspect. I hated that she left, but at least I nailed her twice."

"Ha. It's not as though you didn't give her a little push," Conor said.

"What do you mean by that?"

"You smothered her man. The poor woman couldn't even chat with anyone else without you pulling her away. You can't control a grown woman like that. I wasn't surprised that she left."

"Ah, I sense jealousy, Conor," Ron answered with a grin. "Jealousy leads to the dark side. She was an adult and knew what she was doing. I didn't force her. Besides, she didn't have many friends here anyway, and was seriously anti-social if you ask me."

Terrance walked over to the door. "She wasn't anti-social. She was tired of hearing you chastising her behind closed doors like you were her dad."

Ron pointed at the door. "Why don't you go find Luis and do some work. And yes, I keep my conquests isolated from the likes of you two. I don't like to share."

Terrance nodded. "Whatever, bro." And, without another word, he left.

"Time out." Conor signaled. "On another note, do you want to meet up after work for some drinks at the Tap Room?"

"I would, but can't. I need to save all my socializing time slots for Madison. It's been a few months since the wife and I had our last big falling out, so I don't want to waste my sneak time. You should know that. Or are you trying to throw me off my game plan, buddy?"

"Don't be paranoid. I wanted an excuse not to watch another stupid Lifetime movie tonight with Heather. Terrance and Luis can't go either. It's no big deal. I was thinking about what Luis said, and he has a point. You're married, bro, and you have almost been caught dipping your stick a few times. Kathy is a savvy lady. How you keep avoiding her detection is beyond me."

Ron reclined in his chair with his hands cupped behind his head. "It's easy, young Jedi, when you're a white guy married to a black woman. Kathy thinks that I'm only attracted to black women, and besides Brittany, who she knows and likes, there aren't any other black women working in the office. Kathy never suspects me of being naughty when I tell her that I'm working late. It's as simple as that. Besides, she trusts me."

"If you say so. You are a bold one. I'll give you that."

"You know the saying. Fortune favors the bold."

***

As noon approached, Steve Hyman, the Human Resource Manager, was busy working at his desk when he saw Madison standing in the doorway.

"Hello Madison, come on in."

She entered, handed him a manila folder, and sat down. "I've finished completing the state health insurance forms, my direct deposit, and my relocation reimbursement paperwork. Everything should be in order."

He opened the folder and checked through the contents.

"Thanks. Everything looks good." He closed the folder and removed his glasses. "So, tell me, how is everything going with you? Is there anything I can help you with?"

"I'm doing fine. I'm still getting adjusted. It will take some time to become familiar with my new surroundings and my co-workers. I don't need anything at the moment. I'm good to go."

"You're right, and it will take time. Remember, I have an open-door policy. If you need anything or have any issues, please let me know. You're already an asset to this team, with a good reputation. We need more solid professionals like yourself in that department. Your work ethic and contributions to Traxtonite precede you, and hopefully some of that mojo will rub off on others. Too many of the staff have become complacent in their roles and responsibilities over time."

"I hope to live up to your expectations. So far, everyone has been friendly to me. The work environment feels positive."

"You have an outstanding attitude." He looked at his watch. "It's lunchtime. How time flies when you're having fun."

There was a knock at the door. They turned to see Brittany standing in the doorway.

"Hello, Brittany. What can I do for you?" he asked.

"Hey, Steve. I'm here to escort Madison to lunch."

"Very good." He looked at Madison. "Brittany is the perfect person to show you the ropes around here. You can learn a lot from her."

"Are you ready, Madison, or should I come back?"

"I'm ready now, thanks. See you later, Mr. Hyman."

"Call me Steve, please, and enjoy your lunch."

They left and walked over to the breakroom.

"I didn't bring any lunch today. Where are we planning on going?" Madison asked.

"There are a few places within fifteen minutes of here, but I brought lasagna in today. I made it last night, and there's enough for two to share if you fancy it. Also, we have vending machines with snacks and drinks in the breakroom. It's up to you. What do you want to do?"

"I love lasagna, if you don't mind."

Brittany smiled and opened the door to the bustling breakroom. "I hope you love mine."

Thirty minutes later, when the lunchroom had calmed down, Madison and Brittany began sharing personal details about each other's life. The newly formed bond between the two of them was evident, marked by the natural ease of conversation and mutual pleasantry of each other's company.

"I'm sorry, Brittany. I know we just met today, but I feel like we've known each other for years," Madison confessed.

"Girl, I was thinking the same thing. We've had so many of the same experiences, both good and bad. From being single mothers with deadbeat boyfriends, to relocating for the company, and everything in between. We might as well be sisters."

Madison smirked, then frowned.

"What's wrong, Madison?"

Madison shook her head and looked away. Her eyes watered, and she carefully blotted them with a napkin.

"Nothing. Sometimes I still get choked up when I think about Tony disappearing when I was pregnant."

Brittany reached across the table and patted her arm. "I understand. I do. It depressed me for months after Carlos deserted us. But eventually, I made it through. Sometimes I think if that had never happened,

I would have never met my fiancé, Trent. It's like they say, everything happens for a reason."

"Well, I was more than moderately depressed. If I share something with you, do you promise not to tell anyone? I mean, this is for your ears only.

"Your secret is safe with me. You have my word."

"After I told him I was pregnant, and he disappeared…I had a nervous breakdown. The questions and the anguish that I held inside practically drove me insane, and almost caused me to miscarry Elijah. If it weren't for Traxtonite allowing me time off from my college internment contract for treatment, I would have been fired, and never hired back after graduation. To this day, no one else knows why I had to take those months off from work, except for you."

"And no one will ever know. My lips are sealed, Madison." Brittany shrugged. "Men can be such cold-hearted bastards. But hey, look around, you're in a new place now. Trust me, there is a marvelous man out there, somewhere, who is waiting just for you."

"Thanks, Brittany."

A woman stopped at their table and sat down.

"Hi Brittany," she said while reaching over to shake Madison's hand. "Hello Madison, I'm Trina Berg. It's nice to meet you."

"Hello, Trina."

"Hey, Trina," Brittany mumbled. "What's going on with you today?"

"Oh, nothing much. I'm ready to get off work and have a drink, and that's why I stopped by. Madison, would you like to join me and some of the other girls after work for happy hour? We're planning to go to the

Tap Room in downtown Minneapolis. I would ask Brittany, but I know she won't come."

Madison glanced at Brittany, who was looking away.

"Thanks, Trina, but I can't. I have to pick up my little boy from day-care after work. I'd like a raincheck though. It would be fun to go out with the girls and have a drink. Maybe another time?"

"Sure, just let me know. I'll bring you up to speed on all the hot pros-pects around here. We have our share of cuties if you haven't already noticed."

Brittany held up her hand. "All right Ms. Trina, don't get Madison tangled up in any office affairs. She's just starting here and doesn't need her reputation spoiled by hanging out with the wrong crowd. I'm just saying."

Trina rolled her eyes and stood up.

"Uh, Brittany, don't hate because you're engaged. Once upon a time, you hung out with the 'wrong crowd' yourself, so let's not be hypocritical. I'm just saying." She winked at Madison. "I'll talk to you later, ciao."

Brittany glared at the other woman as she walked off. Then she turned back to Madison. "Yeah, we used to go to Happy Hour back in the day, but she was whoring around then, just like she is now. Anyway, there's nothing wrong with having a few drinks, but I would hate for you to do something that you might regret later."

"Stop. You don't need to explain any of that to me. I'm a big girl, and I can already see what Trina is about. I'm not interested. There has been no one since Tony, and I'm not in any rush to let a man into my life, or Elijah's."

"It sounds like you got your head screwed on right," Brittany said with an approving nod.

"Besides, you and I can have our own girls' night out, right?"

"You know it, sis. We are gonna do our thing."

They giggled and high-fived each other.

***

It was 4 p.m. and the end of the workday for most of the front office employees as they filed out the front entrance and into the parking lot. Madison wasted no time and was among the first to leave, rushing to pick up Elijah from daycare. She prayed that his first day among strangers was as good as hers. He was a small child who lacked the coping skills to navigate an unfamiliar environment, similar to those which she had yet to master as an adult. Being a bi-racial child with an African American father gave her reason for further apprehension.

Would the other kids accept him?

She could only hope for the best. The drive to the daycare center lasted twenty minutes in moderate traffic, and shortly after, she arrived, parking in front. She walked toward the entrance, and the front door opened. Mrs. McGee, the daycare manager, walked out to meet her.

"Hello, Ms. Sanders. I hope the traffic wasn't too terrible for you."

"No, the traffic was fine, but I'm out of sorts thinking about Elijah. How did he do today?"

Mrs. McGee smiled. "Elijah is wonderful. He didn't cry and wasn't shy at all. He made himself a few new friends."

Madison sighed. "I am so relieved, thank you. Did he eat?"

"Yes, he ate his lunch and his snack. He is extremely well-behaved and a joy to have. Let me get him for you."

A minute later, she returned with Elijah.

"Mommy!" he shouted, running up to her and wrapping his arms around her hips. She bent over and hugged him, kissing the top of his head.

"Mommy missed you so much. Did you have fun today?"

Elijah looked nodded. "Yeah."

"Good. Now tell Mrs. McGee thank you and goodbye."

Elijah turned around. "Thank you, Miss Mickey, bye."

The woman chuckled. "Ms. Sanders, next time, just pull up and park. We will bring him out to you."

"Will do, and thanks again."

"You're very welcome. And thank you for choosing us with the care of your precious child. I give Elijah less than a week, and he will be able to pronounce my name. But to tell you the truth, I'd rather have the children fumble it. It's adorable. Goodbye, drive safe, and we'll see you both tomorrow."

They walked over to the car and climbed in. Madison secured her son's safety seat. Then she wound down her window and called out, "Take care, Miss Mickey."

The daycare manager laughed and waved as they drove away.

The trip home took thirty minutes, but Madison didn't mind. Elijah was back in her care now, and the remnants of her anxiety had dissipated. He was her antidote, filling the emotional void of her heart. Her deepest desire in life was to love and to be loved unconditionally. She had experienced no purer devotion than that between herself and her child. Those feelings spurred thoughts of her childhood, of her now-deceased father. Before her son was born, he was the standard-bearer and her solitary measure of what a loving bond should be. Sadly, he passed away when Madison was not much older than Elijah. As she drove, she remembered how she had woken up in the night and wandered into the living room. There, she'd seen him sitting in his recliner, wearing a mask. Being a small child, she remembered being puzzled, thinking that it must be Halloween, but it wasn't. That was the last thing she recalled of that night.

Daddy. I'll never forget you.

He'd been such a jokester and so much fun. He'd loved her and always made sure she knew it. In return, she'd loved him with all her heart, and still did.

Madison remembered that when she woke the following morning, he wasn't home. It was a Saturday. He was always home on Saturday and Sunday mornings. Then her mother, Elizabeth, sat her down in the kitchen and told her. "Your father is in heaven now, Madison. He won't be coming back." Madison didn't know the details of his death, only that her daddy was gone forever. As a child, she often wondered about that word.

How long is forever?

A car horn blew. Madison's heart raced, and her eyes watered, so she deployed the techniques that she learned during past therapy sessions to redirect her thoughts.

You know this is how it all begins. Take action.

She turned on the radio. A familiar tune was playing, a song both her and Elijah knew. So she turned up the volume and glanced in the rearview mirror.

"Sing with me, Elijah. Who let the dogs out! Woof, woof, woof! Who let the dogs out!"

He raised his arms. "Who let the bog down! Oof, oof, oof! Who let the bog down!"

They alternated verses until the song ended, and Elijah threw his arms up.

"Yay!"

She glanced at him in the mirror, then at her reflection. Her tears were dry, and her smile had returned. She knew that the love they shared had made her whole once again. *What would I ever do without him*, she thought.

CHAPTER 3

T he following week, Madison was focused in the workplace, trying to become productive, efficient and comfortable with the unfamiliar environment. She was happy with her performance, feeling a sense of satisfaction with her contributions to the department. Beginning a new job was hard enough but transferring could be substantially more difficult. She knew from experience that managerial expectations did not always align with a job title's reality, and personal office dynamics could add further complications. Madison witnessed that specific scenario while working in Seattle. As she attempted to navigate the various groups and cliques, the personal and company politics can become a virtual minefield of confrontations, disagreements, and feelings of resentment. She wasn't alone. Other peers faced the same challenges, both male and female. But being a woman in the workplace brought its exclusive perils—specifically, the abhorrent practice of sexual harassment. The Traxtonite Corporation would never publicly condone or promote such egregious activity within their company ranks. After settling several lawsuits throughout the years and no proactive follow-up investigations into the individual office cultures that generated the occurrences, the company accepted the infractions by default through its silence and inactivity. Madison hadn't realized it yet, but she had already become the next prime target.

She sat at her desk inside her cubicle with goosebumps on her arms. She couldn't understand why Ron kept the office air temperature set to 65°F when it was freezing outside.

I need to bring a sweater from now on, she thought. This is ridiculous.

Her nipples felt sore, hardening from the frigidity. She sipped her coffee with her arms crossed, checking her work. She finally completed the SWOT analysis report tasked by Ron and hoped that he would stop asking about it. He was irritating and constantly interrupting her. She could smell his overwhelming cologne from across the office space, and it gave her a headache.

"Madison!"

She peeked over the cubicle partition and saw Ron standing in the doorway of his office.

"Yes?" She hated him calling out names from across the room. He did it to everyone. It was a mark of laziness and an indication of narcissism.

He should walk over to her cubicle and address her as a professional. He has to know that.

"I'm still waiting on that SWOT report. How are you coming along with it?"

"I just finished it."

"Well, why didn't you bring it to my office? I need to review it. Come on, let's go, sweetie. You know that I've been waiting for it, and I don't like to wait."

He strode back into his office and closed the door.

Madison huffed, set down her coffee, and gathered up the report. She navigated past her coworkers and through the maze of cubicles to his office. When she went in, he was standing with his arms crossed, leaning back on his desk. She handed him the report. He glanced through the first few pages. "Close the door. You're letting all the heat out, darling."

As she turned around to close it, he stared at her body, inspecting every contour and curve beneath her dress. When she turned around, he focused back on the report. Finally, Madison mustered up the courage to ask the nagging question that had bothered her all week.

"Ron, why is your office warm, but the main office is freezing? It's 65 degrees out there."

He raised his eyebrows and smirked. "My office is warm because I'm so hot. You know, I give off a lot of heat," he winked at her, "or so I've been told."

Madison was unaffected by his comments and remained expressionless. Realizing that his attempt at candor had failed miserably, he reverted to his ordinary chauvinistic approach.

"Well, the guys don't care, but most of you women can't seem to agree on a particular temperature setting. Some like it warm, and others want it cold. Women are going through menopause, pre-menopause, and let's not forget the infamous menstrual cycle, which reduces iron levels in the bloodstream. Did you know that? Low iron can make a woman feel cold. So rather than argue about it, I chose 65 degrees. It keeps the gals moving and keeps them perky."

"Uh, perky? What does that mean?"

He set down the report and stared at her.

"Have a seat, Madison."

She sat down, waiting for him to respond to her question. But he didn't. Instead, he continued to gawk at her. She didn't like where she was sitting. Not because he was making her feel uncomfortable with his silence, but because she was eye-level with his crotch, only a few feet away. She realized from his intrusive posture that this might be a setup of sorts. Telling her to sit down and looming over her while wearing ridiculously tight slacks was his attempt to advertise the bulge inside his pants. This was no coincidence. At that moment, she realized what kind of predator that he indeed was. Regardless, she refused to give him the satisfaction of even glancing at his private area. Finally, he broke the uncomfortable silence.

"Perky as in -," he stared at her breasts for a few moments, ensuring that she saw him, and licked his lips. "I think you understand what perky is."

Madison's exterior remained stoic, but internally she was livid. "Are you finished? I have a lot of work to do."

Ron crossed his ankle over the other, attempting to display the prominence of his genital imprint further. "What's wrong with you, Madison? Are you having a bad day or what? Smile, for Christ's sake. I'm only joking. Lighten up."

"Yes, I'm having an awful day, and I need to get back to work. Is that all?"

Ron walked behind his desk and sat down. "Sure, go do your thing. If I find any issues with the report, I'll let you know. You're dismissed. For now."

He winked as she stood up. Then, as she left the room, she felt his eyes following her every step.

Bitch, I'll have you. Just wait and see.

Meanwhile, Terrance stood at the far end of the office. After replacing a printer, he saw Madison storm out of Ron's office.

I need to pick up my game. Ron is already having closed-door sessions with her. It's my turn to strike, he thought.

***

It was near lunch break, and Madison closed the documents on her computer when she felt a tap on her shoulder.

Oh god, not Ron again.

She turned around to see Terrance.

"Hey Madison, I'm Terrance from IT. I need to do a quick inspection of your computer. It won't take long. Is that cool with you?"

"Thanks." She stood and stepped aside.

He smiled, sat a small tool bag on the desk and slid the computer out. He looked at his watch.

"It's almost lunchtime. You should make a run for it and get a head start before you get stampeded by the others." He chuckled. "Some of them act like they're starving. It makes no sense."

Madison giggled. "I know, right?"

He's funny. He's also cute. Finally, a guy around here that's normal.

He dug into his tool bag. "I won't call any names, but you've seen the people. Most of them need to run away from the lunchroom, and I mean far, far away. That way, they can diet and exercise at the same time."

Madison burst out laughing and covered her mouth. "Terrance, you are too funny."

He smirked, puffing up his chest. "That's what they tell me." He cleaned the dust from the computer's cooling fans. "Why don't you sit down? You're making me nervous, standing over me."

Madison's eyebrows raised. "Really? I don't want to make you nervous. I'll sit and wait until the clock strikes twelve. I'm not very hungry today." She sat and watched him work. "Why does that make you nervous? I'm just curious."

He avoided eye contact and continued to work, shaking his head. "If I tell you why," he mumbled, "you'll think I'm weird and probably tease me."

"No, I won't. I promise."

He stopped cleaning and looked at her.

"Madison, to be honest, I don't have a problem with anyone else standing over me. The reason is simple. You are gorgeous. I've seen beautiful women on television and models on the internet, but they are nothing compared to you. So having you standing over me, and being so close to you, makes me kind of feel like a kid with his first crush. It's not only your looks, but I feel the energy radiating from you. I know that sounds corny, but it's the truth. Now, be honest with me. I know that I'm not the first man to ever confess something like that to you."

Madison was clueless on how to respond. The unexpected words made her feel something. Somehow, they penetrated her emotions before she could ward them off. For a split second, she felt unique, strong, even beautiful.

Does he really feel that way? He seems so sincere, like Tony.

Hinged on that thought, she allowed him deeper and lowered her emotional guard.

"Wow, Terrance, I don't know what to say. Thank you for that wonderful compliment. And no, I have never been told something like that, ever."

He stepped closer and held out his hand. "Do you want to be friends?" he asked.

She thought for a moment and smiled. "Yes. I'd like that."

They shook hands. Then Terrance began putting away his tools, singing softly as he worked. "I got a friend— I got a friend— her name is Madison— and she's my friend."

She blushed. He's such a clown, but a cool clown who sings like Marvin Gaye. She looked at the clock. "Okay, Terrance, I'm going to lunch. Is my computer going to work when I turn it back on?"

"Yes, Ms. Sanders, your computer will be operational upon your return." He bowed and added with a smile, "My queen."

"Uh, thank you."

She grabbed her purse to leave, but Terrance grabbed her arm. "Hold up, wait a second. Let me get your phone number. I have something to talk to you about. Off the job."

Madison eased her arm away from his grip.

"I don't think so, Terrance. It's too soon. Let's get to know each other as friends first. If I was considering a relationship, then we could talk on the phone. But I'm not ready for a relationship right now. So, let's keep this as friends. Who knows what the future may bring? Is that cool?"

He frowned, cocking his head. "Look, I get what you're saying. I'm not ready for a relationship either. So, let's meet in the middle."

She stared at him, puzzled. "What's your idea of meeting in the middle?"

He stepped closer. "Yes, we can be friends. But let's at least be friends with benefits. I promise to keep my mouth shut, and no one will ever know about us. Also, for you only, I'll pay for any motel room where we meet. You won't have to worry about anything. If you tell me what alcohol you like to drink, I'll have that ready for you, every time. I'm for real. I have you covered, princess."

Madison became nauseous, like someone had punched her in the stomach. *You low-life piece of shit,* she thought angrily. *You're pretending to be a friend, but all you want to do is screw me!*

She didn't respond with words, but her eyes screamed insults. He inadvertently mistook the fury in her eyes for a woman burning with lust. He confidently scribbled on a post-it note.

"Look baby, take my cell number, and hit me up when you get free. If I don't pick up, then leave a message and I'll call you right back. Cool?" He reached out to hand her the paper.

She gritted her teeth. "Terrance, that's not my idea of a friend. I don't sleep around. I don't go to motels. I don't do any of that, so you can take that yellow piece of paper, fold it up, and stick it up your ass, player. Don't approach me with that bullshit ever again."

Terrance was beside himself, humiliated and angry. He stuffed the post-it inside his pocket, snatched his tool bag off the desk, and stormed back to the IT Department.

You're gonna give me that tail. You can play hard to get if you want.

***

In the lunchroom, Madison sat at the table with Brittany.

Brittany smiled. "Hey, girl. What did you bring today?"

Madison took out two small containers of yogurt, a banana and a small bag of blueberries.

"I'm eating light for the next few weeks. It's time to get my fat ass back into shape."

Brittany laughed. "Fat? Please. I'll admit, you do have a nice-sized booty for a white girl, but it's hardly fat. I'm sure you've noticed a lot of attention around here to prove that."

"That's the problem. I'm getting too much attention. It's the wrong kind of attention from the wrong people, and I'm getting fed up."

Brittany stopped eating and leaned forward. "I knew something was wrong when you first sat down. What happened? Was it Ron again?"

Madison sighed. "Yes. He called me into his office and had me sit down while he stood in front of me with his junk all but smothering my face. Besides that, his stupid, corny remarks that he calls jokes are getting on my last nerve. I can't stand him!"

"He is an asshole. His wife is gorgeous too. I've met her before. I can't understand what she sees in him."

Across the room, the members of the Wolfpack walked in to eat. Everyone knew which table was unofficially theirs and avoided using it. They sat down and began eating while surveying the lunchroom and mumbling to each other.

Madison glanced over at them and rolled her eyes. "Oh, and just before lunch, Terrance worked on my computer. He had me laughing and giggling before telling me I was the most gorgeous— blah, blah, and then he asked to be friends. I didn't think much of it, so I agreed. Then he asked for my phone number, but I refused. He wanted to give me his, and finally came out and said that he wanted to be friends with benefits. Unbelievable."

Brittany sat quietly, but Madison noticed she'd begun to eat quicker. "Now, what's wrong with you?" she asked.

Brittany shook her head and frowned. "I'll be honest with you, but don't judge me."

"I would never judge you. You're a genuine friend. Now, what's up?"

"Years ago, before I met my fiancé, I hooked up with Terrance. It didn't last long, especially after I found out that he lived with his girl-friend. I'm not affected by what you told me, but it caught me by sur-prise, that's all. I forgot what a big liar he is." She nodded at the group of men. "Look over there. Everyone sitting at that table is part of a little boys club. They call themselves the Wolf Pack."

Madison processed the strange revelation. "He is a dog, isn't he? We are friends, and everyone knows that. That bastard was ready to sleep with me knowing he had already slept with you. That's pathetic. I don't care if he's single and available. I want nothing to do with him."

Brittany's eyebrows arched. She leaned over to her friend and whis-pered, "He isn't available. He still lives with that same woman from years ago. He tried to pick you up using the same line of bullshit that

I believed. He isn't shit. None of them are. They are a bunch of booty bandits. Whore dogs."

Trina walked over and sat down. "Hey girls, how's it going?"

Brittany rolled her eyes. "It could be better. How about you?"

"My day has been super. I'm caught up on my work and have been surfing the net for most of the day. Life sucks, I know."

Trina's laugh echoed throughout the room. But Madison hardly noticed; she was too busy staring over at the Wolf Pack. They were laughing loudly, drowning out even Tricia's annoying laugh.

"Don't pay any attention to those clowns," said Brittany, elbowing her. "They aren't laughing at you. It's only for attention. They want all the attention."

But Madison couldn't help herself and kept staring at the men. "I was looking at the tall one. I think his name is Conor? He hasn't said a word to me. Neither has the short Latino guy. The tall guy only smiles when we pass each other. Now, he is hot. Super-hot. He seems different from the others. Why would a guy like him want to hang around with those losers?"

Brittany wiped her hands. "Well, the short Latino is Luis. He's harmless now, I think. He ran with them once upon a time. That's until Rita got ahold of his ass, and they married. He's a genuine family man. Ron could learn some lessons about being a decent husband from Luis. Conor's story is different. He was getting all the women around here. Once, two of his lovers worked in the same department and got into a physical fight over him. Can you believe that?"

"Yes, I believe," Madison replied, still focused on Conor.

"I think he lives with his girlfriend. I don't know for sure, and I don't have time to keep up with him. I'm too busy with my own life."

Trina cleared her throat. "He lives with his girlfriend. I know that for a fact. We hooked up a few times."

"Oh really, you and Conor?" Brittany asked.

"Yep. I went down on him twice, just before he went back home to her," she giggled.

"And you're proud of that?" Brittany asked.

"Duh, yeah," she proudly answered. "Look at him. Who wouldn't want to taste a bit of that? I took everything that he fed me. I'll tell you another secret. I let Ron bend me over his car last year. Uh-huh, right after the Jay-Z concert."

Madison and Brittany glanced at each other.

Madison leaned forward. "You did that knowing that he had a wife?"

Trina sipped her juice and patted her mouth. "I did nothing wrong. It's not as if I forced him to bend me over and ram me from behind. If there's anyone to blame, it's his wife. She should have been taking better care of her man if you ask me. I know some people don't like him, but Ron is really nice when you get to know him. He told me how his home life sucks, and I truly feel sorry for him. He has an enormous heart."

Brittany stood up. "I've lost my appetite, and I've heard enough from you, little miss fast ass." She turned to Madison. "Are you finished? Are you ready to walk?"

Madison nodded and gathered up her belongings before looking at Trina. "I wouldn't tell that story to anyone else, Trina. Trust me."

"Well, I'm not you, and you are not me, so don't tell me what to do. I'm an adult, if you hadn't noticed. But I get it. Your feathers are ruffled because I gave a blowjob to the guy you're crushing on. I'm sure hundreds of thirsty women have blown him. Grow up and get over it."

Madison was ready to return the insult, but Brittany pulled her away.

"No, don't respond to a slut. You're bigger than that and prettier." She winked at Trina, who displayed her middle finger in return. As they walked toward the exit, Madison debated with herself on taking one last peek at Conor.

Don't do it. He's just like the rest. But she couldn't resist one last look. This time, he caught her. He smiled and waved, making her blush. But she accepted the attraction to him for what it was, a fleeting emotional feeling for a handsome man. She couldn't truly trust any man. Madison had learned that fact in the harshest of ways from the school of life.

***

Later that night, after Elijah had finished his supper, he was ready for a snack. Oddly enough, he liked whole grain granola bars, which was a welcome surprise for any mother attempting to ween their child off sugary snacks. In the daily battle of motherhood, Madison gladly accepted any positive advantages that promoted her child's wellbeing. She handed him a bar wrapped in a paper towel.

"Thank you, Mommy," he mumbled before running off to sit in front of the television.

"You're welcome!" she shouted after him.

It was 7 pm, and she went into her bedroom to lie down for a minute. Her feet hurt, and her lower back felt stiff as a plank. Thankfully, the soft mattress relieved the uncompromising force of gravity, and she moaned with relief. She dreaded the earlier day at work, her mind covered in a black haze from the negativity it left behind. She attempted to focus on unrelated thoughts, but they all returned full circle to the past events of the week. It wasn't the workload or responsibilities that troubled her, but her encounters with Ron and Terrance. They were the same animal with the same intentions, but in different colored skins.

I have to put an end to this. Somehow. But how?

The phone rang. It was her mother. Madison didn't want to answer it, but she needed to. She had only left one message on her mother's voicemail to let her know that she and Elijah had made it to Minnesota safely. Not that her mother would ever worry, God forbid that. It wasn't part of her mother's character to worry or show any emotion, even when situations warranted it, except for anger. Madison had openly defied her only once. It happened when she a child, and she had experienced the full force of her matriarchal wrath.

Ironically, at the time, the younger Madison aspired to be like her mother. Elizabeth Sanders was a biochemist holding her Doctoral in Chemistry. Madison or "Maddy," as she was sometimes referred to, would spend hours reading at home in her mother's study, adjacent to her lab. During adolescence, she would peruse the shelves and read books on biology, chemistry, and psychology. She would ask her mother endless questions, which were answered in detail and with an air of pride, fueling Elizabeth's expectations for Madison's future course of education, namely in Chemistry.

But, after leaving home and away from her mother's micromanaging clutches, the first year of college brought Madison a fresh wind of change. She inhaled her first breaths of adulthood and freedom. The college trust fund that her father had instituted was now active, and so was her spirit. For the first time in her life, she felt alive; she could finally breathe. Elizabeth wasn't happy about her choices or decision to change her college major and vocalized her dissatisfaction at every opportunity. This resulted in Madison further distancing herself from further contact and immersing herself in the new college culture. That's when she met Elijah's father, Tony. Madison kept him a secret from her mother as long as she could, knowing Elizabeth would disapprove of the interracial relationship. But, after Madison became pregnant, the truth became known.

During her last trimester of pregnancy, he suddenly went missing, sparking Madison's first stage of a mental breakdown. Elizabeth was there, not with open arms, but to pick up the pieces and move her back home. In Elizabeth's estimation, her grandson's welfare was much more important than looking after her disappointing, unwed, and rebellious daughter. The day of Elijah's birth marked the end of Madison's secret. When Elizabeth saw her olive-skinned grandson, she pressed Madison for further details about Tony's ethnicity. After finding out he was black, her mother's following words were cold and heartless.

"Why bring a child into this world knowing that they will suffer social rebuke? You are so selfish. You should have aborted him for his own sake."

Although shocked and hurt by her mother's devastating comments, Madison's newfound motherhood inspired an instinctual defense of her newborn son, Elijah. *"This is my decision, mother. It's not 1965 anymore! People are different now. Yes, racism exists and always will, but we live in a progressive society now."*

Elizabeth laughed. *"You sound like a new-age radical with that foolish talk. Your baby is a bastard, who was deserted by his negro father. Your situation is nothing new! Don't you see?"*

"Tony didn't desert me! He could be injured, in a coma, or dead. I know he wouldn't have abandoned his baby or me. He loves me."

That was their last conversation about Tony.

Reluctantly, Madison answered the call. "Hello, Mother."

"Hello, Maddy. Why haven't you returned my calls?" Elizabeth asked in her robotic, monotone voice.

"I apologize. I've been swamped and had intended to call you back, but…"

"It's disrespectful and rude. How is Elijah? Are you taking care of him properly?"

Madison sat up. "Yes, mother. Elijah is doing fine. He likes his daycare, and I'm taking excellent care of him."

There was no response.

"Hello, Mother? Are you still there?"

"Yes. How is work? You have a lazy streak in you. I know all too well. Being transferred to another location does not differ from beginning new employment. Don't assume your new coworkers will pick up your slack. I don't want to receive a call from you crying to me about getting fired. God knows you have disappointed me enough."

It was beginning again. Elizabeth's verbal abuse was her modus operandi, and it was effective. It was the same verbal abuse experienced during Madison's childhood, and it now caused tears to run.

"Yes. Yes, mother, I'm working very hard. I won't disappoint you."

"Are you crying? Why? Stop being weak! For the love of God, grow up!"

Madison composed herself, gathering her shattered confidence. "Yes, mother. I understand. I'm not crying."

"Good. I'm calling you every Friday at 8 pm to check on your status. I don't expect to be sent to your voicemail. Do you understand?"

"Yes, mother. I understand you."

"Goodbye."

Elizabeth ended the call.

Madison got out of bed and went to the bathroom. She stood in front of the sink, looking at her puffy red nose in the mirror, and splashed water on her face. The water helped, and with every swash, a positive thought followed, cleansing the psychological gloom covering her. Usually, she would shower and rinse her entire body off, but this episode wasn't that bad.

She went easy on me this time. Thank God.

***

The following month was unbearable for Madison as the myriad of sexual advances continued to escalate. It wasn't only the pathetic members of the notorious Wolfpack, but also the stares and smiles from several other male coworkers. She eventually crossed paths with Conor at the vending machine and Luis, who came to her cubicle to install a computer update. Both of them acted professionally, but every smile and spoken word during those conversations left her wary. Loneliness was also consuming her, so she was open-minded to a prospective invitation for a date. But it needed to be the right man and for the right reasons. What was happening to her at work wasn't right, and she couldn't take the harassment for much longer.

If one more thing happens, report it to Human Resources, she decided. Period.

Brittany supported her and was empathetic, encouraging her with phrases that summarized the situation.

"This shit is nonsense! Report their asses if you have to!"

Nevertheless, Madison didn't want to cause any waves that might lead to repercussions or retaliation from Ron or his superior. She didn't honestly know how powerful the Wolf Pack was within the company, and the opposing thoughts caused her hesitation.

While in a mental debate, Madison walked to the copy machine to assemble a spreadsheet for the finance dept. The day was dragging, and it wasn't close to lunchtime. She felt a hand on her shoulder.

"Hey Madison, what's shaking?" Ron asked.

His loud cologne engulfed her personal space.

She twisted away and reached for the copies. "I'm compiling a report, that's all."

"Let me help you with that," he whispered from behind, brushing up against her hip. That's when she felt him. His hardness was unmistakable.

She turned away, instinctively glanced down, and saw him aroused.

"No! I don't need your help. You can use the copier. I'm finished."

She hastily gathered the papers.

Ron stepped back. "Whoa— not so loud. Settle down, sweetie. I was only offering help."

She walked away clutching the folder, dropped them at her cubicle, then rushed to the restroom where she sat crying in a stall.

Ten minutes later, she composed herself and left the restroom, looking around the office.

Nobody noticed anything. It was work as usual. They didn't care. No one gives a damn about what is happening.

She marched backed to her desk, picked up her purse, and proceeded to Steve Hyman's office.

Enough is enough!

***

Steve Hyman's door was open, but Madison knocked anyway.

"Hello, Steve. Do you have a minute? I'm having some issues that I'd like to discuss with you."

He looked up from his monitor. "Yes, by all means, close the door and take a seat."

She did as he instructed.

"So, what's on your mind?" he asked.

She sat there, fumbling with her purse and searching for the right words. "I really don't know how to go about this or where to start. I've been having problems with some of my coworkers."

"Really?" He adjusted his eyeglasses. Madison noticed the change in his body language. His smile was gone, replaced by a serious expression and interlocked fingers. "Tell me what's going on. You have no reason to be nervous. What is said here is strictly confidential."

His genuine concern and sincerity were reassuring.

"Okay, here I go. Some of the guys have been getting a little too friendly with me, too comfortable. One of them continues to ask for my phone number after I kindly declined to share it. Even worse, another man can't seem to keep his hands off me, whether it's my shoulder or my back. The last episode was today. He pressed against me at the copier, and I don't know what else to do. I didn't invite any of their advances, and I either verbally protested or removed myself from the situation. This is affecting me negatively, especially my attitude to work. I've debated with myself for a while about reporting this, and I didn't take this step lightly. It's not easy for me. I want to continue working here, but these issues need to be addressed and resolved."

Steve bobbed his head. "I agree with you, and you've done the right thing by reporting this to me. Tell me the names of each individual and which offenses they are responsible for."

She hesitated. "I don't want to get anyone in trouble. One of them is my manager. I just want them to stop, that's all."

"I can't get them to cease if they are unknown, Madison. I know who you report to, but I need you to state their names, and I'll do the rest."

She went quiet, contemplating the repercussions.

"I promise, there will be no retaliation from your disclosure. I will make sure of that."

"Okay. Terrance is the one who keeps trying to go out with me, and Ron touches me inappropriately all the time. There, I said it. That cat is out of the bag now."

Steve clutched his armrests. "So, Terrance Roberts and Ron Tatum?"

"Yes," she replied nervously.

"I understand. You should know that I am required by law to report these incidents to Corporate and begin an investigation immediately." He reached into his bottom drawer and began rifling through folders.

God, what have I done? I don't need any more unnecessary grief in my life. What will mother say? She'll say that I wanted the attention, that I asked for it!

The frantic thoughts unnerved her.

"Wait!" she blurted.

Startled, he froze. "What's wrong?"

"Isn't there something else that you could do besides starting an investigation? Like talking to them or something? I don't want to get anyone fired over this. I just want it over with, so I can come to work and have a normal day."

He leaned back. "I'm legally responsible for initiating the report which outlines your accusations against your coworkers. Traxtonite takes allegations of sexual harassment seriously. This process is for your protection. But allow me to suggest another alternative - if that's all right with you?"

"Yes. What's the other route?"

He leaned forward. "I can call a meeting with Ron and Terrance, letting them know that their conduct is not acceptable. I'll inform them that a formal report is on the cusp of being initiated if there is one more allegation. If they are receptive and compliant, then we can hold the report indefinitely. This option does not follow the mandated protocol, but I also don't want to burden you with any unnecessary grief from the process. Ultimately, it's your decision."

Madison sat quietly, contemplating his suggestion.

"Madison, I want to do what you feel is necessary."

Steve didn't want the headache of filing another report on members of the Wolf Pack. He had done it before, and it was no picnic. He would rather have an informal chastisement session with the two and give them a clear warning of the penalties to follow. This episode was one of many past complaints involving members of the group. Although sexual harassment and discrimination claims plagued the entire company, the Minneapolis division held the lion's share. This was another fight that Steve did not want to referee, and he hoped that Madison would bite on his offer.

She sighed, relieved of the ominous burden. "I would rather go that route. If you talk to them, I believe that they'll get the idea. If it continues, then we can proceed with the report, and I'm fine with that. Thank you," she added.

"Fine. I'll speak with them today. Moving on, I'm curious if there any other individuals that you would like to name? Perhaps Conor? Maybe Luis?"

"No. They've done nothing to me. I understand what you are getting at. I've heard about the Wolf Pack and what they do."

Damn. She knows about them. Then I have to put all those overgrown adolescents on notice, he thought.

"Okay then, I'll take care of this today. I have the names, and I know the details. Why don't you leave early today? You've been through enough and might as well go home to decompress. Don't worry about using your personal hours either; I have that covered. I promise that there will be a positive change in your work experience when you return tomorrow. You'll see. Thanks for sharing this with me and allowing me to do my job."

She was relieved to know that the ordeal was going to be over soon.

"I'll take the rest of the day off. Thanks, Steve."

She stood up and left while Steve fumed. "Immature morons," he mumbled as she closed the door after her and rang his assistant.

"Yes, Steve, what's up?"

"Merilyn, please contact Ron Tatum, Terrance Roberts, Conor Gregory, and Luis Mendoza. Have them report to my office immediately, thank you."

Still livid, he hung up the phone. He began rehearsing his impending verbal counseling of the four. In his opinion, all four were all guilty, regardless of her exemption of two of them. Judging them by their past misbehavior, he surmised that if Conor and Luis hadn't already gotten to her, it was only a matter of time before they would. Steve Hyman was overdue for a promotion, and he wasn't about to let the Wolf Pack stand in his way.

Kill two birds with one stone? I'll kill four instead. They all have it coming.

CHAPTER 4

During the following week, the office environment had drastically changed, and most of the staff noticed a marked difference in the atmosphere. The actual reason was only known by the principals involved. Brittany was the exception, being privy to Madison's visit to Human Resources and knowing the motive behind it. But there wasn't any hot gossip, and everyone went about their daily routines as usual.

The random summoning to Steve Hyman's office culminated in a scathing verbal reprimand and rebuke of the entire Wolf Pack. Conor and Luis vigorously protested their innocence, but their explanations fell on deaf ears, and each individual received the full measure of Steve's chastisement. Their motley reactions spanned the spectrum from anger to humiliation and embarrassment as they listened to his accurate depiction of their corrupt and immature conduct. It was reminiscent of troubled children receiving chastisement in the principal's office. Steve's disciplinary threats concluded the meetings. They had never seen him behave this way. It was as if he was personally insulted and injured. This time he was serious, and the documentation issued during their counseling session confirmed it. The line had been crossed.

After leaving the meeting, they all met in Ron's office to hash out the events. It had been a long time since any of them had allegations leveled at them, including official or unofficial notices of sexual harassment. The situation was upsetting.

Luis was the first to gripe. "This is bullshit, man! I didn't do anything to her. Rita could find out about this - and she might divorce me. Guys, I have kids! I knew that chick was trouble. Something isn't right with her. So, listen up, I'm taking a break. You can say whatever you want about me. I don't care." And, without another word, he stormed out of the office.

Conor appeared nonchalant. The single bachelor seemed unfazed by the events. He understood that his part was one of guilt by association and that he was, in fact, innocent. Regardless, he now had a counseling letter in his information file, along with the rest of his buddies. He chuckled at the irony of it all, knowing that Madison didn't name him.

Why would she do that? This was really about Steve trying to cover his ass, just in case - and showing his due diligence to Corporate, staving off any future harassment complaints. To do that, he had to ding all of us.

Conor shared his feelings with Ron and Terrance before following Luis out the door.

"You guys royally screwed this up. Both of you need to lay low for a while. I've got a bad feeling about her. She's trouble and messing up our program. It's taking the fun out of work. Give me a call later tonight if you want to meet up and have some beers. I'll see you later."

They watched him exit, leaving a dead silence behind. There were no offensive jokes or chatter. The reality of their predicament could not be deflected or dismissed.

Terrance stood by the door. "Ron, buddy, you know that we are tight. But I'm going to have to put the brakes on this one. It's getting too deep, and I need my job. As they say, when you're losing the battle, it's best to run away and live to fight another day. Let me know what you want to do. I'm with you, bro."

He nodded and left, leaving Ron sitting behind his desk, alone.

He felt like a fool who had been bested. And it did not sit well with him. What he had built from scratch was now falling apart. He gathered loose copies of reports from his desk, stapled them together, and looked for something else to do. He had to busy himself. With every breath, feelings of weakness and insecurity grew. Reminiscent of his junior high school years when he was bullied, he was transported back in time and visualized the bathroom stall to sit in between classes. He had to avoid the tormenters and their daily abuse. He remembered them smacking him in front of the pretty girls and slamming him to the ground, emasculating him and laughing about it. He picked that same stall every day. It was safe, and they never noticed. He recalled sitting on the commode and looking at the closed door as clearly as 25 years prior and reading the words that someone inscribed on the inside with a pocketknife.

"RON TATUM IS A FAG!"

He grabbed the stapler and hurled it at the wall. "Bitch!" he snarled. "You goddamn bitch."

He paced the floor while incoherent and illogical thoughts raced through the dark crevasses of his mind.

I'll pay you back, whore. That's a promise.

***

Brittany laughed. "Ha! If I weren't engaged to Trent, I would have given him my phone number. Girl, it was just like a movie. A fine man like him hitting on me in a supermarket. Isn't that some shit? But when I was single and lonely, I couldn't find a decent man to approach me. Now that I have a fiancé, good men are buzzing around me like bees to nectar."

Madison giggled and continued eating, wishing that she had been in Brittany's place at the supermarket. "You should have told him that you had a friend that he might be interested to meet. The way you described him is making me horny. You should have at least asked him if he had a brother."

"I should have, but he had me hypnotized. I couldn't keep my eyes off of him, especially his chest. But you're right. Elijah's daddy is black, so his race wouldn't have been an issue for you. Anyway, I'm keeping my eyes open. No worries, next time I'll keep you in mind."

"Thanks. I don't want to sound desperate because I'm not. You know me. But if you meet someone you think is a good fit, then go for it."

"Consider it done. I must say, you seem different this week. I'm just saying – in a good way. You're more relaxed. I like it."

"Going to Human Resources was the best decision I could have made. Thanks for encouraging me to do it. Ron and Terrance haven't even looked in my direction. Ron speaks to me through his assistant or by email only."

"Really?"

"Yup. And I'm not losing any sleep over it either. I feel much better. Like a weight has been lifted off me. Work is enjoyable now."

"Good. That serves them right. They should have known that their bullshit would catch up with them one day. Still, watch your back, girlfriend."

"Oh, I am. But I'm doing my job and not worrying at all."

Just then, Ron walked into the lunchroom and sat down to eat. Brittany saw him first.

She nudged Madison. "Speak of the horny devil, and he appears."

"He looks lonely. Too bad, so sad."

"Amen. Like my mother used to say, 'You made your bed, now sleep in it.' Momma ain't never lied." Brittany giggled, giving Madison a soft fist bump.

Ron sat stoically, eating the sandwich that his wife Kathy made for him and watching CNN on the lunchroom tv. He didn't want to look around. He felt the true satire of his dilemma—the man who once craved attention and lauding, now sought obscurity among his subordinates.

Laughter erupted from a group sitting across the room, unrelated to Ron's presence. He wasn't on anyone's mind, but he snapped his neck around to look. The second round of amusement exploded, and he became annoyed, scooting his chair back and stuffing his food into his lunch cooler. To him, it was junior high all over again. He left and walked back to his office.

No way. You won't get away with this.

He threw his lunch into the trash can.

This is my house. I make the rules.

He grabbed his cell phone and wrote a group text.

Urgent. I need you all to meet me tonight at 7:30 pm—the Tap Room. Drinks are on me.

He grinned and sent.

***

The music in the Tap Room was blaring. Ron, Conor, and Terrance sat at their regular table in the back corner, waiting on Luis to arrive.

Conor looked toward the entrance. "I wonder if he's going to show."

"He'd better," Ron mumbled, waving his hand at a passing waitress.

"Here he comes now," Terrance said. "I think he had to pick his son up from Cub Scouts or some shit like that."

Luis spotted them and hurried over to sit down. "What's up, guys?"

Ron smiled as the waitress arrived. "Hello, sweetheart. A round of Dos Equis for everyone. Put it on my tab."

"You got it, Ron," she acknowledged, hurrying off to fetch their drinks.

"What's so urgent?" Luis asked.

Ron crossed his arms. "The future, our friendships, and our happiness at the job. I've been thinking and I've come up with some ideas to set things straight. We need to get our shit together and take back what's ours. We all know who the problem child is, and we all know that she has got to go. The sooner, the better."

"What do you mean by, 'she's got to go'? How?" Conor asked.

"She's a snitch and needs to get terminated or transferred. I prefer termination. Since she has a direct line to Steve and knows that he'll act at her slightest whimper, I'm sure her heels are dug in deep. That gives her confidence and will make a transfer difficult."

Luis began shaking his head. "You're confusing me. How can she be terminated? She does her job, from what I hear. Maybe we ought to leave her alone. She isn't bothering…"

"What the hell is wrong with you, Luis?" Ron snapped. "You were right there when we all got our asses written up! And you weren't even in the hunt!" Ron lowered his voice. "I don't mean to yell at you, buddy. I'm sorry. But we are all in this together. She has us by the balls, knowing that anytime her little heart desires, she can push the harassment report and we are finished. So, unless any of you are ready to throw away your hard-earned years of service and look for another job, I suggest that everyone at this table pull your heads out from your asses. Be men, for God's sake."

The waitress brought their beers. "Anything else, fellas?"

"That's all for now, beautiful. You just keep those drinks coming, and I'll personally give you my tip. Pun intended." He smiled and patted her hip. She feigned a smile and hurried away.

"You still haven't told us how," Terrance said.

"It's simple. Everyone keeps a close eye on her. She's been late twice already, and I have that covered. Her next day being tardy will be reported to Steve." He turned to Luis and Terrance. "Go through her cookies and history on the network server. If she visits any non-work-related websites or sends any unauthorized private emails, let me know ASAP. Conor, you dig up any dirt on her through the other chicks. Guys, if we do those things, it shouldn't take long to make a paper trail, and when there's enough ammunition, I'll package it and have a long sit down with Steve. What do you all think?"

Conor grimaced. "It sounds like a plan. But to be fair, everyone is tardy, and everyone abuses the computer policy. To bring up those issues alone still gives her room to cry about being singled out. She can claim retaliation."

Ron raised his finger. "I've thought about that. Remember, the harassment report is still on hold. See? That was Steve's mistake. He can't backdate a sexual harassment claim; he'll get in trouble for not following through when he received the complaint. Our verbal counseling from him was for violating the professional office conduct policy, and she wasn't specifically named in that. Meanwhile, we can make our case with facts and show her clear violation of company policies and anything else that we might be able to dredge up on her. If she does try to initiate the complaint after the fact, then it will look like she is retaliating against me for reporting her. It's perfect. I'm taking the lead on this. You guys need to work your angles from behind the scenes."

Terrance grinned. "I like it. I think it will work."

Ron looked at Conor. "What say ye, oh handsome one?"

Conor smirked. "Okay, I'm in. What the hell is there to lose at this point?"

Everyone turned to Luis and waited for his answer.

"Alright. Let's do it."

Ron beamed with pride, ecstatic to have regained control of the group. "One last detail. Since I'm taking the lead on this and risking the most, everyone needs to keep their findings confidential. Let me know what you find, and then keep it to yourself. I'll be the one to share updates about our progress. Why? There's an old navy saying, 'Loose lips, sink ships.' I don't want to chance anyone of you running their mouths off to their wives, side chicks, or someone in the office about what we're doing. This is top-secret shit. Got it?" Ron held his bottle up. "To the legendary Wolf Pack, the terrors of Traxtonite. We will hunt again."

They toasted.

Terrance laughed. "Wait, we forgot our original toast. 'Bros before hoes!'"

They toasted again.

Ron raised his hand. "And to sweeten the deal, my cabin will be fully stocked this weekend, so how about a hunting party? We haven't hunted coyotes together in over a year. I think it's about damn time. What say ye?"

They looked at each other and barked, making a spectacle of themselves. But they didn't care. The Tap Room belonged to them.

***

Two hours passed before Terrance left with Luis, leaving Ron and Conor binge drinking at the bar. Both should have stopped, but every nostalgic memory accompanied another round. They were doing Tequila shots as their quest to reach inebriation escalated. They hooted repeatedly.

"I love you, man!"

"I love YOU, man!"

Ron looked at his watch, raising his eyebrows. "I've got to get home. Kathy will start calling me soon."

"Say it isn't so," Conor jested.

"I'm afraid that it is. Take my advice. You don't want to get a black woman pissed at you. Ha!"

"How is Kat doing? I meant Kathy."

"She's good. Still walking around the house like she's the Commander in Chief."

"Yea. That's cool. I'm glad."

Ron emptied his glass and slammed it down on the counter. "That's it, and I'm officially done! Whoa!" He looked at Conor in the mirror behind the bar. "Do you still think about her? Be honest, bro."

Conor looked at his reflection. "No. I mean, not like that. Not in that way."

"I don't believe you. Just be honest," Ron slurred.

"I am telling the truth. Of course, right after it first happened, yes, I thought about her. Who wouldn't? Who couldn't? She was like Beyonce and Lena Horne rolled into one. But I got over it. It's no big deal."

Ron stood and grabbed Conor's shoulder. "Thank you."

"For what?"

He patted Conor's back. "For not holding it against me. You're a true friend." He walked towards the exit, hollering, "See you tomorrow. Don't be late!"

"Don't get a DUI!" Conor shouted after him.

He sat there for a few minutes, looking in the mirror, remembering the days when he and Kathy were a couple.

"True friend? Sure, I am," he mumbled. Then he finished his drink and walked out. *But what would you know about either word?*

***

As Conor finished his last drink across town, 54-year-old Don Carson sat in his North Minneapolis suburban home and poured himself another. Like Conor, he also was a fan of Tequila, but without the lime and salt. He believed that combination was only for females and their beta male counterparts, not for real men. He was multi-tasking: watching re-runs of classic hockey games while listening to his police scanner. Carson strove for convenience and organization in all things. He sat in his worn leather recliner, wearing a stained white tank-top and boxer shorts, guarding a Tequila bottle. Within arm's reach sat a shot glass, the television remote, and a handheld scanner spaced equally apart on a fold-up tv tray.

It was a slow Thursday night, and the dispatcher's calls were relatively sparse. Listening to the scanner was only a hobby. At least that's what he told himself. But, if he was honest with himself, it was more than that. He had given into the ritual, the obsession, a year prior. It helped him cope with the reality of being placed on indefinite administrative leave from the Minneapolis Police Department. As an inactive detective, it was becoming unbearable to sit on the sidelines. But he had no choice. Preposterous accusations and an ongoing investigation by IAD had come out of thin air, with unsubstantiated charges. Regardless, they wouldn't close his case.

They don't have shit on me. Nothing will stick.

He repeated those thoughts dozens of times but knew that was only wishful thinking. They had to have something. To add insult to injury, he was only three years away from fulfilling his 30-year retirement requisite to receive his maximum allowable pension. Although he could retire anytime, there was a substantial difference in a financial payout when reaching the 30-year mark, and he was determined to get what was coming to him.

He poured another shot while watching the legendary Gordy Howe march down the ice with the power of a demi-god. Score! He remembered being at that very same game as a kid.

"Calling Homicide. Code 4, priority three at 824 Lakeshore Drive. Requesting a Homicide unit on scene."

Don grabbed his radio and stood while listening.

"10-4, Olson and Schultz in route."

It was Roger Olson responding, Don's former partner.

But who is this Schultz guy?

He probed his foggy past, trying to recount who was on the force before he went on administrative leave. He drank another shot and went to the bathroom. He stared at his reflection in the mirror above the commode and suddenly realized.

No way, not that punk kid, Schultz? Yeah, Schultz. The college boy who had worked in Narcotics. What a joke.

Alex Schultz was part of the modern wave of law-enforcement officers. He was a decorated military veteran who made good on his G.I. Bill, and after four years in the army and two tours in Afghanistan. He had made a name for himself in the Narcotics Division, heavily contributing to three massive drug smuggling busts, resulting in multiple convictions. Schultz was a rising star whose shining light marked the department's future course.

Has he made detective, huh? Don't get too comfortable beside my partner, kid. I'll be back.

He stared in the mirror. He needed a shave, and his potbelly screamed the need for exercise. He flushed and turned sideways, attempting to suck in his gut. Getting back into shape was a long-term goal at best, but he had to shave before his client appointment on Monday morning. Although he was on unpaid leave, that didn't hinder him from working as a private investigator. The side job wasn't making him a fortune, but it kept the lights on and fit his convenience and comfort lifestyle.

There was no shortage of suspicious spouses, male and female, who wanted spying eyes following their partners. Some wanted to know the truth about possible infidelity; others even hoped for it, looking for an exit out of their unhappy marriages. He found that most of his clients were unfaithful themselves and only desired to beat their spouses to the inevitable punch. It was a competition to decide who received the most significant share of the money pot. The fallacy of crushed dreams and a marriage gone sour was never the sentimental response he experienced when turning over incriminating photos and video footage. The client's reaction was either anger or hidden relief, masked by shock. The stereotypical shattered fairy tale, and added waterworks, were few and far between.

He began pacing the living room. *He hadn't returned any of my phone calls, but you know that he's swamped with cases. Should you go to the crime scene? You can catch Roger's attention.* "Hey Roger, I was just passing by and stopped when I saw you. How are things going?

Have you had a chance to talk to the Chief or the Assistant A.G.? The clock is ticking, partner. I only have 18 months left to be reinstated or forced into retirement. I need three more years, Roger. Help me out, partner."

As he worked on his performance, he drank another shot.

Na. What the hell are you thinking? He'll know you've been drinking again. Goddammit!

He slammed his glass down on the tray and ran his fingers through his hair. Then he turned off the table lamp and the handheld scanner before dropping down onto his recliner. The flickering of the television in the darkness lulled him past inebriation, and he dozed off to sleep.

CHAPTER 5

It was 5 p.m. on Friday, and the mass office exodus began. The herd filed out through the four-door entrance, and no one looked back. Madison and Brittany intersected paths as they approached their cars. They were accustomed to parking beside each other, and like most friends, they were creatures of habit and simultaneously arrived at their vehicles.

Brittany opened her door. "TGIF, girlfriend! What do you have planned this weekend?"

Madison shrugged. "Like every other weekend, nothing new. Elijah and I will be hanging out in the house. They say it's going to snow, so I'll probably be pulling him in a sleigh that I haven't even bought yet. I guess that later tonight, or tomorrow we'll run out to Target and see what they have in stock. How about you? Another quiet and romantic night with Trent?"

"Nah. He's helping his brother move this weekend. I won't see him again until Sunday afternoon."

"Okay. Well, enjoy your time off. I'll see you back here, Monday morning."

Madison got into her car and started while Brittany shuffled over. Madison lowered her window.

"What's up, Brit?"

"I have an idea. You've been sitting in that house for months. I get it and applaud you for being a single mother who puts her child first. I know that you aren't actively searching for a man, but you should have some kind of social interaction. You aren't a nun. Since we're both free this Saturday, and both of us are single mothers, then how about we get together and do something?"

Madison nodded. "That's a great idea. What are your thoughts?"

"How about either you or I spend the night and have a sleepover? The kids can finally meet, play together, and be kids, while we indulge ourselves with wine, watch movies or whatever."

"That's a great idea. Do you mind coming over to my place? I'm still not knowledgeable of the area, and Elijah is still so young. I'm unsure how he will adjust to sleeping in new surroundings. This house came furnished, and the living room couch converts to a queen-size bed. Is that alright?"

"Perfect. And I agree with you about Elijah. At four, he's still a baby to me. Ayana is fourteen and too grown-up for her age as it is. She might try to sneak off if I leave her alone. We should come to you. I'll call you Saturday morning. Now, I hope it does snow. I've never been sledding, but I would like to do it once, as long as it doesn't mess up my hair."

Madison giggled. "Girl, you're so crazy. I'll talk to you tomorrow. Drive safe!"

She pulled out and headed off to pick up Elijah.

***

On the other side of the parking lot, closer to the entrance, Ron, Luis, and Conor started up their trucks. Terrance was the only one who drove a car. He was passionate about his Lexus, and even the threat of heavy Minnesota snowfall didn't deter him from going, despite the teasing from the others. He couldn't care less and wasn't a follower. Like the others, he was a confident Alpha male who believed himself a natural leader, doing whatever he wanted to do and making no apologies for it.

Their vehicles were parked side by side in their informally dedicated spaces. Terrance decided to ride with Ron to the cabin and leave his car at work over the weekend. Everyone was packed and ready. Ron rolled down the window beside Terrance and signaled Conor and Luis.

"Terrance and I will head straight to the cabin. I've got two cases of beer in the fridge and frozen patties in the freezer. There are cans of corn and green beans, oatmeal, butter and sugar. That's about it. If you guys want to pick up some Vodka or Tequila, some bread and other shit, get it now and then head on up."

Conor checked his wallet. "I'll pick up a fifth of Jameson and a few bags of chips – maybe some pork rinds, too."

Luis nodded. "I'll follow Conor and pick up some Mezcal. Then I'll stop by Kentucky or Churches Chicken. We need some other type of meat to eat besides steak. FYI, I can't stay the whole weekend. I have to leave out Sunday. I'll miss morning mass, but I can still catch the 6 p.m. if I leave the cabin around 3 or 4 p.m."

Terrance stuck his head out of the window. "You must be kidding. Rita has you on a leash, again? Amigo, was all my advice to you in vain?"

Ron chuckled. "What the hell, Luis. Be a man for once, and tell Rita to 'screw mass.' Grow some huevos."

"Screw you!" Luis barked. He rolled up his window and backed out.

Everyone laughed, knowing how to push each other's buttons. Conor pulled out and left, while Ron and Terrance bumped fists.

"Let's do it, brother," Ron said as they followed behind.

Within ten minutes, the parking lot was empty, except for the janitorial staff's vehicles. Their work started at 5 p.m. Three bantering workers exited their company van and strolled toward the entrance. It was the beginning of the weekend, but their workday was just beginning.

***

On the Southside of Minneapolis, Don Carson pulled into the Timber Pines apartment community's entrance. He leisurely scanned the second-floor balconies while parking his car in front of building 700. *I hope Charlene is home; she should be. Her shift shouldn't start until 7 o'clock.* He looked at his watch and saw it was a few minutes till 6 p.m. He walked up the stairwell to the second floor and turned right. Her apartment was the third door down on the right. He knocked three times, paused, and then knocked once more. It was his personal code. She'd know it was him. A few moments later, the door opened.

"Hey there, what's up, Donny?" she said.

He smiled, looking bashful, but his eyes never left hers. "Hey, beautiful," he smiled. "I hadn't heard back from you in a couple of weeks. I've left messages."

"Oh, sweetie, I'm sorry. I was sick all last week. Besides, I worked over a few times this week. I'm so sorry," she said, smiling at him with a sympathetic brow.

"It's okay, I understand." He tried to walk through the threshold, but she pushed the door forward and stopped him.

"Uh, no. I'm about to leave, babe. I need to do a few more things first. Sorry, I can't let you in right now."

"Come on, Charlene. Just give me a minute. One kiss. That's all." He grinned in what he hoped was a boyish way.

"No, Donny. I have to..."

He grabbed her arm, pushed his way inside, and pivoted around her, pushing her back against the closing door. He gripped the back of her neck and pressed his body against her.

"Donny, no," she mumbled.

He forced his tongue into her mouth until she relented, digging her nails into his chest in submission.

Eventually, he pulled back, panting. "I missed you, babe. Sorry."

"Okay, but I need to finish getting ready. Please!"

He backed out of the doorway.

"No problem, honey. I'll come by tomorrow morning. Be ready. I've got a lot of stress to unload."

She knew what that meant and returned a blank stare.

"Don't come here early. I might be sleeping. There's a hockey team in town, and it's rumored that they might come by the club."

"I don't give a damn who looks at your body or who you give a private dance to, but don't get caught up and leave with one of them. I'm serious. Got it?"

She froze. Don was an alright guy, but he scared her. She was used to his intimidating threats. His delusional thoughts of the two of them as some kind of 'couple' were just that: delusional. In the past, she had been his informant while working at the strip club, exchanging information on drug deals or whatever for some quick cash. But that was business. The few times they had sex were only trivial encounters. It wasn't good or bad. It was just one of those things that she allowed to happen.

But ever since his administrative leave went into effect, he didn't have any more need for information, and she didn't have any need for a 50-year-old boyfriend.

She crossed her arms. "Yeah. I understand."

He grinned and winked. "You better understand. Have a good night and be safe."

She watched him for a few seconds before closing the door and made sure he noticed. It was her form of placation. Otherwise, he might decide to bring it up later as a grievance behind closed doors when she was in a compromised position. She knew that he might use any slight against him to hurt her sexually. He seemed to take pleasure in doing so.

***

Madison picked up Elijah from daycare, and since she didn't feel like cooking, she bought dinner at a Zaxby's drive-thru to eat at home. The house was always cold when they got back. To keep the energy bill down, she kept the heat set to 68°F before leaving in the mornings, and it always took a couple of hours to heat the house when they returned.

After they finished eating, Elijah happily played with his toys and watched television, while Madison cleaned the kitchen before finally collapsing onto her bed. She was physically and emotionally exhausted. It was hard being a single mother, at least a good one. The idea of meeting someone special and having a relationship was briefly entertaining, but her mind always raced back to Tony.

Tony, where are you? I really need you right now.

Her eyes watered.

No! This is one of the triggers. I refuse to give my depression a foothold.

She remembered the lessons from her therapy. After opening her laptop and connecting to the internet, she searched online for vacation destinations within driving range due to her fear of flying. A vacation at this time seemed like a futile fantasy, but it wasn't. Visiting any of the locations was attainable if and when she decided to make it a sincere goal. She smirked and was whisked away by her visualizations.

We're going to do it, Elijah. One day.

Her cell phone rang. It was Mother. It continued to ring while she debated answering.

Just answer it!

"Hello, Mother."

She probed with her monotone voice. "Hello, Madison. What are you doing tonight?"

"I'm on the internet looking at vacation photos, and Elijah is in the living room playing."

"I see. So, you're planning on taking a vacation. That makes absolutely no sense to me at all. You've only been working there for three months. Be warned. It won't reflect well on you."

"I'm just looking, mother. Maybe I'll take Elijah on a trip next year, depending on how my finances pan out."

"Well, at least you are thinking it through. Good. I'm surprised that you aren't out at a bar. After all, it is Friday night. That was your favorite day for mischief."

Madison fumed. "What are you talking about? That was years ago, before Elijah. I'm a responsible mother. "

"Watch your tone, young lady! Don't get sassy with me. I called you out of concern and to check on your wellbeing. You sound like an ingrate."

Why? Why me?

"I apologize, mother," she mumbled.

"That's much better. So, are you dating?"

"No, mother. I'm not dating anyone right now."

"Not right now? I see. But you plan to. What's wrong with you?"

"Mother, I'm 27 years old, and nothing is wrong with me. Eventually, I'm sure that I'll meet a nice man. Someone good, like Daddy was."

"Ha! You know nothing about the kind of man your father was. He certainly was no angel. He had a dark side, just like you. I suppose that's where you get your character. You're a lot like him, but that goes without saying."

Madison cringed at her words. "Please, don't talk about him like that. I'm asking you."

"Fine. But you mentioned him first, remember that."

Madison was both sad and furious, edging closer to her break-ing point. It was already difficult to ward off the thoughts leading to depression, but the weekly, oppressive calls from Elizabeth only compounded her fragile state of mind. She was exhausted, continually having to defend herself.

She is constantly attacking me for dating as if she never dated after Daddy was gone. Madison knew her mother's secret.

"I assumed that you dated after Daddy passed away, even though you never brought anyone home for me to meet."

Madison was purposely coy in broaching the subject, which had never been explored with her mother. She braced herself for the possible backlash.

"That's how you and I differ. I have self-respect and dignity in being a widow. After your father died, I never had a relationship with another man. For all your father's shortcomings, I still honored his memory with celibacy. These are some of the qualities that I've tried to instill in you, but it seems I wasted my time."

Liar! I know the truth, mother. I read your emails to those men. I know where you would meet them. Yes, you tried to cover your tracks, but I found out your password. I was just a nosey college student. I know about your fake email accounts and fake name. Lauren? Really? You must hate the name Elizabeth but love the role play. I read everything. I know all of the promises you made to satisfy them if they met you. I know how many men ran through you. It's too bad after screwing you, they never emailed back. I guess that's why you hate me so much. I remind you of what you could never be; wanted—you hypocrite.

"I understand, mother. I need to put Elijah to bed now. Thanks for calling."

Elizabeth was breathing heavily. "Very well. Goodnight."

She ended the call, and Madison rolled over.

I must have shaken her up with a taste of her own medicine. Good. She doesn't enjoy being on the defensive.

A resolute sense of satisfaction permeated Madison's psyche. The newfound feeling caused her to quiver. With a clear mind and her soul at peace, she thought about Brittany and Ayana's upcoming visit.

"Elijah! It's time for bed, sweety!"

***

It was 6 a.m. the following day at the cabin, and multiple phone alarms sounded, breaking the cold stillness. Ron and Terrance shared one room, while Conor and Luis shared the other. One by one, each alarm was silenced except for Luis's phone. He was a hard sleeper.

Conor stood over him. "Luis. Luis. Luis! Wake up, man. Wake up!"

"Huh? What?" he mumbled.

"Turn your alarm off, dude."

Ron shouted from the other room. "Turn your damn alarm off!"

The alarm went silent.

Ron sat on the edge of the bed. "Rise and shine, sleepyheads. It's time to hunt."

Terrance sat up and rubbed the crust from his eyes. "Damn. I drank too much. Shit! My head is pounding."

Ron put on his shirt and turned on a switch to restart the outside generator. "You'll be fine. Eat something and drink some water."

He stood up and stretched, groaning, while the others, in turn, used the only bathroom. Luis started microwaving frozen breakfast burritos while Conor made the coffee.

After Terence brushed his teeth, he grabbed a bottled water from the refrigerator and sat at the kitchen table. "I honestly don't feel like doing this shit today. Y'all go on without me. I'll hang out here. I think I have a migraine."

Ron walked into the kitchen, fully dressed in his hunting camouflage, and sat down while Luis and Conor brought over the food and coffee.

Ron smirked at Terrance. "Bullshit, you wimp. You're coming with us. Finish that water and drink a cup of java. You'll be fine."

"Not with gunshots going off beside my head."

Ron slid a coffee mug to him. "Bro, we probably won't even see one coyote. Just wear your earplugs. You're coming with us."

Conor and Luis sat down too, and everyone ate.

"It's nice out here, man. I love it," Conor said.

Luis nodded. "It's a cool place and not too far from town. I like it better in the summer, though. I wouldn't want to get stuck out here in the snow."

"Then buy some winter tires for your truck," Terrance suggested. "Your low-profile ones look nice, but they'll get your ass stuck out here."

Luis put down his burrito. "What about you? You have a fricking Lexus with low-profile tires. How can you talk?"

Terrance smirked. "That's why I'm riding with Ron, you knucklehead."

Luis bit into his burrito.

Ron turned to him with a frown. "Are you still leaving on Sunday? The weather forecast is calling for flurries today and a couple of inches on Sunday, but there's no way that you'll get snowed in."

Luis leaned back and sighed. "I'm leaving Sunday. Rita and the kids will be waiting for me. We're going to evening mass together as a family. Plus, I'm not risking getting stuck here and being late to work on Monday."

"Okay, whatever. On Monday morning, we'll be up at 7:30 a.m. and leave the cabin by 8 o'clock. That leaves plenty of time to get to work by 8:50 a.m. and more than enough time to pull you out if you get jammed up. So, think about it," Ron replied.

Luis crossed his arms. "I didn't bring my work clothes, and I'm not gonna wear the same clothes from yesterday."

Ron held up his cup. "Fine." He stood up. "Alright, guys, let's get going. Load up and move out. We'll head down towards the creek and set up our blinds there. Let's hope we catch our furry friends getting a drink of water."

He walked over to the cooler and pulled out a thermos.

"What's that? Are you bringing coffee?" Terrance asked.

"No. It's how real men get rid of a hangover. Drink Bloody Mary's, and the head pressure will magically melt away. Do you want some?"

Ron held out the thermos, shaking it.

"That works? No bullshit?" Terrance asked.

"It works. Trust me."

They loaded their weapons, packed their gear, and left.

***

It was 10:15 a.m., and Don Carson sat in his car at the Timber Pines apartments, debating on when he should knock on Charlene's door.

She's got to be up and moving around by now. She knows I'm coming over to cum. He chuckled and looked in his rear-view mirror, smoothing his hair and swiping his bushy eyebrows. He checked his nostrils, plucking out a long white hair and flicking it to the floor. He opened the glove compartment and riffled through the clutter until he found his favorite cologne. After a few splashes under his armpits, he unbuckled his belt, adding another dose to his crotch. Having taken a Cialis pill earlier, he stared at himself.

Ready?

"Ready," he answered and stepped out. Children were outside playing, and their voices resonated throughout the breezeways. He trotted up the stairwell and approached her front door. There, he paused to listen.

No music or tv. She's still asleep.

"Ouch!"

He heard her yelp.

Nope. She's up. She must have stubbed her toe. Ha!

He knocked three times, paused, and then once more. There was silence.

Come on whore, open up.

He waited impatiently, and with every breath, his blood pressure elevated. He knocked again, harder.

"Hey, hurry up."

There was no response. He was about to knock again but heard a voice mumble. He stepped closer. A few moments later, the door unlocked and parted, with the security chain latched. Charlene's milky white face appeared behind the dark gap. She looked like she'd been in a fight. Her messy hair and bloodshot eyes told a story, one that he soon expected to hear.

"Hey," she croaked. "What are you doing over here so early? I'm still sleeping. Come back later."

She squinted from the light and attempted to close the door, but he wedged his foot in between.

He grinned. "Wait. I'm not coming back later. I'm here now. You can go back to sleep and I'll lay beside you until you wake up. I know you're a fan of morning sex."

She rubbed her eyes. "If I let you inside, there's no way that you'll let me go back to sleep. You'll force me to mess around. Just come back later. Move your foot, please."

"No. Let me in, now."

A deep voice from in the room broke the silence. "I don't care what you two do. Either come inside or stay out, but close the damn door. You're letting all the heat out."

Carson braced himself against the door frame. "Who the hell is that?"

"He's my friend. He's one of the bouncers at the club, and needed a place to crash last night. So, I let him."

"Really? You skank. I knew I couldn't trust you. Cheating is in your DNA. What else did you let him do?"

"Screw you, Don! You're not my boyfriend, and you're not my boss. I don't answer to you. Get that through your thick head! Now move your foot before I call the 'real' police on you."

She struck deep. He gritted his teeth and stepped back, attempting to hide his embarrassment with a noble posture, but he couldn't suppress the expression of his shame.

"Fine. You just saved me from catching Herpes today, thanks." He leaned forward and shouted through the gap. "You can have her, buddy! Enjoy your trip to the health clinic!"

"Don't ever come back here again, motherfucker!" she screamed and shut the door.

He wanted to have the last word, but it was over.

It was fun while it lasted, slut.

He walked down the stairs, noticing that the kids had stopped playing.

They watched him get into his car and back out. He rolled his window down and called out to the group of young females.

"Hey girls, remember this advice, and you will do your parents a huge favor. When you grow up, don't become a stripper. Be good girls."

He drove away, and they looked at each other and shrugged. One commented, "Who is that old fart?"

***

Elijah groaned. "Mommy, I'm hungry. I don't wanna wait."

"Please try and wait a little while longer. You can do it. Ms. Brittany and Ayana will be here in a few minutes."

Despite her reassurance, he pouted and went into his room. Madison sat on the couch, looking out the front windows. It was almost noon, and lunch was prepared. They planned to eat and then go shopping for a reasonably priced sleigh, but it needed to be a two-seater. Brittany was bringing wine and the ingredients required to cook her touted lasagna.

Brittany arrived and parked in the narrow driveway behind Madison.

"Elijah, they're here!"

He came running into the living room to look out the window and began bouncing while Madison opened the door.

"Hey, you two! Do you need any help?" Madison asked.

Brittany walked up the driveway, followed by her daughter.

"No girlfriend, we got it. I hope my emergency brake will hold on this hill."

"It should. I hope so."

She held the door as they walked past her into the living room.

Elijah waved. "Hi."

Madison took the bags from Brittany and stood beside him.

"Elijah, this is Brittany and her daughter, Ayana."

Brittany and Ayana leaned over and shook his tiny hand.

Brittany bubbled, "Hello, handsome. I'm glad to meet you." She looked at Madison. "He's such a cutie!"

"Hello, Elijah," Ayana said.

His eyes widened. "Hi. You're pretty!"

Madison laughed. "Oh my god. Elijah, come help mommy in the kitchen, and then let's show our guests around." She winked at Brittany. "We are going to have to keep our eyes on him."

They left their overnight bags and went into the kitchen to sort the items for supper. After washing up, they ate lunch and finalized their itinerary. They decided to shop for the sled first, anticipating the late afternoon snowfall, before buying a few family movie DVDs. Brittany planned to cook supper early and keep it warm, giving them time to try out the new sled. They expected enough snow accumulation and spending hours outside. After that, it would be supper, movies, and sleep - in that order. Everyone was excited, especially Elijah. This was a welcome change from his usual home environment. He now had a big sister, Ayana, who confirmed it when she pulled him over to her and hugged him.

"You're my little brother now. You're all mine."

***

Late that evening, Ayana and Elijah were snuggled on the couch half-asleep while a movie played in the background. The hours of sledding had taken their toll, and they were exhausted. Madison and Brittany sat at the kitchen table, laughing and drinking wine. Tears ran down Madison's face as Brittany told high school stories of her adolescent escapades in her unique and animated fashion. She was hysterical, and Madison couldn't listen anymore.

Madison begged, clutching her stomach. "Stop! Please! You're going to make me wet myself!"

"Alright, then I'll have mercy on you. I know how that feels. You better go pee now because I'm just getting started."

Madison scampered off to the bathroom but soon returned.

"Ah, you feel so much better now, huh?" Brittany asked.

"All sorted."

Brittany clapped her hands. "Okay, it's your turn. Share something, girlfriend. I know you must have some juicy stories. A pretty thing like you. Go."

Madison looked at the table, smirking. "I have plenty of stories, but none of them are funny." She poured herself another glass of wine. "My experiences were shitty. The only joke was on me."

"Aww, come on now. There has to be something. It was high school, you know?" Brittany set down her glass and leaned forward. "Think hard."

Madison's glazed eyes were making Brittany wonder if she was even listening.

Madison huffed. "I was a bad girl and sort of rebellious when away from my home. I had fights and other issues when I started high school. My mother finally had enough and sent me to an all-girls Catholic high school. None of that was funny though. But I had some funny dogs. I love dogs. All kinds, big, small, beautiful, ugly, funny-looking, you name it. They used to do hysterical things. Once, I had this German Shepard named Max. He was so cool. He was like a human but trapped in a dog's body. He always wanted me to play with him. When I was on the phone, he would get jealous and keep nudging me to pet him.

"That's cool."

"Okay, the funny part. When I would take a nap during the day, he wouldn't like that, oh no. He would climb up on my bed and lick my face, trying to wake me up."

Brittany frowned. "Yuck."

"No, that's not the funny part. When he would do that, I would just turn over and ignore him. Then he would nudge me in my butt. No, wait. He would try to burrow with his nose through the blanket, into my ass."

Brittany cackled. "Ha! What in the hell?"

"The funny part is that I would let him do it until I couldn't stand it anymore. I kind of liked it, weirdly."

Brittany burst out laughing. "It felt good, huh?"

"In a weird kind of way. Not sexually, but like, my ass must smell good?"

Brittany cheered. "I'm sure it does!"

They both bawled.

Madison put her finger to her mouth. "Shush. The kids might hear us."

Brittany looked past her into the living room. "Those kids are knocked out. So, how is Max doing these days? He's probably sniffing your mom's ass now."

Madison gulped her wine.

"He's dead. Just like the rest of them. Niko. Butch. Rosco. They eventually got sick, and mother had to put them down."

The mood had changed in seconds. Brittany wasn't interested in exploring any further, but Madison continued.

"They would all get sick sooner or later. My mother would handle the situation. She didn't believe in taking them to the vet, except for certain shots. If they didn't eat or drink after a few days, she would do it herself."

"She would do what?"

"My mother was a chemist for over thirty years. She knew what was used at the vet's office to euthanize animals. She believed there was a better way and refused to pay for a sick pet's vet visit, a diagnosis, or even having them euthanized, so she would do it herself. I remember she used Hydroxy-Methaburate and Tricozomine combined at three parts to 1. The chemicals were easily purchased, and she kept a supply. She would take away their water for an entire day, then put it in their water bowl and wait. After a day without drinking, They would lap up the entire bowl and be dead within five minutes. Mother said, 'Too little will make them sleep for days, and too much would stop an elephant's heart. One teaspoon of the mixture is all that's needed to kill a 100-pound animal'."

Brittany was silent, not knowing what to say. She could tell Madison didn't enjoy the dark memory. More questions would only encourage the sad reminiscence. "I'm sorry you lost so many. I wanted a..."

"She forced me to prepare it. She instructed me like a college student in the lab. I refused to give it to them. I begged her to take them to the vet. 'Use my allowance!' I pleaded, but she ignored me, and I hated her for it. The dogs would stumble around and drop. She would try to force me to watch, but I couldn't. I'd run to my room and cry and cry. Then the bitch would wait until night and drag their corpses out by the curb, and the next morning call animal control to report a dead dog in the neighborhood." Madison smirked, with her eyes full of tears. "That way, she didn't have to pay the vet for disposal."

"That's terrible. To not have enough money to pay for..."

"No, Brittany, my mom is wealthy. She had plenty of money. She never shed a goddamn tear!" Madison bawled and began to sob. Brittany rushed around the table and hugged her.

Brittany grabbed a napkin and handed it to her while rubbing her back. "It's alright. That's all in the past. Just don't think about it."

Madison nodded, wiped her eyes, and blew her nose. "I sure know how to ruin a good time, huh?"

Brittany smiled. "Hell no. We're all good." She peeked in the living room. "The movie is over, and I don't hear them anymore. They must be asleep. Let's get them into bed and get some sleep ourselves."

"That's a good idea. I'm so tired."

As Brittany started to walk away, Madison grabbed her arm.

"Brittany."

"Yeah?"

"Thanks for being my friend. I love you."

Brittany smiled, and they hugged.

"I love you too, Madison. I'm glad you're in my life."

They got the kids up to brush their teeth and unfolded the couch bed, dressing it with fresh sheets and a quilt. Within thirty minutes, the house was dark, and everyone asleep.

***

The following day, they all ate breakfast, and afterward, Brittany and Ayana left to go to church. Elijah was sad to see everyone leave and tried to leave with them, but Madison picked him up.

"Don't cry. Next week, we'll visit their church. But not today."

He pouted, laying his head on her shoulder. She waved as their car drove away, went inside, and sat him down.

"I know you're sad about them leaving, but guess what we can do?"

He looked up. "What, mommy?"

"We can go sledding again!"

His frown turned into a smile as he bounced. "Yay! I want to go. I want to go!"

"Then let's get dressed and go!"

She felt invigorated by the events over the last 24 hours. Madison's defiant conversation with her mother had left a negative cloud over her, but Brittany's positive visit had instilled hope in her wavering confidence. The psychological grip that once seemed unbreakable now showed cracks and flaws.

I can break away. I can.

She was reassured by Brittany's emotional support and everything that she brought to the table, namely honesty and sincerity. She was the only true friend that Madison knew, whose love was genuine.

Madison and Elijah went sledding, played in the snow, and ate supper before cuddling on the couch to watch tv before going to bed. The weekend was over, and she usually dreaded Monday mornings. But not tonight.

She chuckled to herself. I believe my mojo is back. She kissed Elijah on the cheek. "I love you, Elijah."

"I love you, mommy," he mumbled, his eyes closed.

Rather than have him walk, she carried him to his room and tucked him in bed, noting that soon he would be too heavy to pick up. She wanted him to grow up, but also wanted everything to stay the same, dreading the vision of his adolescence.

He's going to grow up, and you'll have to get used to it. It's part of life.

She smiled, and went into her room, turned off the lamp, and laid down. Her mind was quiet. The still silence of the darkness gave her clarity, and she could feel herself. Her heart was smiling. Finally, all was well again.

***

Ron rested his cards on the table. "Four of a kind, punk asses."

"You cheating, motherfucker," Terrance cursed. "Screw this. I'm going to sleep."

He pushed off of the table and went into the bathroom.

Conor scratched his head and yawned while looking at his watch. It was 11:47 p.m. "Yep. Time to hit the sack." He looked at Ron. "I guess you'll just have to play with yourself. But we know you're used to doing that."

Ron sat back with his arms opened wide. "Come on, boys, don't cut out early. I'm getting rich from you two clowns. Give me three more hours so I can enter early retirement."

Conor stood up and walked toward his bedroom. "What time are we getting up?"

Terrance left the bathroom and went into his room. "I ain't getting up until eight."

Ron stretched and yawned. "We're all getting up at 7:30 a.m. That'll give us all until eight o'clock to piss, shit and shower. 7:30 a.m.! Set your alarms!"

"Got it," Conor shouted from his room.

Ron went into his room and saw that Terrance was already in bed. He undressed and laid down.

"Did you get that, too, brother?"

"Yeah, I got it. Hey, don't be farting and stinking up the room, like you always do. Did you get that, Ron?"

"Yeah, I got that. Do you got this?" He farted. Terrance covered his head, and Ron turned off the lamp. "Don't worry about the farts. Worry about getting up early."

Ron was at peace. He had his gang back. His marriage was going well, and all his girlfriends were satisfied. Only one bump remained in his road, troubling him.

That bitch, Madison. Oh, you're going to get it.

He couldn't strike directly at her. It would take time to cut her loose from the herd. He hoped that she would soon be erased from his memory. But, until then, he assaulted her in the only way that he could - mentally.

Take that, you whore! Take it all!

He imagined holding her arms back and pulling her hair.

It hurts, huh? Shut your mouth and take it!

He went to sleep with a smile on his face, lulled to slumber on the cusp of his twisted fantasies. With Ron, all was well.

Hours passed as a mild but steady wind whistled through the trees. An owl's hoot and faint calls from coyotes peppered the pre-dawn darkness. The solitude of the cabin imprinted itself into the natural landscape, embodying tranquility.

The engine of a truck started, disturbing the silence before moving out of sight - and sound. Within a minute, serenity revisited the dark panorama, and the owl's hoot returned, answering nature's beckon and call.

CHAPTER 6

Don Carson rolled over and looked at his clock. It was 7:45 a.m. He sat up on the edge of his bed and began hacking, coughing up the previous night's cigarettes, before hobbling into the bathroom and emptying his bladder of last night's Scotch. He went over to the sink and sprinkled out the daily dosage of heart and blood pressure medications into his hand. A sip of water from the faucet and they were down. He debated taking a shower or just washing his face. His client wasn't due to arrive until 9 a.m. He sniffed his armpits and decided that a shower wasn't needed.

After hastily throwing water on his face and brushing his teeth, he started his morning routine of making coffee, heating one frozen breakfast biscuit, and turning on his handheld scanner. Meanwhile, he drank a full glass of water to begin rehydrating. It was one of the most important steps of his ritual. The combination made it possible for him to continue to function as an alcoholic physically. He knew what was required to keep going.

He sat in the den with his biscuit and coffee, looking out of the window and allowing his eyes to adjust to the bright sunrise. He added of few ounces of Scotch to his coffee, stirred and sipped.

"There we go," he murmured.

He lit a cigarette and blew out a plume, filling the room and crisply defining the rays of light as it expanded.

The scanner came alive. A traffic accident downtown. He turned on the television to the local news station and leaned back in his recliner, thinking about his upcoming client visit.

I need to vacuum and clean the guest bathroom.

The scanner sounded again. Officers were requesting homicide at a scene—one fatality. A few moments later, he heard Roger Olson responding. Don looked at the wall clock. It was 8:05 a.m.

This might be the perfect time to show up unexpectedly. The address is 20 minutes away. I can make it back here by 9 a.m. He hopped to his feet, and gulped down his coffee, then rushed into his bedroom. After throwing on the previous day's slacks, shirt and tie, he put on his overcoat and left the house. He sucked on two breath mints while entering the crime scene address into his GPS. It read 25 mins to the destination.

I can make it.

There were a few inches of snow on the road, but he wouldn't allow that to slow him down.

***

"Thank you very much for your time. You have my card, and I have your information. If you need to contact me at any hour, just call my cell phone. If we need anything else from you, you'll hear from us," Detective Olson told the man. The neighbor was visibly shaken, having been the first responder to the incident.

"Yes. Okay. I just wish I could have done more," he replied.

His hands were trembling as he attempted to slip the card into his wallet. Olson understood. He gripped the man's shoulder.

"Listen to me. I understand how shocked you are feeling. You didn't wake up today expecting any of this to happen. But it did, and although it was too late for the child, you handled the crisis professionally and achieved the best possible outcome. You tried your best, and I commend you. Do not feel any guilt."

The man nodded, and they shook. As the man walked away, Olson's partner Detective Schultz arrived and parked. He stepped out, holding two covered cups of coffee.

"Here you go, Roger," he said.

"Thanks."

Olson took a cup and walked toward the victim's vehicle. It had been hastily parked, with its front tire butted against the curb. The door was open, and the scene untouched, save the footprints in the snow made by paramedics and the first responder.

Schultz peeked inside the car. "What happened here?"

"A tragic Monday morning incident. From the initial interviews, it appears that a mother and her 4-year-old son were on their way out before exhaust fumes overcame them. The child didn't make it. The mother should pull through. We'll check on her later today at the hospital. She was still unconscious when the paramedics took her. Her CO_2 blood levels were off the charts."

"That sucks." Schultz walked over to the driveway. "Can you walk me through?"

"Sure. It's cut and dry." He pointed at the top of the driveway. "The scene was witnessed by a bunch of kids waiting on the bus, and also by a neighbor on his way to work. He was the first responder. He sees the unconscious mother hanging halfway out of the vehicle. He reported smelling overpowering exhaust fumes as he approached. It was unmistakable. He turned off the car and dragged the mother away. He sees the kid, and pulled him out, and checked for vitals. No vitals were detected, so he performs CPR. He realizes the child is not reviving. Now, my take, from the beginning. Mother and child are inside the car. She starts it, probably lets it heat up. Maybe she let it heat up first before coming back. Either scenario is logical. Anyway, you can see that the driveway is steep, and there are a few inches of snow. She must have backed down very slowly, all the time inhaling the CO2. She should have noticed the odor unless she had a cold or something. By the time she gets to the bottom of the driveway, she must be aware of the effects. She tries to pull over and get out, hence the car against the curb. Somehow, she opens the door, probably just before succumbing. Being overcome with Co2 and losing consciousness, she barely makes it. She falls out, hitting her head against the pavement, hence the blood in the snow by the driver's side door. The engine is still running. Her poor kid is still inside. By the time the neighbor gets him out, it's too late." Olson sipped his drink. "Even the paramedics smelled the exhaust when they arrived, and the car had been off for minutes."

Schultz nodded. "That sounds about right. It seems to fit. If that neighbor would have gotten to them a minute earlier, there could've been an entirely different outcome."

"Yes, sir. I agree."

"Do you want to make the call to have the car towed to impound and wait for forensics, or should I?" Schultz asked.

"I don't think any of that is needed. There's no suspicion or evidence of homicide. I don't see manslaughter through neglect or otherwise. We'll have to get the mother's statement, but this was accidental death by all indications. Also, to note, I've already peeked underneath the car. It's rusted to hell."

Schultz walked over to the open driver's door, reached inside, and unlocked the hood while Olson walked to the front.

"Let's take a look at the engine," Schultz said and raised the hood, peering inside. "Look at this. There's tons of rust and corrosion. It's full of crud, too."

Olson coughed and spat. "This car needs to go to the junkyard and be scrapped or sold at the County Police auction with full disclosure. Let's inform the mother at the interview. I bet that she doesn't ever want to see this piece of a shit car again. But that'll be her call."

Schultz whipped his head around. "Roger that, Roger. No pun intended."

Olson smirked. "That's a good one, junior."

Olson removed the keys, closed and locked the door. "Let's mosey on back to the office and update the status board."

They walked to their vehicles and noticed a car barreling down the road toward them.

"That dumbass is driving way too fast. Another Monday morning idiot," Schultz said.

Olson shook his head.

"That's my ex-partner. Fasten your seatbelt, young man, and hold on for the ride. He's a character."

Carson saw them and slowed down. Pulling along beside them, he lowered his window and stopped.

"Morning, Roger. It's been a long time. What's going on, pal?"

Olson walked over to the car.

"Well, well. Good morning Don, how the hell are you?"

"I can't complain. I could, but who else would listen to me besides you?"

"What are you doing out here?" Olson looked at his watch. "At 8:35 in the morning?"

"You know me. I was up early with the scanner on and heard the call. I hadn't heard back from you for a while, so I thought I would swing by. I do need to get back to the house. I'm meeting a client at nine o'clock."

Olson chuckled. "Yeah, that sounds about right. You're staying busy, I see." He turned and pointed at Schultz. "This is Alex Schultz. Alex, this is my old partner, Don Carson."

Schultz nodded.

Carson glared at Schultz. "Stick with Roger, and you'll learn a lot. Trust me."

Schultz smirked, walked over to his warm car, and got inside.

Carson watched him and lowered his tone. "That kid has a chip on his shoulder or something. How's he doing?"

"You know. He's still green but has a lot of potentials. He's part of the new generation. The kind of people that are textbook smart and always trying too hard to prove their worth. He seems like an alright guy, but we're still in the trust-building stage. You know what I mean."

"I know exactly what you mean, which brings me to another subject. Have you talked to the Chief or the Assistant AG about my situation? The clock is ticking, and I'm still in fricking limbo. I need help with this, buddy."

Olson tapped the door. "Relax, I spoke to the Chief and Angelletti two weeks ago. I reinforced my past recommendations to have you reinstated. From the feedback I received, they're moving on it. Just be patient."

Carson pointed at Schultz. "Patient? What about the kid sitting over there? He's filling my slot. That sure doesn't reassure me about the situation."

"Don, the kid is being fast-tracked. By the time you return to work, he'll probably be our boss. Besides, your slot hasn't been filled. Alex is here in the interim. I'm only mentoring him. Trust me."

"Okay then, I'll fall back as long as you're handling it. We've been through a lot, Roger, and we're way past our trust-building stage. I'll talk to you later. I've got to run."

He made a U-turn and drove away as Olson walked back to his car. Schultz lowered his window.

"Damn, Roger. The term 'old partner' is accurate. That guy is in rough shape. He needs to hang it up and move to Florida."

"Probably so, but his type won't go into the night quietly. Don't mind him, detective." He got inside, and they drove back to the precinct.

***

Twenty minutes later, the Traxtonite executive parking lot began to bustle. Ron and Terrance arrived first, with Conor trailing, and parked next to Luis's empty truck.

Terrance was the first to hop out. Carrying his travel bag, he walked around his Lexus to inspect.

He opened the door and threw his bag in the back seat. "Perfect. Not a scratch. Just like I left it."

"Why would it not be?" Conor asked as he and Ron walked toward the entrance.

Terrance trotted behind them. "Because I never know when one of my crazy side chicks might get emotional and get key happy with my car. It's happened before."

Ron palmed Terrance's head. "That's because you don't know how to keep your hoes walking the line, brother man."

Everyone casually diverged toward their work areas except for Ron. He hustled over to his office to prepare his talking points and look over any new emails. It was another typical Monday morning for the staff. Save one.

***

The staff meeting consisted of the same bland subject matter. Besides one or two unnecessary questions from the usuals, nothing new further extended the session with needless jabber. When the meeting ended, Ron happily walked back to his office and sat at his desk, waiting for the others to arrive. One by one, they came in and took their places. Luis and Terrance sat while Conor stood with folded arms.

Ron swiveled back and forth in his chair, grinning. "This is going to be easier than I thought. She's put the lid on her coffin."

Everyone was baffled.

"What are you talking about?" Luis asked.

"What? You didn't notice? Madison wasn't at the meeting. I've checked the sick call line, and there are no messages. The meeting is over, and she's still not here. That's a no-call, no-show," Ron replied. "I'll wait until lunch, and then go talk to Steve. She's getting written up for this."

"Good," Terrance said. "I don't have time to spy on her snitching ass anyway. I'm ready for her to be gone."

Ron leaned forward. "Maybe I'm too negative. Maybe, she had car problems. But also phone problems? Hell no, I'll tell you her problem. Ever since she went to Steve, she feels untouchable. It's the sexual harassment card she's playing. She has dumb ass Steve quivering in his shoes while holding it over his head."

"She'll probably be here soon. But she deserves a reprimand or something," Conor added.

Ron stood up and grabbed his crotch. "She deserves something alright. I got something for her right here."

Terrance and Luis laughed as Conor walked toward the door.

"Whatever you say, pee-wee," he said and left, with Luis and Terrance following.

***

It was 10:00 a.m., and Brittany sat at her desk, checking her phone. Her calls and messages to Madison remained unanswered, which worried her. She could feel that something was wrong. She left her office to recheck Madison's cubicle. Empty.

Jesus, please let everything be alright, she prayed. She walked over to Steve's office, knocked, and went inside.

"Good morning Brittany. What's up?"

"Steve, I need to take an hour off."

"Of course, that's not a problem. When?"

"Right now." Within minutes, she explained her concern about Madison's sudden absence and the inability to contact her. Steve had been unaware of her absence.

"Ayana and I spent Saturday night at her house, and everything was fine. I need to check on her."

"Sure, I have no problem with that, as long as you understand that your visit is not an official company visit. The company policy states that Human Resources will attempt to contact an absent employee after 4 hours of the start of their workday. But I know that you are very good friends, and I understand your concern. Let me know what's going on when you can."

"Thank you. I'll be right back."

***

There were fifteen minutes until the lunch bell sounded, and Conor, Terrance, and Luis hovered around Ron's computer watching YouTube.

"Here's the one. Check this out." Ron grinned and played a video of college girls twerking and dirty dancing.

Terrance squinted and leaned closer. "Make it full screen."

Their juvenile grunts and hoots drowned out the music. Conor looked up and saw Steve opening the door. He tapped Ron's shoulder and coughed. Ron quickly ended the video while the others circulated to the front of his desk.

Ron stood. "Hey, Steve, what's shaking?"

Steve closed the door. "Hey Ron, guys. Have you heard the news about Madison?"

"Nope. I was waiting until after lunch before visiting you. I haven't seen or heard from her today. She's now been late twice, including today's no call, no show. That's all within three months. I'll come by after lunch and discuss my thoughts on discipline with you. I know you'll have the final word, but this shit has to stop. This is a business, and we need..."

"There's been an accident. Madison is in the ICU at Abbott Northwestern Hospital. She's in stable condition." He sniffled and choked. "But her 4-year-old son died."

The atmosphere turned somber, along with everyone's expression.

"What happened? Do you know any details?" Luis asked.

Steve wiped the corner of his eye. "Brittany told me that they both received toxic CO_2 poisoning from her car."

Ron folded his arms. "Whoa, that's terrible. Poor kid."

Steve nodded. "We've spoken with Madison's emergency contact, her mother. She's flying out of Seattle today and should be at the hospital by early evening. That's all I have for now. I'll keep you informed of her leave status and if or when she decides to return to work." Steve shrugged. "I'm planning to take donations from the office for her this week and send around a card for those who wish to sign. I'll email the notification of the visitation and funeral arrangements when I get the specifics."

"That sounds good, thank you," Ron said. Steve left and closed the door as Ron collapsed in his chair.

"It's damn a shame," Terrance mumbled.

Luis hung his head and covered his face. "Oh my God. I can't believe it. She lost her child."

Ron noticed that Conor had moved next to the wall and was staring at him.

"What?" Ron asked. Conor scowled as he walked to the desk and knocked on it. "All that bullshit we talked about before, getting dirt on her, spying on her, yada-yada. It all ends here, and it ends now." He turned to Terrance and Luis. "I mean it. No more."

"I agree with you a hundred percent. It's over," Ron said.

Conor walked to the door, brooding, and looked back. "It's lunchtime. Let's go."

As they exited the office quietly, each man's attention diverted from the sad news, except for the guilty party. Their remorseful thoughts intensified and grew louder.

Jesus Christ! What have we done?

***

Later that day, around 5:30 p.m., Elizabeth Sanders arrived at the Saint-Paul Minneapolis International Airport. Within the hour, she claimed her checked baggage and signed the receipt for her car rental. The visiting hours for the ICU ended at 7:00 p.m., which left little time for her to get there due to the tail end of rush hour traffic. Regardless of the time crunch, she showed no sense of urgency or emotion as she entered her sedan. She had always been stoical and deliberate, with conservative mannerisms and staying true to form. These tragic family events also appeared to have no emotional bearing on her. She started the car, entered the hospital address into the vehicle's GPS, and left.

The white noise from the road inside the insulated interior was relaxing and caused her mind to drift. With each passing thought, her blank stare evolved into a frown of disgust. Her elegant and attractive facial features now morphed into an offensive, regal visage of the former as her obsessive thoughts rambled onward.

Madison, the idiot! You're just like your father, stupid and irresponsible. You don't care about this family's reputation. I sometimes wish that you were never born. She continued to fume as the frustration from the traffic encouraged her negativity.

After arriving at the hospital at 6:37 p.m., she found her way to the ICU ward and checked in at the reception desk.

"Hello. I'm here to see my daughter, Madison Sanders."

"Hello." The nurse looked at her tablet. "Yes, she's in Quad B, room 442. She has a visitor with her now, but we're only allowing one person in at a time. I'll inform her that you're here. One moment, please."

The nurse walked down the hall and returned with Brittany, and motioned toward Elizabeth.

"Hello Ms. Sanders, I'm Brittany Lewis, Madison's best friend. We work together at Traxtonite."

As they shook hands, Elizabeth gauged her, examining the company that Madison kept.

"I'm Elizabeth Sanders. I'm pleased to meet you."

"I wish it was under different circumstances. First, let me say that I am so sorry about Elijah. He was the sweetest boy. My daughter and I were with them this past weekend." Brittany pulled out a crumpled wad of tissue paper from her purse and wiped the tears from her eyes. "We had a beautiful day." She covered her face and began sobbing. Elizabeth nodded and watched Brittany attempting to compose herself. She sighed. "I'm sorry."

"It is a tragedy. I was briefly told what happened, but I haven't been truly informed of any specifics."

"I see. I can tell you that two detectives came to visit Madison earlier, but she was still dazed, so they told me that they would have to come back again. Madison has their business cards if you would like to contact them. I put them inside her purse. Her car had a horrible exhaust leak that overcame her and Elijah this morning, from what I was told. Madison went unconscious before she could react fast enough to get herself and Elijah out. The nurse said that she has a bad cold and is congested. That must be the reason she couldn't smell anything."

Elizabeth appeared surprised. "I see. How is it then that Madison survived, and Elijah didn't?"

Brittany was astounded.

What kind of question is that? Amazing.

"Ma'am, Madison went unconscious as she opened the door and fell out, hitting her head on the pavement. So she wasn't only poisoned by the CO2; she also has a concussion. She barely survived. They're treating her for both conditions right now."

Elizabeth looked down the hall. "I was merely curious. I guess her hard head was good for something." She signaled to the nurse at the desk. "May I see her now?"

"Yes. I'll escort you," she replied.

Elizabeth turned to Brittany. "There's no need for you to stay. You may leave. I'm sure Madison will be in contact with you after a few days. Goodbye."

She followed the nurse to the room.

Brittany stood there livid before walking away.

Madison was right. Her mom wasn't any ordinary bitch. She was a queen bitch. Unbelievable!

***

Madison was on her side, facing away from the door. Both her tears ducts and her soul were empty. She knew that her mother's entrance was imminent. Everything felt surreal, including her guilt. It smothered her. The detectives, the doctors, and her best friend had reassured her that the accident was not her fault. But the facts didn't matter.

I should have known! I could have done something different!

The thoughts of regret were anchored within her psyche, shackled to her natural motherly instincts. Such instincts were non-debatable and non-negotiable.

I failed him. Elijah! My baby boy!

Despite the powerful tranquilizers and her near-comatose condition, the repetitive mental dialogue continued. She heard the door open and shut. Mother was here.

As Madison heard Elizabeth's footsteps, a blanket of childhood fear and mental abuse covered her, adding another layer of turmoil and anxiety on her bed of despair.

"Hello, Madison. I know that you're awake."

There was silence.

"I met your friend Brittany. She appears to be a decent person."

Elizabeth walked over to a chair and set her pocketbook down.

"Madison? Madison!"

Madison cringed before curling up. "Yes, mother?" she slurred.

"Turn over, and look at me," Elizabeth whispered.

Madison's heart rate monitor increased. Elizabeth noticed the digital display and smirked.

I've got your attention. Good.

Madison rolled over and fixated on Elizabeth's stomach, unwilling to look up. With Elizabeth, prolonged eye contact could be misconstrued as a sign of defiance.

"I found out what happened. We both know that this entire situation was avoidable. You could have done more. I know that you..."

"Mother, I didn't know. How could I have known what..."

"Shut your mouth, and don't interrupt me. I have a lot to say, but as drugged up as you are now, you probably wouldn't remember a word. I am here now, and we'll have ample time in the future to review all of today's events." She shouldered her pocketbook. "I'll come back in the morning. First, I need to check in to my hotel room for the night. I'm exhausted from the flight and need to eat supper. I'm staying at Le Meridien Chambers, room 205. I'll let the nurse know since your obviously incapable of writing it down." She walked to the door. "Here's something to think about tonight. The word 'preventable.' Goodnight."

Madison rolled toward the window, utterly numb to everything but the pain of remorse. Although her eyes were physically incapable of shedding any more tears at the moment, her heart grieved with the invisible tears of misery.

CHAPTER 7

Six weeks had passed since Elijah's funeral, and each day appeared as a blur to Madison. Time seemed to stand still, as did her progression toward recovery. Mourning filled her days as she repetitively switched between a catatonic state and incessant sobbing. Elizabeth wouldn't stand for any of it. Her hawkish and controlling nature forced Madison to retreat into her bedroom during those grief-stricken outbursts and bury her face into the pillow, muffling any sound or whimper. But Elizabeth knew Madison and could hear every sound from Elijah's room. Madison wanted his room to be empty, at least for a few weeks. But she was afraid to make her request known. Besides, Elizabeth would never sleep on a pull-out sofa.

Brittany, on the other hand, was a godsend. She stayed in close contact and consistently visited each passing week, never deserting her friend. A simple trip to the store or a bite to eat with Brittany seemed like leave from prison. Outwardly, Elizabeth appeared unconcerned with Brittany's friendly visits. However, she was suspicious and vigilant. Her absolute ownership of Madison would not be challenged. Brittany sensed this, and besides a few minor verbal altercations between her and Elizabeth, there remained a fragile peace.

The one subject that both Elizabeth and Brittany agreed on was the poor state of Madison's mental health. Brittany somewhat knew of Madison's past mental breakdown, but Elizabeth experienced it first-hand. It was no surprise when Elizabeth insisted that Madison immediately begin trauma therapy and grief counseling. Brittany agreed, and not only in front of Elizabeth but also privately with Madison. Initially, Madison resisted, feigning illness, migraines or excessive menstrual cramping. But Elizabeth was relentless in her prodding. Her motives were not driven by her love, but by necessity.

Elizabeth had her reasons and her own life to live. There were many things she planned to do. Another mental breakdown would cause Madison to become once again non-functional in society. Besides being marginalized as a professional, and the stigma of social disgrace, Madison's condition would require Elizabeth to table her agenda and sacrifice valuable time from her own life to care for another adult. Whether that adult was her daughter mattered not. It was a violation of her principles and her freedom.

Madison had attended three weekly therapy sessions during the past month with the psychiatrist of Elizabeth's choosing. In that decision, there was little discussion. Madison went into the sessions and contributed to some degree, but she never truly opened herself fully. She guarded her most intimate secrets and past childhood events, not wanting to give the psychiatrist consent for deeper exploration and further extending the sessions. She accepted the prescribed medication, which helped some, but she wanted the sessions to end, Elizabeth to leave, and everything to return to normal. But that could never happen. Elijah was gone, and she was the reason why. That fact would never change.

Ironically, it was work that gave her the most comfort. She returned to Traxtonite three weeks after the funeral and buried herself in work assignments. It temporarily kept her mind from thoughts of Elijah and her miserable life. The eight-hour break from Elizabeth was much needed, and she found short-term solace. But every day, close to quitting time, she would instinctually look at the clock, remembering how excited she was to pick him up from daycare, before stumbling back to reality. Several times a week, she would rush to the women's restroom to sit in a stall and cry. Quietly weeping there on the commode was preferable to crying at home, where unsympathetic harshness awaited.

***

It was noon at Traxtonite, and while everyone else in the office ate in the breakroom, Madison and Brittany were eating lunch at Madison's desk. Madison felt more comfortable there, and the quiet time eased her nerves. Brittany wouldn't allow her to be alone, catered to her, heating any food in the microwave as needed, and brought it back. Madison finished her sandwich and stared out of the window at the bright green spring grass. It was beautiful outside, and she daydreamed. For a moment, a rare but happy imagination caught hold of her mind, resulting in a faint smile. But her thoughts soon returned to Elijah.

I'm sorry that you never got a chance to see spring. You would have liked it.

Brittany finished reading a magazine article on her tablet. "That was a waste of my time. It had nothing to do with the title. I can't stand clickbait." She noticed Madison daydreaming. "What are you thinking about? Your new car? How is it driving?"

There was silence.

"Madison."

Madison flinched. "I'm sorry. What did you say?"

"What are you thinking about?"

"I'm just thinking about how pretty it is outside," she replied, cleaning up her desk.

"It's nice. I love the smell of spring. It's a great time to get outside and do something. Mother Nature is calling."

"What is there to do?"

"Everything. You could go to the park and walk or go hiking. There are lakes and ponds everywhere. Some of the marinas on the lake rent peddle boats too. Hmm, that's something that we can do together. I'll find a place for us to visit."

Madison began staring out the window. It was understandable why Madison seemed off; nonetheless, Brittany stood, attempting to break Madison's repetitive trance.

"What do you think about that? Do you want to do it?"

Without looking up, Madison responded. "You've spent a lot of time helping me through this and sacrificing a lot of your time babysitting me. Thank you so much, but it's not fair to you or your family. You should be with them more. Time is precious, Britt. Spend it with them. I'll be alright."

Brittany frowned. "I don't think that I'm babysitting you. I'm being there for my best friend, who I love very much. I know you would do the same for me."

Madison sulked. "I don't want to be a burden on you anymore."

"You're not! Never that, Maddy."

She held Madison's arm and then hugged her. Lunch was nearly over, and the noise from the emptying breakroom trickled into the hallways.

Madison wiped her eyes. "It's time to get back to it. I have a ton of copies to make before the 2 pm meeting today. What do you have going on?"

Brittany giggled, grabbed her bag and water bottle. "Me? I'll be hiding. I've done all that I'm going to do today."

"I'll do it myself," Madison said.

"Do what?"

"I'll look around for a park where I can walk. That's a good idea. I need time alone, away from my mother. The exercise will be good for me."

"Great, I agree. I'll see you later. Call me."

Brittany smiled and walked away, feeling concerned. She understood that anyone grieving must have time alone, but the uncertainty of Madison's mental stability gave her pause, and she was worried. *Please, God, don't let her hurt herself.*

***

The early birds exited the lunchroom, exercising their pride in being the first to arrive at work and being the first to come back from lunch. For them, it was a badge of honor. Ron and Terrance sat at their table, packing their lunch coolers before leaving. Conor and Luis had been absent from their dedicated table for the past month, deciding to eat at another table with other office peers. This new development, along with their infrequent rendezvous in Ron's office, caused speculation that the two had 'dropped out' of the Wolfpack. Ron wasn't sure if their new routine was temporary or permanent and decided not to confront them directly. But it was eating at his pride.

I'm not going to beg and chase those jerks for friendship. I'm a grown man.

He watched Conor and Luis walk past.

Terrance tapped Ron's shoulder. "I'm heading out. Luis and I have to set up the main conference room for the meeting. What are you into?"

Ron was fixated on Conor, hoping to catch his attention. "What do you think, Terrance? Do those two think that they are better than us? We don't hang out anymore, and they don't even eat with us. What the hell is up with that?"

"Man, you need to quit with that shit. I'm glad to get a break from Luis. I work with him every day. He's cool."

"Yeah, but what about Conor? Ever since our last camping trip, he's been treating us like red-haired stepchildren."

Conor dumped his trash as he and Luis passed Ron and Terrance.

"What's up, guys?" Conor smiled. "Did you get your bellies full?"

Ron stood up, patting his stomach. "I didn't want to overeat today and ruin my six-pack."

Luis looked at Terrance. "Don't worry, Terrance, I ate plenty. Plenty of beans, mucho! In twenty minutes, I'll have a sweet-smelling surprise for you. Can you smell what Luis is cooking?"

Terrance's nostrils flared. "Please don't fart in the conference room. Not today, man. I can't take it."

Luis chuckled. "Don't knock it until you try it, homeboy. You have to sample it first."

They all walked out together snickering, with Ron laughing the loudest. For the moment, his apprehensions seemed unwarranted, so he muted his concern for the time being.

The hallways rumbled as the staff deviated in different directions toward their work areas. As the other three disappeared, Conor walked down the main corridor. Being over six feet tall, he towered over the others. Ever since his growth spurt during high school, he treasured the ability to look above the heads of everyone. He didn't know or care why he felt that way, but it was empowering.

He casually bopped down the hall. Further ahead, he saw Madison at the copier. His eyes fastened on her, and his mood began changing. He wasn't sure if it was a feeling, emotion, or both which caused the shift, but it was strong enough to notice. It wasn't only because she was attractive. It was more profound than that and unfamiliar, which naturally made him apprehensive. He recognized that only the mere sight of her had triggered it, and because of that, he intentionally avoided her. He continued his course while observing her discretely and masking his attention.

Madison turned around and collided with a passing employee. The folder in her arms flipped open, causing a stack of reports to spill onto the floor.

"Watch where you're going," Trina blurted.

Madison dropped to the floor to gather up the papers. "I'm sorry. It's my fault."

Trina looked down at her and walked away as Conor watched.

Trina, you tramp. Are you not even going to help her?

Still on her knees, she slid her hand under the copier, trying to retrieve the papers which slid underneath. She couldn't reach them. Conor stopped and knelt.

"Let me help you, Madison," he said and looked underneath, shining his penlight. "Hang on a second." He hopped up and went to the closest cubicle, and borrowed a ruler. She stood while he laid on his stomach and used the ruler to coax the paper out. He stood and handed her the sheets. "Most of the copiers have wheels, but these particular units don't. Here's everything that was underneath."

She glanced at him, never making eye contact. "Thank you," she mumbled and hurried away.

He watched her leave. "No problem."

He walked to his office and began sorting through his inbox. He was anxious and fidgety while he reviewed memos and shuffled through the pile. He dropped the stack of papers on his desk and interlocked his fingers. He couldn't avoid the obvious anymore and submitted to the truth. It was Madison. He wanted her and always had. It was clear to him that she was a shell of her former self, and understandably so. His heart was empathetic for what she had experienced and had to live with for the rest of her life. He replayed their recent interaction at the copier and relived his feelings at that moment. It was the closest, physically, they had ever been to each other.

Her scent.

He closed his eyes.

There's no possible way that I'm falling for her. Nope, not me. Not the legend.

He dismissed the romantic notions and impulses, chalking them up to a lack of sex. He had been extra horny since the recent breakup with his girlfriend.

It all makes sense now—close call.

***

A few hours later, Madison arrived home and went inside. It was quiet.

Hopefully, mother is napping.

Then she heard the toilet flush.

Damn.

She hurried toward her bedroom, as water from the bathroom sink ran, and scooted inside, closing the door. She kicked off her shoes, dropped her purse, and flopped on the bed. Then closed her eyes and curled up with a pillow. Besides Brittany, sleep was her best friend, and she welcomed it. Madison believed that it was the only natural condition besides its cousin, death, in which she could exist in nothingness. A place where pain, and thought, don't live. Her breathing reduced to a slow rhythm as she relaxed within her fragile biosphere. She heard Elizabeth's footsteps, then a knock on the door.

"Madison, I need to speak with you. Come to the kitchen."

And then she was gone.

What now? Why now?

"Yes, mother."

She rolled out of bed, changed into shorts and a t-shirt, then went into the kitchen. Elizabeth sat at the table with her laptop.

"Good. That's a fair price." She removed her eyeglasses and turned to Madison. "The time has come to make some important changes. I've been here five weeks, and I believe it's time to leave."

Madison was speechless but wanted to shout for joy. *Thank you, God! Thank you so much!* Instead, she crossed her arms and nodded.

"Do you agree? You have no issues with my decision?"

"No, mother. I'm ready as well. I know that you are too."

"Good. I've just checked the pricing on our tickets and found some acceptable rates. I'll purchase them now."

She put on her eyeglasses, and Madison walked over.

"Our tickets?" Madison asked.

"Yes, of course, I'll purchase your ticket. Save your last paycheck. You'll need it as you look for a new employer in Seattle. Don't worry. You need not pay me back, similar to the down payment I provided for your new car. Before it skips my mind, I also have a shipping estimate for your car. You need not worry about that. By the way, your old bedroom is still the way you left it. As I said, you need not reimburse me. However, a simple 'thank you' would be in order. You're mature enough to show a glimmer of gratitude. I have done, and am doing, quite a bit for you."

"Mother, I'm not leaving with you."

"That makes no sense at all. Why not travel together? Are you still afraid of flying? Grow up."

"Yes, I am, you know that. But that's beside the point. Mother, why should I leave at all? I'm getting better every day. I only need time. But I do thank you for offering."

Elizabeth pointed a bony finger at her. "Madison Sanders, you're coming home with me! I'll not hear another word about it!"

Her voice penetrated deep into Madison's brittle core, and tortuous silence followed. Madison struggled to remain straight-faced and hold her composure, but it became impossible. She turned away from Elizabeth in a feeble attempt to hide her contorted expression of shame. It was the shame of submitting to Elizabeth's control, and it crushed her confidence. Madison felt like a helpless child with no self-value.

Those feeling of helplessness suddenly stirred memories of another child, Elijah. This time, his memory invigorated her. She had given birth to him and been his mother.

I'm not a child. I'm a grown woman.

As the keystrokes from Elizabeth's fingers grew louder, Madison's emotions intensified until she could no longer resist. She whipped around.

"No!" She went to the opposite end of the table. "I'm not leaving. I'm an adult. I thank you for everything that you've done for me, but you don't get to tell me what to do anymore, mother. No more. Never again! Got it!?"

She stomped out of the room and into her bedroom and slammed the door.

Silence ensued as Elizabeth sat with her finger still pointing and trembling. A moment later, she finalized the purchase, buying one, not two, airline tickets. She shut down her computer, turned off the light, and went to bed.

Madison was on her bed, crying and biting the pillow to muffle any sound. Although upset by her outburst, Madison staunchly refused to let Elizabeth glean any weakness. By exploding, Madison had crossed into the unknown and was in the right to do so. But these new and contrary emotions were alien to her. She felt terrified yet emboldened. She was filled with grief but felt a sense of satisfaction. It was all becoming too much for her and had to be controlled.

I'm losing my mind. I must be going insane. I have to be. Help!

Hold on, Maddy, you can do it. You'll get through this. Just hold on.

How? I wish that Daddy was here right now. I miss him. I miss him so much!

She cried desperately before pleasant memories of her father replaced the sorrow and made her smile. She was emotionally wired but exhausted and mentally drained. She expected to stay awake all night, being vexed by her newfound manic impulses, but the tranquility of sleep was only a few breaths away. It took her without warning and silenced her misery.

***

Across town at the Foxy Diamond Strip Club, the music was deafening, as were the clouds of smoke passing through the multi-colored flashing lights. It was crowded, packed, and suffocating as half-naked women danced on four stages, with raging males of all ages swarming everywhere.

Don Carson sat in the back, at his table, with his bottle. He'd been inside for a few hours, drowning his frustrations. The clock was ticking closer toward his retirement, and nothing on the horizon was changing that inevitable outcome. He finished his drink and poured another.

I can't believe that no one is going to bat for me after all of the favors that I've handed out. I should have squeezed more drug dealers before I got pulled. That was stupid. All those missed opportunities. Dumb ass.

He checked his phone. No messages.

Fucking Roger!

He gulped down his drink, then stood up to adjust his belt. A young man sitting across the room caught his attention, mainly for the jewelry he was advertising. The man's large platinum and gold chains, rings, and money thrown at the dancers were apparent clues to his profession. Carson assessed the man's overweight body type and build.

He's no athlete; that's a fact. But he sure is full of himself, throwing around that dirty money without a care in the world. Okay, I'll save him for later.

Don was planning a shake-down. The department had his badge, but he always kept a spare. It was a trick from the old-school Blue. Report your badge lost but stow it. You earned it and had the right to keep it. Use the replacement. You never know when you might need it later. Carson had everything needed. A gun, a badge, and a blue light. Within minutes, he planned to follow the man as he left, and stop him somewhere on the road and roust him. Carson didn't view himself as impersonating a detective. He lied to himself instead.

It's just the natural order of things—the weening of the herd. No harm, no foul. Within his mind, the justifications abounded.

Presently, he was horny. He'd taken his blue pill in advance, and the effects were active. He looked around for his regular, his favorite. She walked out from the private section with a satisfied customer trailing behind. Carson weaved his way through the patrons to intercept her.

He grabbed her arm. "Hey!" he shouted over the music. "Let's go. I'm in a hurry!"

"Okay, but would you please stop squeezing my arm!"

"Oh, sorry!"

He let go and followed her into a small room in the private section. She closed the curtain for privacy.

"What do you want to do?" she asked.

"Blow me."

She held out her hand. "Fifty. In advance, as usual."

He opened his wallet, handed her money, and she began to count.

"There's no need to count it, sugar. It's all there," he whispered while placing his hands on her shoulders and forcing her down. She shook him off and stepped back.

"Bullshit, Don! This is only forty-six bucks. Where's the other four?"

He opened his empty wallet and turned it upside down. "Damn, I'm out of cash right now. I'll make it right the next time and give you a good tip. I promise," he slurred.

She stared at him, debating the deal. "This is the last time that I let you come up short." She knelt. "And don't take long. I have paying customers waiting."

He grunted and unzipped his pants. "This won't take long if you'd stop flapping your lips, so stop talking and get to work."

He was on a tight schedule, needing to be in the car and position as his unsuspecting victim exited the premises. This wasn't Carson's first rodeo. He was a pro, having no qualms about it.

***

The following day, Madison woke up feeling refreshed but hungry, having slept through the night without eating since noon. After using the bathroom and showering, she brushed her teeth and went to the kitchen. Elizabeth was on her mind, along with the possible ramifications of last night's outburst. Surprisingly, there were no overwhelming feelings of anxiety or angst, but she left a message on the call-in work line anyway, expecting another emotional confrontation.

She looked for Elizabeth, who was in her room with the door shut, and noticed her mother's luggage sitting by the front door.

Wow. She really is leaving!

She tensed with excitement, anticipating her departure. She wanted something quick to eat and grabbed a yogurt. She popped the lid and stirred.

"Good morning."

Madison flinched around to see Elizabeth dressed and holding her purse.

"Good morning, mother."

"I was fortunate enough to book a flight out this morning. There's no need to delay any further since you feel confident in handling your affairs. Goodbye." She walked to the front door as Madison followed her. Every step brought Madison closer into the shadow of unfounded guilt from her eruption, but she resisted those old demons by mentally repeating her defense.

I did nothing wrong. I did nothing wrong.

"Mother, thanks for all your help. I want to ap...I hope you have a safe trip home. Let me carry your luggage."

"I can carry my luggage, thank you," she hissed, yanking open the door. Madison stood in the doorway, watching her load up the car and leave. There was no smile or goodbye wave. When the red taillights disappeared from view, Madison closed the door and walked into Elijah's room. She texted Brittany the news, dropped her phone, and collapsed on the bed, bawling. The collective release of relief and grief somehow gave her a sense of balance. She accepted that healing from sorrow would take time, but standing her ground the night before sparked a newfound sense of liberation. Rebelling against Elizabeth's misplaced authority sparked a new awareness of freedom within her core being.

"The thought of you helped me do it, Elijah. My sweet baby. Elijah? Mommy is so sorry. Please forgive me. Please forgive me."

***

Later that morning at Traxtonite, Ron walked into his office and was surprised to see Conor, Luis, and Terrance sitting together, hooting with laugher.

My boys have come back home. It's about damn time.

He grinned and sat behind his desk, witnessing the ruckus response to Terrance's storytelling.

"There were five of us in the express checkout line. I was in the middle. A fitness chick in spandex was in front of me, and an old lady was checking out at the register. Then the smell hit me. It was so bad that my eyes began watering, and my nose hairs were on fire! I looked at the two people standing behind me. They were straight-faced. The odor hadn't hit them yet. I say to the chick in front of me, 'Excuse me, but do you smell that?' She snaps, 'No, I don't smell anything.' She says it loud enough for everyone to hear, which made everyone think that I was the one who had farted, when it had to be her!"

Conor laughed. "Right, she framed you, bro, putting you under the 'Whoever smelt it, dealt it' rule. That's pretty slick."

"It could have been the cashier. No one ever suspects them!" Luis said, adding to the laughter.

"That's funny shit," Ron commented. "So, what do you guys have going on?"

"Work. What else?" Luis replied.

"This week has been boring as hell," Terrance said.

"I'm finishing up the draft for Rexor and Ingersoll-Rand, then chilling out for the rest of the day. What about you?" Conor asked.

"I'm skating today, right after I drop off the attendance report to Steve. Do you want to cut out of here early today? Maybe hit the Tap Room?"

Conor gave a thumbs up. "Okay, let's leave after lunch. That way, we'll already have food in our stomach before getting slammed."

Terrance's jaw dropped. "That's just plain wrong. Why should you guys get to leave early?"

"Because we can, man, understand?" Ron laughed. "Check out my rapping skills, bro, and don't be hating on me."

Terrane stood. "You can't rap, you're not funny, you sound like a clown; with that shit on your face, you should be wearing a frown!"

They burst into laughter as Conor and Luis high-fived Terrance.

Ron nodded, wearing an embarrassed smirk. "You got me, bro. Good one."

Their amusement dissipated, and they stood to leave.

"Why don't you guys leave early today and come with us?" Conor said. "You two never leave early. The four of us haven't been out together in a while." He looked at Ron.

Ron shrugged. "They can't come with us, at least not today. Two people have already called out. If the four of us leave, it reduces our office totalization by six, under the forecasted limit. It's not a big problem, but I would have to update Steve. It raises red flags, and questions would be asked, like, 'Why are you guys pulling this shit again?'."

"Fuck Steve," Terrance grumbled.

"Who called out sick today?" Luis asked.

"Gabrielle and Madison," Ron replied.

"Madison? I wonder what's wrong with her," Conor asked.

"I don't know, and I don't care. I hate even speaking her name," Ron replied.

"I'll catch up with Brittany later. She'll probably know," Conor said.

Ron frowned and crossed his arms. "Why do that?"

"Why not? I'm only checking on the woman through her friend. I'll tell her to keep it between us. What's wrong with that?"

"It's not smart. No, it's fucking stupid, okay? With all the shit that we've been through with that chick, you want to stir some more shit up. No, don't do it."

"Motherfucker, you're not my boss – or my father. I'll do whatever I want. I'm curious how she's doing, that's all. She's been through some rough times, so excuse me for having a heart."

Ron's face turned red as if he'd been slapped.

Terrance raised his hand. "Conor, I agree with Ron, man. Why even open up that box? Leave it alone, bro."

Luis leaned forward. "It's not a good idea, Conor. I'm sure she's doing fine, but don't you realize that anything you say to Brittany will get right back to Madison? They are best friends. You don't want Madison to freak out and think she is being harassed again. She'll run right back to Steve and complain. We just got out of that situation. That's what Ron is saying."

"But I never harassed her!" Conor yelled. "Neither did you, Luis." He waved his finger in anger. "It was you two that created the entire situation."

Ron shrugged. "That doesn't matter anymore. This is where we are at now, period. I get it. You broke up with your girlfriend, and Madison is at her weakest. At any other time, we all would take the same route as you toward her panties. But not this time."

Conor stood in their midst, feeling betrayed.

These assholes don't care about anyone—heartless bastards.

He walked to the door. "No, guys. You're wrong. I've had enough of your bullshit. From now on, you do you, and I'll do me. You can kick me out of the Pack. At this point, I don't give a shit."

He slammed the door and marched towards Brittany's office. He was furious but managed to calm himself down as he arrived in her doorway. As gently as he could, he knocked.

"Hey, Britt," he smiled. "How's it going today?"

Brittany looked up from her monitor. "Hello, stranger. It's going. That's all I can say. How have you been doing these days? It's been years since you took time to stop by my office."

He stepped inside. "Yeah, I know. I've been a bad boy; forgive me." He smirked. "But all is well with me. I'm glad to see that spring is finally here."

"I know, right?" She leaned back. "So, what's up, playboy?"

"Oh, nothing much."

"Ha! Boy, don't even try it. We go way back. I know you. So what do you want? What's up?"

"I know, right? You've exposed me." He chuckled. "Okay, Britt, I want you to keep this between us. Do I have your word?"

She winked. "My lips are sealed."

"Brittany Lewis. Just between us."

She held up three fingers. "Girl Scouts honor. I promise. I can also knock on wood." She winked.

He closed his eyes and grinned. "I was wondering how Madison is doing. I heard she called out today. Is she sick?"

Brittany cocked her head. "Come again? I don't believe I heard you correctly."

Conor shrugged. "I'm only checking on Madison out of my concern as a co-worker. It's no big deal. Don't play around."

Brittany bounced from her chair and closed the door.

"Do you like Madison?" she whispered.

"No. I mean, yes, but not in the way that you're thinking. And stop whispering, silly."

Brittany crossed her arms. "What way am I thinking? Either you do like her, or you don't. Don't start with your games. Do you like her and want to get to know her better? Or do you like her just enough to have sex with her? Be honest with me. This is Britt that you're talking to, and you know that I can't be played for a fool."

"I swear, this has nothing to do with the other guys, a scheme, or any of that shit. I've been thinking about her lately. I've watched her change and go through a lot. With everything that has happened to her, I don't know, but she seems fragile. Since her son died, she's been alone. She seems like a sweet person. Anyway, I was just checking on her through you."

"Do you have a girlfriend?"

"No. I broke it off weeks ago."

Brittany searched his eyes.

He seems very sincere. Maybe, he's changed for the better. Time will tell all.

She sat behind her desk. "Madison is fine. She decided to take the day off because her mother had been staying with her since Elijah's funeral and flew back to Seattle this morning."

"Really? Okay, that's cool. I'm glad to hear it. Thanks for the info, Britt. I'll talk to you later," he said and reached for the doorknob.

"Conor."

"Yes?"

"I love Madison. She's my best friend, and I won't allow her to be hurt in any way. You need to understand that fact. You seem sincere. I hope so. It would be nice for Madison to meet an honest person who sincerely cares about her welfare. She needs someone in her life that's dependable and trustworthy. She has a lot to offer a partner in a relationship, but she needs to heal first. Having another 'friend' added to her circle would be great and make a huge impact on her life. Maybe you could be that friend? Or maybe not. We'll have to see what happens in the future."

Conor leaned back on the door. "She's special, I know that, and I swear that I only have good intentions. Don't worry about that. But can I ask you one more thing?"

"Sure, what?"

"In the future, whenever I come back here to check on her wellbeing, would you skip all the hyper-sensitive monologue and keep things simple?" He smirked.

"Get out of here. You're dismissed," she growled.

He left smiling. Her grimace changed into a grin as she picked up her phone and texted Madison.

Hey, Maddy. Enjoy your day off and celebrate your freedom. I hope you find a peaceful place to walk. Let me know where. Btw, Conor asked about you. He wanted to make sure you were doing well. Just letting you know. Love you!

Send.

***

Madison's newfangled sense of freedom was intoxicating. With her windows down, she streaked through the outskirts of town while following her GPS to the destination. She located a battery of hiking trails on South Lake, southeast of Lake Minnetonka. Many of the online photos reminded her of another picturesque location in Seattle that she was fond of visiting. It was a secluded area where she and Tony spent time.

The thought of him didn't spoil her warm memories of that area. Her obsessive feelings about him had faded long ago. As she pulled into a lake parking area, her phone vibrated with a message from Brittany. Madison began reading it and smiled, but her smile turned into a frown when she got to the last sentence.

Conor asked about me? That's not a big deal. It was a nice gesture, but I can't trust him. She thinks that the news makes me happy, but it doesn't; not really. She means well.

Madison thanked her and turned off her phone. She didn't want any distractions from the outside world during this therapeutic moment and walked toward the trail, reviving herself with every step and inhaling the cool lake breeze. She stepped onto the path and looked around, then turned left to begin her exploration along the lake's edge, grateful for nature's scenic blessing of awe and harmony. She was at peace and felt indebted for the opportunity to be part of it.

***

The Spring blooms signified new life and new beginnings. Similarly, the following months for Madison were therapeutic and transformative. She would never be who she once was again, but she firmly picked up the pieces of her life and decided to become the very best person she could, if possible. If not for herself, for Elijah. She had an epiphany and concluded that she would best honor his memory and life by being her best self. The pain of his loss was stubborn. It lived deep within her bones. But the intensity and duration of the waves of grief and guilt were slowly diminishing as time passed.

She began eating in the lunchroom with Brittany again, without apprehension or paranoia. She was learning to adjust and understood that no one was in her way anymore, not even her mother. Elizabeth hadn't called, which was a blessing for Madison. There weren't any more dark clouds of humiliation hovering in her mind, and that aspect gave the sun a chance to shine in her life, allowing all good things to grow.

Conor was her secret admirer. He watched her recovery and transformation from a distance while never exposing himself. He was happy to see her doing well, but he wanted more. His not being able to speak to her openly while at work made him want her even more. One day, during his weekly visit to Brittany's office, he made a breakthrough.

"Hey Britt, how are you?" Conor asked.

She continued typing without looking. "Ugh," she sighed. "I'm fine."

"How's Madison..."

She paused and looked. "Stop. If you want to know how she's doing, then ask her yourself. I'm tired of being your mediator."

"You know that I can't talk to her around here. I'm not going to toss her into the rumor mill. I thought you understood that."

Brittany scribbled on a post-it note and handed it to him.

"What's this?" he asked.

"It's the location of the trail where she walks after work every day. You can check on her there. I'm busy." She continued typing. "Bye, Conor."

He looked at the note.

"Thanks, Britt."

It was close to quitting time. As he walked back to his office, he debated what he should do - if he should do anything at all.

***

It was a gorgeous Friday afternoon, and while most commuters were fighting the traffic to get home, to school, or to socialize, Madison was completing her second lap on the trail. The past months of regular exercise had made her fit and her body lean. The walk served the dual purposes of mental relaxation and physical fitness. She pushed herself harder.

I should be sweating like a pig by now.

She increased her stride while thinking about what she wanted to eat later.

Madison felt fortunate that this particular trail was usually unoccupied, and she wondered why. It was beautiful, but there were dozens of similar hiking trails and parks around all the lakes. She appreciated the solitude even more while passing the rear of the person ahead of her.

Several weeks had passed since she had to share the trail with anyone else.

Don't mind them. You can't have everything you want in life.

She looked ahead and ignored him. Then, she increased her speed and overtook him.

God, he's so slow. Get out of the way!

"Madison?" he called out. Surprised, she slowed down and looked at the man's face.

"Conor? What are you doing here? I've been walking this trail for two months, and I've never seen you here before."

"I have a confession to make. A while back, I asked Brittany about you and how you were doing. Today, she finally got fed up and told me to ask you myself. She wrote down this address, so here I am. How are you?"

Madison's expression went blank. "Uh, I'm fine. But I still don't understand why you would drive out here to ask how I'm doing when you could ask me at work. That doesn't make sense to me."

She stood with her hand on her hips, sweating and looking at her watch.

"No, it's not like that. If I talk to you at work, it will start rumors, no matter how innocent it is, and with the history between you and some of our peers, it wouldn't be a good idea."

"You mean that piece of shit, Ron? Yes, I can see him running his mouth. Even Terrance. But so what? You're probably here for your little boy's club. What do you call it? The Pack? No, the Wolf Pack, right?"

"Absolutely not, Madison, I swear. I never did anything to you or said anything disrespectful to you, right?"

She thought for a moment. "That's true. I'll admit, you were never rude to me. When I think of it, neither was Luis. But those other two friends of yours are scumbags. Months ago, I reported them to Steve for harassing me. I could have gotten them into big trouble, but I blew it off. They should realize how lucky they are."

"I agree with you, but Luis and I got caught up with them and reprimanded also. We didn't deserve that."

Madison was stunned. "What? I never mentioned your names to Steve. I only reported Ron and Terrance." She looked at the ground, attempting to recall the past events. "No, I never brought you up. Why would I?"

"It's not your fault. It's my fault for choosing the wrong people to associate with at work. You know, guilt by association. But anyway, I don't want to talk about them. I see you're doing good, looking great, and, well - I'm happy for you."

His concern was disarming, and she appreciated his sentiments.

She shook her head. "I'm very sorry that you were dragged into any of it. That was never my intention. I'll talk to Steve and let him know that you and Luis had nothing to do with anything. I'll make it clear. I feel bad."

"No, don't do that. It's not necessary. It's old news. But I'm glad you understand the truth. So, are we good now?"

She smiled. "Yes, we are. Okay then, see you at work. Have a good weekend." She waved and walked away.

"Wait."

She turned around. Conor appeared lost and at a loss for words.

"What?" she asked.

"Do you mind if I walk with you? I could use the exercise if you don't mind the company."

"Conor, I don't think that your girlfriend would appreciate that. I know that I wouldn't if you were my man."

"I'm not in a relationship. I'm not even dating anyone. I'm putting dating on the shelf for a while. I need to put more time into myself. Do you know what I mean?"

"Yeah, I know all about that. Okay, come on then. Hopefully, you can keep up with me," she added with a smirk.

He grinned. "I'll try my best."

They started down the trail, beginning their first of many treks together during the weeks to follow. No one needed to know, except for Brittany. She was her best friend and the architect of the encounter. That couldn't be avoided. But Conor kept his silence about their routine, not wanting the glow of his new interest to become tarnished by the brutes he called friends. He would not disrespect her or allow anyone else to do the same.

Madison and Conor's personalities clicked immediately and effortlessly, making each rendezvous an enjoyable affair and something they looked forward to daily. It was no surprise when their feelings and emotions began to simmer due to the mixture of time and chemistry. This inevitable fact came to fruition on the day that Conor surprised Madison at the trail with flowers, along with a request to join him for dinner.

Her eyes began to water when she asked him, "Why me? Why? There's nothing special about me."

"Madison, I've wanted you since the first time I saw you. After these past months of getting to know you, I realized something. I can't see myself with anyone else but you. You are all I want," he said before pulling her close. She yielded to him as they kissed, and their mutual desire breached the floodgates. They no longer held back their desires and allowed the ignition of their hidden passion. Madison never imagined feeling this way again, after so long, and after so much. But she felt safe within Conor's solid arms and reveled in ecstasy as his gentle hands lay firmly against the small of her back.

They ended their hike prematurely and walked back to their cars, holding hands. It was all wonderfully new and, in a strange way, frightening. But it felt right and proper. Summer was quickly approaching, and everything was heating up.

CHAPTER 8

S pring, the Following Year

It was Friday morning, and Madison's alarm sounded. She stirred in bed while Bob Marley's Three Little Birds' easy listening tones played in the background, replacing the former new wave punk sounds of Jim Carroll's People Who Died. The marked change in her musical taste was representative of her new mindset. She found herself engulfed in contentment as the morning adrenaline pumped through her veins. Mentally, she sang with the chorus, confirming the words and claiming them as her mantra.

Don't worry about a thing, Cause every little thing gonna be alright, Don't worry!

She felt lazy this morning and didn't want the music to end or go to work.

His warm hand brushed across her belly and moved toward her thigh.

"Morning," Conor whispered, with half of his face sunken into the pillow. She ran her fingers through his dark hair.

She silenced her alarm. "Good morning, sweetheart. I don't want to go to work today."

He smiled. "At least it's Friday, babe. Only one more day till the weekend."

He yawned and rolled onto his back to stretch.

"That's true. I don't know why I feel so lazy."

He flipped onto his stomach and kissed her legs, easing his way towards her belly button. "I know what you need to get you started. Energy. Let me charge you up."

He began kissing her neck before moving to her lips. She turned away, grimacing.

"Morning breath. We need to brush our teeth."

He caressed her. "Just turn around and face the other way."

"Conor, we'll be late."

He rolled her over onto her stomach. "So what? It's Friday. Plus, it won't take long. I'm about to explode."

She relaxed. The heat from his hot body radiated against her skin, melting her as he kissed the back of her neck. As always, she submitted to his erotic nature, endlessly craving his caress. His touch fulfilled her. Not only mentally and physically, but emotionally as well. It became, of all things, a form of therapy. In her opinion, the tsunami of endorphins experienced during intercourse with Conor rivaled the effects and benefits of medical drugs or psychiatry sessions. There was no comparison.

"Take me," she moaned.

He did just that and fulfilled his claim.

He was right again. I do feel energized.

After the two separated, they showered together as usual. Afterward, Conor kissed her.

"I told you that it wouldn't take long. We won't be late," he said.

"Yep, you said it. It was short but very, very sweet."

"Just like you, babe, short but very, very sweet." He winked.

She laughed. "Get out!"

She closed the door and began to put on her makeup. She decided to wear her hair differently for a change. The change was good, and she embraced it with open arms.

Twenty minutes later, she applied the last touch of her eyeliner and stepped back from the mirror for a final inspection.

Looking good, Maddy.

She reached for the door and fixated on her engagement ring, then smiled and turned to the mirror. *You look like a new person. You've come a long way. Be proud of yourself. You did good!*

At that moment, her mind was filled with rogue thoughts and flashbacks from the past December. Christmas without Elijah was painful, at times even excruciating. She visited his gravesite once since the funeral but couldn't endure going back; not yet. She wanted to be closer to him and his memory. Still, it was excruciating, torn between honoring his last physical resting place and accepting the reality that his spiritual resting place was elsewhere. The thought of him being alone and buried deep within the cold ground was overwhelming.

Had it not been for Brittany's support, along with Conor's marriage proposal and unwavering dedication, she doubted her ability to reach the new year. There was no Christmas phone call or correspondence from Elizabeth and no response either, even after Madison reached out several times. She left a voice mail informing Elizabeth of her engagement to Conor, but still nothing.

Her eyes began to water. "No, you don't. Don't you dare," she mumbled while tearing toilet paper from the roll and blotting her eyes.

I didn't spend all this time putting on makeup to look like the damn Joker.

"I didn't hear you. What did you say?" Conor shouted from the living room.

"Nothing. I'm not crazy, but I was talking to myself!"

"You're not crazy, as long as you don't answer yourself!"

He went to the bathroom as she opened the door.

She struck a seductive pose. "It's your turn now. The princess has finished her work."

"Damn, you're a hot babe. Do you want a second round?"

He slipped past her and squeezed her butt.

"No way, you sexy beast. I tap out. Hurry up in there, and I'll start on breakfast."

***

They rode in Madison's car with Conor driving and arrived with five minutes to spare. He shut off the car and turned to her.

"Have a good one, babe."

"You too, sweetheart." She gave him a peck.

The passing employees paid no attention to the couple. They were old news from last year, and the rumor mill's initial shock value had dissipated. Madison and Conor had kept their relationship a secret during the first three months, but eventually resented hiding their commitment within the shadows. By the sixth month, they decided to live together in Madison's house. Initially, Conor preferred renting a new place, believing that it would help Madison let go of memories of the house, but her feelings were contrary to his suggestion. She needed those memories and wasn't ready to move on or let them go. He recognized and accepted that fact and didn't press the issue.

As they walked inside, he held the door for her, and they parted ways toward their desks. He strolled through the main office in a terrific mood, greeting the passing peers with his charming smile. His chipper disposition wasn't only because of the countdown to weekend bliss, but it was because of Madison. Even though he thought of her as a wounded bird, he realized the positive effect that she had in his life. While dealing with her emotional issues, she prodded and encouraged him toward his full potential by sincerely listening to him, supporting his endeavors, and believing in him. Unlike the other women he dated in the past, Madison wasn't afraid to show him an appreciation for minor acts of kindness and consideration. She even treasured his surprise displays of affection. The result was that he trusted her completely, and she loved him deeply.

He passed Ron's office and glanced in to see his three former comrades inside.

He waved without stopping. "Hey, guys!"

They stopped talking and returned the greeting as he passed by.

Ron frowned, and Terrance dropped his head.

"So, our boy is getting married in September. Unbelievable," Ron said.

"Yep. Madison has him whipped for sure. I heard that he sent out wedding invitations already. Are you going?" Terrance asked.

Ron contorted his face. "Ha! Yeah, right. I never got one. How about you?"

"Hell no, and I know it was that bitch's doing. She blacklisted us. You can be sure of that."

Ron clapped. "He's the bitch. He could have stood up to her like a real man. But that's alright. Get married, sucker. That'll leave more skirts for the Pack. It all works out."

Ron snickered, and he and Terrance bumped fists.

Luis stood up and stretched. "Rita and I got an invitation. He'll send yours, I'm sure. They probably haven't finished mailing them. It's a lot of work. I remember it took Rita a month to get ours out to everyone. Remember, this is Conor we're talking about."

"Luis, shut the hell up!" Ron snapped while Terrance crowed.

Luis walked out. "Screw you assholes!"

Ron stood up and adjusted his belt. "To hell with Conor. He's been deleted and soon to be replaced."

"Oh, right, that new kid out of college. What department does he intern for?"

"He's interning in finance, and Trina is his mentor. It won't be long before he sticks her. We need to start reigning him in and get him acclimated to the rules around here."

Terrance nodded. "Indeed."

Ron wasn't concerned with future comradery. He was a married man and didn't like anybody digging in his backyard and having relations with any of his former conquests. His affair with Trina had ended years ago, but Ron's insecurities ran deep, regardless of his attempts to mask them with ridiculous self-assurance.

I could care less about Trina, but it's a violation of the principle that matters. It's all about respect.

***

It was lunchtime when Madison stopped by Brittany's office.

"Hey there. Are you ready?" Madison asked.

Brittany shouldered her bag and picked up her cell phone. "Yes, I am. Don't you hear my stomach growling?"

Madison laughed. "I thought that noise was my stomach. Before I forget to ask, are you and your handsome husband still meeting us for lunch tomorrow at Excelsior Bay?"

Brittany's eyes widened. "Definitely. Trent is looking forward to finally meeting Conor. It's a good thing that Conor decided to go. Trent didn't like the idea of being the third wheel. He'd rather be playing basketball on a Saturday morning."

"Conor would rather be playing soccer on Saturday mornings."

They left and went to the lunchroom. Conor had already claimed their regular table, and they joined him.

"Hey, Britt. Are you and your man ready for our double-date tomorrow?" he asked.

"Yes, sir. I was telling Madison that Trent is looking forward to meeting you."

He leaned forward. "One question. Who's buying?"

Madison patted his arm. "You two can decide that tomorrow. Brittany and I will happily accept either of your hard-earned dollars."

"I couldn't have said it better myself," Brittany added.

"Equal rights, huh? Not fair," he whined.

They all greeted Luis as he walked over and sat down with them to eat. Across the room, Ron's crowded table decided to make them the subject of attention.

"Is that his girlfriend?" the new intern asked.

"No, that's his fiancé and soon-to-be wife," Ron replied.

The young man gushed. "She's fricking hot, man. I can see why he's marrying her."

Ron and Terrance looked at each other and rolled their eyes.

Terrance rubbed his forehead, "Is this our future? This younger generation? Please, shoot me now."

Across the room, Brittany nudged Madison. "Look over there. That intern hasn't been working here for a month, and they're trying to corrupt him already."

Conor listened but kept quiet, ashamed of his former affiliation with the juvenile bunch. That unsavory chapter was an embarrassment for him, but Madison never brought up his dubious history. She knew the past was something that you couldn't change. You could only learn from it.

The rest of the day flew by, and soon the cramped parking lot was empty. There were no special plans for Madison and Conor besides eating dinner and watching a movie. The quiet life suited Madison, and Conor seemed to echo the same sentiments. She was glad that his rambling days were over and relieved that he wasn't like other boyfriends. Particularly those who professed a deep love for their partners, but yet always wanted to spend most of their time elsewhere, out hunting or fishing for hours, and even days on end. Those men only showed their love when they wanted to have sex. Madison knew that sex did not equate to love. The two words were not synonymous.

That night, after the credits rolled at the end of their last movie, they got into bed, kissed, and prepared to sleep. The final ritual was to follow. Madison turned, took ahold of Elijah's picture from her nightstand, and kissed it.

"I love you, Elijah," she whispered, placing it back. Those words were a necessity, bringing peace and order to her psyche through repetition. The four words reverberated in her mind as she drifted off to sleep. I love you, Elijah.

***

The next day, Madison and Conor walked onto the outdoor dining deck overlooking the stunning Excelsior Bay, where Brittany and her husband Trent were seated. After introducing Conor and Trent, they placed their orders with a waitress.

"How about strawberry margaritas to start?" Brittany asked the group.

Conor grimaced. "Uh, okay."

Trent raised his hand. "We'll drink one, but then Conor and I will order some real drinks. Man drinks."

Conor winked, and they fist-bumped. The waiter took the order and returned with a pitcher.

"I'll just sip on one glass," Madison said, pouring herself a half glass. "I'm not a big drinker,"

Conor chuckled. "That means you're the official designated driver."

"And? So? What else is new?" Madison replied and bumped fists with Brittany.

"Good one, Madison," Brittany cheered. "You boys can have all the hard liquor you want. We like the girly drinks. Either way, you're paying!"

"So, what else is new?" Trent asked.

Conor laughed, choking on his drink. "I see that she hasn't tamed you yet. I can respect that and salute you, sir." Conor smiled and saluted.

Trent patted his back. "Thanks, future husband. Soon, your eligible bachelor days will come to an end, and you'll have to retreat into your man cave to defend your freedom. You'll think of that room like it was the Alamo. No retreat, no surrender."

Conor played along. "That bad? Really?"

Brittany slapped Trent's arm. "Oh yeah, answer him big mouth. Is it that bad?" Her piercing eyes were never wavering from his. "Trent Daniels, think before you speak."

"Na, it's not so bad," he replied. She frowned and pinched his arm. "Ouch! Alright. No, Conor, it's not bad at all. It's wonderful."

Madison and Brittany could not stop laughing as Brittany rubbed Trent's arm.

"That's correct! You see, my husband likes to joke a lot." She leaned over and kissed Trent on his cheek. "I love you, honey."

He looked at her, nodded, and smiled until her glare reappeared and her hand prepared another assault.

"Wait. I love you too, Brittany." He attempted to stand. "I want everyone who can hear my voice to know that I love my wife, Brittany!"

She smacked his butt. "Trent! Sit your crazy ass down. You're embarrassing me."

Conor nearly spilled his drink as the table fell into an uproar.

"I like you, dude. You are hilarious!" Conor said.

"Did you catch what she said, man? I'm embarrassing her. She slaps and pinches my arm. I then stand up to declare my undying love for her, but I'm the one embarrassing her! Go figure that one out, come back, and we'll have another drink."

"I know, man, it's not fair," Conor consoled him.

Trent smiled and sipped his drink while Brittany rubbed his leg. "Whoever said that life was fair was a damn liar."

Brittany turned to Madison. "All jokes aside. The big day in September is moving closer, and I know that you're super-excited. I can't wait to be your matron of honor."

"I felt the same way about your wedding. That was my first wedding party. Being chosen as your bridesmaid meant everything to me. It was a huge honor."

"Aww, I didn't consider anyone else but my bestie."

"I only wish that my father was alive to give me away. But I'm sure he's looking down and happy for me."

The lively atmosphere stalled.

Brittany nodded. "I believe that he is too. On another note, more independent women are choosing to walk down the aisle alone nowadays. But I understand your feelings. Have you heard any word back from your mother?"

"No. She hasn't returned any of my calls. She didn't even send a Christmas card last year."

Brittany rolled her eyes. "That's ridiculous. I don't ever speak badly about someone's mother, but I just don't get her at all."

"You and me both. She's complicated. That's all I can say."

Trent tapped Conor.

"So, who is your best man?"

"My brother, Jack. He's driving up from Ohio. I'm glad we are having a small wedding. That was Madison's idea. It cuts out a ton of expenses and the need to have a bunch of guys fitted for their tuxedos."

"In other words, it saves a ton of money," Madison added.

Conor winked at her and smiled. "Which allows me to treat everyone to lunch today. I'm starving. Let's order the food."

They stayed for over an hour, eating, laughing, and sharing good times under the beaming sunlight as the boats crisscrossed the water. Their meeting was to be the first of many future gatherings between old and new friends. As they hugged and parted ways, Madison looked into the powder-blue sky. *Could this day be any more perfect?*

***

Madison was too intoxicated to drive, so Conor took the wheel. It was amazing how drunk she was, considering she'd only had one 8 oz glass of margarita. But Conor condoned her lapse of sobriety, believing that she deserved to loosen up and not have a care in the world. At least not for a few hours. He laughed as she attempted to sing along to a song on the radio: Crazy by Cee-lo Green. She was adorable, and he encouraged her.

He cheered while she tried to keep up and finally ended the last verse. "Sing it, Madison. Sing louder!"

"But maybe I'm crazy, maybe you're crazy, maybe we're crazy, probably..."

She ended the performance and raised her arms as he honked the horn.

"You're a badass, babe. Well done!"

She leaned over the armrest and rested her head on his shoulder. "I know, right?"

A chime inside the car sounded. It was the low fuel warning.

Conor hit the steering wheel. "Shit. I almost let us run out of gas. We need to fill up."

She raised her arms. "Yes, sir! You big strong man. Go for it!"

He drove another quarter mile and pulled into a rundown gas station.

"I have to take a leak. How about you?" he asked.

"Uh, no. I'm good."

"Okay. Do you want something from inside?"

"Huh? Why? We just ate all that food. My tummy is stretched. Look at it."

She pulled up her shirt and poked at her belly.

"Alright, I'll be right back." He clambered out of the car and went inside.

She began to doodle with her phone and noticed that the alcohol intensified her happy mood. *I might need to start drinking more. I forgot how free I feel when buzzed. When was the last time I felt this way after a Margarita? My sophomore year in college? Yep, that's right!*

She looked around and saw that Conor was already fueling the car. She smiled. *My man.* She glanced around at the gas station. It was dirty. *Why don't they have someone clean the trash up? It's not like that's a hard job.*

Then she saw it. It was parked at the far left gas pump across from them. She looked away and back again.

My mind must be playing tricks on me.

"No. It can't be."

She stepped out and walked towards it, leaving the door ajar. Conor didn't notice her exit and was fixated on pumping gas. She walked around a car and stepped on top of the gas pump's raised concrete foundation to look. It was her old car. But she wasn't positive and walked around to the rear, ignoring the apparent owner, a white male dressed in overalls. She bent over and looked for a specific mark on the bumper and verified the familiar long, vertical scratch. The horrid memories of that fateful morning bombarded her mind, as fresh as the dreadful day of their creation.

She covered her face, swaying from intoxication. "Oh my God. This isn't happening."

The owner whipped his head around in surprise and tightened his gas cap.

"Can I help you, miss?"

She didn't know what to say or how to react. Her anxiety had risen to critical levels, and the familiar feeling of helplessness crept back inside to unhinge her. It was imminent.

Conor replaced the gas nozzle. He screwed the gas cap and noticed Madison standing talking to a man at the far pump station.

What the hell is she doing?

Being spurred by the concern for her safety, mingled with jealousy, he marched over to investigate.

The owner of the car became wary. "Hello? I said, can I help you, miss?"

She stared blankly at the car, trembling. "That's my old car, and no one should be driving it. It was supposed to be destroyed in a junkyard." She crossed her arms.

He raised his eyebrows, "Really? I wonder why you say that because this car runs great. I bought it last fall at the Hennepin County Sheriffs auction."

"An Auction?"

"That's correct. The vehicle's description stated that it was being sold under a salvage title and had a minor exhaust leak. I'm a car mechanic by trade, so I checked the entire exhaust system thoroughly. I only found a minor leak at one of the exhaust manifold gaskets, but I changed all four of them anyway. The parts cost less than $40 bucks."

Madison exploded. "My son died inside that car from carbon monoxide!" Her tears began to flow. "I was there, and it nearly killed me too!"

Conor walked over and hugged her. "Madison, I'm here. It's alright, calm down." He looked at the man. "What's your problem, man? What did you say to her?"

"You need to calm down, partner. She walked over and was staring at my car. I asked could I help her, and she started in with how this was her car, and that it shouldn't be on the road. I explained how I bought this car legally and that it runs great. Man, I'm not looking for any trouble. I just mind my own business. Ask her for yourself."

Conor looked at her. "What's going on, babe? Tell me. Is it the alcohol?"

Madison wiped her eyes. "Conor, the car shouldn't be on the road. Mother was to make sure of that."

The man was planning his exit but, while they spoke, he relented. His first impression of her was a drug-crazed, delusional woman who was harassing him. But that observation was quickly replaced by a grieving mother's apparent reality, inadvertently reminded of her deceased child.

"Miss, sir, I'm very sorry for the loss of your child and offer my sincere condolences. But I'm not convinced if this is the same vehicle. This isn't a rare make or model. By any chance, do you happen to have your old vehicle registration? We can compare the VINs. This may not be your old vehicle, is what I'm getting at."

She broke away from Conor and pointed to the rear bumper. "We don't have to do that. This is my old car. There's a long scratch in the middle of the bumper. I owned it for three years." She looked at the owner, and Conor, who were staring at each other.

Do they doubt me?

Then she remembered. "The rearview mirror. I remember a crack, a small one, on the lower right corner." She walked around and bent over to look through the driver's side window. "There," she said, pointing. "Look for yourselves."

The owner shrugged and nodded. "I don't need to. It's there. You're right."

Conor walked over and held her hand. "I know this was unexpected and shouldn't have happened, but this man isn't responsible for anything. Let's go home, come on."

He put his arm around her, but she wouldn't budge.

"It makes no sense. He said the car is fine. How can that be?"

The owner raised his finger.

"Let me clarify a few things and share my thoughts, if that's alright with you. I've been a licensed automotive technician for over 30 years. In my lifetime, I've purchased hundreds of cars and repaired them as needed for resale. I perform a thorough inspection of every vehicle because it's what I do. I'm liable if I knowingly sell a dangerous vehicle. This car is my personal vehicle, and like the others, I checked the engine compression, emissions, and electrical systems, among other things. Every test passed. The only minor issue was a slight leak on one exhaust manifold gasket. There's only one way to cause the situation that she described. There would have to be a physical blockage or obstruction in the exhaust."

"What do you mean?" Conor asked.

"What comes to mind first is the old saying that when a car doesn't start, 'there's a banana in the tailpipe.' Well, it doesn't have to be a banana. It could be a potato, a lemon, or anything that will fit. Also, being stuck in a snowdrift could do it. I remember when I was a boy, kids would stuff snowballs into the neighbor's tailpipes so that they wouldn't start. After the snow melted, the car would start. But if the snow were powdery, some would blow out, and the car might start. For example, if I partially blocked the tailpipe on this car before repairing the small exhaust leak, then there is a chance that the car might be able to operate. But that small leak would now become a severe leak due to the increased backpressure. The exhaust fumes would build up under the hood and eventually seep into the interior cabin. If you don't mind me asking, was your car in a snowdrift, or maybe stuck in the mud when this accident happened?"

"No," she mumbled.

He shook his head. "I don't know what else to say, but again, I'm sorry for your loss. I do need to leave. Take care, and may God bless you. Goodbye."

He got inside and drove to the main road, waiting for an opening in traffic. Madison pulled away from Conor and pointed her phone at the car, fumbling to activate her camera.

Conor threw up his arms. "Madison, what are you doing?"

"I'm trying to take a picture of his license plate, but I can't pull up the camera. Help me!" She handed him the phone. "Hurry, take a picture!"

Her phone was alien to him. When he finally located the camera app, the car was gone.

"Did you get it?"

"Shit! No. I'm sorry."

She wandered back to the car, sobbing, as he followed, and got inside. He laid the phone in her lap and gently stroked her hair before kissing her cheek.

"We'll be home soon, babe. We can talk about this later. Try to relax. Lay back."

She reclined the seat and stared out of the window. Her tears subsided, along with her anxiety, and she transitioned to a near-catatonic state. The unforeseen event was surreal and shook her otherwise stable perception of reality, smothering her feelings of accomplishment and progress. The light of hope from her emotional recovery had been snuffed in an instant, bringing her mental fragility back to the forefront. She dreaded the future.

It's all happening again.

***

They arrived home at 5 p.m. Madison used the bathroom, then headed directly for the bedroom, stripped off her clothes, and hid underneath the covers. Conor looked in on her. He was upset that the fun day had ended so badly. His happy bride was regressing toward her former depressed and troubled self.

"Hey, Madison," he whispered. "Do you want me to get you a couple of Xanax's? I know you stopped taking them months ago, but they can help. They work fast."

"No. I don't want any," she mumbled from beneath the blanket.

He eased the door closed and walked away, believing that she would work this out and return to normal.

She was almost there, and now this happens. It's Murphy's law at its best.

Six months had passed since her last relapse, brought on by the last vestiges of the strangling mental images from that tragic day. The episodes stemmed from the guilt that she was responsible for everything that day.

Poor girl. I wish she knew that it wasn't her fault.

Conor lamented and hoped that she could move on with her life, for her sake and his. They were to be married soon—the institution where all problems are shared and bared by husband and wife.

In the bedroom, Madison was fast asleep. Sleep was her trusted refuge in chaotic times, providing a temporary escape from everything contrary to her peace of mind. The only exception was the nightmares that sometimes came along with it. The horrible dreams raised hell and heartache to epic levels. They had lasting effects as well, adding psychological and emotional chaos to her mind upon awakening.

This night was no exception, as she found herself immersed in the reality of a frigid winter morning standing outside her car.

Elijah was inside, struggling to get out of his car seat amidst billowing clouds of vaporous fumes. "Help me, mommy!" His muffled screams echoed from within, but she couldn't move. She was frozen, like the snow around her. She tried to shout, scream, cry out, but her voice was muted. She watched in horror as he disappeared, covered by a thick dark fog.

"No...No!" She screamed and tried to raise herself, but Conor was already holding her.

"I'm here, Madison! Wake up, wake up!"

Fully awoken and panting, she instinctively grabbed for him.

"My nightmares are back," she whimpered. "I can't handle them again, Conor. It's too hard."

He kissed her forehead. "I know it sucks. Seeing that car today had to trigger it. Hopefully, this will be the last one."

"I don't think so. I really don't. I need answers to make sense of this. On Monday morning, I'm calling that detective who visited me in the hospital. I still have his card in my wallet."

"What will you say to him?"

"Uh, why is my old car still on the road? Or why the hell is my old car on the road?"

"Madison. Remember to be nice. Trust me, and you'll get more accomplished that way. This is only a suggestion, but why not call your mother and ask her about it. She's the one who handled it, right?"

Madison scooted out of bed.

"Because she won't return any of my calls! Who knows, she probably wanted me to see it again. She knows that it would cause me heartache, and that's what she wants me to feel. I know her too well. She wants me to have another nervous breakdown so she can come back and save me, then takes me back home where she can keep her foot on my neck. No, I won't give her the satisfaction. I'll handle this myself, like a grown adult." She stamped her foot and stormed into the bathroom.

"Go for it, babe. I'm behind you!"

***

The Monday morning meeting had adjourned. Madison and Brittany stood while the room emptied.

Brittany whispered to Madison. "Are you going to make that call now? Your foot was tapping through the whole meeting. I can feel the heat from you."

"I was going to wait until lunch, but screw that; I'm going to my car right now and call him."

"Good. Let's see what's up. I'll be in my office. Let me know what he says."

Brittany squeezed her hand, and Madison headed to the parking lot.

When she was in her car, she riffled through her purse, eventually finding the card and dialing the number. After two rings, he answered.

"Hello, this is Detective Olson. How may I help you?"

"Good morning, Detective Olson. This is Madison Sanders. I don't know if you remember me. I lost my son Elijah last year, and you visited me while I was in the hospital. I live at..."

"Of course I remember you, Miss Sanders! I hope that all is well. Please forgive me for not following up with you at some point. That is something I regularly do. We make it a point to look in on individuals and families who have suffered the loss of a loved one, or victims themselves, after a few months to see how they are recovering. That's when time permits, and I failed to do that in your case. I apologize. We have a huge backlog of active cases and are short-staffed, making it very difficult at times. So, Miss Sanders, how are you today?"

"To be honest, I'm not doing good. This past Saturday, my fiancé and I stopped at a gas station, and I saw my old car where my son died. I remember my mother explicitly telling me that the car had been junked. I was told that it was taken to a salvage yard and destroyed. My question to you is, why is that car still on the road?"

"Hmm. How can you be certain that it was your car?"

"I spoke with the owner and verified all the defining marks that are still on it. Scratches and cracks. But the owner shared some disturbing information with us. He stated that he was a professional auto mechanic and bought the car from a police auction. But this last part is the main reason why I'm calling. He inspected it and said that nothing was wrong with my car. He mentioned the exhaust and emissions specifically and was positive that the car was safe."

Olson took notes. "That's interesting. Ms. Sanders, I can verify the car's disposition and processing paperwork by giving our motor pool a call. If you can hold the line for a few minutes, I will give you a definitive answer. As for the owner claiming to be a mechanic, I would take that with a grain of salt. Backyard mechanics get paid for their work, and some think of it as their profession. It can be a play on words, but I wouldn't put faith in his statement."

"He said that he was licensed," she said.

"Did he verify that? Did he show you proof?"

Madison was frustrated with his challenges and struggled to maintain her composure.

"Sir, I'll be happy to hold on. Thank you."

"Sure, no problem, please hold."

While waiting, she used the time to unwind and destress. *Bring it down a notch Madison. Don't let him set you off.* She closed her eyes and meditated. Five minutes later, he returned.

"Hello, Miss Sanders?"

"Yes, sir."

"I have answers for you. The disposition paperwork shows that your signature is listed, giving the authorization to impound the vehicle. You signed over the vehicle to the county as a salvage vehicle, meaning that we take possession of the vehicle and dispose of it as necessary, saving you any costs that may be incurred from towing, demolition, etc., for a small fee, of course."

"I don't remember signing anything. I don't even remember being asked about it. My mother told me that the car had been destroyed."

"I wouldn't expect you to remember very much. We had to cut our interview short and come back the next day. I do remember giving the forms to your mother to give to you. Oh, and also that she had just arrived from out of town. She was a very nice woman. As to the vehicle serviceability inspection, a notation was made stating that it had an exhaust manifold gasket leak. I recall looking at the vehicle with Detective Schultz after arriving at the scene. I can tell you without a doubt that your underbody and engine compartment were in terrible condition, and pure rust was caked up throughout the underbody as well. Nevertheless, our mechanics made the final determination and felt that it could be repaired or restored, and if not, it could be used for parts. So, yes, it was sold at auction."

"But the new owner told us that the car is in great condition! How can that be? He is driving it and still alive!"

"Please calm down. I can hear you just fine, Miss Sanders. I understand that it was disturbing to see your car again. But your signature is on the paperwork. Yes, it's unfortunate, but if possible, try and let it go. I sincerely doubt that you'll see it again."

"I am calm! Listen to me, please. I told the man about what happened to us in that car, and he said that the leak alone couldn't cause that to happen. He clearly stated that something had to block the tailpipe."

"What? What in the world was he talking about?"

"He said that someone would have to have put an object in the tailpipe for that amount of exhaust fumes to get into the car."

"Miss, we didn't find any objects inside the tailpipe. Neither did our mechanics. The new owner didn't either. So, that takes us back to our initial findings. I believe the new owner repaired more than what he told you."

Madison huffed. "He also said that it could have been snow. Like kids playing pranks on their neighbors with snowballs. He was familiar with that type of thing."

"Let me stop you right there. There was no evidence found to substantiate that scenario, which would lead me to another conclusion. I'm sorry. It was a horrific accident due to the vehicle's condition, and there was no way you could have known that it was going to happen. There was the exhaust leak that we know of, along with excessive rust. Rust is in an unstable condition. The metal will perform its function, then suddenly give way, and that's what happened here. If the new owner is indeed a professional automotive mechanic, he would have already replaced the entire exhaust system. For that car to be roadworthy, it would have to be done."

"Would you at least recheck the vehicle? It would help me with closure."

"I don't see why that's necessary. As I mentioned, we have priority cases to work on, and even if I thought that another inspection might be warranted, I have to receive approval to reopen your case. That mountain is almost impossible to climb and requires approval from the District Attorney, Joe Angelletti. I know him very well, and he wouldn't consider such a request without solid justification. I'm afraid the answer is no."

His words faded into obscurity after his first sentence. There was nothing left to say. Her questions remained unanswered, and her attitude experienced a drastic shift. The debilitating anxiety that flowed through her over the weekend was nonexistent. Now, a new sensation engulfed her body and mind, and it burned.

"Thank you for your time. Goodbye," she said.

"Thank you for giving me an opportunity to..."

She hung up the phone and walked back inside, dazed and detached. She sat at her desk and stared out of the window.

I'm not buying it. Something isn't right.

A few moments later, Conor walked through her office and drifted over to her. He tapped her shoulder. "Hey. Are you alright? You look like you're spacing out."

She rolled her head and looked up. "I just got off the phone with that detective."

"What did he have to say?"

"He thinks what the guy told us is bullshit. He blew me off."

"What an asshole. Screw him. At least you tried."

"I need to think about this."

"I understand. Just try not to get yourself worked up about it. It kills me to see you hurting, babe."

"I'm past being worked up, Conor. I'm tired of hurting."

"I know that you are. We'll talk about it on the ride home," he said and walked away.

She gazed out the window again. There was office work to get done, but that could wait. More critical issues held priority, and they couldn't be closed until she was satisfied with the answers. Everything was dark to her at the moment, but she knew it was her responsibility to turn on the light, whatever that meant, someway, somehow. There was no other path in sight. To do nothing would be to surrender her sanity, and she wasn't prepared to do that.

***

During the ride home from work, Madison relayed her earlier conversation with the detective to Conor and then went silent. He sensed her ill-mood and was accustomed to her emotional swings, so he kept his chatter down and let the radio play in peace. After arriving home, Madison skipped her usual nap and opened her laptop on the kitchen table.

"What are you doing?" Conor asked.

She leaned forward and started to type. "I talked to Brittany about this, and I've thought it over. Since the police won't give me any answers that make sense or help me, I'll hire a private investigator and help myself. Brittany said that her cousin once hired one to investigate a police brutality case, and they won a lawsuit. I'm searching for one in Minneapolis."

Conor grabbed a beer from the refrigerator and went to look.

"Wow, that's far out, like the movies. Cool. I bet they are pricey, though, but I'll chip in to make it happen."

She reached up, pulled him close, and kissed him. "I love you. Thanks for supporting me through all of this. You've always been in my corner, and I appreciate you. I really do, sweetheart."

"That's my job, dear. I love you too." He nodded toward the screen. "Let's see what we can find out there in P.I. land. I wonder if Magnum P.I. is still working cases." He chuckled.

Madison sifted through the matrix of private investigation services and, within thirty minutes, decided on her first prospect. She chose Don Carson, Private Investigator. Like all the other listings, he didn't advertise the pricing for his services, but he did have a large web banner stating, 'I'll Beat Any Other Price Out There!', which was a strong incentive for her. Her college trust fund had paid for the first two years of school, but she still had a large student loan debt and credit cards that weighed on her finances. Although Conor was helping her pay for the investigation, she didn't want to take advantage of his kindness. Aside from Don Carson's cheesy, used-car salesman advertising gimmick, he did promote an impressive resume with sterling credentials.

Madison pointed. "Look, he has over 25 years of experience with the Metro Police department and served 15 years as a detective. Look at his medals and awards. Fancy. I pick him. What are your thoughts?"

Conor chugged his third beer. "Go for it."

She filled out her contact information and submitted her online request for an appointment.

"There. Done," she declared.

Conor set his beer down. "I'm proud of you, babe. You're a fighter. That makes you even hotter."

He kissed the back of her neck while massaging her shoulders. She arched in pleasure and pulled on his pants, aching for him.

She moaned. "I need you to investigate something for me in the bedroom. But I don't have any money."

"Let's go now. We'll work out a trade. I want to show you my private eye."

"Yes, sir!" she squealed as he pulled her into the bedroom.

An hour passed by, and they were snuggled on the couch, watching television. Madison's phone rang. The caller was unknown, but she stood up and answered.

"Hello? Yes, sir, this is Madison Sanders. Yes, sir, I'm doing fine. Tomorrow at 4:30 p.m.? Yes, that will be fine. Okay, thank you. Goodbye." She turned to Conor. "That was Don Carson. We have an appointment scheduled for tomorrow at 4:30 p.m. His office is at his house, and he said to use the side entrance. There's a sign hanging by the door."

"Cool, sounds good. I bet that you're not going to be able to sleep tonight, thinking about tomorrow."

She plopped down beside him. "I'm excited and a tad bit nervous."

He put his arm around her. "I'll be with you every step of the way. No worries."

They continued watching the hilarious sitcom, and her nervous energy subtly dissolved due to one of the most effective forms of therapy, unadulterated laughter.

CHAPTER 9

The next day after work, Madison and Conor arrived at the home of Don Carson. Her leg had been bouncing for the duration of the ride, expelling her nervous energy like a pressure relief valve.

They pulled into the driveway of the small brick house and parked behind a car.

Madison pointed at a small sign posted next to the side entrance. "That's where we go in."

"Yeah." He shut off the car. "Remember, you don't have to be nervous. If you are, don't tap your foot so much."

"I'll try not to. I don't know why my heart is beating so fast. Let's just get it over with."

They went to the entrance and rang the doorbell. A few moments later, the door opened, and Don Carson appeared, groomed, wearing a suit and necktie.

"Hello, Miss Sanders." He smiled, shaking her and Conor's hands.

"This is my fiancé, Conor Gregory," she introduced him. "I hope it was okay for us both to come."

He nodded. "Please, come on in."

They followed him into a small office and sat down. He walked behind his desk and sat down too. Behind him, on the wall, hung a variety of framed awards and medals from the police department. Above them all were his most prized accomplishments, his university degree in Criminology and an Honorable Discharge certificate from the United States Navy. He shuffled through his desk while Madison and Conor panned across the impressive display that dispelled any doubts about his competency as an experienced professional investigator. Carson opened a manilla folder, then sat a small video camera at the front of the desk and turned it on.

"Miss Sanders and Mr. Gregory, do I have your permission to record this consultation interview? I will also take notes, but the ability to review our meeting will ensure that every detail about your case is captured. This recording is part of my standard protocol to help provide you the best service possible. That is if you decide to retain my services."

The couple glanced at each other and agreed.

Madison recounted her story from the morning of Elijah's death until her conversation with Detective Olson. It was challenging to present the sad events without being overcome with emotions, but Conor's supporting hand rubbed her back for encouragement. She did well and maintained her composure. Particular details about the events sparked Carson's memory.

"What's the name of the detective you called a few days ago?" Carson asked.

"Roger Olson," she replied. She picked through her purse and handed him Olson's card. "Have you ever heard of him?"

He smiled with a boyish grin. "Sort of. He was my partner for fifteen years."

"Really? Okay. That's a good thing, right?" she asked.

"It is. That's one of the benefits when choosing my investigative firm over others. I have numerous active duty contacts inside and outside of law enforcement."

"That's impressive," Conor added.

"Yes, but that's not as impressive as having the ear of the Assistant District Attorney, which I currently do." He focused on Madison. "I know what you want. It's what everyone who comes to me wants, and that's the truth. But in your own words, tell me exactly what resolution you are looking for."

She sighed, thinking how to condense her desired outcome into plain words. "I want the truth so that I can have closure. Maybe some of the neighborhood kids were playing a joke and put something inside my exhaust? The new owner mentioned snowballs, but I don't know. That's why we need your help. We need real answers."

He nodded, made a note on a pad, and then reclined. Seemingly in deep thought, he repeatedly clicked his pen.

"I understand. I've found out many times through investigation that freak accidents, or the like, actually end up as unintentional crimes. You've got my dander up. The evidence doesn't appear to add up with the summary investigation. I've decided to take your case and check under every rock for you. But, first, I want to revisit the facts."

She grabbed Conor's leg. "That's great news! Thank you!"

Carson smiled. "You are a young couple about to get married, and usually this type of investigation would be quite expensive. But this case is different from most others. The gravity of the terrible event and the long-lasting emotional burden you as a mother still carry gives me pause and time to reflect on why I do this work. It's to help people. I don't need the money. I do this because I care. So, I won't break your bank. I'll use my time and energy efficiently. Once you sign the agreement and the disclosure, I work for you. You're my boss. I'll continue exploring the facts and hopefully find new ones on your behalf while keeping you informed of my progress. Presently, I'm working on another case, but that won't interfere with your investigation."

"That's good," Conor said.

Madison clutched her purse. "We appreciate any discount on your fees and are ready to proceed."

"Good. I'm only charging you $40 per hour, with a 4-hour per day minimum and an 8-hour maximum. You can set a weekly dollar amount cap. I recommend a $640 weekly spending cap. Fuel and expenses are itemized separately and will be included in your invoice at the end of each week. A written report of my activities, findings, or discoveries will be attached to that invoice, along with a status summary report containing my recommendations. Lastly, you can nullify our agreement at any time and request a final bill for services rendered. Do you agree with the terms?"

She looked at Conor, who dipped in approval. "Yes, we agree," she acknowledged.

"Excellent. Please read, sign, and date these, then I'll notarize them. This is the agreement contract, the disclosure form, and a Proxy Release of Information form to gain access to the police and coroner's report, as well as all hospitalization records."

He removed the forms and slid them to the front of his desk as she walked over.

"May I use your pen?" she asked.

"Of course." He held it out, but it dropped to the floor. "Oops, I'm sorry," he said, getting up.

"No, sir, it's my fault. I'll get it." She bent over and picked it up. She quickly read and signed each one, then returned his pen and sat back down. He checked the dates and placed them in the folder.

"Everything looks good. To get started, I'll need a deposit of $200 today. This amount will be credited against your first week's billing invoice. How will you be paying? Cash or credit? I don't accept personal checks, but I will accept a bank cashier's check."

Madison picked up her purse, but Conor stopped her.

"I got this one, babe." He went to the desk, opened his wallet, and handed over a credit card. Carson turned around and swiped it into his mobile card processor. He then handed back a receipt for the transaction, and they both sat down.

Carson's demeanor changed. "Now, we can begin. I'll be sending you an email with instructions to list all the names and contact information of your friends and associates first and then list anyone you believe might have a grudge against you. This can be any and everybody: coworkers, ex-boyfriends, a neighborhood youth who you might have slighted. Simply list anyone who comes to mind. Complete the list and send it back tonight if possible. I'll begin accessing the reports and tracking down the owner of your old vehicle. He'll be easy to locate. Where do you work again?"

"Both of us work for Traxtonite," she replied.

"How do you get along with your coworkers?"

Madison shrugged. "I keep to myself. I always have. I might not be the most likable person at work, I suppose, but I can't imagine that anyone hates me."

"Not hate Madison, dislike. That's one reason that I request information about close friends and associates. They can be aware of the sentiments and attitudes of others concerning you. Also, they may remember social situations or personal interactions that you've had with other people, which you may feel are irrelevant. Take your time and try to be thorough."

She looked at the ceiling. "The only instance that comes to mind is when I first moved here. But it was nothing—just a few guys who couldn't take a hint. I talked about it with my Human Resource manager, and it stopped. No one got into any trouble over it."

Carson frowned. "Remember to list their names. What is the Human Resource manager's name who you spoke with about that matter?"

Madison tensed. "Steve Hyman. Do you have to talk to all of these people? I don't want to start any confusion at work. My job environment is good, and I don't want to mess it up."

"I don't expect to speak with everyone on your list unless the investigation warrants it. But remember, if you want to find the truth, you may have to move a few stones. Don't worry about any retaliation stemming from my inquiries. I keep detailed records that can be used as evidence, should you feel the need to report any negatively related repercussions. Also, I can be called as a witness on your behalf to testify in any civil or criminal proceedings."

"That's reassuring and good to know," Conor said.

Carson began clicking his pen. "While I have you here, are there any ex-boyfriends that might feel scorned by you in some way?"

"No. Conor is the only man who I've dated since moving here. We've been together almost a year."

The couple looked at each other and squeezed their hands.

"Okay. So, are you all in? Are you committed?" Carson asked.

"Yes. I am," she answered. She looked at Conor. "Yes, we are."

"Then let's go find you some answers," he said with a smile.

He stood up, shook their hands, and followed them out to their car.

"I'll update you in two, maybe three days. Thank you for your business, and have a nice day."

He went inside, and they left.

As they drove home, Madison rested her head on Conor's shoulder.

"I feel good about this. Thanks for coming with me, sweetheart," she gushed.

"No problem, princess. I'm glad I did. I can tell that this guy means business. Whatever it is, he'll get to the bottom of it."

"I believe he will."

Her mind drifted toward her evening chores and the rest of her day. First, she planned to phone Brittany, share the exciting news, and then inform her that she should expect a call from Don Carson.

Meanwhile, Don Carson looked at his checking account balance after the last deposit. The $200 had brought him out of a negative balance, leaving him $53.98 available.

Just in the nick of time.

He crooned, grabbed his car keys, and pulled a nearly empty pint of Scotch from his bottom drawer. He slurped it down. Then he left for the liquor store. *I'll start working on Miss 'sweet cheeks' case tomorrow. There's no rush. Her kid is already dead.*

***

The next day, after finishing his morning breakfast of Bailey's Irish Cream with coffee and a donut, Don Carson lit a cigarette and started the investigation. He needed to find Madison a glimpse of hope early on to keep her motivated. He learned that lesson through past clients. Typically, after paying their first few invoices, they expected drastic results. Without a speedy resolution to their case, the client would become disillusioned, indifferent and terminate their contract. The exceptions were those who sought proof of their partner's infidelity. Other motivations drove those individuals, and they were adamant to prove what they thought to be true at any cost.

Carson's finances were tight, and his debt was mounting as he sat in the limbo of unpaid administrative leave. He also had health issues which only added to his stress. Alcoholism was the primary culprit perpetuating his destructive cycle, and his victim mentality kept him blind to his condition. Nonetheless, he was an impressive investigator and interrogator. The fact that he could sniff out lies like a bloodhound was no surprise because he was full of them. His deviant and opportunistic nature provided him with an inclination and resonance toward the criminal likeminded.

Armed with the documents required to release Madison's information, he pulled out of his driveway and headed into the city. His first stop was at the Police precinct, where he retrieved a copy of the investigation and incident reports, along with photos and the medical examiner's findings. During this visit, he didn't hang around the precinct chatting with his former peers, but he showed a sense of urgency and kept to his schedule.

He drove across town to the hospital and secured Elijah and Madison's medical records. He checked his watch. It was time for a break, so he decided to drive home, where he topped off his flask with Scotch, but not before drinking another glass first, to reinvigorate himself. After scarfing down a pack of peanuts, he dialed the police motor pool and called in a favor from an old friend, the Maintenance Supervisor. His friend located the new owner of Madison's car, and Carson documented the information, updated his agenda, and contacted the owner.

Two hours later, he visited the owner at his repair shop and obtained an affidavit from the car's owner and a consensual audio recording of their interview, attesting to the vehicle's serviceability. Carson concluded the interview, and drove away, convinced that the initial investigation had been botched.

That's not like Roger Olson. Not the detective that I know. That kid Schultz has got Roger off his game. This slack shit didn't happen when we partnered up. Not on our watch. Hell no. Now, where to next? What else could they have missed?

He tapped the steering wheel. "Bingo," he muttered, turning right onto the expressway.

Thirty minutes later, he parked in front of Madison's house, having recognized it from the previous year. The house and steep driveway were familiar, but the snow had melted, and the landscape was unrecognizable.

Holding his leather carry case, he stepped out and lit a cigarette, assessing the neighborhood before sauntering off. It was 2:58 p.m., and he knew the neighborhood children would be coming home from school soon.

He walked up and down the road leisurely, looking for any houses equipped with security cameras pointed toward Madison's home. The house across the street had one, but it was at the wrong angle and positioned to capture video from their front porch. He opened his field case, retrieved the police report, and shuffled through witness statements.

Well, at least those idiots spoke with the neighbor and confirmed the absence of video footage.

He critiqued the statement from the first responder but decided against attempting an interview with him.

He's clean. There's only one more thing to do.

Ten minutes later, the school bus pulled up, and children filed off, dispersing in several directions. Carson sat in his car and watched, counting the eight students who lived on Madison's street as they walked in his direction. They appeared to be middle and junior high school students. He checked the time and nipped from his flask while watching each one. Their behavior, mannerisms, conduct, and interactions with the other kids were indicators of their character. It could expose those who had the potential of being troublemakers and who might be inclined toward neighborhood pranking. This was one of Don Carson's shortcuts. Why attempt to interview an entire list of residents to inquire if they've experienced community pranking when you might locate the pranksters first?

A minute passed, and none of the students sparked his interest. As the mixed group of boys and girls streamed by, Carson started his engine and drove off, flicking his cigarette out of the window. One of the boys noticed.

"Hey! Be a hoot! Don't pollute!" he shouted. His pubescent voice crackled above the engine's acceleration. Carson heard him and responded with a hand wave as he sped onward.

Good kids. Just like I thought.

It was time to go home. He wanted to make one more phone call later that evening before writing the first day's progress report.

***

The following day, after Carson ate breakfast, he commenced the day with more enthusiasm. His conversation with Brittany clarified the specifics of Madison's accurate work environment. Eager to help her friend, Brittany recounted every detail and shred of gossip concerning Madison. While embellishing some particulars and negating the less salacious, she explained events on behalf of her best friend with honorable intentions. After giving her consent to record their phone conversation, Carson eagerly recorded field notes as the Wolfpack's existence was disclosed. It was an important revelation to explore and was never investigated by Olson and Schultz.

Roger's head is definitely up his ass. How could he have missed this?

Both investigators were derelict in their probatory duties to the corrupt former detective and showed little due diligence.

And I'm supposed to be the screwup? Give me a break—self-righteous bastards.

Equipped with the new ammunition, he headed to Traxtonite.

He arrived, checked in with the receptionist at the front desk, and waited in the lobby. The meeting was easy to arrange, with Steve Hyman eager to accommodate. Steve assumed that the meeting was a request for probatory information gathering on behalf of someone representing Madison. He dreaded the thought that she was either exploring or pursuing a sexual harassment lawsuit. Before referring the matter to Traxtonite's legal department, Steve needed to confirm her intentions. Carson had already faxed over the required documents to release her information and act as Madison's proxy.

For Steve, this was a moment of truth, and he questioned himself about the handling of Madison's initial complaint.

Did I do enough? Could I have done more?

He walked out to meet Carson and invited him into his office. After exchanging polite chitchat, Carson turned on his audio recorder, opened his field notes, and informed Steve that he would be recording the conversation.

"Mr. Hyman, please recount the events and conversations that you had with Ms. Madison Sanders relating to her claim of harassment by her peers. Also, expand on what actions you took to address her concerns."

Steve raised his finger. "Wait. Excuse me, is this about a lawsuit against Traxtonite? If so, I'll have to refer you to our legal department. I can give you their..."

"No, sir. This information is not relating to any lawsuit against Traxtonite or yourself."

"Really? Do you say this unequivocally?"

"Yes, I do."

"Then what is this? Why do you want to know these things? Since you represent Madison and act as her proxy, she can tell you everything herself. I don't see what you gain from speaking with me."

"Mr. Hyman. You misunderstand the purpose of this interview. Ms. Sanders has retained me to investigate another matter entirely. As part of my investigative canvass, I gather information from all facets of her life, both personal and professional. What you say to me here benefits her greatly. I'm not at liberty to discuss the investigation's specifics due to privacy laws, as you well know, but I can tell you something personally. I commend you for being cooperative in this matter, and so does Ms. Sanders. She holds you in very high esteem and looks at you as, well, sort of an uncle."

Steve adjusted his necktie. "Really?"

"Don't be surprised. She told me that you took her under your wing and ensured her smooth transfer from the Seattle location. When she reported issues of inappropriate behavior, she stated that you addressed them to her satisfaction. You accommodated her every request. She's learned to depend on you and, of course, admire you."

Steve nodded. "That's true. Everything you said is true. I acted appropriately, and she thanked me for helping her."

"I know that, and she knows that. But I'm looking for something else. What you can recall during this interview may help me in that pursuit, or it might not. Either way, don't be afraid. There's nothing to worry about, Steve."

"I'm not afraid, Mr. Carson. I'll answer what I can. As I stated before, this is information that Madison is already aware of, and I hope that I can help her. Please be sure to tell her for me."

"Excellent, sir. Now, let's begin again. "Mr. Hyman, please recount the events and conversations that you had with Ms. Madison Sanders relating to a claim of harassment by her peers. Also, expand on what actions you took to address her concerns."

Steve relayed the events, giving accurate dates and times. He was a meticulous note keeper, saving every digit of data crossing his desk. He confidentially explained the circumstances surrounding Madison's arrival and his summary actions. But his confidence faltered when confronted with Carson's final question.

Carson leaned forward. "What exactly is the Wolfpack, and who are the members? That's what this is all about, isn't it? You mentioned employees in general, but not that they belonged to an unauthorized workplace fraternity. I know that you wouldn't sanction any of this behavior, and maybe you just simply forgot. But I'm asking you now to verify their names. That's the last answer I need, and I'll leave you to your business."

Steve's heart sank. He couldn't admit knowledge of the group. The years of his neglect to properly discipline its members now made him guilty in one way or another.

"I don't know exactly what you're talking about, not offhand, but I can verify the names of the employees that I verbally counseled for the harassment. Ron Tatum, Conor Gregory, Luis Mendoza and Terrance Roberts." Steve watched Don document the names. "But I can't give you any of their personal contact information. Our privacy policy covers that.

"No worries, I don't need that from you. I can get that information myself." Carson stood up. "Thank you for your time and cooperation,"

"I'm glad to be of help. Will I see you again?"

"Ah, I doubt it. Have a good day, Mr. Hyman." They shook hands and Don exited.

Steve walked behind him and closed the door. He paced the floor, thinking of the potential outcome, then froze.

She's preparing to file either a criminal or civil suit against them. Oh, boys, you're in a world of shit now! But my ass is covered, I'm sure. Pretty sure. Of course, you're covered—you worrywart. For God's sake, you're like her uncle.

Carson winked at the receptionist as he passed by and out the front door.

What a wimp. I turned him on and off like a water faucet. Sucker!

Inside, Madison sat at her desk, staring out of the window, and watched him drive away. While finalizing a report, she noticed his arrival and tracked his time on company property. The realization of his investigation became evident.

Who did he talk to? Steve? I hope he doesn't start questioning anyone else here. Please don't. I don't need this right now.

She tried to remain calm, not wanting any negative implications or gossip to flourish, but seeing her hired investigator at her workplace shook her. She wanted to believe that the positive work environment she fostered wouldn't be affected by any of this, but her gut feeling knew that wouldn't hold. Anything too good to be true couldn't last. It never did.

***

Later that evening, around six o'clock, Madison and Conor sat on the couch watching a movie. She was calm and sustaining a fragile peace of mind, thanks to Conor's reassurances. He had a unique way of quelling her fears before they turned her manic.

Conor's phone rang, and he answered it.

"Hello?"

"Hello, Conor, This is Don Carson. I'm sorry to bother you at this hour, but I need to ask you a few questions in person. It won't take long. It's too late to come over, but there's a restaurant only a few miles from your house. It's called Zellie's. Have you heard of it?"

"Yeah, I know where it is. What time do you want to meet?"

"I'm here now, sitting at the bar."

"Okay, I'm on my way. I'll be there in 15 minutes."

"Great, thanks. See you soon."

Conor hung up and rubbed Madison's back.

"That was our 'private eye' calling. He wants to meet at Zellie's for a few minutes and discuss something with me."

"What does he want?" she asked.

"I'm not sure, but I'll fill you in when I get back."

He kissed her, put on his shoes, and scooped up his car keys.

She always worried when he went out late, but she smiled bravely. "Okay, drive safe, and be careful."

"Yep. I'll be back soon."

He arrived at Zellie's and walked inside. The restaurant was at half capacity and, as he looked toward the bar, he saw Carson.

"Hey detective, what's up?"

Carson put down his drink and turned around.

"Hey, Conor, pull up a seat and order a drink. I'm way ahead of you." He grinned, raising his glass as Conor sat.

"Thanks, but I try not to drink during the workweek." He patted his stomach. "I'm working hard to get these abs tight, but don't let me hold you back. Madison is waiting for me. So, what do you need to know?"

Carson sipped and signaled the bartender for another.

"I had a meeting with Steve Hyman today. It was productive and informative. He's a good guy, that Steve. Anyway, he shared a few interesting facts with me, which corroborates statements made by other individuals."

The Barkeep brought his drink and walked off.

"Wait," he motioned, then sipped. "Oh, that's very good, well done." He turned to Conor. "I have a few questions for you. My first question is, how does a guy who gets reported for sexual harassment end up engaged to the victim whom he sexually harassed? Please answer that for me because I've never seen that one before. No, not in all my miserable years investigating. My second question is, why was this fact not mentioned during our first interview? Madison never listed the names of the other assholes harassing her, and neither did you. To be clear, I'm not accusing you of anything, but even you must admit that these are red flags. Don't get defensive. I'm sure that you have a rational explanation. Those two questions have been ruining my buzz all day."

"It's simple. I wasn't mentioned because I never harassed Madison, and you can verify that with her. The other guys I associated with kept hitting on her when she first got here. They were aggressive and cringy. They couldn't read the signs of a woman's subtle rejections and couldn't take a hint. They pushed her until she got fed up with their shit. I told all of them that they were crossing the line. One day, four of us were called to a meeting with Human Resources, hosted by Steve Hyman. He counseled all of us when, in fact, only two people in the room were responsible. Luis Mendoza and I protested our innocence, but Steve didn't give a shit. But that counseling session wasn't official anyway. There was no reprimand, and none of the accusations were documented and placed in my personnel file. It was more like an informal warning. The reason why that I didn't mention it during our interview was that it wasn't relevant. We hired you. Remember? What clients hire a private investigator to investigate themselves? So there's your answer."

Carson listened but made minimal eye contact with Conor. He didn't need to focus on Conor's facial clues and body language to determine truth or deception. Carson's peripheral vision was always activated and processing data. He was more interested in what he had to say.

"Those answers make perfect sense to me. I'm clear now. Thanks. Are you sure that you won't have a drink? Just one."

Conor looked around and at Carson's half-empty glass.

"Sure, why not. What are you drinking?"

"Johnnie Walker Red, what else?" Carson hailed the bartender and signaled for another drink. "I got this one, Conor."

"Thanks, I appreciate that."

The bartender sat the drink in front of Carson, and he slid it over to Conor.

Carson raised his glass and toasted, "Here's to Madison and her peace of mind."

"Amen," Conor seconded. Carson raised his hand, signaling for two more.

"Let's go easy, Mr. Carson. We both have to drive. I don't have cop friends like you. A DUI won't go well for me."

"We're big boys. We can handle a few drinks, right?"

Conor checked the time. "Sure we can. After this one, I need to get back to Madison."

The bartender brought their last round.

"Check please, barkeep," Carson said and turned to Conor. "To Conor and Madison. May their future be filled with prosperity, happy children, and laughable arguments."

"A double amen to that," Conor replied, and they gulped in unison. Conor shook his hand. "I appreciate the drinks; that was cool of you. Do you have any more questions?"

"Sure, you're welcome, anytime. Questions? Okay, where were you the night before Elijah's death?"

"I was with some friends camping in a cabin about an hour away,"

"Would these friends happen to be Ron Tatum, Luis Mendoza, and Terrance Roberts?"

"Yeah," Conor burped. "Damn, excuse me."

Don laughed. "So, you four went camping. Were you all on vacation? Or just camping for the weekend and reporting to work on Monday morning?"

"Nah, we didn't use any vacation time. This was a weekend excursion. Luis left on Sunday afternoon and went to mass with his family. I, Ron, and Terrance stayed that Sunday night and went to work on Monday morning. We have this worthless Monday morning meeting every week that Ron leads."

"Did you all ride together?"

"Hell no, we rode separately. Terrance rode in Ron's truck. I would never ride with Ron; he farts too much."

Carson doubled over, laughing. "He sounds like my old partner. Let me get this story straight. You three stayed Sunday night in the cabin, except Luis, who left earlier. Right?"

"Correct."

"And everyone stayed in that cabin all night long? No other trips were made? No dipping out to a bar and coming back?"

Conor paused momentarily, staring. "To the best of my knowledge. I think so. I mean, yes."

"Which one is it, Conor? You gave me three different answers."

"I'm sure, but I'm not sure. I remember waking from my sleep Sunday night, but I wasn't sure why at the time. I tried to go back to sleep, but we had been drinking all day, and I had to take a wicked piss. I remember looking out of the bathroom window and noticing that Ron's truck was gone. I was half-asleep and went back to bed, not sure if he had parked his truck in a different spot or if he had gone back out during the night for the last chance to kill a coyote. We've had a $50 standing bet for years as to who gets the first kill. I know how competitive Ron is, and I figured that he was trying to show us up. That's Ron for you."

"Did you ask him about it the next morning?"

"I didn't remember to ask. We all were hungover and rushing around to get ready, trying to make it to work on time. Imagine three hungover guys fighting each other early in the morning to be the first to shave, shower, and shit. But there was nothing weird about it to me. I'll tell you what I can do. I'll ask Ron about that night and why his truck was gone, and then I'll tell you what he says. Is that cool?"

"No, that's not necessary. I plan to contact Ron and Terrance tomorrow or the day after. But you've been accommodating, thanks."

"Anything for my girl. I love her, man. I really do."

"You better love her. She's a special woman who has truly suffered - and still is suffering. Take good care of her, young man. I'll be in touch with you both soon. My weekly summary is on the way, so keep a lookout."

"Will do. Take it easy, Don," Conor replied. They shook, and Conor left, leaving Carson alone. He signaled the bartender again. "One more for the road barkeep and bring a new bill."

Carson saw a clear trail of smoke over the horizon. The new information validated his new course of the investigation and also verified his instincts. There was more to this.

Only time will tell. I'll have to wait and see what panders out, but I see something. It's been a long time. I thought it was gone. But that gut feeling; it's still there.

He paid his tab and drove home. He stumbled into the dark house, and turned on the lights, settled himself, and went to bed. The lights didn't make the place any less void of warmth, and a prevailing atmosphere of loneliness cloaked the home within its shadow. Don was oblivious, and while drifting off to sleep, his thoughts were directed toward the future.

Six months remained before his retirement. Barring the fortune of him landing extraordinary cases which might lead to criminal prosecution, this case alone was a possible game-changer. He convinced himself that a crime had been committed and saw his redemption potential through his reinstatement.

The case is a Godsend. This is your last shot, your last goddamn rodeo, cowboy. If you have to pull a rabbit out of your ass, then fucking do it! Get Angelletti something, anything, to work with and make your star shine bright. This is it. You're almost there, only a few more pieces to find. You can't depend on Roger alone to get you reinstated. You have to help him. He needs motivation. Give it to him.

***

When Conor arrived home, the living room was empty. He found Madison in bed, reading a book and waiting for him.

"That didn't take long. How did it go?" she asked.

He stripped off his clothes and crawled into bed.

"He wanted to know why we never mentioned me hanging around with Ron and the guys during the interview. He also knew about the time that Steve chewed our asses."

Madison put down her book. "That was a mistake. You never did anything to me. Did you tell him that?"

"Of course I did, and he understands. Then he grilled me on my whereabouts the night before the accident. I told him that the guys and I were camping at Ron's cabin. He asked if anyone left, and I told him that I wasn't sure. I saw that Ron's truck was missing, but that's all I remembered."

"His truck was missing? Where was he?" Her jaw dropped. "Conor, do you think Ron had anything to do with the car?"

He touched her face. "Don't get riled up, babe. No, I don't think that at all. Ron probably went out to try for a kill. He hates hunting all week-end and coming back empty-handed. Hell, every hunter feels that way. I told Don that I would ask him about it, but he said that he was planning to interview Ron and Terrance in a couple of days. Don't worry about it. Don will get to the bottom of everything. If you let your mind run wild, you won't sleep a wink." He kissed her cheek and played with her hair. She closed her eyes and laid flat.

"I'm not going to be able to sleep after hearing these things. I just can't."

He crawled on top of her, kissing and caressing her, until she grabbed his hips, moaning in anticipation.

"Let me help you," he whispered as they intertwined.

Madison ignored the troubling thoughts temporarily, knowing that they would be patiently waiting for her in the morning.

***

The following day, after lunch break ended, the office staff trailed each other through the cafeteria doors. Oddly, Ron and Terrance weren't present. Conor asked Luis about their absence, but he didn't know why they weren't there. They concluded that the pair must have gone off-site to eat and shrugged it off. Conor followed Madison through the door and stealthily pinched her rear.

"Luis, please don't do that. Conor might see," she whispered without looking behind.

He gritted his teeth and whispered. "What the hell? It's me."

She laughed. "No shit, Sherlock."

"Ooh, you're gonna get it when we get home."

She turned and headed toward her cubicle. "Promises, promises," she teased.

He liked her great sense of humor, that is, whenever she loosened up. A good sense of humor was a requirement for Conor when choosing his women. He gravitated to those that didn't take life too seriously.

What's the point in being serious. Life is short, and then you die.

He walked over to his office and heard someone whistle.

"Hey, Conor."

It was Ron, hailing him through his open office door. Conor snapped out of his daze, stepped inside, and noticed Terrance standing to the left.

"What's up, Ron? Hey, Terrance."

Ron walked past him to close the door. Then he sat behind his desk, spreading his arms wide. "What's up? You tell us, and we'll both know."

"Don't give me the runaround. What do you want, man?"

Terrance stepped to Conor. "Cut the bullshit! Stop pretending that you don't know," he shouted.

Conor pressed his hand to the other man's chest, holding him off. "What I do know is that you better chill out and lower your voice. You don't have any reason to come at me like this."

Terrance pushed his hand away. "I better? I better or what? What are you going to do about it?"

Ron stood up. "That's enough, Terrance. There's not going to be any fighting in my office. You can meet after work somewhere and duke it out on your own time. Everybody, calm down. Both of you, sit your asses down."

Terrance sighed and did as he was told, his nostrils flaring with every breath. Conor sat next to him, both of them looking moodily down at their respective shoes.

Conor broke the deadlock and looked at Ron. "Tell me what the problem is. I have shit to do today."

Ron ballooned his cheeks. "Terrance and I got a call today before lunch from a private investigator claiming that you and Madison hired him. He wanted to set up a time for an interview concerning our work relationship with her. I told him to fuck off, and Terrance told him..."

"I told him that I was busy and not to call my goddamn phone again," Terrance barked.

Ron pointed at him. "Exactly. What the hell happened to you, Conor? Why wouldn't you give us a heads up? I don't get it. All of us were best friends, man. How can you be silent and just stand by when you see that we're about to be sued by your woman? All that shit from the past has been overdone. Everybody moved on. Now, this comes back to haunt us. We want to know why you didn't tell us. That's all."

Conor hung his head. "Jesus. Is this why you guys are about to murder me? Let me explain what's going on. Last week, Madison saw her old car at a gas station, and she freaked out. Her mother was supposed to have it scrapped, but instead, it wound up at the police auction and was sold. The new owner said that the car ran awesome, which freaked Madison out. So, she asked the police to investigate why the car was still on the road when it was supposed to be a rolling death trap. The cops refused to help, go figure. She got pissed off and hired a private investigator to determine if the police were wrong the whole time. She's got the idea in her head that some kids in the neighborhood somehow tampered with the car."

"What does any of that have to do with us?" Terrance asked.

"It doesn't, but the investigator told her to list anyone that she knows at work or in her social life. That's what she did. This guy, Don Carson, is just doing what he's paid to do. Milk the clock and cash the checks."

Ron squinted and glanced at Terrance.

"Then it sounds like she's planning to sue the Metro Police," Ron said. "We thought for a second that she was planning to hit us with a sexual harassment lawsuit."

Conor waved his hands. "Christ, no. She has no intention of doing that. She's never discussed anything like that with me. That harassment fiasco is forgiven and forgotten."

Terrance coughed. "She's not the only one forgetting things. I see it has rubbed off on you. You forgot to send us wedding invitations. Thanks a lot, my brother."

Ron laughed. "Oh yeah, the wedding invitations. Did you forget how to spell our names? Huh? Friend?"

Conor clamped the arms of the chair. "Honestly, I had no idea that you two wanted to come, or I would have told her to add your names to the list. Since when do you two go to weddings?"

Ron frowned. "We go to weddings that our best friends are in, dumbass. Did you forget about Luis's wedding? We were all there. Why would your wedding be any different?"

"And why would you invite Luis and not us? Answer that too, smartass," Terrance chimed in. "Man, we used to be tight. Nowadays, you walk around here like you never met us. I know you love your girl, but dammit, Conor, we go way back. It's a messed up situation, bro."

Conor stood up and faced them both. "You're both right. I screwed up. I'm sorry. I got caught up in my relationship and forgot about my boys."

"Damn right. You forgot where you came from," Terrance grumbled.

Ron walked up to Conor. "Yep. He forgot about the Pack. But it's alright now." He looked at Terrance. "The man apologized." He held out his hand. "Apology accepted." They shook and looked at Terrance, who was still fuming.

Terrance looked up. "That shit hurt, Conor. After all that we've been through together. Why?"

Conor held out his hand. "All I can do is apologize and do better from here on out. I'm sorry, bro."

Terrance grinned, and they shook. "Okay, we're good now, but do that shit again, and we will be fighting."

Conor raised his finger. "I have an idea. I want to make this up to you two with a rendezvous. Tonight, the Tap Room at 8 p.m. There's a band playing, so you know the girls will be out on the dance floor. But most importantly, tonight's drinks are on me."

Ron and Terrance stared at each other, speechless.

"Did he just say what I think he said?" Ron asked.

Terrance smirked. "I'm not sure. I think he needs to repeat it."

Conor walked over to the door.

"There will be no repeat. You ladies heard me loud and clear. You've busted my balls enough for today, so if you snooze, you lose. Bitches."

"I'll tell Luis and see if he wants to come," Terrance said.

"Don't bother," Conor replied. "I eat with him every day, and he's all about church and family these days. Let him be. He gets so uptight that he tends to ruin a good time."

"True," Ron said. "It's only us three tonight. Cool. We'll see you there, my prodigal son."

Conor left, and Ron smirked at Terrance. "I knew that he couldn't stay away for long. He's one of us. Don't forget that. It was only a matter of time."

CHAPTER 10

At 7:30 pm, Conor grabbed his car keys from the coffee table to leave for the Tap Room. Madison sat on the couch watching him, pouting. She disapproved of him meeting up with his old friends, even to calm their fears, especially after their tainted history, but he tried to quell her anxiety.

"Babe, I won't be much longer. As I said, I'm buying them a few rounds to calm them down." He chuckled. "I can't believe they thought that you were taking them to court over all that old shit."

"Fuck them! I should sue their asses. It doesn't sound like a bad idea," she hissed.

He walked over and kissed her. "Now, now, be nice."

"Don't drink too much. And don't come back smelling like a whore. I know they'll try to hang all over you."

"Me? Nobody is interested in me," he said and left the house.

"I'm not playing with you, Conor Gregory!" she shouted after him.

Thirty minutes later, he burst through the doors of the Tap Room. The cover band began their second song, and couples bounced to the dance floor below. The band was popular and a people's favorite within the metro, covering the hottest genres flawlessly. Conor looked around for the guys. He noticed Ron's car in the parking lot.

"Hey! Conor! Over here!" Ron shouted from the bar as Terrance sat beside him.

Conor walked over and sat between them.

"We're already three drinks ahead of you," Ron said as Terrance held up his glass.

"Cool," Conor said. He looked around the bar, then faced the dance floor. "Let's get a table. Then we can pull up more chairs if you guys bag some chicks. Plus, it's not as loud over there." He pointed.

Terrance gulped. "Hell yeah, let's do it. There are some fine ass women in here tonight."

"Let's get it!" Ron said.

The three weaved past clusters of patrons and seized a table. The waitress took their order while Conor grabbed Ron and Terrance's shoulders.

"I'm ordering for the table. Whatever they get goes on my bill. Start us off with a bottle of Jameson and a bucket of Dos Equis Lager."

"Dammit, Conor! That's what I'm talking about! Woo-hoo!" Terrance crooned.

Ron grabbed the back of Conor's neck and leaned into his ear. "I knew you'd come back, you handsome son of a bitch! I love you, man!" Ron kissed his cheek.

Conor pushed him away and laughed. "Don't kiss me fool, kiss one of those hotties over there!" He pointed across the room at a collection of females.

Terrance stood. "He's right. The jars of honey are in the house! I'm gonna have to make a move."

The waitress returned with the order and poured their first round.

Ron stood. "Fill those glasses up!" He looked to his friends. "Raise them. You know the drill."

Conor jumped to his feet.

Ron nodded. "To the brotherhood. To the Wolf Pack!"

They emptied their glasses and howled in unison. As Conor sat, he felt out of place. It had been years since they toasted that way. It once was a cherished ritual to him, but now it meant nothing. Madison was on his mind, no matter how hard he pretended that she wasn't. He would rather be home with her, but he had arranged this outing for a purpose and had to go through with it.

Ron looked down at him. "Okay, let's pick our targets."

"I found mine already," Terrance replied, his eyes already engaged on a victim.

Conor waved them off. "Nah, I'm not here for that. I'm covering the drinks, that's all."

"Wow. You are whipped! But that's cool; you just left more for us," Ron mocked as he and Terrance high-fived each other.

Terrance sat and began texting. "It's gonna be a long night. I better start covering my tracks right now."

Ron sat and opened a beer. "I can smell the poontang. It's like a slut bakery!" He laughed. "Terrance is right. I need a new excuse for Kathy. She isn't falling for my old shit anymore. I'm running out of lies!"

Conor smirked and sipped a beer. "Get your lies straight. Don't get busted. Who can lie faster? On your mark, get set, go!"

Ron and Terrance glanced at each other and raced to finish.

Ron set his phone down and raised his hands. "I won! Again!"

Conor clapped.

Terrance stood. "Alright, we need to get busy."

Ron finished his beer and staggered to his feet. "Are you gonna dance?" he asked Conor.

"Nope, and after this beer is finished, I'm done drinking. My ass will stay planted in this chair until I leave. My woman is waiting for me. Have at it, boys. I give you my blessing. Go forth and spread thy seed."

"Oh, we will be spreading some seed tonight. You better believe it!" Terrance shouted.

"Watch our stuff then, water boy. The real men are going out to hunt," Ron said and followed behind Terrance.

Conor sat for the next two hours, watching the crowd's ebb and flow while they danced and partied into pandemonium. The music and alcohol filled the souls of the patrons, removing their inhibitions. Scores of women reverted to their base liberated nature, becoming sensual, seductive, and predatory. The men became desperate and subservient as the night dragged onward, at times showing aggression when in direct competition with another male. Conor once lived for nights like this. But that was the old Conor, and this night confirmed that fact to him. He decided that this was the last time that he would associate with Ron and Terrance socially. The longer he watched them dance and be themselves, the more he counted them as pitiful.

I have something better waiting for me at home. These jerks don't care about me. Following behind their stupidity has only caused me trouble. I won't let them ruin my life and lose Madison.

Spurred by that thought, he stood and got their attention. They put their dance partners on hold and walked over to him. The three shook hands and headed in opposite directions. Conor paid the bar tab and went home to the arms of his loving fiancé while Ron and Terrance rejoined the crowd. No one there was a stranger. They were all the same passing shadows, sharing the pretense of love, but not wanting any attachments or expectations to follow.

***

The following day, Detective Alex Schultz locked the front door to his apartment and drove to the precinct. It was a short drive, lasting fifteen minutes in the morning, which gave him time to get his mind up to speed. He was a go-getter and an overachiever in everything that he set his mind to do. From Pee-wee baseball to Military Special Operations Intelligence, he excelled in everything. Being socially introverted was also helpful and conducive to his focus in life and on any task at hand.

He was where he wanted to be in life at the moment, but his appetite for professional achievement was never satiated. Time was the only roadblock in attaining his goals, but just as time teaches patience, his senior partner taught him like a college professor's aide. Schultz respected Olson, just as one respects a retired champion boxer. Both shared the same sentiments about the future and passing greatness, but time was on the side of the young and robust. Schultz knew that he could outperform his mentor. Still, for now, he had to fake the role of an eager-to-learn greenhorn, pretending to be appreciative for every morsel of investigative wisdom that Olson would gracefully bestow up him. Playing the game infuriated him.

Give me a break! You can't show me anything. I can't wait for the day you melt away and ride off into the sunset.

But Schultz knew that emotions and petty feelings had no place in the situation. He was patiently waiting to receive the keys to the kingdom and become a Lead Detective. Olson was holding on to that post until either retiring or somehow getting the coveted promotion to lieutenant. Schultz could, and would, grit his teeth and bear the burden. He counted this episode as a mere speed bump and nothing more in the unwritten record of his past life's trials and tribulations.

He pulled into the Metro police parking lot and noticed one of the clerks walking in.

Hmm, now she's hot. Look at the legs on her.

It had been weeks since he had gotten laid, and the clerk triggered his male instincts enough for him to make a note and visit her later. He wouldn't mind having a steady girlfriend if it weren't for his irregular working hours. It was the primary reason that all his relationships had turned to dust within months. Their reasons were all similar. Either he wasn't physically or emotionally available, and he knew that they spoke the truth. His saving grace was that he was a handsome young detective, and in his opinion, that alone was enough to open the sexual interests of most women. To them, he was like a celebrity actor, and they were willing to sleep with him to see for themselves.

He walked in the front door and saw Olson in the lobby talking with a group of officers.

Olson saw him. "Here's my partner now; I have to run. Don't forget to check on that for me," he added before joining Schultz in the elevator. "How's it going, Alex?"

"It's going. I was checking out that clerk. The blonde, who works in dispatch. What's her name again?"

Olson grinned and sipped his coffee. "You're talking about Jessica. She is a beauty."

"Yeah, Jessica. So, what our first point of business? Oh, wise mentor."

"We're gonna check the S.A. log."

Schultz was puzzled. "S.A. log? What's that?"

"It's the Smart Ass log. I thought you were familiar with it, oh wise student."

The door opened, and Olson walked out first.

"Good one, Roger."

"Thanks, it comes from wisdom," he winked as they walked toward the Investigative unit. "We need to check the status board. The Chief hinted at a meeting today, but I'm not sure why. I have a feeling it's something to..."

His voice tapered off as the sound of laughter echoed down the hallway.

"Someone's having a hell of a party this morning," Schultz commented as they opened the doors to the unit.

Don Carson was surrounded by a group of detectives, hooting at their longtime investigative peer as he delivered one of his famous punch lines. Olson approached from behind, shedding his grimace for a smile.

Olson tapped his shoulder. "Hey, partner. What the devil are you doing here so early this morning? You don't even get out of bed until noon."

Don turned. "Good morning Roger." He turned back to the group of old comrades, "I'll catch you later, guys." He put his arm around Olson and led him toward an empty corner of the office while Schultz stood by, loathing the intrusion. The former partners stopped in an area of privacy, and Don began his well-rehearsed pitch.

"Roger, I'm on my way to meet with Angelletti. You know that he has an open-door policy, and I'm still on the roll in this department. I've got a client who believes that the investigators who worked her homicide case may not have performed their due diligence. You know, they may have cut corners and such. I've been gathering affidavits and evidence all week long and compiled some compelling facts."

"Who's the client?" Olson pretended to show interest, but he didn't care what Don had cooking. He merely wanted to patronize him so that he could continue on his way.

"Madison Sanders."

Her name seemed to echo aloud as Olson looked around the office. His reaction was the type of indicator that Don was hoping for as he chuckled inside.

That's right, partner, hello!

Olson appeared concerned. "Really? Hmm, that's odd. You already know Schultz, and I worked that case, so cut the shit. So, what new facts did you discover? We were thorough. All i's dotted, and t's crossed."

"It's about her old car. That exhaust leak alone wasn't severe enough to cause the death of her son. There had to be another component which caused the chain of events leading to the CO_2 poisoning."

"No, Don. She called me last week and was upset that her car wasn't crushed. I checked with the Motor Pool and confirmed the disclaimer written for the vehicle before it was sold. It disclosed that there was an exhaust leak."

"She's not disputing if there was a leak, but she now knows that the leak alone didn't cause the accident. Take a look at this."

Carson handed him a folder and stood by as Olson donned his eyeglasses and sifted through the information. Despite his mixed feelings about his former partner, Olson respected Carson's experience and abilities. When not drinking or violating the law, Carson was second to none among the other detectives in the unit. He was also known as a human lie detector.

After reviewing Carson's findings, Olson closed the folder and handed it back, looking down and away as he thought.

Carson stepped closer. "For God's sake Roger, at least call in the four of them for questioning. Keep it light and see who lawyers up. There are motives and opportunities for half of them, and the fiancé may be the key. He's a non-prejudicial witness whose sworn statement contradicts the potentially weak alibi of the others. If you catch even one of them in a lie, then request a warrant, and take a look at their cell phones. Check their GPS locations."

Olson pondered the offer. "I'm not sure about it."

"What? I'm giving you this on a silver platter, Roger. I'm doing you a huge favor. Let's appreciate the scenario. If there's nothing to any of this, then you and your minion standing over there have done your duty. All bases will be covered, and you both can rest easy. I'll convince her to drop any potential litigation against you, your partner, and the department. But, if you blow her off and ignore her, then expect a childless mother's fury to rain down hellfire on you and that kid. I'm saying that if you don't follow up on this for me within the next couple of days, then I'll be forced to assist my client in every way possible to get satisfaction. She will file a suit against you. You better believe me."

"Give me the file, and I'll take care of it. I'll talk to Schultz, and we'll call them in for questioning."

Carson handed the file to Olson but wouldn't release it. "No more bullshit, Roger. This is what we've been waiting for, and it's my last chance. It's a win for us both. Do you copy?"

"Yeah, and I'm on it."

Carson released the folder. "You better be. For both our sakes." He smiled, patted Olson's cheek, and handed him a USB flash drive. "Here are the audio and video files to go with my report. You have all that you need. I'll call you tomorrow to get an update."

"You're acting like you're my Lead detective again."

Carson scoffed. "When was I ever not?"

Olson watched him leave and then saw Schultz staring at him from across the room, knowing that he would ask about the private conversation.

Goddamn Carson! He's worse than bed bugs. You can't ever get rid of him.

***

The following day, Luis Mendoza, Conor Gregory, Ron Tatum, and Terrance Roberts were contacted by Detective Schultz, requesting if they would voluntarily come in for questioning at the precinct, and all consented. Olson ensured that Schultz scheduled the interviews thirty minutes apart, all required for the initial probatory phase.

Each interview lasted approximately twenty minutes. Everyone recalled their whereabouts the night before the accident, but there were no inquiries about Madison's sexual harassment. Ron and Terrance were relieved by the omission of those potentially damning questions. Luis and Conor were the first to conclude their interviews, which contained a variant line of questioning separately from the others. The detectives knew what they were looking for, and Carson's work had provided a readymade template for their inquiry. It wasn't long before they began to sense that he was correct.

Olson sat in a room with Ron and asked the basic questions.

"Where did you go? Who were you with? Who did you text or call?"

He concluded the interview with one final request.

"Mr. Tatum, would you mind if we look at your cell phone? It will only take a few minutes."

Ron turned red. "I don't think so. Why?"

"You have no reason to be concerned. This is only a formality. We are covering our bases to give a grieving mother closure, that's all."

"Do I need a lawyer or something? I've got a funny feeling about this."

"Lawyer?" Olson laughed. "Why do you think that you need a lawyer? The others didn't ask for a lawyer. That's interesting. If you feel like you need a lawyer for some reason, then, by all means, call one."

"I didn't say that I need one. Am I the only one who you asked to see their cell phone? I have personal conversations and photos stored and things that I wouldn't want my wife to find. Do you get me?"

"I figured that's why you might be reluctant. I tell you with certainty that we do not care about any of that. Again, this is only a formality. They've already returned Mr. Roberts' phone, and he's leaving now. You're the only person who we are waiting for to cooperate with us. It's your prerogative if you want to help Ms. Sanders or not. It's your call."

Ron sighed. "Okay, it's not a problem. Here."

He handed his phone to Olson.

"Thank you, sir. I'll be right back."

Olson left and rode the elevator down to the 2nd floor, where he handed off the device to a waiting forensic technician. "This is the last one, Tommy." He filled out an evidentiary disposition form. "Be sure to clone two copies—one for me and one for Alex.

"No problem, just give me a few minutes," the technician replied and began the cloning process.

Olson leaned against the counter, relieved. He wasn't sure if Ron and Terrance would allow their phones to be looked at, but he was prepared for that. They had no idea that the investigators had cloned their phone data, which they were not legally sanctioned to do. Still, Olson's finesse and deception circumvented their commonsense defenses, causing them to turn their property over willingly. Olson never understood why ordinary citizens were ignorant to the fact that investigators can lie during questioning.

They're too stupid to be educated professionals. That was too easy.

After the technician finished his work, he handed the phone to Olson, who hurried back to the interview room and returned Ron's property.

Ron stood. "Is that all?"

"Yes, sir, and thank you again for your cooperation."

"Anytime, detective. I'm glad that I could help."

Olson walked him to the elevator to see him off, and as the elevator door closed, Schultz walked over.

"Did you get it?" Schultz asked.

"Yep. He was beginning to kick a little, but after I rebaited my line, he bit."

They went to their desks and sat down.

Schultz leaned back. "I hate to admit it, but your ex-partner was right. There was more to this. I wish that I could have called his bullshit."

"Forget Carson. We need to root this thing out and figure out why Mr. Tatum is lying about his alibi. Let's get down to forensics and make sure they stay on this. I want to look at some of the data before we go home."

***

"I like him, but I don't know how much longer we can afford him," Madison told Brittany while standing in her office. "A $740 invoice is not exactly pocket change."

"But is he getting results?"

"I guess. I know that he interviewed a lot of people. He did get that asshole detective, Olson, to bring in Conor and the others a few days ago for questioning. But what now? I can't keep paying out money like this. I'm trying to save for the wedding."

"Just put the P.I. on pause for right now, and budget his work."

"I'll have to. I don't have a choice."

Brittany checked the wall clock.

"We get off in ten minutes. Do you and Conor want to have a drink after work? We'll be just in time for Happy Hour. That will save you some money."

"I'll ask him when we walk to the car and let you know. I don't mind going."

Madison went to her cubicle and cleaned off her desk in preparation for the next day's workload. She sat and stared out of the window, passing the final minutes until quitting time. Her frustration from the lack of progress and a resolution caused her to feel that she was letting Elijah down, which saddened her. She prayed but felt unworthy.

Please, God, help me find peace. Help me find the truth.

Madison wasn't the praying type and felt hypocritical by imploring an almighty deity to assist her in this predicament. But she didn't know what else to do. She sat with her eyes closed in prayerful meditation, making her heartfelt requests known.

When finished, she opened her eyes, squinted from the brightness of the sun. When she was eventually able to focus, she noticed police cars in the parking lot.

That's odd.

The intercom chimed, signaling the close of the workday. She shouldered her purse and went to meet Conor in the front lobby. Brittany was there first and tapped her shoulder.

"I'll pay for your drinks today. I know that your finances are tight, so don't worry."

"Aw, Britt. You don't have to do that. I'm not that bad off."

"But that's what best friends are for."

Conor met them, and they walked to their cars.

"I wonder what the cops are here for?" Conor asked.

Brittany smirked, looking over the roof of her car. "It looks like someone didn't pay their child support."

"Three police cars is a lot of manpower for a deadbeat dad. Don't you think?" he replied.

Madison sat inside. "Conor. Brittany invited us out for cocktails. Do you want to go?"

Conor got inside. "That's a great idea." He peeked at Brittany. "You lead the way, sister."

They started their cars and noticed movement from the police cruisers as six officers stepped out and marched toward the front. Seconds later, they pulled two men from the crowd.

"Holy shit! They're arresting Terrance and Ron!" Conor yelled.

Madison stiffened. "Oh my God. Oh my God..."

Brittany stepped out to get a better view. "I don't believe it. What did they do?"

The entire parking lot watched Ron and Terrance handcuffed, placed in the backseat of separate cruisers, and driven off. The events stunned everyone within the vicinity. The staff stood in awe of the unexpected arrests of their coworkers.

"Why are they being arrested, Conor?" Madison asked.

"I'm not sure, babe, but I have a feeling that Don Carson will know. Let's skip the drinks today and go home. We'll call him and find out what's going on."

She told Brittany about the change of plans, and they left.

Madison's mind was foggy during the drive home, and Conor's chatter became inaudible. Her thoughts were miles away, contemplating the implications. She now knew that Ron and Terrance were somehow involved in Elijah's tragedy.

How? What did they do? What did they do to my child?

Mixed feelings of hate, happiness, and satisfaction flowed through her veins, overwhelming her with emotion. Her hands trembled while texting Brittany, and Conor noticed. He massaged the nape of her neck, noting that despite being emotionally shaken, she hadn't cried at all. No, not one tear.

CHAPTER 11

Ron Tatum and Terrance Roberts were both charged with violating Minnesota statutes § 609.195 and § 609.505, Murder in the Third Degree, and Obstruction of the Legal Process. After a detailed review of the new evidence discovered by Detectives Olson and Schultz, Joe Angelletti confidentially brought the matter to Minnesota's Attorney General's attention, who gave his approval to proceed. Facing up to 25 years imprisonment, with fines and penalties in the tens of thousands of dollars, Ron and Terrance demanded to contact attorneys as they were transported.

Schultz and Olson transported Ron in the backseat while he berated them.

"This is bullshit! Fucking bullshit!" he yelled.

Olson sat in the passenger's seat, trying to maintain his patience. He didn't want to look back at Ron and give him the attention he sought, so he remained face-forward. But halfway to the precinct, Olson couldn't restrain any longer.

"Mr. Tatum, you lied to us. You said you were at the cabin all night long and had an alibi. But your alibi says otherwise."

"What? Who said that? Terrance? Oh, please. He sells Ecstasy! You're going to believe a goddamn drug dealer?" He gritted his teeth. "Give me a fucking break."

"I didn't mention Terrance, but thanks for that information," Olson said while scribbling on his notepad. "Don't worry about who our witnesses are. You've demanded your right to speak with an attorney. You'll find out during the discovery phase. That being said, let me remind you that you have the right to remain silent. I would exercise that right, sir. You already have enough to contend with."

"Silent? Fuck that shit! I want to scream from the goddamn rooftops!" He leaned forward and lowered his voice. "You morons screwed up. You did. I'm going to sue your department and both of you stupid assholes. That's a promise."

Finally spent, Ron leaned back to catch his breath, panting, and closed his eyes until they reached the precinct.

When they arrived, Olson cracked his door and turned to Schultz. "I've got to hit a toilet first. Those burritos at lunch went straight through me."

Schultz snickered. "You better hurry then."

"I hope you shit your pants," Ron jeered.

Olson grinned and looked back. "After your first month in prison, you'll be shitting your pants daily. Not from fear but from the burrito-sized cocks that will be decimating your asshole. Remember that, Ronda."

He smiled, closed the door, and went inside. Schultz drove to the reception area. He turned off the car and sat staring at Ron in the rear-view mirror.

Schultz smirked. "So, you're going to sue us. Good luck with that."

"What's so funny about that, shithead?"

"I'll tell you. After we cloned your phones and sifted through the info, we located your cell phone's GPS location to be 30 miles away from the crime scene, which would exclude you from having any viable window of opportunity to commit the crime."

"Right! Exactly man. I didn't do shit!"

"Wait a second, let me finish," he smirked. "That doesn't mean much by itself. You and Terrance could have simply left your cell phones at the cabin. Anyway, that doesn't matter right now. Next, we checked all your phone calls and messages. Nothing much to see there either."

"Then why am I in handcuffs, motherfucker?!"

"Calm down and be patient. Are you ready for the punchline? When we recovered the deleted messages from both your phones, we noticed two text messages between you and Terrance. The first text was from him to you. The second was your reply. These two texts seal the deal. We have the motive, opportunity, and a confession in your own words by your hand. You don't even have a solid alibi. I want to be the first to say thank you, sir. Job well done." Schultz looked away, snickering.

Ron appeared puzzled, confused. "Huh?" He stared at the back of the seat, attempting to recollect the past. "What texts?"

Schultz opened his pocket pad and flipped through the pages. "Oh, I thought you might get amnesia, but don't worry, we're aware of every word. Listen up, and I'll read them to you. Here's Terrance's text to you. *"I'm worried about that guy Don Carson, bro. He might find out what we did to Madison's car."* Forty-five seconds later, you replied. *"It was an accident. We packed too much snow. Be cool and keep your mouth shut.!"*

"We have all the evidence we need, and all your screaming and kicking isn't going to change the fact that you and Terrance are going to prison. You're a piece of shit, and I don't have anything else to say to you. Now, shut your mouth before I kick your teeth in."

Ron was speechless and withdrew. He realized that something was wrong and didn't struggle as Schultz brought him inside for processing.

Terrance arrived afterward, outwardly angry, but stopped short of rebellion. Both were processed within the hour but would have to wait until the next day for their arraignment hearings in front of a magistrate. Ron contacted his attorney first and then made preparations to contact his wife. Terrance decided to wait and see where his bail would be set. With limited funds at his present disposal, he was unsure if he could afford both the attorney's retainer fee and the anticipated bond to be released. Although his immediate freedom was paramount, he felt no trepidation by spending a few days in jail. He always maintained various contacts throughout the city and had certain business dealings with criminal elements, including gang affiliations.

As the holding cell doors closed to their separate quads, both the men sat down with the others on worn metal benches. Some contemplated various ways to escape the repercussions of their bad decisions, while others adamantly reaffirmed their innocence. Even a few believed that one universal fact covered them all under its umbrella.

Every man is guilty of something. Karma will be the judge.

***

Madison collapsed in tears on the floor of the living room as Conor dropped to console her. She knelt in the fetal position, wailing, as he held the phone in one hand and turned on the speaker.

"Thank you, Detective Olson! Madison is overcome with emotion right now, as you can hear. Me too."

"I understand, and I'll let you go. The prosecutors will be in touch soon. Take care of yourselves. We got them for you. It's time that Elijah and you both receive justice."

Conor hung up and sat on the floor, hugging Madison. The release of guilt struck her suddenly after hearing of the arrest charges.

Elijah, see? Mommy didn't hurt you. I would never hurt you! My sweet baby. I'm sorry I couldn't stop them. I didn't know. Please forgive me.

They sat for a few minutes before she wiped her eyes and stood, with Conor beside her. She held his face. "Conor, I did not kill my child." She smiled, and tears streamed again.

He pulled her tight. "No, babe. I know that you didn't. Those two are going to prison," he hissed.

She squeezed him back. "Yes, they are. But it won't bring him back. He's gone, and they should be too." She bobbed her head. "Yes. They both deserve to die."

He led her to the couch and brought over a box of tissues as she sat. She blew her nose and wiped her eyes.

"Did you know that your eyes turn deep blue when you cry?"

She squinted. "Really? I know that my nose gets as red as Rudolph's when I cry."

He chuckled. "That too."

She thought about what he just said and smiled. He had a way of helping her through emotional barriers with small comments like that. He was good at redirecting her negative thoughts.

"Your eyes get bluer," he said, sitting down next to her. "Your nose looks cute too; all swollen, red, and puffy,"

She reached for her phone. "I need to call Brittany and tell her."

"Wait. I have an idea. Let's get out of this house and do something."

"Do what? I don't feel like eating right now."

Conor stood. "We don't have to eat right now. We can go to the lake."

She slumped. "But I don't feel like walking either. We hike that trail all the time."

"No. Let's rent a boat. You're always talking about that when we're out there. We can rent a boat for an hour or two. Think about it. The wind in your hair. The calm of the water, right? If we leave now, we could be on the lake and watch the sunset."

"Conor, are you serious? Would you do that for me?" She stopped dialing.

"Would I? Get your stuff, change clothes, go potty, or whatever. We leave in ten minutes." He stood with his hands on his hips. "Up! Get moving, beautiful."

"Okay. Alright. Let's do this." She stood up and kissed him. Then she began gathering her things.

***

The next day around noon, Terrance and Ron were arraigned in court. Ron stood confidently as his attorney requested a reasonable bail amount set and that his client would be released pending trial. Alternately, the lead prosecutor put forward a compelling argument, alleging that due to the defendant's history of sexual harassment and concerted efforts to cause the victim harm, they posed a danger to her and the public. She requested bail to be set to the maximum allowable amount and that the defendant be placed under house arrest with electronic monitoring.

After patiently listening to both requests, the judge set bail at 1 million dollars and that he be remanded under house arrest with monitoring, surrendering any firearms, voiding his firearm permits, and having no contact with Madison Sanders or her family. Ron's mouth fell open as the judge's order was read, and the deputies led him away.

Terrance was next and decided to forego the cost for private counsel. The public defender stood beside him, echoing the same request as the previous counsel. Likewise, the lead prosecutor requested her same terms, but with an additional caveat. She informed the court of an active search warrant of Terrance's house and an ongoing investigation into his involvement in narcotics trafficking. Without deliberation, the judge decreed the identical order and set the same terms as his co-defendant. Terrance dropped his head, not knowing if he would be spending his next few months, or years, in confinement.

Ron's problems further escalated while speaking to his wife Kathy on the phone. They discussed their available finances needed to pay his bail, and after contacting friends and family, they ultimately lacked sixty-two thousand dollars. But he had a plan and shared it with her.

"Okay, that's not a problem. We have more than enough equity in the house to cover that. I need you to get the papers together and contact the Bail Bon.."

"Oh no, I won't!" she shouted. "I am not putting up our house so you can make bail. No, sir. I'm not going to jeopardize this family's home or put our children through that stress. You'll have to find another way."

"Stress? What about my stress!"

"Don't yell at me! I'll hang up on you right now."

"I'm sorry. Please, Kathy. We won't lose the house. It's not like I'm going to skip town."

"Honestly, I don't know what you might do. You're in jail for messing with some woman's car, and her child died. What am I supposed to think that you'll do? Huh?"

Ron was desperate. "If you won't do that, then sell my truck. I hate to do it, but..."

"I'm not selling shit! What if you go to prison? What then? After you're finished with everything, the kids and I won't have a pot to piss in! No, Ron. You're going to have to call some more of your family, friends, or whoever."

"I own half of everything, bitch!"

"Go to hell!"

She ended the call. Ron dropped the phone handset and turned to the guard.

"Take me back. I'm through," he mumbled.

"You'll be through after you hang up the damn phone properly. Now do it," the guard barked. Ron replaced the handset and was handcuffed. "Don't ever let me see you do that shit again. Do you understand?"

Ron nodded.

"Motherfucker, you better open your damn mouth before I do it for you."

"Yes. I understand."

"Good, now move your ass. Wannabe Rockstar." The guard laughed while towing Ron behind.

***

Don Carson pulled into a restaurant parking lot and turned off the car. He bobbed around in his seat, looking for Olson's car, and he saw it. He straightened his necktie and walked inside. This was the meeting that he had been waiting for, although it was impromptu. Carson had gotten word from the precinct that Olson, Schultz, and Angelletti were having lunch together at the restaurant. He considered it an opportunity to casually discuss his contributions to solving the Sanders' case. But the expectation of discussing his official reinstatement was his main objective. This was the finale. There wouldn't be another opportunity.

Carson strutted into the foyer. "I'll be joining that group over there," he informed the host, who had rushed over to greet him. "I'll take it from here, honey," he said and went to their table.

The three paused their conversation and looked up, unable to disguise their irritation of the uninvited visitor.

"Hello, gentlemen. Mr. Angelletti, Olson, Schultz. How's the food?"

They nodded, responding in kind.

Angelletti wiped his mouth and smiled. "How are you doing these days, Don?"

"I've never been better." He beamed brightly at them. "And I'm still performing at my best, as you can see from my work on the Sanders' case."

"Oh, that's right. I think I heard something about that. Thanks for the tip."

The first sign of disrespect tested Carson's chipper smile. "Tip? I think that turning over a fifty-page file filled with affidavits, interviews, and audio qualifies as more than a tip. Don't you?" Carson looked at Olson, who continued to eat his meal, seemingly unaffected by the comments.

Angelletti wiped his mouth. "I'm not entirely aware of the totality of your contributions, but whatever you did is appreciated. I don't intend to minimize the weight of your efforts. I'll tell you what I can do. Stop by my office later this week, and I'll authorize a $500 payment for all your work."

To Carson, the offer was a slap in the face. An insult. Nevertheless, he maintained his composure.

"Sir, with all due respect, you can keep the $500. Instead, let my work in the case stand as an indication of my fitness for duty. I'm ready to be reinstated. I've been..."

Angelletti held up his finger. "One moment, Don." He turned to Olson and Schultz. "Would you please excuse us for a few moments?"

"Yes, sir," Schultz replied, standing up. "I have to use the restroom anyway."

Olson nodded without saying a word and followed him. Carson watched them walk away before pulling out a chair.

"No, please don't sit. This won't take long," Angelletti sighed. "So, this visit is about reinstatement. You want back in."

"Yes, sir. What I did in the Sanders' case should prove my readiness. I haven't lost a step. I hope that you can see that fact. Talk is cheap, so I proved myself."

"Don, what you did in this case doesn't make up for what you did in the past. That's why you haven't been reinstated."

Carson leaned on a chair. "I understand that, but you've had that investigation open for two years. All that time, I've been hanging by a thread, waiting for the conclusion. I only need six months, Joe. Six months active, and I'm out of your hair for good."

Angelletti crossed his arms. "The answer is no. You will not be reinstated. Since you are a short-timer now, I'll break the news to you. My office uncovered enough irrefutable corruption in your case to send you to prison. And now you have the nerve to complain about being in the dark for two years. Let me be clear. I decided to keep your case on the bottom of the stack. Why, might you ask? To let you make it to retirement. Why? Because of your years of valuable service. Consider it an early retirement present. I'm not going around in circles with you on this, Don. The decision has been made."

Angelletti stared at him before continuing with his meal. Carson stood there, his cheeks flushed with embarrassment, at a loss for words. His past sins had crushed his cocky demeanor. He looked around, feeling awkward as if the entire restaurant was privy to their conversation.

"Sir, is the $500 still on the table?"

Angelletti nodded without looking up. "Enjoy your retirement, detective. You've earned it. Goodbye and good luck."

"Thanks, goodbye," he replied and wandered out to his car.

A shortly after, Olson and Schultz returned and resumed their meal.

Olson turned to Schultz. "Well, speak of the devil, and he comes." They all chuckled. "Anyway, like I was saying. I got tired of his shit. The job is hard enough without having to babysit your partner, and it's a double disgrace if that partner was your former mentor. At the end of the day, I did what was best, and the department is better off because of it. You're a prime example, Alex. You're a notch above."

Angelletti winked. "That was courageous, Roger. Not many officers have the ethics to turn their partners in. That's the type of character the department is looking for when considering promotion from Sergeant to Lieutenant."

"Evidently, Carson never figured out that it was you, who reported him," Schultz said.

"He doesn't have a clue, but putting him out to pasture was the best thing for that pitiful bastard. Believe it or not, he wasn't always like this. He was impressive. Hey, would you mind passing me the hollandaise sauce?"

***

It was a bright Saturday morning as Madison sat on the floor of her bedroom with Brittany, sorting out old clothes to drop off at the Goodwill. The past two weeks brought forth more details on the scheduled court proceedings, and the trial dates were set. Madison was not happy about the timing.

"Why do they have to wait three months? I don't understand," Madison complained.

"That's how the system works. Be patient."

"I'll have to move the wedding back even further now. Maybe Spring. Conor was disappointed, but I don't have any other choice. There shouldn't be anything else on my mind, except for the man that I'm about to marry."

They heard Conor's footsteps approaching.

He peeked in the room. "Babe, I'm going to the gym." He looked at the piles of clothes on the floor. "That's gonna take all day."

Madison jumped to her feet and opened the closet door.

"Wait. Look in the closet, and take out what you're donating because I'm ready to give it all away."

He looked inside. "Huh? Hell no, I'm keeping everything in that closet."

She spread the hangars apart. "No, you're not. You don't wear half of this crap." She pulled out a coat. "A Green Bay Packers camouflage winter coat? You're a Vikings fan." She grabbed a hanging sweater. "You've never worn this Christmas sweater either. I kind of like Frosty the snowman plastered across the front." She laughed.

"Okay, you win. But don't you dare touch any suede or leather. That goes for my shoes too." He kissed her on the cheek. "Alright, I'm out. See you later."

"Bye, Conor," Brittany shouted.

"Bye, Britt!" he called over his shoulder.

They returned to sorting and bagging the items, none of which belonged to Elijah. Madison wasn't ready to take that step yet, clinging steadfastly to anything he had ever touched. Especially his clothing. It contained his scent, an instant reminder of him. When the pain of missing him became too much to bear, she would inhale his fragrance until the agony subsided.

"Have you heard back from your mother?" Brittany asked.

"Nope, not a word, and I don't care. I've done my part to keep her informed. Since she doesn't give and damn, neither do I."

Brittany frowned. "I know, but I hate that you don't have support from your mother. It's a shame."

"Brittany, please. Pretty please, don't bring her up. I'm not trying to be a bitch. The thought of her ruins my day every time."

"Bring up who? I don't know what you're talking about." She giggled, and Madison smirked.

***

Conor exited the main highway heading toward the gym but passed it by. He drove another fifteen minutes toward the outskirts of the city, pulling up in Ron's driveway. He tossed a breath mint into his mouth and walked to the front door, looking around nervously as he rang the doorbell. A few moments later, the door opened wide.

Ron's wife, Kathy, stood in the doorway, wearing a long t-shirt with nothing underneath.

"I was beginning to think that you weren't coming," she said.

"You know that I can't stay away," he whispered as he stepped inside and closed the door.

"Really? I couldn't tell after you pounded me last week. You were too quiet. I thought that guilt had gotten the better of you."

He pulled her close and fondled her breasts. She closed her eyes and melted, allowing him to do as he pleased. He pulled her head back with one hand and kissed her while exploring her vagina with the other.

"I told you, don't bring her up. This is about you and me." He snatched off her t-shirt. She stood completely naked, withering under his control. "How bad do you want it?"

She moaned. "I want it bad. Give it to me."

"Do you want mine more than Ron's?"

"Yes. Yes."

He enjoyed degrading her this way. It was a satisfying form of redemption. The woman Ron took from him many years ago deserved to feel the same humiliation that she forced on him. He smacked her on the butt.

"Bitch, get upstairs and into my bed. Hurry up, move that ass!" He smacked her again.

She trotted upstairs while he walked into the kitchen and opened up the refrigerator.

What do you have for best friends to drink, Ronnie? Let's see.

He took out a beer and popped the top, flicking it to the floor, then strolled up the staircase, admiring the family portraits with each step. He stopped at Ron's photo and laughed.

"Here's to you, Ron." He held up his bottle and then sipped. "Like you always said, payback is a bitch." He winked and went into the bedroom.

CHAPTER 12

It was a Friday, and three weeks had passed since Ron and Terrance's incarceration. Madison sat at her desk, waiting for the lunch bell. As the trial date drew closer, she struggled to keep focus in her daily life. Her mind constantly drifted away from any task at hand, whether at home or work. She became easily agitated and wasn't sleeping well, feeling engulfed by the slow, methodical drudgery of learning patience through time.

The office atmosphere at Traxtonite had changed. The Monday morning meetings once hosted by Ron were now being conducted in the interim by Steve Hyman. Positions had to be filled, and Luis was responsible for Terrance's workload until a replacement could be hired. Both men were terminated promptly after the official criminal charges were filed, but after a few days of sporadic office gossip, the news became old, and no one mentioned their names. Both were put on the back page until the trial began. Only then could they return to the front page news and be worthy of being catapulted back into social relevance.

At that moment, no one at Traxtonite had an inkling that Ron and Terrance were in a literal 'fight for their lives. Both men were genuinely ignorant of the inner workings of prison and the politics governing the convict population. While being processed into the general prison population, they neglected to submit a request to be placed into a more suitable environment, like protective custody. Their alleged crimes resulted in a child's death and, although the official trial had not begun, an unofficial tribunal by their fellow cellmates had already concluded. The verdicts were read, and the penalty swiftly delivered by two ruling but separate entities. The prison population considered crimes against children, and those of any sexual nature, as anathema and would not tolerate those particular offenders to live among them. Those who controlled the prison yard and housing units, or blocks, dispatched their representative teams of soldiers. Each group was comprised of five convicts tasked with beating Ron and Terrance within an inch of their lives. At the appointed time, the 'Green Light' was given, and the mission commenced in separate areas of the prison. The two friends were repeatedly slammed against the concrete floors and brutally beaten.

Ron endured his retribution curled in the fetal position, squealing, sobbing, and begging for mercy. His assailants answered his cries for help with laughter and increased brutality while jeering and mocking him. It was a treat for most but redeeming for the group, being motivated by the thoughts and memories of their children. Despite the malicious attack, Ron found fortune. A new corrections officer whose ethics had not yet been comprised happened to hear Ron's screams from his cell and went to investigate. The aftermath would reveal the extent of Ron's injuries to include multiple flesh wounds requiring stitches, a broken arm, and a head fracture. Still shaken and in excruciating pain after leaving the infirmary, Ron was immediately placed into protective custody. He would live, but Terrance wouldn't.

While the Whites dispensed prison justice to Ron, the Blacks handled their own kind without leniency. If Terrance would have humbled himself to his attackers, then his outcome would have been similar to Ron's, but he chose another path. He fought back ferociously in an attempt to uphold his pride and street credibility, which was his fatal mistake. As his executioners efficiently and repeatedly plunged their prison shanks into his neck and torso, the light from eyes faded, then extinguished.

Ironically, at the moment of his death, the lunch bell sounded at Traxtonite, and the breakroom filled with the chatter and chuckles of his former coworkers. It wasn't until the end of the workday that Madison heard the news of Terrance's death from Brittany. While the three walked to their cars, Brittany received a text from an acquaintance and stopped.

"What's wrong?" Madison asked.

"It's Terrance. No. They killed him in jail. He's dead."

Conor whipped around. "Dead? No way, it can't be. Are you sure?"

Brittany's eyes welled up, and she broke down in tears.

"Are you crying for him?" Madison challenged.

"No. I'm not crying for him," she sniffled. "It's more shock than anything else. I wanted him to be punished and get what he deserved, but the text says he was stabbed to death. Stabbed, Madison."

Madison turned to her. "That is shocking. I'd never imagined that happening to him. I'll talk to you later after you get home. I see that you're upset."

They hugged, and Conor started the car. Madison got inside, noticing Conor's reaction. He hung his head in disbelief, and they drove away.

"Not Terrance. My bro. Not this way," he lamented.

Madison snapped. "Screw Terrance! He can rot in hell! I only wish that they would have gotten Ron, too. Why waste the taxpayer's money on a trial?"

"I know, I understand. I'm only saying that the guy was once my friend. Getting stabbed to death in jail wasn't how I pictured him dying."

She gritted her teeth. "Yeah, well, I had a son once. His name was Elijah. Getting suffocated in a car wasn't how I pictured him dying either."

Her last words ended their conversation during the drive home and also for the night. Conor, regretting his insensitive comments, stayed out of her way for the rest of the evening. But Madison, stretched out across her bed with the door closed, repeatedly imagined Terrance's final bloody moments with pleasure. She even added in her own creative twists to the morbid scene, attempting to satisfy her hunger for vengeance. Her macabre fantasy was short-lived. With tears streaming down her face, she returned full circle to reality and faced the truth.

Terrance's death wouldn't bring Elijah back, and gloating over his death wasn't a remedy for her pain. Madison's pain was a mother's pain, shared by all women who suffer the loss of their child, and there was no reprieve. While Madison groaned for Elijah, Terrance's mother, Beatrice Roberts, walked into the prison morgue to claim the body of her only son, shedding the same tears of sorrow and repeating Madison's same question.

Why?

Likewise, both women received the same answer. Silence.

***

In his dark living room across town, Carson watched past video recordings of his former clients. His finances were in shambles, and most of his bills were overdue, leading him to escalate his alcohol consumption. Troubles were a convenient excuse to fuel his addiction, not that he required one. It was the easy way, the shortcut, and his preferred method to cope with any adverse situation. It absolved him of his responsibility for the bad decisions that he made leading up to this point. Self-pity was ingrained within his psyche, and accountability absent during these stressful moments. He couldn't afford to go out to a bar or a strip club and instead accepted home entertainment as his only source to exercise his perversions. He stopped and repeated the video, savoring Madison's first interview. It was his favorite. Especially the recorded part where he purposely dropped his ink pen on the floor when handing it to her. That moment aroused him as she bent over to pick it up.

I can still smell you, even through those tight jeans. Bend over a little more.

She owed him $740 for his work, but that wouldn't be past due for another ten days. And the gears in his depraved mind began to turn.

I can surprise her at home tomorrow—just a friendly visit to check on her and see how she's doing. Then I'll casually bring up the balance of her account. I might get lucky and get paid early. Yeah, that's it. That's what I'll do. Oh, yeah, oh yeah, ugh!

He groaned and panted as he climaxed. A moment later, he picked up the towel beside him and cleaned himself.

With glazed eyes he stared at the screen. "Thank you, Miss Sanders. Great job. I'll see you tomorrow, sweet cheeks." He winked and closed his laptop.

***

The following day, Madison woke up refreshed. The deep sleep seemed to balance her emotions and help her reset. She turned over and watched Conor sleep. It was hard to stay mad at him, especially for a dumb slip of his tongue. He hadn't lied about anything. He and Terrance were once best friends, a fact that couldn't be changed. His reaction was normal, she thought, but some things need not be said, and that was his undoing on the day before.

He needs to know that I've forgiven him. I was mean.

She reached under the covers and began playing with him until he woke.

"Babe. Morning," he croaked, still half asleep. But her hands were soft, gentle, and active. She touched his spot, and he stiffened. "Good morning!" he barked, accepting her affection and forgiveness. Within a few minutes, it was over, leaving him panting while she kissed his cheek.

"Good morning, Mr. Gregory. I've got chores to do. What are your plans?"

"I was thinking about going to the golf driving range with Luis around noon. Then maybe going to the gym after that. Is that's cool with you? I don't have to go anywhere if you..."

"It's not a problem at all. I want you to enjoy your day. And I apologize for yelling at you yesterday. We both were wrong."

He kissed her. "I'm sorry too."

Madison slid out of bed and strutted to the bathroom, wearing a grin. All was well now.

Today is going to be a great day.

She hoped. It was a daily battle to affirm her positive thoughts, and consistency was paramount, so she pressed forward and encouraged herself. Conor reached for his cell phone, planning to take full advantage of the day.

It doesn't get any better than this, he thought.

***

A few hours later, Madison ate lunch. She made a sandwich, grabbed a diet Sprite, and sat on the front porch steps. It was a bright Saturday, and the subdivision bustled with weekend activity. The lawnmowers and rambunctious children echoed throughout the neighborhood while subtle breezes dispersed freshly cut grass and floral aroma.

Across the street, a few houses down, Madison noticed that her neighbor, Cindy, was having a yard sale. She looked toward the subdivision entrance, wondering how she could have missed seeing the homemade sign posted the day before. She scarfed down her sandwich and hurried inside to wash her hands before coming back outside with her purse. She hoped that all the 'good stuff' hadn't been sold and walked over to the house and joined the small group perusing.

Cindy watched Madison crossing the road. The two were community acquaintances but not friends in the traditional sense. But the tragic event during the previous year disturbed most of the neighborhood mothers, like Cindy. The sad event had been discussed among many households, generating blather, and judgment, as uninformed adults chose sides. Some unfairly blamed Madison for being irresponsible, unfairly casting negative dispersions, and unfounded accusations.

Others opened their hearts with sympathy, understanding that everyone is fallible, and accidents are inevitable.

Despite the gossip, Madison's public vindication came through the hands of the media. The arrests of Ronald Tatum, and Terrance Roberts for causing the death of four-year-old Elijah Sanders, made the 6 o'clock news, and the subdivision chatter ground to a halt. Cindy was of the latter school of thought and beamed as Madison approached, walking around the display tables to greet her.

"Hello, Madison. Thanks for coming over."

"Hey, Cindy. I didn't know that you were having a sale today until I looked over. I would have been here earlier."

"That's alright; we haven't sold much. Let me know if you have any questions. Everything is on sale," she giggled.

"Okay." Madison smiled and began her search. There were a few quaint pieces, bicycles, and older electronic devices, but mostly women's clothes.

Cindy noticed her looking through the garments and giggled. "Unless you're buying something for someone else, don't even waste your time. I wear a size eight. Two of you could fit into one of my dresses."

Madison replaced a blouse on a hanger. "I'm a size four. It's a shame because you have great taste in clothes. Fudge! I wish, I wish," she lamented while rifling through the rack.

"I'm sorry. Even my shoe inventory isn't going to be of much help either. We have a lot of 'guy stuff,' as you can see. Maybe your husband could use something?"

"Now, that's an idea. His name is Conor, but he's not my husband, not yet. Our wedding was planned for this September, but I had to push it back until the Spring."

"Oh, no. That's a shame. That's a bride's nightmare. Is everything alright?"

"Sure, we're fine. We had an unexpected conflict of interest arise and thought it best to reschedule. You know us brides, everything has to be perfect," she smirked, "As if any wedding can ever be truly perfect."

"Well, I hope it all works out for you. I'll have to make sure that I buy you a wedding gift."

"Aw, you don't have to do that, but thank you." Madison scanned the tables one last time. "I'm sorry. I hate to leave empty-handed. I hope you sell out."

"That's fine. It was nice talking to you. I'm glad you came over. You're welcome to come by anytime. I'd love to chat with you."

"I'll do that. Good luck," Madison smiled and walked away.

"Wait! I almost forgot. Are you interested in buying a MacBook? My husband gave me a new one for Christmas, and I don't need both. It's in great condition. It has a few years on it, but it works great."

"Where? I don't see it."

"It's inside. I'll get it. I was going to create a listing online, but I dreaded getting calls from strangers. Do you want to see?"

"Sure. I've been using Windows forever, but I always wanted a Mac. People seem to rave about them. Conor has one. We could become a matching Mac couple," she smirked.

"Awesome! One sec, I'll be right back."

Cindy skirted through the garage and into the house, returning with the MacBook. She set it on the table and pressed the power button. Then initiated her rookie sale's pitch.

"This baby has been my daily workstation since I bought it. He's, I mean, she's seven years old and has never let me down. I've never been hacked, and it's never frozen on me. All my files and history have been deleted, but I left most of the software installed. If you want it erased, you'll have to do it yourself. Don't take it to the Geek Squad. It's easy. Anyway, I've had no problems whatsoever."

Cindy logged in as a guest, connected to her home Wi-Fi, and navigated the features and software. Madison took control and explored the machine.

She was impressed with its performance and capabilities. It was a considerable upgrade from her current laptop.

"I want it. How much are you asking?"

Cindy sighed. "I checked online for current prices and saw that this same year, and model, listed from $550 to $900."

"Ouch."

"I know, but hold on. Those prices are marked up because of a middleman. Right? I'm not looking to make a fortune, and you're a good neighbor. How does $425 sound?"

"Really? Yes, thank you!"

"Wonderful. I'll get the charger and the carry case that it came with."

She went inside and brought out the accessories.

"Cindy, I'll have to run to the ATM. I don't use checks."

"Don't worry about that. You can pay me later. Take it home and enjoy."

"Thanks, but no, that's not right. You deserve to be paid right now. I'll be back within an hour."

Madison walked to her house, grabbed her car keys, and left.

***

Ten minutes after Madison left, Don Carson pulled into her driveway.

Shit, no cars. Where the hell could she be? I'm wasting gas. Screw it, hang out and wait for a bit.

He walked to the front door and rang the bell a few times while peeping through the window. He checked the time, and scoped the surroundings, then sat on the top step. Madison's front porch was the highest point among the adjoining properties and overlooked the surrounding area, giving him an unobstructed view of the subdivision entrance. He wanted to see her coming.

Goddamn, girl, hurry up.

He was aggravated. His low cash flow forced him to ration his alcohol intake. He was running on fumes. He lit a cigarette and loosened his tie. He should have been wearing shorts in the warm weather, but he took issue with that. Shorts violated his warped code of appearance standards. He believed that wearing a tie distinguishes a man rather than without one. It set him apart. His validating mantra explained all.

I might be broke, but I don't have to look like it.

He observed Cindy's yard sale and Cindy in particular.

Now there's a thick one. Oh, yeah. I think she's checking me out.

Cindy was aware of Carson's presence. She attempted to be inconspicuous while making a mental note of his every movement and reporting it to Madison. But the veteran detective was a formidable target to spy, and when he caught her peeping, he waved at her and smiled.

"Good afternoon!" he called out from the step. "How is business going?"

Cindy looked away, ignoring him. She strutted into the house and told her husband that the sale was over. "Take everything down. I'm done for the day."

After using the bathroom, she went upstairs to the second floor and peeked through the front blinds.

Who is he? A bill collector?

Carson snuffed his cigarette on the step and plucked the butt into the shrubbery.

That wasn't very friendly, lady.

Carson checked the time and decided to wait five more minutes. He began to daydream, gazing into the distance, and noticed the window blinds moving at Cindy's house.

You have to be kidding me. She must want me. But why so cold? Oh, I get it. Her jealous hubby must be home. Just walk over and look at what she's selling. Then the chubby bird will come down from her perch. Easy work.

He walked down the steps while adjusting his necktie but stopped short when Cindy's husband began clearing the tables.

Abort, abort. Damn it.

He looked at his watch and decided to leave. He slowly walked down the steps, hoping to catch one last glimpse of the woman behind the blinds. Then, it caught his attention, and he stopped. To the right of the house, in the backyard, was a large storage shed. Attached to the shed's gable, just under the ridge, sat a small, mounted video camera.

Carson vaguely remembered the shed from his canvassing of the neighborhood, but he did remember the house and Olson's entry in the official report. The owners had confirmed the absence of video footage from their home.

How the hell did they miss that? No, how the hell did I miss it?

He maintained focus on the camera in the distance while slowly walking down the steps. Then it was gone, behind the foliage of the trees. He stopped and stepped backward until it reappeared into view. He continued to his car, never breaking his gaze.

Well, I'll be damned.

He walked to the bottom of the driveway and squinted into the sun. There was a clear line of sight through a myriad of tree leaves. He searched for an answer.

Why didn't they see it?

He lit a cigarette and picked at his nose.

If I can see it now, with the trees in bloom, why couldn't they see it without any leaves?

He smacked his forehead.

Dumbass, it was the snow. It snowed that week and the night before. Snow built upon the branches and the camera was hard to see. Out of sight and out of everyone's mind to look in the backyard.

He got into his car, debating whether to secure any video footage. His agreement with Madison had officially concluded. Although his investigative work had led to arrests, there was no reason for her to incur any more fees from his services. Carson believed that the State's case against Tatum and Roberts was strong, but anything could happen at trial. There was no way that he could know the outcome, just as he didn't realize that Terrance had been killed a day before.

Hold onto this nugget. Who knows? It might become useful in the future. Keep close tabs in the department. If the prosecution runs into evidentiary issues during the trial, this video footage may be worth more than a few dollars. Besides, she already owes me, and I'm not working for free.

He backed down the driveway and left.

Five minutes later, Madison pulled into her driveway and parked. Cindy sat on a stool inside her garage with her new computer, diligently supervising her husband's labor. Madison met her on the sidewalk and handed her the money.

"That's $425, and thanks again. I'm so excited! I'll be playing with it all night."

Cindy handed over the carry case.

"You saved me a lot of time and effort. By the way, while you were gone, a man pulled into your driveway. He was at your front door for a least ten minutes."

"What did he look like? What was he driving?"

"He was tall, maybe six feet? He had dark hair and looked to be an older man, possibly in his sixties? He drove an older model car. I think it was a Lincoln. Also, he had a short-sleeve shirt and wore a necktie. Now, why would anyone want to wear a tie on a warm day like this? I know what you're probably thinking, but he didn't look like a Mormon or Jehovah's Witness type of person. That's just my opinion."

Madison realized that it was Don Carson. He fit the description.

"It sounds like the private investigator that we hired to investigate my son's death."

Cindy's expression changed from suspicion to concern.

"Oh. I had no idea. I apologize. I wasn't trying to disparage the man."

Madison shook her head. "No, Cindy, you're fine. There's no need to apologize. I'm sure you've heard on the news that the police caught the men responsible. Mr. Carson was the sole reason for that."

Cindy rubbed her chin. "I did hear about that, but I didn't want to ask you about it. We were so glad to hear that those monsters got caught. We pray that they'll get what they deserve."

Madison smiled and hugged her. "I'll talk to you later, Cindy. Take care."

Madison walked across the street and went inside, sat the laptop on the couch, and called Don Carson. He answered on the first ring.

"Hello, Madison. How are you doing today?"

"Hi, Mr. Carson. I'm fine. I was calling to ask, did you come by my house today?"

"Yes, I sure did. I was in the neighborhood and giving you a courtesy visit to see how things are going. I should have called. I'm sorry about that."

"No, don't be sorry. You just missed me. I stepped out to go to the ATM, but I'm home now."

"Aw, shucks. Well, since we're talking, is there anything that you need from me? I'm here to serve you."

"No, sir. We're good to go. But I want to thank you again for what you did. I feel like I can't pay you enough. I can bake you something, though, if you'd like. What's your favorite dessert?"

Dessert? Didn't expect that. She's fond of me, after all. That's a good starting point.

"Hmm, let me think. I do love banana pudding. Yep. Do you think you can handle that?"

"I can."

"Great. Let me give you a tip, okay?"

"Please do. I'll prepare it exactly how you want. I want you completely satisfied."

You bet your ass you will, 'sweet cheeks.'

Carson pulled over to the side of the road and parked. "The secret is in the size of the main ingredient, the banana. When you go to the store, pick out the longest, thickest bananas that you can find. Then squeeze them, and make sure they are firm. You don't want any mushy ones."

"Uh, okay. I got it. It may be a couple of weeks before I can get it to you."

"You take your sweet time, darling. I'm not in any rush."

"Okay, good. Well, I hope you have a super day!"

"You too, sweetie, bye."

He sipped from his flask.

There's a spark of magic there, somewhere. Too bad that she's getting married. But then again, they could be swingers. The game is not over yet.

***

Conor sat in his truck parked outside the gym. He propped back and zipped up his shorts while Kathy looked in the vanity mirror and wiped her mouth. She leaned to kiss his cheek, but he drew back.

"No, don't do that. You might get something on me," he said and started the car.

She jerked back. "That's why I left you the first time. You're an asshole."

He smirked. "And you married a gentleman instead. I get it. Just get out. I have to get home."

"With pleasure, you son of a bitch. This is over! Don't ever contact me again."

She bolted out and slammed the door. He shrugged and saluted her before driving away.

It was 8:32 p.m. when he walked into the house. He knew that Madison was waiting for him - and wanting him too! He planned to oblige her. He found her sitting up in bed with a new laptop.

"Hey, babe. I missed you. What are you into?" he asked while stripping off his clothes.

Madison broke her gaze from the screen. "Hi, sweetheart." She smiled. "I missed you, too. I'm glad you're back. Look at my new Mac! Well, it's not new, but it's new to me. I bought it from Cindy from across the street. I love it!"

"Oh, yeah? How much did you pay?"

"$425. That's a sweet deal."

He frowned. "That's a good price, but..."

"But, what?"

"Remember, Don's bill is due this month."

"I know. I thought you were going to pay half of it."

"That's not the point. I don't want to get into an argument tonight; I'm in a good mood. But, after we get married, you're going to have to cut down on your spending. You're a compulsive shopper. For instance, you already have a laptop. Did you need a MacBook?" He stood naked, with his hands on his hips.

She closed the lid. "Why are you so grumpy? I wanted a MacBook, and I bought one. At least it's used and not new. Besides, what's it to you?"

He rubbed his chest. "You're right. I'm frustrated. Sorry. I played soccer and went to the gym, but I'm still horny as hell." He walked around to her side of the bed.

Her forehead wrinkled. "And what do you expect me to do about it?"

"Oral," he mumbled.

Her head dropped. "Please, I don't feel like doing anything tonight. Okay?"

"No, it's not okay. You said that you would never refuse me. What's this?"

"Okay, after you get out of the shower." She opened the laptop.

"No, right now."

He moved the laptop to the side and pulled her off the bed.

"Please, just take a shower," she pleaded.

"Shush." He coerced her to her knees.

Five minutes later, he was finished and stepped into the shower while Madison brushed her teeth. She climbed into bed and opened up her MacBook. She'd already copied her data over and was deleting the last of Cindy's files.

Conor crawled into bed and kissed her. "Goodnight. I love you."

"I love you, too."

He rolled over and went to sleep.

It was 11:37 p.m., and Madison could barely keep her eyes open. She was addicted to her new toy and unable to shut the lid. She stretched her arms out wide and yawned.

She rubbed her eyes and took a deep breath to receive a moment of clarity. She pushed at Conor, breaking his snore. Madison never worried about waking him. He slept like a rock. She looked through her folders and saw that all was in order, but one.

Crap, how could I have missed that? Solex Vid backdoor 01.

She selected the folder for trash but paused.

"Solex Vid backdoor 01," she mumbled.

Don't be nosey. It's none of your business. Respect the privacy of others.

"It's the last file left. Indulge yourself. Be a bad girl," she whispered.

She opened the folder to find hundreds of folders inside, all dated chronologically.

Out of curiosity, she opened a random folder, which revealed video clips, and picked one. As the video played, it became apparent that it was camera footage of Cathy's back door. Half her house was in view, and across the street, Madison saw her own home.

That's neat.

Madison chuckled as she watched the motion-detected clips of daily life in Cindy's backyard. Squirrels played, competing with birds at a hanging feeder, and kids raced by on their bicycles. The highlight was Cindy sneaking out her back door and smoking a cigarette. Madison giggled.

A closet smoker. Who would've guessed?

But as a group of children walked by, Madison's mood changed. Tears welled in her eyes. This time, she allowed it. She was on guard for any emotional triggers, pursed her lips, searched for a file dated when Elijah was alive. She closed her eyes, imagining what she might feel if she viewed the footage. She had stopped herself from obsessively watching phone videos of him in an attempt to retain her sanity. Seeing new videos of him could send her over the edge, forcing her to another part of the house in seclusion to bawl.

No. You can't do it. Not tonight. Don't look.

She wiped her eyes, sniffling. Then she stopped breathing. Anger raged against sorrow as she thought about her loss and the cause of it. She frantically searched the folders by date, finally locating the video file from the day of Elijah's death. She began to realize the detectives must be unaware of the camera footage because neither they nor the prosecutors made any mention of it. She had to watch. She wanted to see Ron exposed with her own eyes and promised herself to end it before Elijah appeared.

You can do this, Maddy. Then contact the detectives in the morning.

She started the video at the 12:01 a.m. timestamp.

There was no traffic for hours as the video timeline advanced, intermittently activating as the trees would gradually sway. But at 5:44 a.m., light illuminated the snowy road as what appeared to be a pickup truck came into view, performed a U-turn, and parked at the curb near her front yard. The video at that distance was dark. Her house and its surroundings appeared small. Her heart thumped as she watched the hooded figure exit, creep up her driveway, and kneel behind her car. She looked closer but was unable to decipher if it was Ron or Terrance.

It doesn't matter. Even the getaway driver is an accomplice. You're both murderers!

Tears rolled down her cheeks. With their back to the camera, the culprit kneeled, meddled with the snow behind her car and then brushed the nearby area.

I could kill you!

She bit her lip and replayed the clip but zoomed in and expanded the video. She wanted to see his face. She watched him walk up the driveway, noticing something familiar about his clothing. It was his hooded jacket that struck her curiosity. As the man feverishly pushed snow into the tailpipe, Madison was fixated on his coat.

What is it about that damn jacket? Camouflage, Green Bay Packers...

The figure turned around, and Madison paused the frame. She looked closely.

It was Conor. His image was unmistakable. She went catatonic, unable to move, unable the think. Her instinct was to look at him.

Why look? He's not real. I'm not real. None of this is real.

Those were her last memories before her vision faded, the base of her neck tightened, and she went unconscious. Her body stiffened involuntarily as her back arched and teeth clamped shut. She convulsed in total seizure, her legs partially covering Conor's, who remained asleep, unaffected. The episode lasted five minutes, and when she revived, her vision slowly returned, and nausea followed.

Her laptop was on its side between her and Conor. She grabbed it and slid out of bed. Her footing was unstable, and she groggily stumbled toward the bathroom, dropping the laptop on the couch as she passed. She staggered into the dark bathroom and dropped to her knees in front of the commode. She vomited until nothing remained and dry heaved until her ribs and stomach ached. While on the floor, she flushed the toilet, grabbed a hand towel next to the sink, and bit down, muffling her cries of anguish. She kicked the door closed.

Why Conor? Why?

She couldn't comprehend, eventually gathered enough strength to stand.

Where's my laptop?

She eased out of the bathroom, vaguely remembering tossing it on the couch. She stopped to listen. Conor was snoring, so she sat down and opened the lid. The paused video of his face filled the screen.

Immediately becoming nauseated again, she frantically tried to close the video, but her shaky hands were uncoordinated, and the image moved around the screen. She tossed the laptop to the side and rushed to the toilet. She shut the door and dropped to her knees, violently dry heaving. The pain was excruciating. She calmed herself and controlled the impulses until the urges eventually reduced into sporadic gagging.

Conor knocked. "Madison. Are you alright? What's wrong."

She froze, not knowing what to say. The sound of his voice made her queasy, and she caused her heaving to return. He heard eased the door open.

"Don't! Get out..." she squeaked and gagged.

He backed out and shut the door. "Holy shit, you're sick. It couldn't have been from swallowing. You always swallow. Maybe it was something else that you ate. Do you want me to bring you some water? Or a ginger ale?"

She wiped the spit from her chin. "No. Just go."

"Alright. But you should sleep on the couch tonight if you have a stomach bug. I don't want you to give it to me."

"Uh, huh," she groaned, her stomach cramping.

He walked back to the bedroom and noticed her open laptop sitting on the couch. He walked over to it and shut the lid as he passed by.

She ruined a perfect dream, waking me up with all that noise. Yeah, she's sick alright, but not too ill to be on the damn computer.

He went into the bedroom and closed the door.

A few minutes later, Madison wandered out of the bathroom. She took a knife from the kitchen drawer, grabbed a blanket from the closet, and walked over to the couch. She noticed the laptop lid closed and brought it into Elijah's room, laid down, and covered herself. The house was quiet, except for Conor beginning to snore.

He must not have looked before closing it. It doesn't matter anyway.

She was exhausted physically and emotionally drained, but her mind was in an uproar.

I could go to the police. Or I could plunge this knife into his heart right now and kill him while he sleeps. That would be justice. What other penalty is there? You killed my child. You deceived me. Lied to me. You made me fall in love with you. Ron is innocent, and Terrance was, also. I could put a stop to the trial right now. I could end it all. I could do that. I could.

She started to sob, but her tears were cut short.

Fuck them! None are innocent! They are all guilty, guilty, guilty.

Part of her conscience protested, appealing to her rational mind, and warned her that the vengeful thoughts of rage were blinding her to the absolute truth. She struggled, but her logical mind was overcome. It would not rule the day. She relinquished control to her other half and free-fell into that unknown place, the place that she somehow knew existed deep inside her core. She pulled at her hair.

Calm down. Think.

She contemplated her future, choosing alternate paths of action to achieve her desired result. There was a flash, and a recollection resurfaced in the form of a childhood memory. Oddly, she smiled and remembered Elizabeth's method for euthanizing the family pets. Her mother's macabre words were as clear as the day when they were first spoken.

"Too little will make a dog sleep for days, and too much will stop an elephant's heart. One teaspoon is all that is needed to kill a 100-pound animal."

Madison's new question was a simple one.

How much does it take to kill a man?

CHAPTER 13

The following day, Madison hid away in Elijah's room, venturing out only to use the restroom and bring back food from the kitchen to eat. She feigned a stomach virus to validate her isolation, and a depressive state of mind, hoping that the combination of both would excuse her lack of interaction with Conor. The surrealness of the situation was suffocating, but her hatred for him was revitalizing, giving her the clarity to focus on what she had committed to do. There were no protests of conscience this time or any reason to dissuade her from the resolution. She didn't care about the resulting ramifications as long as her goal was achieved. Madison was fully determined and set her plan into motion.

Conor wasn't eager to cater to her. Instead, he used the opportunity to conduct his personal affairs around town. He left the house at noon, and that's when Madison got busy. She searched the internet for the products she needed, hoping to find them. Within the hour, she located two chemical suppliers in Canada which carried both items required, specifically, Hydroxy-Methaburate and Tricozomine, and selected the smallest quantity available of each, 250mL. Both chemicals were inexpensive, and the total was less than seventy-five dollars. But there was a problem. Madison didn't want them shipped to her house, fearing that Conor might become inquisitive. She picked up the phone and dialed Brittany.

"Hey Britt, I need a favor."

"Hey girl, sure, what's up?"

"I'm ordering a present for Conor, but I can't ship it to my house. Mr. Nosey will sniff it out and ruin my surprise. Is it alright if I ship it to your address?"

"Sure, that's no problem. How's your Sunday going?"

Madison despised misleading her best friend and would never put her in danger, but felt it necessary under the current conditions to bend the truth. Madison needed her to execute the plan, but the less Brittany knew, the better off she would be.

Madison groaned. "Thanks, sis'. I appreciate you. My Sunday sucks. I've come down with a stomach virus and have been up all night with it, coming out of both ends."

"Ugh! I hate it for you. I hope that you feel better soon."

"Me too. I'm sure that I'll have to take tomorrow off from work. I can't keep anything down, and I'm feeling dehydrated."

"Oh no, please don't bring that mess to work. Rest, and don't exert yourself."

"I'll take your advice, and on that note, my stomach is cramping right now."

"Okay, hurry up, or you'll be cleaning up! Bye."

"Bye."

Madison continued with her order details, optioning for the fastest shipping offered, 2nd-day air.

Done.

Completing the order satisfied and empowered her, cracking open a small window of hope and allowing a sense of freedom within the confines of Elijah's room. She hadn't a clue how or when she would carry out the act but knew it was inevitable.

The sooner, the better. One step at a time, Maddy. You can do this. You have to.

***

For the next two days, Madison called in sick to work and played the waiting game, practicing evasion and avoidance from her enemy. For Conor, the absence of affection and intimacy for two days only compounded his frustration. By Tuesday night, he was at his wit's end and reached out to Kathy, requesting an intimate rendezvous, but she refused to respond to his calls or texts. The aggravation of talking to Madison behind a locked door for days, and the inability to release his sexual frustration with her, had become too much. He felt that the time had arrived to re-evaluate their relationship.

Give her an ultimatum and be done with it all.

He schemed a manipulative plan to attack her verbally but decided to give her another day to see a change. But Madison stood resolute. She didn't waver or falter from her routine, and she didn't argue with him, no matter how hard he tried to provoke her. She maintained physical distance and emotional composure. On Tuesday afternoon, she received a text from Brittany.

I have your package. What do you want me to do with it?

I'm feeling a little better today. I can come to work at noon tomorrow and wait for you in the parking lot. I'll drive my car, so put it in your trunk, and I'll get it from you during lunch. I'll text you when I get there.

I gotcha. I'm glad to get a chance to see you. I missed you, girlfriend.

I feel the same way, Britt. I'll see you tomorrow.

***

The next morning, as Conor was about to leave for work, he knocked on Elijah's bedroom door. "Hey babe, I'm about to leave. How are you feeling this morning?"

"About the same. A little better. I'm not cramping as much."

"I can wait for you if you're going."

"No, you go on. Don't be late on my account."

"Okay, cool. I'll see you later."

He left the house and drove off. Madison peered through the blinds watching him go. Then she went into the kitchen, retrieving a small glass bottle of vanilla extract and a bottle of water. She emptied them down the sink. After rinsing out the vanilla jar, she grabbed a measuring cup, a tablespoon, an empty water bottle, brought them back to the room, and hid them under the pillow. She sat on the bed, waiting, and reaffirming her next steps.

Get the package, use the water bottle as a beaker to mix the chemicals, and use the small extract jar as the delivery device. It's tiny enough to hide. Then trash the box along with the original containers. Only the water bottle and the jar will remain, each filled with the recipe. Everything left is easily hidden and disposable.

Systematically, she rehearsed the motions, shunning the apparent gravity of her lethal intentions. She didn't know precisely when the appointed time would be and wasn't sure of the dosage needed to achieve death. That worried her. She planned to spike one of his drinks and hope that he didn't notice any taste.

Shit. What if he can taste it? What if he already figured out that I've known it was HIM all this time? He'd probably kill me. Or would he? It doesn't matter. Nothing else matters. You're ready to die, so stay calm.

***

Before noon, Madison sat in her car, texting Brittany that she was waiting in the parking lot. Five minutes later, Brittany walked out the front entrance and to the rear of her car, opening the trunk. Madison walked around to meet her, and as Brittany leaned in to hug her, Madison drew back.

Madison frowned. "No, Britt, I don't want to get you sick. I could be contagious." Ignoring her, Brittany turned her head and opened her arms.

"You better hug me and stop acting crazy."

They embraced, rocking back and forth. They missed each other for different reasons, but each with sincerity.

Brittany eventually released her. "You take it out, and I'll keep a watch out for Conor," she laughed.

"Ha, ha, thanks." Madison picked up the small box, wedging it under her arm. "Thank you, sis."

"You're welcome. It's nothing. What did you buy him?"

"A cologne that he mentioned. It's nothing special."

"There's nothing wrong with helping your man smell good. I'll call you later. Are you coming to work tomorrow?"

"I'm coming. I feel much better."

The two hugged again and went their separate ways.

The lunch bell rang, commencing the migration to the breakroom. Conor was walking with Luis and passed Madison's empty cubicle.

Luis noticed. "Madison's been out sick for a while. How is she?"

"Not too good. She's sick, and I think 'on the rag.' Double trouble."

Luis glanced past her desk and through the front window. "Hey man, isn't that her car." Luis stopped and pointed. "There's Brittany, too, walking inside."

Conor saw Madison drive away and became irate.

You bitch! What the hell are you doing here? You said you were still sick.

"Yeah, that's her." He looked at his watch. "Man, I'm going to catch up with her. I want to make sure that everything is alright. I'll be back soon."

"Okay, man. I'll see you later."

Conor marched down the hall and burst out of the front entrance towards his truck, neglecting to inform his superior. He didn't care.

Enough of this bullshit! She's going to get her act together, or I'm fucking out of here!

He started his truck and barreled out of the parking lot.

***

Madison got home and hurried inside, going to the bathroom first, and then to Elijah's room. She closed the door, locking it behind her, and sat on the bed. She tossed the pillow aside and unpacked the box's contents, pulling out two small glass jars. The labels were small but legible. She held them up, looking closely. The sunlight through the window reflected against the brown glass bottles, and old memories returned. She remembered the painful tears and grief from the loss of her beloved pets, never imagining that she would use the same method to kill HIM.

She sat on the floor with her legs crossed and set each item on the floor. After removing the plastic seals, she carefully poured both jars into the empty water bottle and stuffed the trash into the open box. She was nervous, and her hands trembled while handling the deadly concoction. She capped the water bottle and shook it vigorously for fifteen seconds. After stopping and watching the bubbles rise to the surface, she shook it again and looked. Madison was dazed but not confused by the process and transferred the poison from the water bottle to the smaller vanilla extract jar.

Slow and easy. Breath, Maddy.

Bam! Bam! Bam!

Conor pounded on the door. "Hey! We need to talk right now!"

The surprise took her breath, and she flinched, almost spilling the liquid. She was at a loss for words. Speechless. But she focused and continued the transfer.

"I saw you at work just now. It's fucking embarrassing! Everybody saw you. What the hell, Madison, what were you doing there? Huh? I thought that you were supposed to be sick."

She ignored him. The jar was filling.

Just a bit more.

"I know that you're awake, so talk! Fuck it. I'm coming in."

She stopped and looked at the door.

It's locked. He won't break it down.

She continued with the task but then remembered.

The key above the door!

A slot key sat on the molding above each door for anyone that locked themself out of a room, courtesy of the property owner. She heard the doorknob rattling.

No. Hurry! Hurry! Hurry!

She shuddered. Her shaky hands became uncontrollable. "Don't come in! I can hear you! I can explain!"

The knob turned, and the door flung open.

Conor bolted inside. "What the hell are you doing?"

Madison lay on the floor with her hands behind her head, having kicked everything underneath the bed seconds before.

She looked at him and sat up. "Let me explain."

"Yeah, you do that. Start talking."

He slammed the door. His paper-thin pride was injured, and he was intent on coming getting answers.

Madison put on a pitiful expression. "I thought that I could go to work. I felt better. But on the way there, I got sick again. I only stayed there for a second, and Brittany came out to check on me. Then I left."

Conor was huffing, and his nostrils flared. The answer was acceptable to him. But more essential issues remained, and his grievances boiled over.

"Okay, whatever. I'm going to be straight with you. I'm not feeling any love around you. You won't talk to me, fuck me, hell; you won't look at me. What the hell? I'm tired of the shit. So, let's not waste anymore of each other's time. If you don't want to be with me, then just say so. If you do, then you need to get your shit together, pronto."

Madison stared blankly.

What am I supposed to say, you bastard? Motherfucker, I'm going to kill you!

She covered her face with both hands.

He pressed his attack. "You better not start crying again! I'm tired of that shit!"

He raged, hoping to humiliate and intimidate her, but she understood his tactics.

She adapted. "You changed, Conor! You don't treat me that same. You treat me like shit!"

He appeared to be shocked, bewildered. "Huh? Don't even try that. What do you mean?"

Madison stood, glaring. "When is the last time that you took me somewhere? Well? Answer me, big mouth! All you want to do is play with your friends, get drunk, and come back here and screw me. Conor, I can get any man to do that."

Caught off guard, he looked away in thought.

"Where do you want me to take you? All you had to do was say something."

"I shouldn't have to say anything! If you loved me, then you would know."

"I'm not a goddamn mind reader. Where do you want to go? Tell me." He folded his arms.

"I don't know, anywhere. I've been sick, but I feel fine now. Take me out on the lake again. I don't know."

"The lake? Cool. We'll go this weekend." He stepped closer, sensing reconciliation and temporary closure.

"No. Let's go now," she snapped and stepped closer.

"Now?"

She turned her back to him. "Forget it."

He grabbed her shoulders. She shuddered, despising his touch, but tolerated the outrage.

"Okay. You got it. Get your shit ready, and I'll call the marina."

He kissed her neck as his hands moved to her waist.

She shook her head. "Just like I said. All that you want to do is screw me. I'm just a piece of ass to you."

She shrugged him off and walked to the window.

He raised his palms. "I'm trying to make up with you, shit. Get your stuff together. We're leaving soon."

"I want to drink today. Bring alcohol."

He jerked around, surprised. "Hell yeah, babe. You got it." He walked out, and his voice trailed behind. "Understand that we're screwing on the boat, so don't be surprised when I bend you over the pilot's seat. Get your bathing suit on!"

She closed the door, locked it, then dropped to the floor and reached underneath the bed. She rose to her feet, holding the small jar in her hand.

I won't be surprised. But you will be.

***

At 5:30 p.m., Conor launched from the slip. He chose the same 26 ft Bowrider they previously rented, already familiar with the boat characteristics and handling. Madison sat in the aft, near the outboard motor, as Conor sped off, disregarding the marina rules and the no-wake zone buoys.

She spread her arms wide across the seat, tilting her head back, and absorbed the sunshine. She wasn't wearing a bathing suit. Instead, she chose to stay wearing her shorts and t-shirt. Her short hair flickered in the wind as the boat accelerated with Conor at the helm, chugging a beer. He turned around.

"Hand me another," he shouted over the engine's roar. She reached into the cooler and offered it to him.

He looked away. "Open it."

She used her shirt, twisted the top off, and handed it over.

I hope you enjoy it, you thankless sonofabitch.

He glanced at her and grinned. "I saw a spot last time we were here where we could have some privacy."

She began to plot and organize her garbled thoughts, remembering the purpose, the goal, and the vendetta to be accomplished. Everything seemed to be falling into place naturally, or so she hoped.

Twenty minutes later, Conor slowed down as they entered a secluded cove and turned off the engine, letting the boat drift into the middle. He grabbed his beer and stood in front of Madison, surveying the area.

"I told you. Total privacy," he mumbled and sat beside her. "Hand me another one, babe," he burped. She opened the cooler and handed him a beer. "You're not gonna open it for me? Aw, man."

Disgusted, she twisted the top and handed it to him. "Open it yourself, next time."

His forehead wrinkled. "What's with the attitude?"

She closed her eyes and rested her head on the seat. "Can we just enjoy the silence for a little while?"

He guzzled the entire beer and dropped the bottle. "Grab me another one."

"No. Get it yourself," she murmured.

"Really? Is that how you want to play?" He snatched a beer, opened it, and chugged. He staggered to the pilot's seat, turned on the radio, and searched for a rock station but stopped when hearing the rock band Metallica and turned up the volume.

"Unforgiven. That's your song."

She ignored him. It was infuriating, but he held back his retaliation. He was horny and would be damned if the outing ended without his sexual satisfaction while she patiently waited and hoped, praying for the right time. He sat in the pilot's seat, and belched, then patted his leg.

"Madison, babe, I'm sorry for being an asshole. Let's make a truce."

She raised her head and stared. She stood, steadying herself with the motion of the boat, and walked to him. He grabbed her waist and tried to kiss her, but she turned her head, frowning.

"You have beer breath. It stinks. I don't want to kiss you."

"Fine."

He caressed her and squeezed her breasts. His once sensual touch was now revolting, but she endured the torment.

Hurry up! God, how much longer?

He groped her butt and spun her around, pulling her against him.

"Do you want it?" he whispered. "I want you to beg for it."

She felt trapped, desperate, helpless.

No, this can't happen!

He stopped and pushed her aside. "I have to piss," he slurred and staggered to the aft.

Yes! Thank you!

He stood on atop the backseat, urinating, while she quickly pulled the small jar from her front pocket and emptied it into his beer bottle.

"I know what you're thinking. You think that I'm going to rent a boat every time that we fight. You're wrong. I won't. I mean that shit." He zipped up his shorts and sat down in the pilot's seat. "Now, let's get this party started." He grabbed her and reached inside the front of her shorts.

She tried to push away from him. "Stop!" But he was too strong. He held her firmly and turned her around, grabbed her hair, and bent her over the chair. "No! Let go!" she yelled.

But he wouldn't and held her still with one hand, and he began pulling down her shorts. She reached back, clawing at his arm, and wiggled away. He went for her, and after a brief struggle, she rushed to the aft and sat.

He snarled while she sat with her arms crossed and snapped. "Fuck you! The wedding is off! I'm done!"

He guzzled his beer. She watched his tantrum unfold while remaining expressionless. Her incessant foot-tapping advertised her angst, but she was powerless to prevent it.

"That's fine," she murmured, never breaking eye contact.

"Oh, it is?" he laughed. "I should've never gotten involved with your crazy ass. That was my big mistake. Just know that there are plenty of women who want me. They want this." He grabbed his crotch. "And I'm gonna give them every inch."

Madison waited patiently, longing for the moment.

"You're quiet as a mouse now. Why aren't you running your mouth? You spoiled bitch."

Just then, his left leg buckled, but he recovered. Instinctively, he grabbed the back of the chair. He swallowed the rest of the beer, emptying his bottle, and threw it overboard.

He scowled at her and held up his middle finger. "I'm taking your ass back to the house, packing my shit, and hauling ass. Baby, you just messed up the best thing that ever happened to you."

He turned to sit down, reaching for the keys but was confused when he couldn't grab them. A warm rush circulated through his body, and he became nauseous.

What the hell? I only drank three beers, and I'm drunk as shit already.

He rested his head on the steering wheel. Madison observed the effects, her heart pounding. She leaned forward, enthusiastically witnessing his deterioration. As the endorphins rushed through her bloodstream, a smile cracked her dormant lips.

"I think I'm gonna puke," he moaned, trying to stand up. Madison stood up as well and went over to him.

"Don't throw up on the boat, idiot. Throw up in the water."

He stumbled past the pilot's chair to the starboard side and leaned over the side, gagging. He spat into the water.

She followed behind and put her hand on his back. "You're fine. Just throw up. You'll feel better."

He nodded and began to heave, but he couldn't vomit. Suddenly, his knees gave way, and he dropped to the deck, still holding onto the side. Madison helped him to his feet.

"Lean over the side, hurry!" she barked.

He stood, teetering on the railing, and then went motionless. She used both hands to support him and looked around the cove.

Yes. Complete privacy.

This was the moment that she had been dreaming of and her opportunity of chance. She wrapped her arms around his right leg and swung it over. He was now straddling the side, his body limp. She thought that he had already died and put her ear to his back, listening for the breath of life; there was nothing. She repositioned herself and grabbed his left leg to heave him over the rest of the way.

"No," he mumbled. "What – what are you doing?"

She flinched in surprise.

"Help. Help me," he slurred, clutching the side with his left hand.

She strained, lifting with all her might. "That's what Elijah tried to say while he choked on exhaust fumes. I know you did it. I saw you on video. You lied to me! You said you loved me. How does it feel to be helpless?"

"Sorry," he panted. "mistake...wait...please...plea - ." His speech failed him, slurring into incoherency, leaving only his feeble whimpers.

The pitiful cries only escalated her fury. "Just die and go to hell! That's all I want."

She threw his left leg over, and he splashed into the water. She leaned over to watch him thrash about, basking in the bliss of his pathetic struggling. The thrill was short-lived, as the paralytic effects took hold and ended her satisfaction.

"Hel..." he gurgled, choking as the water filled his lungs. Within seconds, he slipped beneath the surface and troubled the water no more. She fixated on the last mental image of his suffering while gazing at the water, yearning to relive it again and again in real-time. Gradually, she came back to reality, breaking free from wrath and the thrill of revenge.

She dropped to her knees, weeping, emotionally releasing the grief and anguish that fueled her constant despair.

"I got him, Elijah! He can't hurt you again!" she shouted.

I'm still sorry. Mommy is so sad for not protecting you. Forgive me, Elijah!

She wiped her eyes with her shirt and looked at the sky. Then reality dawned.

What am I going to do now? Oh my God. Oh my God.

She had no plan, or idea, of what to do afterward.

Think Maddy, think! You're not going to prison over, HIM!

She stood up and paced the boat, looking around the cove. The wind increased, raising the lake swells, causing the vessel to drift toward open water. Her heart pounded with anxiety as she rehearsed her upcoming performance to the 911 operator.

"Please, help me! I'm on a boat at South Lake. My boyfriend jumped into the water, but he never came back up! Please, send help! The boat is drifting, and I don't know what to do. Hurry!"

***

Within fifteen minutes, the Minnesota Department of Natural Resources and the Boat and Water Recreation Patrol Division were combing the lake. They located Madison within an hour. Since a fatality was involved, they contacted the Homicide Investigative Unit for assistance. When the Unit's night shift status board received the update, listing Conor Gregory as the victim, the Lead Investigator on duty recognized him as a State's witness in an active murder trial and gave a courtesy call to Detective Olson. Olson was obliged to accept and contacted Schultz, informing him to meet at the marina.

When they arrived on the scene, they were surprised to see Madison sitting in a squad car's front seat. By then, Conor's body had been recovered by divers and sent to the medical examiner's office for processing.

"That poor woman can't seem to catch a break," Olson said. "First her son dies; now her fiancé."

Schultz observed her. "She's had her share of tough breaks. That's a fact. How about I take the lead on this?"

Olson shrugged. "Sure, you've got this one."

Schultz signaled an officer before sitting in the driver's seat of his squad car.

"Hello again, Ms. Sanders. I'm Detective Shultz. You may remember me from last year. Detective Olson and I visited you in the hospital."

She glanced over, expressionless "Yes, I remember you."

"I'm sincerely sorry for your loss. I do need to ask you a few questions if you don't mind."

She nodded, seemingly unaffected, and they began.

For fifteen minutes, she recounted her fictitious version of events, leaving no cause for suspicion. Her fabricated story was simple but, more importantly, believable, occurring hundreds of times each year around the country. Her intoxicated boyfriend jumped into the lake without a life jacket, possibly caught a leg cramp, panicked, and drowned. When asked why she didn't throw a life preserver into the water, her lies were elementary.

"I never saw him again after he jumped in. I thought he was joking around. After a minute, I knew something was wrong, but he could surface somewhere else if I threw a life preserver just anywhere. I would have jumped in myself, but I can't swim."

Her answers were consistent with the purported events, so Schultz concluded the interview and handed her his contact card. "Thank you for your time, Ms. Sanders. Do you have a way to get home tonight?"

"I have his truck keys, but I'm not going to be able to drive it home. I can't do it. Not tonight. I can't."

"I understand. I wouldn't recommend that you operate a vehicle right now. I'll have an officer take you home. Okay?"

"Thank you."

He stepped out and informed the officer standing by to drive her. He then rejoined Olson, and they walked back to their cars.

"So, what's the story, Alex?"

"Nothing seems out of the ordinary. He was allegedly drunk, jumped in, and went underneath. She says it happened within seconds. She can't swim or drive a boat. We'll wait for the medical examiner and toxicology report to confirm the presence of alcohol and anything else that she might have failed to mention or didn't know. We'll have to wait and see if that pans out."

"I'm sure that it will."

Schultz grimaced and appeared aggravated. "There is something odd, though. She didn't shed a tear. Hell, her eyes didn't see water at all. She was stoic, which is something that I wouldn't expect."

"Don't be such a hard ass, junior. She's been dealing with a traumatic event for over three hours and has probably cried a river already. I wouldn't look too much into that. You know that people deal with death differently."

"I understand, Rog, but she still has makeup on, and there are no tear streaks, no signs of running eyeliner or mascara. Unless she decided to put on makeup after the fact, she hasn't shed a tear. I find that odd. You should too."

Olson pounded the hood of his car. "What's wrong with you, man? Hasn't she cried enough? Try having a fricking heart sometimes, Jesus!"

Olson got in, slammed the door, and drove away, leaving Schultz standing there. He turned and watched the squad car transporting Madison move out of the parking lot. For a moment, he thought she was staring at him when passing by.

Okay, now you've got my attention, Miss Sanders.

***

Madison was dropped off at home shortly after 9:00 p.m. She walked into the bathroom and stripped naked. She avoided looking in the mirror and immediately showered, scrubbing her body feverishly, intent on removing the self-projected layers of impurity and defilement covering her. After her scoured skin became red and raw, she dropped the soap and exfoliating pad, allowing the water to christen her from top to bottom.

Earlier, during her ride home, she informed Brittany of Conor's death by drowning.

"I can't talk right now, Britt. Please understand. It's too much."

"I want to come over and sit with you. You shouldn't be alone tonight, sweetie."

"No. I need to be alone. I'll be alright. I'll call you tomorrow. I promise."

"Okay, but I love you, and you know that I'm here for you."

"I love you, too, Britt."

Madison wanted to share the truth but knew that was impossible. And when Brittany attempted her calling later that night, Madison rejected it. She feared the abandonment of her only true friend, and the potential loss of love and support was too great a risk to take.

She turned off the shower, wrapped a towel around her body, and laid down in Elijah's bed. After kissing Elijah's photograph, she closed her eyes, gratified, and drifted off to sleep.

CHAPTER 14

The medical examiner released the reports on Conor's cause of death five days after the accident. It was deemed Death by Accidental Drowning. Excessive alcohol was found in his system, but no identifiable narcotics or drugs. However, they did find the presence of two unknown substances. The specific identification of these elements would require further testing by the Minneapolis VA HCS Pathology and Laboratory Medicine Service. Still, the Chief Coroner decided not to authorize it and avoid the expense. Her opinion was that the unknown substances were not pertinent, a significant factor, and did not contribute to the cause of death.

For Conor's family, the conclusion was inconsequential. When Conor's only brother drove from their hometown to claim his body, he met Madison for the first time and was stunned to learn of her engagement to Conor. He, nor his family, knew anything about it, which puzzled them. Still, they knew Conor and how unpredictable and private he was. If he never mentioned his engagement to the family, then he had his reasons.

Against Madison's wishes and to avoid suspicion, she attended the funeral, wearing her sunglasses as much as possible to disguise her absence of grief. Dozens of coworkers from Traxtonite made the two-hour drive upstate. Conor was well-liked by many, as evident by the immense support shown to the family, but Madison remained completely apathetic until the director seated her beside Conor's mother.

As the priest conducted the Rite of Committal, Conor's mother clenched Madison's hand for encouragement, sharing, and transmitting grief unconsciously to her once future daughter-in-law. His mother's pain was sincere, relatable, and so intimate that Madison could not hold back her tears. She wept for Conor's mother and her pain, but not for him.

Madison returned home from the funeral, exhausted and drained but comfortable. She had no regrets about her actions that day and wanted to move onward with what was left of her life. It was time to glue the broken pieces of her life together if possible. She planned to take another week of bereavement leave from Traxtonite, although her vacation and sick hours held a negative balance. Despite the loss of pay, a brief respite was deserved and needed.

***

It was eleven o'clock the following afternoon. Don Carson sat in his living room with his feet resting on the coffee table, sorting through old newspapers and cutting out grocery coupons. While his retirement paperwork was processing, his active clients dwindled, leaving him ample time to do absolutely nothing but to drink and budget his shrinking savings. His romantic life remained in shambles, and his financial debt continued to accumulate, but he saw the finish line.

He would have to "Suck it up," quoting his favorite unofficial U.S. Navy vocabulary and deal with it. It wasn't all bad. He still had enough money to keep up with his mortgage payments for a while and stay intoxicated. For him, all was not lost.

He sipped his morning coffee, spiked with Captain Morgan's Rum, and smacked his lips while flipping through the newspaper. The obituary page caught his attention. A particular name stuck out. Conor Gregory. He continued to read with surprise, then tossed the newspaper aside and opened his laptop, looking for more details on the death. He began searching the local newspaper archives from that date and read other articles about the accident from different news outlets. He leaned, reclined, and processed the data.

That's too bad—what a shame. Little Miss Madison is all alone now. I wonder, did she ever make my banana pudding?

He looked at his calendar.

Lucky me, her balance is due today. Check on that and your pudding ASAP. Give her a day or two. She's probably still bawling her eyes out.

He contemplated the new events, wondering why his curiosity was peaked and what was nagging him. He rationally sorted, separated, and disposed of extraneous thoughts, but Conor's death remained in the forefront of his mind, and he was puzzled as to why.

Shit. I hate it when this happens.

These instances were rare and usually a waste of his time. He considered these strange episodes to be a bi-product of his career as a detective and an investigative glitch. It was being caught between a pestering thought and a viable hunch. He sorted through the files on his laptop and replayed Madison's initial interview, but this time he focused exclusively on Conor, assessing his body language, projections, and reactions during key questions to Madison. He replayed the interview several times before he stood and stared at the screen.

Tell me it isn't so, Don. Did you screw this up? She had your nose wide open, and you ignored him—you idiot.

"You were guilty of something, pretty boy. I'm not sure of what, but you were involved, somehow, in some way."

He left the room, took a shower, and got dressed while assessing the facts of Madison's case under a new light and with an added variable, Conor Gregory.

"What's the strongest evidence in the State's case?"

The self-incriminating text messages between Ronald Tatum and Terrance Roberts.

"Why not talk in person? They see each other every day at work and hang out frequently after work. Why would they text each other self-incriminating messages at all?"

They wouldn't.

Carson already knew the 'what,' but he needed to find out the 'when' and the 'where.' He placed calls to his department contacts. Within an hour, he had elicited the exact time, location, and origin of the original text messages. It was The Tap Room. He had heard of it but had never been. He grabbed his notebook and headed out the door. The hunch was perplexing, but the potential video footage of the crime from Madison's neighbor's camera could settle the entire matter. Obtaining the footage, if any, would be tricky but doable. He decided to climb that hill later if needed.

***

Carson walked into Tap Room around noon and sat at the bar before surveying for video cameras. Besides a few customers eating lunch, the place was bare, except for the bartender who was stocking stations.

The bartender approached. "Hey bud, what can I get you?"

"Nothing, pal, but would you mind answering a few questions for me?"

"I'll try. What do you want?"

"My name is Don Carson, and I'm a private investigator. I recently worked on a case scheduled for trial and compared my notes with the State's evidence. I'd like to know about your cameras. I've seen the two covering the parking lot and one here at the bar," he pointed, "but are there any other cameras that capture the seating area, the stage, or the dance floor?"

The bartender wiped the counter. "Oh, you must be talking about Ron and Terrance getting arrested. Nope, those three cameras are all we have. The cops asked about that months ago. I guess they were looking for the same thing that you are. It didn't matter much. A bunch of us confirmed that they were here. Conor was with them, too."

"So, you know them by their first names?"

"Of course I do. Everybody does. Those guys have been coming here for years." He laughed. "They're practically wall fixtures."

Carson smirked. "Really?"

"Yeah. We told the cops everything that we knew and saw. A band was playing that night, and we were slammed. They were sitting right over there," he pointed. "That's all I have for you, bud. I'm kind of busy now and need to get back at it."

"Sure, thanks. Just one more thing. What was the name of the band?"

"Tokyo Jack played that night."

"Okay, thanks."

Carson walked out, taking notes as he left, and drove back home. He rushed inside, shakily poured a double-shot of Scotch, and gulped it before searching the internet for information on the band, Tokyo Jack. He perused their social media, and YouTube videos, until stumbling across a playlist of their taped sessions.

He smiled. "Bingo." He clicked on their dated performance at the Tap Room. The video quality of the actual band was excellent, but everything outside of that, including the dancing patrons and crowd, was shadowy and grainy at best. Still, he decided to capture it and downloaded the file. Carson's experience as a seasoned investigator had led to the development of a multitude of techniques, or 'shortcuts,' as he referred to them. One such skill was video editing. There were instances in the field when an investigator didn't have the time, or patience, to wait in line for the Forensics Unit to process work. Carson learned to circumvent these delays, and this was one of those instances.

He opened the newly downloaded video file with his video editing software and began adjusting it to sharpen and enhance the images. Then he viewed it again. The video was much clearer. When the band reached the halfway mark of their performance, he spotted them.

"There you are," he mumbled. The euphoric feeling of discovery returned as his hunch dangled on the precipice of truth.

Old-timer, you still got it.

He watched and rewound as Conor, Terrance, and Ron sat down at the same table, drinking. He observed Ron and Terrance using their phones and texting. He stopped the video, checking the time stamp.

That's too early. The time doesn't match up.

He saw women join the table for drinks and then dance with them. Except for Conor, who remained seated, never using the bathroom.

He must have a bladder the size of Texas.

He doubled the video speed, then paused it, replaying the same fifty-second clip. He could see Conor sitting alone in the shadows but couldn't tell why he appeared to be moving around.

If he's moving to the music, the boy has terrible rhythm.

He changed the video overlay from normal to negative and replayed the clip. As he watched, he saw Conor texting from the cell phones of his friends. He replayed it three times before hopping to his feet.

"You slick sonofabitch. Well done. Well done!"

He poured another double shot to celebrate.

"Why would you do something like that?" He swallowed the Scotch. "Never mind, I already know the answer. Plus, you're already dead. You dirty dog, you," he chuckled. He looked out of his front window, feeling redeemed from his first failure to uncover the truth. The cogs of his mind rotated, powered by resentment and payback.

Roger, Roger. You shouldn't have screwed me, partner. Now, it's YOUR turn to get bent over. I want you to watch me burn your case down to the ground. Fuck you, Schultz, and that cocksucker Angelletti! I'm going to make you all look like fools. I promise.

He held up his middle finger.

I swear by my Detective's honor.

***

The next day, while driving home after work, Brittany called to check on Madison. Her empathetic heart, and extended hand, reached out to her friend in sympathy for the unimaginable loss of Conor. His death affected everyone at work, even those who disliked him for one reason or another, and in conjunction with the loss of Terrance, the office atmosphere would never be the same. Brittany didn't attend the funeral. She didn't do well at them, always being overwhelmed with grief, regardless of her relationship with the deceased. It was the finality of death that she took issue with and its uncompromising prerogative to snuff the life from anyone it desired. She was mature enough to understand the privilege of life and its delicate, temporal, and endearing nature.

The phone rang, and Madison answered.

"Hi, Britt."

"Hey, Maddy. How are you feeling?"

"I'm doing okay. How was work?"

"It was...work, and it sucked. It's always that way when you're gone. What have you eaten today? You probably don't have much of an appetite."

"I cooked a grilled cheese sandwich earlier, but you're right. I haven't been very hungry."

"That's not enough to sustain you. I can come over and cook you something that'll make you want to eat. I just left work and can swing by."

"That sounds great, but Britt, I want to be alone for a few more days. I know that you're worried about me. I love you for caring, I do, but I'm working everything out in my mind. Slowly, but surely."

Brittany sighed, straining to remain upbeat and encouraging. "I got you. I'm wearing a big frown because I miss you, but I understand."

"I'm still coping with what happened, and Conor being gone forever. I can't believe that it happened."

"Oh my God, Madison, I want to help you so bad, but I don't know how." She pleaded. "Whatever you need, just open your mouth, please."

"I will, I promise. Don't be upset with me. Please realize that your friendship is what's holding me together. I mean it, Britt."

"I believe you. Call me later if you need to talk."

"Will do. Drive safe, bye."

Madison stretched out across the couch, shielding her face with a pillow.

I hate lying to her! It's not right, Maddy, but you have to hide it. You have no choice.

Her soul was in turmoil, with no place to go and no one to tell. A week prior, she would have become anxious, then depressed, and the tears would have flowed. But not now. She had changed. Even before murdering Conor, she felt altered and believed it was necessary to cry for something, for anything. Her mind was willing, but her heart seemed unmovable, unaffected, and fearless. If she dreaded anything, it was only the thought of becoming unrecognizable to herself.

The doorbell rang, and she sprang to her feet like a startled cat. She was wary and cautious yet ready to strike out if cornered. She crept to the front window and peeked through the blinds.

Mr. Carson? What is he doing here?

Her mind raced with possibilities.

Oh, shit. I owe him. Dammit, I'm broke until payday!

She retreated from the window.

Maybe, he'll go away. Be quiet.

She patiently waited for him to leave, but her car was in the driveway, and he continued to ring the bell. Since he wasn't leaving anytime soon, she eventually opened the door.

Carson stood, appearing contrite and humble. His meek facade disarmed her anxiety.

"Hello, Madison. I just learned the news yesterday about your fiancé. I wanted you to know that you have my deepest condolences. I am so very sorry."

"Hello, Mr. Carson. Thank you."

"You're welcome. May I come in?"

She hesitated, not wanting any visitors. "I wish you hadn't driven all this way to stand outside, but I'm not ready for any visitors yet. I'm sorry."

He stepped closer, and his musty scent crept through the door opening. "I'm afraid that I have some disturbing news to tell you. You need to be informed today. You'll want to be sitting down when I share it with you."

What in the world has happened now, she thought. "Alright."

She opened the door, and he walked inside, gesturing towards the couch. They both sat as he regurgitated his prepared statement.

"There has been a new development in the case for Elijah. I'm about to tell you things that will be very hard to accept or even comprehend, but they are the facts, not my opinions, and nothing can change that. First, I want to ask you a question."

She nodded, concerned about the unknown.

"Do you trust me?"

"Yes, I do. Why?"

"You're already intimately aware of the facts about the case, so I'll get right to it. I have in my possession video evidence of Conor, Ron Tatum, and Terrance Roberts at the Tap Room on the night that they allegedly sent each other text messages, implicating and incriminating themselves."

"Okay."

"Here goes. The video recording clearly shows that while Mr. Tatum and Mr. Roberts were out on the dance floor, that Conor picked up both of their phones and used them. He was the one who sent the erroneous text messages before deleting them."

Madison feigned shock, although she was mildly surprised. "What? Really?"

Did he set up his friends? He did that? Ron and Terrance weren't involved at all? I can't believe it. That means...

Carson reached over and patted her knee. "I know the news is shocking. Take your time to process it." He sighed. "I hate being the bearer of bad news, but when the truth rises to the surface, it must be told."

"Wait. How did you learn this?"

"By good old fashion detective work. I revisited the evidence, investigated, and got lucky."

She leaned back, folded her arms, and stared out the window. "It's hard to believe."

He scooted forward. "Believe it, and trust me. There's more."

"More? I don't know how much more that I can handle."

He loosened his tie. "May I trouble you for a glass of water, please?"

"Sure. Yes, sir."

She walked into the kitchen while his lustful eyes followed behind her. She came back and handed him a glass.

"Thank you, darling." He sipped and set it down. "Now, continuing. Those text messages were the strongest evidence that the State had at its disposal. Now, the stakes have been raised and changed the dynamics of the case; Mr. Tatum won't be convicted, not now."

"Are you sure?"

"I've been doing police work for nearly thirty years, and I'm sure. At least 99.9% positive. The reason that I'm here is to request your help."

Her face contorted. "I can't imagine how I can help."

Carson pursed his lips and sipped. "I'd like to take a look at your laptop if you don't mind."

Her jaw went slack, and her anxiety skyrocketed. "Laptop? What are you talking about?"

"You know, the MacBook you bought from your neighbor across the street, Cindy."

She looked down at her bare knees, and her cheeks turned pink.

Oh my God!

"How do you know that I bought anything from her?"

"Well, she told me. I was just over there, introduced myself, explained who I was, our professional relationship, and my contributions to the case. I talked with her and her husband about their video surveillance system and asked about the footage. He told me that the video software was installed on Cindy's MacBook and that it also was the storage for the video footage history." He snickered. "He said that he wasn't paying a red cent to back it up on the Cloud. I like his attitude. Anyhow, you purchased it two weeks ago, in fact, on the same day that we spoke. Remember? I came over for a courtesy visit."

"Oh, okay. I remember now. Sorry. But why do you want to see it? What's the purpose?"

"Good question. I mentioned luck. Well, I found something that the other investigators missed. Your neighbor's backyard camera was originally hidden from sight, so it was initially overlooked, not only by Detective Olson, but to be fair, I missed it, too. But now that it has been located, the positioning, and possible field of view, lead me to believe that it may show the entire front facade of your house, the driveway, and the road. If it was active and recording during those early morning hours, then we might be able to make a definitive determination of who perpetrated the action resulting in Elijah's death."

Madison was frozen, void of thought, as fear revisited her. Her lip quivered, and Carson noticed it. He was curious.

He gripped her knee. "Madison, are you alright."

Her foot began tapping, but she was powerless to control it.

Carson's antenna raised.

Women are the worst at holding their cards. She knows something.

"Madison, I asked if you were alright. What's the matt..."

"I'm fine!" she barked.

He stood up and buttoned his sports jacket. "I know that these are new revelations, and have you shaken. I don't blame you. You have every right to be upset. I mean that. I merely need to borrow the Mac-Book for a few hours, and I'll bring it directly back."

She stopped. "There's nothing to see. Cindy erased everything. Sorry."

"That's not a problem. Everything deleted can be recovered, just like a cell phone. I want to clone the hard drive, and then I'll give it right back to you. I promise."

With her arms still folded, she walked past him and plopped down on the couch.

Think! Don't make a mistake!

She shook from adrenaline. "I don't think I can do that. I'm sorry. I can't seem to get over this. Every time I take a step forward, something else comes up, and I get knocked back. I'm tired. I'm fucking tired of it all!" She hung her head. "The answer is no. Goodbye."

Carson appeared stunned until his devilish grin appeared, and the power play began.

"Goodbye? Are you telling me goodbye? No, you've got it all wrong. You might want to say goodbye to everyone that you know and care about if there is anyone left in that selfish heart of yours."

She snapped her head. "Don't talk to me like that. I said goodbye, now please leave."

He towered over her. "You heard me. You're selfish!" he yelled, deepening his voice and frightening her. "Two innocent men went to jail. One is dead. The other is fighting for his freedom, looking at a decade or more in prison for something he didn't do. Meanwhile, we find evidence that your fiancé was most likely the culprit, and you want to sit here and withhold the evidence that will exonerate him? Yeah, that's the definition of being selfish."

He took off his jacket, folding it over his arm, and pointed. "Listen, young lady. I'll say this once. Tomorrow morning, I'll be meeting with the Assistant Attorney General and informing him that you are withholding potential State's evidence in the case against Ron Tatum. He's going call a judge, who will issue a search warrant, for your laptop only, but the entire premises. We'll have your financial records, too, for good measure. You can expect your house to be ransacked in a few days. If that laptop isn't found, then know that you'll be charged for obstruction of justice and whatever else they want to throw at you!"

Madison covered her face, slowly crumbling, her self-esteem fading. On the precipice of tears, she had nowhere to hide.

"Please. Don't yell at me," she squeaked from behind her hands.

He smirked.

Just a little bit farther, 'sweet cheeks.' You're almost there. Give me what I want.

"Or." He bent down and rubbed her knee. She peeked at his hand.

No. No, please don't.

His eyebrows rose. "Your other option is simple and better. Let me make a copy, and I'll give it to the proper authorities. Those are your two choices. Pick one. I have somewhere to be." He stepped back and slipped on his sportscoat.

She wanted to speak but was lost, mute.

He cocked his head sideways. "Hold on a minute, don't you owe me a payment for services rendered? I believe so. While you're making your decision, I'll take your payment now. $740, please. You can run to the bank. They're still open. I'll wait in the driveway."

Despite the changing direction of the conversation, she found the wherewithal to respond.

"I can't pay it all today. I've taken so much leave time that I won't even have a full check this week. I have other bills, food, my utilities, besides the rent. I promise to pay you by the end of next month. If you can.."

"Enough, shush, quiet." He sighed, running his fingers through his receding hairline. "Let me think for a second, sweetheart." He contemplated his next play and snapped his fingers. "I tell you what I'm going to do. I want you to come over to my house tonight at eight o'clock. Use the front door. Bring the MacBook and whatever money you can scrape up. I'll clone the hard drive while you're there, and you can take it when you leave. That's my last and final offer."

She stared, without saying a word, enflaming him even more.

He smiled and casually strolled toward the front door. "You've made your decision. Goodbye."

"I'll come," she mumbled.

He stopped and turned around. "What? I can't hear you. Speak up, honey."

"I said, I'll come."

"And bring the laptop. And some cash."

She nodded.

He walked over to her and extended his hand. "We're not going to end like this. We both got heated, but honestly, we are coming out of this as winners. You get to learn the truth, set an innocent man free, and put all this shit behind you. Let's shake, so there are no hard feelings." She hung her head and shook his hand, but he held on. "Hey, I know you're strapped for cash, but when you come over, we'll work something out, clear your debt." He winked and walked over to the door. "I'll see you tonight at eight. Don't be late."

He closed the door, put on his sunglasses, and stretched his arms in victory, then backed down the driveway, and waved to Cindy as she nosed about in her driveway.

Well done, Donny boy. Tonight, you get paid and laid. A double whammy! Yee-haw!

He turned up the radio and barreled out of the subdivision.

Madison was curled up on the couch, crying. She hated herself for allowing him to intimidate her but more so dreaded what would be found on her computer, and paranoia took hold.

They'll see everything—the video of Conor. The chemicals I ordered. They'll know. They'll figure out that I killed him and throw me in jail! God, please, please, help me!

The intense pressure became too much, and she released a blood-curdling scream.

Those were her last thoughts before her eyes rolled backward, and she lost consciousness, arching, contorting, and stiffening until becoming rigid as the seizure commanded control of her body.

***

Carson sprayed cologne on his hairy chest, rubbed it dry, tied his bathrobe, and strolled into the kitchen. He poured a drink and checked the time. It was 7:55 p.m. He picked up the Viagra tablet next to the glass and popped it into his mouth, chasing it with the Scotch. The house was dimly lit, contrived to set the mood of his pleasure, as he mixed it with business and extortion. His morally defunct conscience regretted none of it, nor his past unethical and criminal escapades. He wallowed in it.

I can't wait to pop this babe.

He lusted, fantasizing about the sexual positions he would impose on her.

She's petite and tiny; I can throw her around. Ha. Get a little rough.

The doorbell rang. He hurried to the front, almost losing one of his house slippers, and smoothed down his hair. Freshly shaven and smelling good, he prepared his best Hollywood smile before opening the door.

Madison stood wearing jeans and a sweatshirt, shouldering her purse and holding the laptop travel case.

He sized her up. "Hey, darling. I'm glad that you decided to make our date. Come inside."

As she walked by him, he inhaled her passing scent, "I was running late and just got out of the shower," he told her, shutting and locking the door.

She stood there in the corridor and nodded.

"Come with me." He led her into his living room, waving her over to a comfy-looking couch. "Sit down. Make yourself comfortable. Would you like something to drink? A beer? Or something stronger? I've got Scotch, tequila, rum, and vodka. Pick your poison, and don't be shy."

The moldy smell of his house combined with the aroma of household disinfectant repulsed her, as did his very presence, but she remained expressionless.

"I'll have a beer," she replied.

"You got it, doll." He stepped into the kitchen, grabbed a beer, and opened it. Then, after refreshing his glass, he came back to the couch to join her. "Here you go." He handed over the bottle, sat down beside her, and held out his glass. "Let's toast. Here's to a bright future, and both of us getting what we want and what we deserve."

She reluctantly held up her bottle, ashamed, humiliated by the charade and her compliance. He gulped down half of his glass while she sipped in pretense, refusing to dull her senses.

You're not getting me drunk, filthy pig. Whatever happens to me, I want to be sober.

He set his glass down on the coffee table and rested his hand on her knee.

"Now, down to business. What do you have for me?"

She went into her purse and handed over cash bills. "That's $175. It's all I can give you right now. I swear."

His forehead wrinkled, and he tossed the money onto the table. "Like I told you at your house. You'll have to work this out. We can start that part of it tonight. Now, give me the laptop." He held out his hand.

She unzipped the case, setting the MacBook on her lap. Her foot began to tap. "How long is it going to take?"

He grabbed it and stood up, looking at his watch.

"To clone the hard drive? Not long, maybe an hour. How long am I going to take with you? A little longer, maybe two hours." He winked and walked to his office.

He turned on his desk lamp and powered up the device. Minutes later, the cloning procedure was in progress, and he returned to the couch.

"It's in the works," he said, finishing his Scotch. "How are you coming along with that beer? Do you need another?"

She looked at the bottle in her hand. "I'm good. But can I have a napkin? The glass is sweating."

"One napkin, coming up." He walked into the kitchen, raising his voice. "You sure are a cheap date! One beer and a napkin? Where have you been hiding all my life?" He laughed, returned, and leaned up against her. "Here you go, precious."

She wrapped the napkin around the bottle, set it on the table, and folded her arms. He sipped his Scotch, smacking his lips, and put his glass down.

"Do you want me to play some music?" he whispered while easing his arm around her.

She looked down, avoiding his hot breath, but noticed that his genitals were exposed from his robe.

She leaned away. "Stop. What are you doing?"

She tried to stand up, but he grabbed her arm and yanked her down. She froze.

"Sit down," he growled. "What the hell is wrong with you? You know what kind of party this is, so cut the shit."

His grip was firm, strong for a man of his age, and he forced her closer. He glanced at his penis and smirked.

"It's huge, I know. But I promise to go slow - at first anyway. I won't hurt you, sweetie. I guarantee."

He kissed the side of her head and pecked at her neck while groping her breasts.

"No! Stop!" she yelled, squirming and trying to push him back. But he was too strong.

He grabbed both of her arms, twisting her onto her back, and straddled her. "Enough. Stop fighting me." He spread his robe, exposing his full erection.

"Get off of me! Help!" she screamed.

He raised to his knees and stroked his member. "Dammit, girl! Keep still! Let me squirt it all over you," he moaned.

She tried to wiggle out from underneath him, but he held her down with one arm and continued his perverse assault toward the climax.

"No! I said NO!" she cried. She closed her eyes, waiting for the humiliating conclusion.

But the arm forcing her down suddenly weakened, and his groans of pleasure changed into grunts of pain. She opened her eyes to see him fall to the floor.

A vein popped out in his neck. "Call 911! Now. Hurry. I'm having a heart attack. A stroke," he mumbled. "Water. Bring water."

She laughed cruelly. "Ha-ha! Water? That's not going to help you."

He collapsed to the floor and rolled onto his back, wheezing and coughing. She tiptoed around the couch and stood over him as his shallow breaths slowed.

"Your dick's not hard anymore. What's wrong? Why can't you get it up?"

He lay exposed, clutching at his motionless chest, and then went still.

Madison was huffing, overcome with excitement. The experience was exhilarating.

A few minutes passed before she cautiously approached his corpse and bent over to check his neck for a pulse, but stopped.

You monster. I don't even want to touch you.

Happy with her decision to double the dose she had given to Conor, she checked her purse to make sure that the small extract jar wasn't left behind. Then she hurried into Carson's office. She looked around and saw her computer on his desk, connected to a small hard disk. The screen showed the progress bar, indicating the current progress at 27%.

Good! It didn't finish.

She snatched out the cable that connected both devices, shut the lid, and carried the laptop into the living room, placing it into the case. After grabbing her purse, she wiped off her beer bottle with the napkin and exited out of the front door, using the napkin to open and close it.

You're almost home, Maddy. Calm down. You did it. You did it!

She was relieved that Carson's front porch light was off, easing her way through the darkness to her car. She backed out and drove off, warily surveying the area. Within a minute, her lungs began to burn, and she realized that, at some point, she had started holding her breath.

Breathe. Breathe.

She inhaled fully and deeply while her quaking hands manipulated the steering wheel. Her mind was clear of thoughts and memories as she basked in the freedom of the moment, glimpsing the fury inside her soul. For the first time, she felt the power, the purity, and the sincere honesty of its elusive purpose. It had been dormant during her entire life, patiently biding its time in ignorance while cloaked in the moral hypocrisy of denial. The hidden now became visible, and the glass barrier between her two minds shattered, splitting her psyche asunder. This was Madison's truth, and there was no turning back from reality.

CHAPTER 15

Early the following day, Madison woke up exhausted and completely drained. She crawled to the edge of Elijah's bed and sat, staring at the floor. The events that transpired the night before seemed a distant memory. She wanted it to remain so and compartmentalized the ordeal's intermittent flashes using the hope of forgetfulness. She knew that one negative thought could begin her escalation towards anxiety, to be followed by paranoia. Instead, she chose to rely on the power of denial and amnesia. She looked around, dreading the isolation and loneliness that the day would bring, and decided to go to work. She called Steve Hyman and left a voicemail that she would be coming to work.

Why not? Everything is normal. This is just another day. Get off your lazy ass.

She got ready, prepared her lunch, and left the house.

Thirty minutes later, she parked next to Brittany's car and walked inside. As she passed through the doors leading to the main office, she was immediately engulfed in the usual daily office bustle and commotion. Her breathing became rapid, and her mouth went dry as she looked straight forward and hurried to her cubicle. She huffed and turned on her computer.

What's wrong with you? Relax. Calm down. This is only another day at work.

"Good morning, Madison! It's good to see you," Trina yelled from behind.

"Good morning. Thanks."

"Let me know if you need anything or you want to talk. I'm here for you. I'll see you at lunch," she smiled and walked away.

Are you here for me? To do what? Gossip behind my back? Or tell me who you've been screwing? Do you have another story about Conor?... Stop! Maddy, stop it right now! That's how it starts. Haven't you learned yet?

She logged onto her computer while incessantly tapping her foot and opened her emails. The time away from work was apparent by the deluge of messages, requests, and priority tasks that required her attention. This was a good thing. Madison knew that burying her head in work kept her mind focused and off her life issues.

"Good morning, Ms. Sanders. We're glad to have you back." Steve Hyman said.

She twitched in surprise. Steve stood beside an unknown man.

"Good morning. I'm glad to be back. I'm swamped, as you can see." She motioned toward her monitor.

"I see that. I want you to meet Fred Hinkley. He's been hired as our new Office Manager."

Fred smiled and extended his hand. The sweat from his balding head glistened beneath the ceiling lights.

"It's nice to meet you, Miss Sanders."

She hesitated but shook his hand. "Same to you."

She turned to her computer.

Steve's eyebrows raised, and he glanced at Fred, who shrugged and stepped closer. "After you catch up on things, maybe later this week, we can sit down together, and you can fill me in on what you do. I'm open to any thoughts or suggestions that might improve our office productivity as a department. Whenever you catch up, that is."

"Okay," she replied without looking.

"And if you need anything from Human Resources, let me know," Steve added, and they walked away.

Madison shivered. She already detested the new manager.

The way he looked at me. He was smiling, like he couldn't wait to get me behind closed doors. Improve office productivity? Bullshit. If Steve weren't standing next to him, he'd be all over me, just like Ron. There's no way that I'm going through that hell again. Never again!

She fumed and continued trudging through her backlog.

At noon, the lunch chime sounded, startling her again, but this time she bolted to her feet and looked around. Brittany was approaching, with her arms held wide.

"Girl, you didn't tell me that you were coming in today!"

They hugged, but Madison felt guilty for forgetting. Regardless, she soaked up the positive energy from the physical embrace.

"I wanted it to be a surprise," Madison said as they separated.

"Well, you did it. Surprise!" she giggled. "Did you bring something?"

Bring something? Bring what? What does she know?

Madison appeared disheveled.

"Did you bring something to eat?" Brittany reiterated.

"Oh. Yes, I did."

"Then let's go." Brittany turned to walk away.

Madison bent over to picked up her purse and lunch bag, then noticed something from the corner of her eye. She jumped back behind the cubicle partition.

No. It can't be. He's dead! I know that he's dead.

But are you sure?

Brittany stopped walking. "Come on. What are you doing?"

Madison peeked over the partition and looked across the room.

I saw him. I thought I saw him.

But are you sure? Are you sure that you're not crazy?

"Madison. Madison," Brittany called out and walked over, touching her shoulder.

Madison flinched. "Huh! I don't know. I don't know what's going on, Britt."

Brittany rubbed her back but was suspicious of the strange behavior. She had seen Madison do weird things, but never to this extent.

"Come, Madison. Let's get some food inside that belly and relax in the breakroom. You may have overdone it on your first day back.

You're a classic workaholic." She smirked, nudging her along. Madison was suffocated with apprehension but followed Brittany to the breakroom. Every foreboding step felt as though it would be her last, as her body trembled nervously under the crushing weight of her developing psychosis.

When Brittany opened the door and entered the breakroom, Madison stood motionless under the threshold, glaring inside. Overcome by the noise, the stares, and fear, she panicked.

Brittany didn't realize that Madison had left until she sat down with Luis.

Brittany looked around. "Where did she go?"

"I saw her when you walked inside, but then she turned around and left. She probably had to use the restroom," Luis replied.

Brittany thought for a moment, then stood up. "I need to find her."

She walked into the hallway and looked inside the nearest restroom, but it was empty. She hurried to the main office, only to find Madison's cubicle empty.

Where in the world have you gone? Oh, Jesus! Please let everything be alright. Please, help her.

Brittany looked through the front window beside Madison's cubicle and watched her car speeding out of the parking lot.

You knew that something wasn't right with her! Why didn't you keep a closer eye on her!

Brittany paced the floor.

She needs you. Now. Go!

She searched for Steve to let him know that Madison had to leave early, and so did she.

What if he asks, why? This is an emergency!

***

Thirty minutes later, Brittany turned into Madison's subdivision. She didn't know what to expect, or even if Madison went home, but she hoped for the best. She parked behind Madison's car and ran toward the front door.

"Britt!"

She heard Madison and turned around to see Madison getting out of her car.

"Madison!"

Brittany trotted to her, and Madison collapsed into her arms, crying.

"I can't live like this, Britt," she sobbed. "I give up. I can't do it anymore. It's too hard."

Brittany pulled her until they were cheek to cheek.

"What are you doing sitting out here?"

"I was afraid."

"Afraid of what?"

Madison cried out. "That someone is inside the house!"

"It's going to be alright, sis. Let's go inside. No one is inside. Come on now, walk with me."

Brittany kept her close as they walked to the door and went inside. They walked to the couch and sat. Madison covered her face, blubbering, and Brittany went to the kitchen and brought back a paper towel.

Brittany looked at the ceiling. "How can I help? Lord Jesus, please tell me what to do."

Madison repeatedly shook her head and quietly sobbed while Brittany stroked her.

"Britt, I did something bad. I can't hide what's inside anymore. But I can't tell anyone. I feel like I'm losing my mind," she whined in agony.

Brittany turned Madison's head and looked into her teary eyes.

"That's a lie. You're not losing your mind. You can tell me anything. You need to tell me everything that's happening to you."

Although near hysterics, Madison understood that divulging the truth would cross a threshold of no return.

You have to tell her. Something has got to change, or you might as well kill yourself!

But don't tell her everything.

Madison wiped her eyes. "Please don't think bad of me. I know you will. I know it."

"I promise that I won't. Tell me!"

"Do you promise not to hate me?"

Brittany dropped her head and sighed. "Of course. I promise not to hate you. Now tell me."

Madison took a deep breath. "I killed Conor."

The room went silent. Brittany squinted her eyes and cocked her head, attempting to process the unexpected confession. But it simply didn't compute.

"I'm sorry, but please repeat that."

"I killed Conor. I found out that he was the one that hurt Elijah. I bought a..."

Brittany leaped off the couch. "Stop. Just stop! That's enough. You did not kill Conor. Do you hear me? Conor did not hurt Elijah! Oh my God!" She grabbed Madison's shoulders. "I love you. You mean more to me than any best friend ever could. But you've been through too much, and it's time to get you help."

"What do you mean, help?" Madison wiped her eyes and blew her nose. "I'm trying to tell you the truth."

Brittany took out her cell phone.

Madison was dumbfounded. "What are you doing?"

"I'm looking for psychiatric counseling in this area. Madison, today, mark my words, you're going to talk with someone. A professional."

Madison bolted for Elijah's room, brought back her MacBook, and set it on the coffee table.

"You think that I'm crazy, but I can prove what I know. Sit down, and I'll show you the video. This is from the house camera across the street."

"The video? What? How?"

"Sit down and watch it for yourself. You can turn me over to the police after if you want, but at least look!"

Madison began the clip as Brittany sat to watch. Her initial expression was doubtful, then she went blank, and as Madison zoomed closer and paused on Conor's image, Brittany fell into utter shock.

She covered her mouth. "Oh, my God. Oh, my God. I can't believe this." Her eyes watered as she turned to Madison. "He did do it." She stumbled around the room, thinking, and then stopped. "The police! You need to give this to the police!"

Madison closed the lid. "It's too late for that."

"No, it's not. Why?"

"I killed Conor. He didn't drown on his own. I gave him something. If they see this video, they'll investigate me. They will know my motive to kill him."

"What? That doesn't make any sense. How long have you had this?" Brittany thought about Terrance. "How long? Maybe Terrance would still be alive..."

"I found it two weeks ago after I bought the computer from Cindy, across the street. Terrance was already gone by then."

Unable to contain her emotions, Brittany broke down in tears. "Why did Conor do that? Why?" she sobbed. "Elijah, Terrance. They're gone because of him!"

Madison began crying. "Do you hate me?"

Brittany took the used paper towel from Madison and blew her nose. "No. It's just hard to believe that this actually occurred and everything else that is happening, now," she choked. "No wonder you've been acting so strange. I knew it. I knew that something was very wrong with you."

They sat together without saying a word, both only breaking the silence with intermittent sniffles.

Brittany stared out the front window, rubbing her temples. "I would've probably done the same thing if someone hurt my baby. Then he blamed it on someone else, and the whole time he was pretending to love you." She looked at Madison. "That sonofabitch took advantage of you."

"Yes, he did." Madison stared at the floor.

"It just occurred to me that I received that package for you on the same day that Conor was killed. Did it have anything to do with how he died? Or was that a coincidence?"

Madison hesitated to find the right words. "It was for him. I needed it. That's one of the reasons that I don't want the police involved. If they search my computer, they could see my internet history, my purchases, and they might get curious. I tried to be sneaky and thought..."

"I thought that we were best friends. You're supposed to be my sister. What the hell, Madison? Have you got me caught up in a damn murder? You made me an accessory?"

"I'm sorry. I wasn't thinking straight. I should have told you everything, but I was afraid that you would have tried to talk me out of it."

Brittany waved her hands and stood up. "In other words, you didn't give a shit about me, my family, or my future. I can't believe you did that to me. I'm leaving now, and please don't call or text me."

Brittany walked to the door.

Madison reached. "No, please, I'm sorry. I really am. Don't leave me! Please, don't leave me!"

Brittany slammed the door.

Madison fell to her knees. "No!"

She curled up on the couch, moaning in distress like an injured animal, alone and isolated, while her solitary source of love and support drove away.

Within the hour, Madison's psychological condition rapidly deteriorated from the newly formed void in her heart, encouraging another relapse into psychosis. But she fought back and resisted the impulse to relinquish her control to that which seemed uncontrollable. Youthful memories flowed through her mind as she reminisced of the safety and solitude of her childhood bedroom. It had always been her sanctuary, and she attempted to project herself back into those surroundings, and into that mindset, in efforts to stave off her lunacy. It sparked her craving for the maternal, as a daughter, intrinsically seeking safety from the woman who gave her life.

Another hour passed, and Madison barely held on to her sanity when she dialed her mother's phone. It rang and went to her voicemail.

"Hello, Mother. I'm calling to apologize to you. I'm sorry for offending you. And Mother, Conor is dead. He died two weeks ago. I'm all alone. I went to work today but couldn't stay. It's really hard to focus and think straight. Again, I'm sorry, mother. Goodbye."

She ended the call and stared at the ceiling.

Take me away. Take me far away where I am nothing. Tear me into a million pieces. Make me forget.

She burst out in tears.

But I could never forget you, Elijah. Never.

Her phone rang. Without looking, she knew that it was Elizabeth.

"Hello, Mother," she croaked.

"Hello, Madison. I just listened to your message. I accept your apology."

Madison blubbered, her thirst for forgiveness partially quenched. "Thank you."

Elizabeth exhaled. "You don't sound well. I think that it's time for you to come home for a few days. The visit will benefit you. I'll purchase a plane ticket for you. Let me know when you are ready to leave."

Madison sat up on the couch.

Oh my God. Does she miss me?

She wept, unable to hold her emotions at bay, and was grateful for the lifeline thrown.

"Thank you, mother," she sniffled, "I want... I'm going to come home, but you know that I'm afraid to fly."

"You haven't overcome that phobia yet?"

Madison blew her nose and composed herself. "No. It would be ten times worse if I tried to fly now. I'll drive home instead."

"Fine. When are you leaving, and when should I expect you?"

"I'll leave early tomorrow morning. I should be there in two days."

"Very good. Drive safely. Goodbye."

"Goodbye, mother."

Madison tossed the phone aside and ran to the bathroom. It had been days since she passed a bowel movement, and she was grateful to have one, unexpectantly triggered by the good news of her temporary get-away. She sat on the commode, thinking.

You need this, just for a week, to clear your mind. Thank you, God. You're right on time.

Before going to bed, she packed her suitcase and emailed Steve Hyman, requesting a week of unpaid FMLA leave. He would approve it. He had no choice. She completed the necessary forms, and forwarded them, then laid down to sleep.

At 5:00 a.m. the following day, Madison backed out of her driveway, beginning her 1600 mile trek toward Seattle, Washington. Armed with $318 and a full tank of gas, she packed enough clothes for a week. She stocked a cooler with food to eat along the way, tossing the half-filled vanilla extract jar inside too. She turned up the music and drove off, rhythmically tapping the MacBook in the seat beside her. She was confident of making it to Seattle, but not returning to Minnesota without financial assistance. Elizabeth had never refused to render loans in the past, and Madison believed that this time wouldn't be any different. At least, she hoped.

***

Charlene drove out of the gas station, having pumped her last six dollars. Times were hard, again, but she wasn't worried. She was determined to replenish her bank account by hustling or any means necessary. Her latest boyfriend didn't stay around long, but it was fun while it lasted. But fun couldn't pay the bills. Her finances were cyclical, and income from the strip club wasn't dependable. This month, the ends didn't meet, and she came up short.

All was not lost as she scrolled through her long list of Sugar Daddies and selected the easiest sucker to manipulate first, Don Carson. After sending him multiple texts without receiving any responses, she decided to call him. He didn't answer. Frustrated and consumed with scoring cash, she drove by his house. She'd been there several times in the past, doing that special thing he liked, but that was a long time ago. Although their last meeting ended with an argument, she knew that Carson was no cream puff. He knew the rules and understood how the 'pay to play' game worked.

She pulled up to his house and parked behind his car.

So you're going to ignore me, asshole? You better not have another bitch in there.

She walked to the front door while dialing his phone and leaned over the railing to peek through his blinds. She heard a faint ringtone from inside and rang the doorbell, but no answer.

She banged on the door and poked at the doorbell button relentlessly. "I know you're in there, Don! I don't have all day! Open up the goddamn door!"

Still, no answer. Irate and reckless, she turned the doorknob and opened the door.

Instantly, she was forced backward by the stink of rotting flesh. She covered her nose, gagging.

Oh my God. Don?

She knew that smell, and now, it all made sense. Against her will but powered by the compulsion of female curiosity, she crept inside. She held her breath, moving through the foyer and into the living room, where she saw his legs protruding from behind the couch. Tears fell as she leaned over the couch and saw him on the floor, naked, swollen, and dead. His tight grey skin appeared on the verge of bursting open from the internal pressure.

She ran out of the house, wailing, and called 911.

"Oh, Donnie!"

All her bad memories from their past were washed away in a moment. The authenticity of death reminded her of life's fragility. The first police cruiser arrived within fifteen minutes, but it felt like hours. Charlene had no idea that the putrid smell lingering inside her nostrils would remain in her mind, and memory, for years to follow.

***

Olson and Schultz sat at their desks, trading stories about their past military exploits when Detective Songetay walked over to share the news about Don Carson.

"They assigned the case to Phil and me, but out of respect, we both thought that you should get it. You make the call, Roger," Songetay said.

Olson dropped his head. The morbid news's impact was apparent to all those watching, but especially Schultz, who was amazed by his partner's emotional reaction.

He had feelings for the guy? I don't get it.

Schultz stood and leaned over his desk. "Hey, partner. I'm sorry for the bad news. Make the call. I'm with you, man."

Olson wiped his eyes and stood up, buttoning his coat. "Thanks, Alex. Let's go."

They arrived on the scene, and after reviewing Charlene's initial interview, they questioned her again before she left. Both detectives donned their respirators and inspected inside. Olson viewed the body for a moment before being overcome with emotion and returning to his car. Schultz watched him and finally understood his pain, having witnessed his own fallen comrades' corpses in Afghanistan. He was intimate with that type of pain and knew how it penetrated the heart and mind. He continued his exploration, taking notes, and photographs, while carefully manipulating the corpse to check for wounds and injuries.

Twenty minutes later, he walked outside, peeled off his respirator, and met with Olson.

"This is what I see, Rog. He has been dead for at least a couple of days. The front door was closed but unlocked—no signs of forced entry. There are no signs of struggle, no indications of defensive wounds, no signs of strangulation. Nothing in the house appears disturbed, and there's at least $150 lying on the table beside him so that rules out a robbery. I guess that he had an aneurism, heart attack, or stroke. I looked in his bathrooms. He took many meds, some for his heart, blood pressure, and others I'm not sure about. It appears that he was drinking alcohol when it occurred."

Olson was glass-eyed and visibly shaken but calm. "Yeah. That sounds like him. He was a hard charger." He exhaled. "Everything looks clean. Let's get the toxicology and autopsy initiated and wrap it up."

"I'll take care of it. But there is one unclear issue. I'm not sure how it fits, but he wasn't alone."

"Why do you think that?" Olson asked.

"There's a half glass of alcohol and also a full bottle of beer sitting on the coffee table next to him."

Olson glared. "So what? The man was an alcoholic. Maybe he intended to use the beer to chase the liquor. Or maybe he was going to drink the beer, but he keeled over first."

Schultz folded his arms. "You would know better than me, but Carson didn't strike me as the type of man who needed a chaser. I could be wrong. I'm only sharing my thoughts."

"I don't think it means shit. He wasn't robbed or assaulted. We'll wait on forensics before jumping to any conclusions. There are no signs of homicide, so document the findings accordingly."

"Gotcha, will do," Schultz sighed. "Other than that, there's nothing else of interest. A few external hard disks are on his desk, and one has a data cable connected. He has a pile of past-due bills on his bedroom dresser. He was taking Viagra, and..."

Olson grabbed Schultz's shoulder. "Hard drives?"

"Yes."

"Have I taught you how to clone those?"

"No, but I already know how. It's child's play."

Olson pointed. "Good. I need you to take them with you, clone them at your place tonight, and bring them back here tomorrow."

Schultz's eyebrows raised. "You've got to be kidding. I can't do that. If you want to process them, fine, but I'm not going to violate the procedure. It makes no sense."

Olson turned red. "I'm not asking you, Alex; I'm telling you to do it. And don't give me any of that honor and ethics bullshit. None of that data can be used in court, but I still want to sift through it. It may hold information that we can use in the future. Anything could be on those drives about ongoing cases or new ones. Look at it as information sharing with a former colleague. You want to play a bigger part, right? Then do it."

Olson got inside and started the car, staring at Schultz.

It was Detective Schultz's moment of truth. To be entangled in procedural violations was something that he wanted to avoid at all costs, but his experience as a military intelligence officer contradicted his hypocritical ideology. He had bent the rules before egregiously. However, that was during the war and not in the civilian sector. He recalled James Lyly's quote, 'All is fair in love, and war,' struggling to justify Olson's demand, but that idiom didn't apply either. He watched his partner drive off and shuffled back inside against his better judgment.

***

That same night, Madison exited the interstate on Seattle's outskirts, fifteen minutes from home. The long crossing was exhausting but eventful, bringing revelation and a new resolve to her troubled mind. As she passed the familiar towns and landmarks along I-94, surreal memories of Elijah resurfaced, convincing her that his spirit was present. She reached I-90 by the end of the first night and rented a room in Billings, Montana, from the same motel where she, and Elijah, previously stayed. After learning that the same room was already occupied, she was disappointed but managed to book a room only a few doors down. That night, she awoke from a deep sleep, shedding guilt-ridden tears, painfully aware of her homicidal acts, and made a vow.

God, you made me. I am what I am. I'm sorry for what I've done, and I swear to you, I promise, to never kill again. Please, protect me. Please, help me. Save me from others. Save me from me.

It was a vow that she intended to keep. The next day, after exiting the interstate in Idaho, she parked at Higgens Point, overlooking the lake. The midday sun shimmered against the calm water as she left the car carrying her laptop and climbed a trail leading to higher ground. She stopped along a ridge overlooking the clear water below and launched the computer from the edge.

Splash!

The vanilla extract jar followed behind.

Splash!

As both sank to the muddy bottom, out of sight and mind, she imagined that her murderous deeds, and haunting memories, would follow. She adopted a new mindset of personal convictions and continued her quest in the hope of a new beginning.

She arrived before 10:00 p.m. and parked in the driveway behind Elizabeth's car. The house looked the same as the day when she and Elijah first departed. She remembered leaving that day and vowing never to return, elated to be released from Elizabeth's control.

I can't believe that I'm back home.

The front porch lights brightened the path as she strode to the door and rang the bell. Elizabeth opened.

Madison smiled. "Hello."

"Good evening. I see that you made it intact. Late, but intact," she scolded, walking inside and into the kitchen. Madison closed the door and followed behind, absorbing the house's recognizable scent while childhood memories swirled within her mind.

Elizabeth stood in front of the kitchen sink, rinsing the utensils used during supper. "You're hungry. Find something in the refrigerator to eat, and don't forget to clean up your mess."

"Yes, mother. Thank you."

Elizabeth sat at the kitchen table, next to the wall, and she dried her hands. "Sit down. We need to have a discussion."

Madison sat across from her, with her suitcase in her lap.

"We need to revisit the house rules, which should need no clarification, only compliance.

Madison nodded.

"I've made up a list of daily chores for you. There's nothing new. You've been doing them all your life, but in case you forgot what they were, I've written them down."

She handed the list to Madison. "Number one, curfew. The time is the same as when you were in college, or rather, after your nervous breakdown during college. You are to be inside the house, no later than 10:00 p.m."

Madison squinted. "Ten o'clock, mother? I'm 28 years old. Is that necessary?"

"Absolutely. You can come, and go as you please, when at your own home. But in this house, you will follow my rules. There's no exception, and I won't accept any excuses. Is that understood?"

"Yes, mother."

"Good. There will be no eating in your bedroom. You are to eat in the kitchen. Lastly, I shouldn't have to repeat this, but there is to be no loud music. If I can hear it, then it's too loud."

"Yes, mother, I understand. There won't be any problems."

Within one minute, Madison's newly regained self-esteem was reduced to her former preadolescent levels. It wasn't because of the rules, specifically. It was the demeaning and condescending method in which they were communicated.

She'll never change. Never, Madison thought.

"Your room is clean. The linens have been washed. Nothing else has been touched," she said and retired to her bedroom.

Madison sat for a moment, breathing slowly to calm her nerves and wondering if the police had discovered Don Carson's body. She was afraid to check the obituaries online, choosing to ignore the entire matter entirely. Denial always offered her a reprieve, and together with her solemn vow, it preserved her solace of optimism. She walked toward her bedroom, took the shortcut through the living room, and passed her father's recliner. She stopped and stared as her ominous childhood emotions bubbled to the surface.

Why did you have to leave us, Daddy? Why couldn't you stay? I need you more than ever.

Snapping out of her trance-like state, she went to her bedroom and turned on the light. The scene matched perfectly with her mental snapshot. The good and the bad memories were extensive and exhaustive. Although she promised never to return, she was relieved to be standing there. She plopped on the mattress, spreading her limbs as if making snow angels. The quiet reassurance of her square refuge had been sorely missed. Not even Elizabeth could denigrate that feeling of safety or take it away, even though she had tried to in the past.

At 8:00 a.m. the following day, Madison woke up in a daze, but ironically, felt refreshed. The time zone change took effect, but she shook off the mental fatigue and brain fog while soaking in the shower. After getting dressed, she went into the kitchen and found a note on the table from Elizabeth.

"Madison, I'm running errands. I'll be back in a few hours. Have your chores done before I return home." Signed, "Mother."

She crumpled up the note and threw it in the trash before making herself breakfast.

While eating, she looked around the kitchen, noticing that nothing had changed. The same drab blue window curtains, and dusty valance above, had been there since she was eighteen years old, along with the worn navy blue floormat in front of the sink. Nothing in the house appeared different.

Madison finished eating, washed her hands, and planned her day.

I might as well get these stupid chores done.

She opened the cabinet doors beneath the sink and looked for the bucket. It was there. The same bucket that she had used since junior high to clean the house. Inside were rubber gloves, glass cleaner, toilet bowl cleaner, paper towels, and sponges. She held it up and spun it around until she saw her name, sloppily scribbled 15 years prior with a magic marker, done during another humiliating episode and at Elizabeth's behest.

Madison's Cleaning Bucket.

The unpleasant memory didn't affect Madison anymore. It was merely a reminder.

She began cleaning her assigned areas, starting with the two bathrooms first, before moving into Elizabeth's office study, combination makeshift laboratory. It was always cleaner than the rest of the house, and today was no exception, as Madison began sponging dust from the marble countertops. She cleaned, covering every area thoroughly, knowing that Elizabeth would perform a post-cleaning inspection. But Madison soon became distracted.

She focused on the numerous books shelved behind Elizabeth's desk and remembered how interesting they had been to her during adolescence. The questions asked to her mother while reading from them were the only non-criticizing discussions between the two. After finishing with her desk, Madison stepped from the carpet onto the room's tiled section and began wiping down the small sink and stainless steel countertops. She carefully dusted five medium-sized glass beakers before looking around to check her progress.

That's all, folks.

She checked the time.

Forty-five minutes? That's not bad.

She stretched her arms wide and arched, loosening the tightness in her lower back, and her eyes fixated on the glass-paned cabinet doors before her.

"Dang it. How could you forget these?" she huffed, and sprayed the glass, then wiped them. Within a few minutes, she was done, checking her reflection in each to make sure. She stopped at the seventh door and peered through the glass at the jars behind. The lettering of the two chemicals kept her attention, as well as their placement. They were Hydroxy-Methaburate and Tricozomine.

Three parts to one. Three parts to one.

The reflexive thought about the recipe snuck through her mental defenses unopposed, and the sight of the familiar jars repulsed her. She scampered toward the guest bathroom and dropped to her knees to vomit. She waited for it, blowing and bracing herself. After a minute, her nausea subsided. She hobbled to the sink, splashed cold water on her face, and looked into the mirror.

Forget about it. It's never going to happen again. It didn't happen anyway. No. You didn't do anything. You're innocent, Maddy! You need to leave the house for a while.

She grabbed her keys and purse, then left. Her destination, unknown.

***

Five days had passed since Don Carson's body was discovered. The autopsy and toxicology reports had been uploaded, and Schultz sat on his couch with his laptop, checking the online department database. It was almost midnight when he found them.

Don Vincent Carson. Death by Natural Causes: Cardiac Arrest.

There were contributing factors noted in the toxicology findings, such as Viagra and excessive alcohol intoxication, but these substances were considered ancillary to Carson's overall poor state of general health. His prescribed medication regime substantiated that fact, and his unseen decadent lifestyle confirmed the same. There were two unknown substances found in his blood, but they were dismissed as non-relevant and not requiring further testing for specific identification. Case closed.

Schultz inclined forward, and sipped his beer, then connected one of the three cloned hard disks to his laptop and searched. The data files were a mess and not categorized or appropriately labeled. They appeared to reflect Carson's life. Schultz probed through dozens of videos mixed with client interviews but became inundated with Carson's deluge of pornographic videos and was disturbed.

I didn't sign up for this bullshit.

He decided to view the files by date and ultimately uncovered Madison and Conor's client interview. With his interest peaked, he relaxed and began watching it and watching her. He was captivated by her persona, the way she spoke, and the way she moved. It surprised him, and he replayed the interview several times. It was Schultz's first time viewing Madison's normal demeanor under ordinary circumstances. Although he had prior contact interviewing her, they weren't a fair representation of her true personality.

She'd make a good girlfriend. Possibly a good wife. She's feisty, loyal, and passionate about what she says. She seems sincere—what a damn beauty.

He thought about the last interview and her lack of emotion. He wanted to dismiss the notion, but his gut held the hunch close for safekeeping. He checked the time, and yawned, needing to sleep, and paused the video. It was Conor. Schultz noticed him throughout the interview and detected several visual inconsistencies in his mannerisms and comments that screamed of deception and guilt.

Mr. Gregory, you were into some shit. I'm not sure what kind shit. But it had to stink.

He shut down his computer and went to bed.

CHAPTER 16

Early afternoon the next day, Madison left the dreariness of the house behind and ventured out into the city again. With her anxiety held at bay, her mind clear and stable, she knew that it was time to leave Seattle. After calculating her much cash she had left, she realized there wasn't enough money for gas to return to Minneapolis. So the subject of a loan would have to be discussed with Elizabeth.

Madison dreaded the exchange to come but knew that her mother would comply. It was the conversation accompanying the loan which bothered her.

Maybe I can catch her in a decent mood. She's socializing outside the house more than ever these days. That's unusual for her, but it could be good for me.

Elizabeth had left the house twice in the early evening during Madison's four-day stay, returning near midnight. Her reasons were always the same: she was meeting former colleagues for supper. But Madison knew better, and Elizabeth's makeup and clothing only confirmed her suspicions.

She's not fooling anyone, all dressed up, with her hair done and wearing perfume. There must be a man in her life. She's hiding him from me. I know it.

Madison remembered snooping on Elizabeth's unattended computer while home from college and discovering a secret email account. She read Elizabeth's correspondence with several men and gasped at her mother's guarantee of sexual satisfaction. Madison resented the hypocrisy of it all.

Maybe that wasn't only a brief period of loneliness in her life. Perhaps she truly is promiscuous after all. But is she getting freaky with strangers? Ugh!

She shook off the untasteful thoughts. After all, Elizabeth was still her mother.

Madison had been driving around each day, exploring the city where she grew up while avoiding those areas attached to sad memories. But she was becoming bored with the excursions and was beginning to daydream as she cruised the busy streets.

The car's low fuel bell chimed, and she pulled over to a small gas station on the other side of town. It looked familiar like she had been there before. It was grimy, run-down, and peppered with loose trash dancing in the wind while indigents meandered around the front. She stepped out and marched to the entrance, ignoring the requests for loose change from the non-patrons lined up against the storefront.

As she opened the door, a foul stench overwhelmed her. She held her breath while paying for gas and a bottle of orange juice, then burst through the front doors and hustled to her car, gulping fresh air.

"Excuse me, Miss."

She heard a man's voice behind her but ignored him. The little money she had left wasn't to be shared.

"Excuse me. Hey, wait for a second!"

The voice was closer, and she walked faster.

"Madison? Madison!"

She stopped. She recognized the voice. Only one man pronounced her name that way. She turned. It was Tony. Her first love stood there, no longer fit and vibrant, but skinny, unshaven, and filthy. Nearly unrecognizable to her, Madison could not speak or react as a storm of emotions overwhelmed her heart. He walked over to her, smiling, and opened his arms, exposing his partially missing and rotten teeth.

"Damn, girl, where have you been? I haven't seen you for a few years. But you're still fine as wine!"

She was paralyzed. The horde of jumbled feelings bottled up inside her was sealed tight, with nowhere to go and no place to vent. She became lightheaded, weak, and thought that another seizure was imminent.

He noticed her reaction. "What's wrong, Maddy?"

She burst into tears and covered her face as she went for the car door handle.

"Wait, hold up, don't go. It's been a long time, girl. Don't do me like that," he pleaded.

She stopped, wiped her eyes, trying to find the courage to turn around. Finally, reluctantly she did.

"Tony." She began to cry but quickly squashed the impulse and wiped her eyes. "I don't know what to speak to you. I don't. I haven't seen you in almost seven years, and then you pop up out of thin air."

She grabbed a tissue from her purse and blew her nose.

"Yeah, I'm sorry about that, but a lot of shit happened to me." He searched his baked brain for any information to recall. "When we were messing around back then, I had to visit my cousin in California to help him out with something. I ended up getting locked up out there. They gave me a year for some shit that I didn't even do. When I got out, I came back here looking for you. I remember that you told me to never show up at your house because of your mama, so I think I tried calling you. Yeah, I did, but your cell phone was disconnected. I figured that you had moved on. You were gone. But we found each other again! Damn baby, give me a hug or something."

He lurched forward and wrapped his arms around her. She wanted to push him away but couldn't. She felt powerless to express her rage and escape from his hold and putrid odor.

He released her and stepped back. His excuses made sense to her. They fit the timeline of events, and she recalled that Elizabeth had disconnected her cell phone service during the mental breakdown.

Madison stared at him, searching his droopy eyes for authenticity. "Tony, I told you that I was pregnant. I had a baby. A boy. His name was Elijah. He died over a year ago."

He tilted his head and frowned. "Oh shit, for real?" He scratched his ashy scalp. "I thought that you were getting rid of it. Damn, I'm sorry to hear that. What happened to him?"

"Someone killed him."

His eyes widened. "That's messed up. Did they go to jail?"

"No, the man who did it is dead. Someone killed him, too."

"Cool." His grinning expression returned. "I need a favor. Do you have a few dollars that you could loan me? I'm having a hard time out here in these streets. Please, for old times' sake?"

Cool? Is that all you have to say? Cool! And you want money?

"Where do you live?" she asked.

"I ain't got nowhere to stay right now. I can't pay rent. I do have a couple of job interviews coming up soon. Why? Can I live with you?"

She rolled her eyes, reached into her purse, and handed him a five-dollar bill. "I don't know, Tony. We'll have to talk about that later. Take this for now. Do you have a cell phone?"

He patted his pockets. "Hell no. I just told you that I'm broke as a joke. I can't afford any shit like that.

"Okay, I get it. Do you remember back in the days, we used to go to the Aqua Theater, and after, make out at our favorite spot on Green Lake?"

He thought for a moment. "Oh yeah, I remember that! I gave you some good loving back in the woods."

"Listen. I'm staying with my mother right now, and she still hates your guts, so you can't come to the house. I'm low on money, too, and can't afford to rent you a motel room, or I would. But my mother is about to loan me money, and I'll use some of that to help you get back on your feet. Okay?"

His cracked lips parted, and he smiled, bouncing in place at the good news. "Hell yeah, that's what I'm talking about."

"I want you to meet me at eleven o'clock tonight, at our old spot. I'll bring you more money, and some food. We can lay out behind the trees and talk and get to know each other again. We can try to work things out. It's going to take time, Tony. Can you do that? Will you do that?"

He grimaced and then pouted. "Why can't you pick me up here? It's gonna be a long-ass walk to get out there."

"I can't take the chance of my mother seeing us together. She was out late last night, but hopefully, she will stay home today. That's why I picked tonight to meet. Are you coming, or not? I want you to be there. You owe me that."

"You're damn skippy. I'll be there; just don't forget the money."

He hugged her again and then went in for a kiss, but she dodged and pushed away from him. "I'll bring a toothbrush and toothpaste tonight. I can't let you kiss me when you're like this. I'm sorry. Don't be mad."

She ducked inside her car and let the window down. He was stunned, and his ignorant pride was injured.

Don't kiss me then, bitch! Just give me them goddamn dollars.

He smirked. "Nah, that's cool. I'm good with that. I'll be there at eleven. You better not be bullshitting me. Don't stand me up, girl."

"I promise that I won't. I have to get back home, but I'll see you tonight at eleven. Bye."

She started the car and left, watching him in her rearview mirror, hurrying through the front doors of the station. Cold chills crept down the back of her neck, and she shivered.

I can't believe that he's alive. He's back. Tony is back.

She drove home, clutching the steering wheel while planning her subsequent movements carefully.

***

It was 5:15 when Madison walked inside the house. Elizabeth passed her on the way to the door, holding her handbag and a shopping list.

"It's about time that you came home. I wanted to talk to you before going to the grocery store. You did a terrible job cleaning my study. It's horrendous. Redo it," she ordered.

"Yes, mother. I'm sorry."

Elizabeth glared momentarily, as always, measuring Madison's sincerity of repentance. "I'll be back within the hour."

"Mother, I need to ask a favor of you. I wish I didn't have to do this. Would you loan me some money? I don't have enough to make it back to Minnesota, and I know you're ready for me to leave. I don't need much. $400 would be more than enough. I promise to pay you back by the end of next month. I need to get back to work."

Elizabeth wasn't surprised, having anticipated the request.

"We can talk about this later. I'll give you some money to purchase your hygiene products." She reached inside her handbag and handed over $40. "You need to consider staying home and looking for employment locally. Think about that over the next few days, then we'll revisit the subject."

She brushed past Madison and out the front door.

"Wait, please! I have to get back home."

"This is your home," Elizabeth responded and shut the door.

Madison stormed into the kitchen, gulped her orange juice, and snatched the cleaning bucket from beneath the sink. She snapped on her rubber gloves, mumbling profanities, and went to the study. Her newly formed plan to secure a loan, take care of Tony and then leave straightaway back to Minnesota tonight was unraveling. Her plan was desperate, but she had to escape from her mother's overbearing control.

She's trying to cage you again. Don't let her do it! You promised yourself! She has controlled you for your entire life, and you continue to let her do it. Silly girl.

She forced back tears as she sponged down the counter and began cleaning the glass, becoming hypnotized by its reflection. She saw herself and then the chemicals that waited beyond.

She's stood in your way for far too long. Stick with the plan. Silly girl.

***

At 10:00 p.m., the countdown timer for the house alarm chimed throughout the house, preparing to arm itself for the night. Madison lay on her bed, wearing shorts and a t-shirt, waiting patiently. She refused to eat supper with Elizabeth, feigning stomach cramps instead, but her mother knew better. Elizabeth hadn't gone out tonight, which allowed Madison to salvage a portion of her scheme and meet with Tony. She was eager as the seconds ticked closer towards the surreal rendezvous.

Please be there, Tony. I have to see you. I won't let you leave me again. I wouldn't be able to live with myself if I did.

At 10:25 p.m., she put on her shoes and grabbed her purse before quietly sneaking out of her bedroom window. Reminiscent of her high school years, it wasn't her first time, and she was careful not to make a peep. She didn't worry about waking Elizabeth, a sound sleeper by nature, and within a minute, she was inside her car, backing out of the driveway.

On the way to Green Lake, she stopped at the Kuzo Burger drive-thru, one of Tony's favorite fast-food restaurants. She remembered what he liked, ordering a double cheeseburger with no pickles and a Dr. Pepper before driving away.

By 11:05 p.m., she arrived in the area, then detoured off the asphalt and onto a dirt road leading through a forest of trees. The scenery appeared vaguely familiar, but the vegetation had grown exponentially, causing her to doubt her memory. Just then, Tony appeared to the right, from behind the trees. She parked as he trotted to the passenger's side door and tried to open it.

"Unlock the door," he snapped, his mood irritable.

She pocketed her keys and stepped out, holding the bag and soda and bumping the door closed with her hip.

"Hello to you, too, Tony. Let's go right to the spot and lay back on the tree. Don't you remember? I'm tired of being couped up. I want to be outside in the fresh air."

They walked through a small opening in the brush, near the water, where a large White Elm stood alone, slightly leaning toward the water.

He grabbed the paper bag and looked inside. "Damn, girl. Is that all the food you brought? I'm hungry as hell."

"I made a special trip to Kuzco Burger for you. It remembered your favorite. A double cheeseburger without pickles and a Dr. Pepper."

He unwrapped it, tossed his trash on the ground, and took a bite.

"You should have gotten two," he mumbled with a full mouth and took the soda from her. "Where's the cash?" He sipped and burped.

"Be patient. The money isn't going to disappear. There's no rush."

They walked around the massive tree and sat reclining against it. The half-moon showed dimly in the sky, covered by a thin sheen of clouds, and reflected hazily against the calm liquid swells. She sighed and smiled, gazing into the distance.

He burped again. "Yeah, you're right. Hey, what about that toothbrush?"

"Oops. I forgot about that. Sorry."

He swallowed that last corner of his burger and sucked the cup dry, belching again.

"Sure, you forgot. Then don't talk shit when I kiss you and get my desert."

He grinned and palmed the back of her head, tossing the cup aside.

She knocked his hand away. "No. Stop."

"Bitch! Don't ever push back on me," he barked. "I'm tired of these games. Give me the goddamn money so that I can go."

She broke her skyward gaze. "Please wait. I promise to give you what you need."

He gripped her arm and dug his hand into the front pocket of her shorts. She grabbed his skinny wrist and hopped to her feet, glaring down at him.

He began to raise himself, chuckling, until his nostrils flared. "Bitch, now I'm gonna have to beat your ass."

Madison tensed herself and stepped backward, preparing to dart back to the car. As he stood, he wiggled his head and reached back for support. He staggered backward against the Elm, his legs losing strength by the second, and dropped down to his buttocks.

"What the hell?" he panted, grabbing his chest. "Get me to the car! I'm sick. Take me to the hospital."

Madison appeared to glow as the moonlight contrasted the dark waters against her milky white skin. "You're out of shape, Tony. You should take better care of yourself. Stop eating so much fast food. It's not good for you."

He tried pushing himself up off the ground, but his arms went limp, and his legs were unresponsive as he struggled to breathe.

Madison began undressing. "You need to wake up. The cold water will make you feel better." She giggled. "And clean you up. I'll get in with you."

Completely naked, she grabbed his ankles and pulled him toward the lake's edge.

"No. I'll kill you...You crazy bitch. Stop...," he mumbled, helplessly, desperately.

Madison huffed, straining to bring him closer to the edge, not anticipating the physical effort required, but remaining determined.

When her foot struck the cold surface, she exhaled and tugged him off the solid ground until he was floating on his back in waist-deep water. She grabbed the front of his shirt and his waistband, then looked around for witnesses. He coughed and gagged, helpless to keep his head above water. After Madison felt reassured of her privacy, she pulled him closer until their eyes met.

"You shouldn't have deserted us, Tony. Your son needed you. I needed you. Everything that happened to us is your fault! To make things right between us, you need to give me something—your life. You owe Elijah and me. Goodbye."

She held tight and pushed him downward, silencing his gurgles and submerging him. She delighted in the moment and his twitching. Minutes after his hypoxic convulsions ended, she continued holding him there while gazing at the moon.

The experience was cut short as she heard faint sounds of music from across the lake. She left him floating beneath the surface, submerged, and trudged back onshore. Dripping wet, she dressed. Consciously aware that she was tingling from excitement, she wondered why it was so much easier this time. She didn't know the answer but knew that she felt amazing, and that was enough. She walked back to the car while picking up the trash that he had left behind. She planned to discard it during her ride home, along with an empty orange juice bottle that held the mixture. Momentarily oblivious of her broken vow not to kill and filled with adrenaline, she made light of the tragedy, noting her twisted contribution to society.

You did a good thing, Maddy. There's one less litterbug in the world.

***

It was 12:05 a.m. when she returned home, creeping along the side of the house to her window. She slowly raised the window, climbed on top of the garden hose reel sitting below, and eased her body inside the darkroom. She turned and quietly lowered it.

"Welcome home, Madison."

She screamed instinctively, and the lamp turned on.

Elizabeth was sitting on a chair, blocking the door. "Sit down. I have questions."

"I'm sorry, mother. I can explain..."

"Sit down!" Elizabeth roared and leaped out of the chair, pointing her finger. "Right now!"

Madison rushed over to the bed and sat, staring at the floor. Elizabeth towered above her, breathing heavily and incensed. Madison's childhood instincts controlled her body with immobilizing fear.

"I've been calling your phone, but you haven't answered. It's my time to talk. Don't speak unless spoken to. Do you understand me?"

Madison quivered. "Yes, mother."

"After you re-cleaned my study today, I inspected it. It was cleaned properly, as it should have been done the first time. But I noticed something odd. The chemicals inside of the cabinet appeared to have been disturbed. To be certain, I measured each jar's levels and vial, then compared them with my records and inventory logs. The volumes matched precisely for all the chemicals, except two. The Hydroxy-Methaburate and Tricozomine were both low, and strangely enough, their levels had been decreased by a ratio of three to one." She brought her hands to her hips. "I remembered that particular formula. It's the recipe that I developed to euthanize the animals years ago. That's when I thought about you."

"Mother, I can explain, I..."

A flash of light, and a sharp pain, was all that Madison could remember as Elizabeth's hand returned to her side. Madison held the side of her face as it throbbed.

Elizabeth leaned close. Her graceful features were now appearing beastlike. "Shut your mouth!" Her dark eyes appeared as black marbles under the shadow of her brow ridge.

"Why did you steal my chemicals?"

Madison frantically thought of a lie. "It's not what you think, I..."

Elizabeth slapped her again, more brutal, knocking her flat on the bed.

"Please, stop! No more! Don't hit me! Please!"

She grabbed Madison's shirt, pulling her upright with one hand and raising the other. "Tell me the truth!" Madison covered her face, bawling, while Elizabeth shook her. "Tell me! Or I swear, I'll..."

Madison surrendered. "I killed Tony! That's why I did it! I saw him today for the first time in years, lured him to Green Lake, and killed him! Just like you killed the animals!"

Elizabeth released her and stepped back, clasping her hands in shock, while Madison shielded her beet-red, puffy face. She couldn't contain her guarded secrets any longer and launched a cascade of confessions.

"I killed Conor, too. He didn't drown on his own. I gave it to him, just like Tony. Mother, he killed Elijah! I couldn't stop myself! I had to do it! So, call the police. I'm ready! I don't care!" Within moments, Madison's shouts of rage deteriorated into beleaguered whimpering of submission. "Mother. I can't hide what's inside anymore. It's too hard. I need to be put away."

Madison sobbed, and Elizabeth gently placed her hands on Madison's head. Madison flinched in fear but became bewildered when witnessing Elizabeth's eyes filled with tears for the very first time. Madison became transfixed and stiffened as Elizabeth kissed her forehead.

Elizabeth beamed with pride. "Don't cry. Shh. You're not going anywhere. Madison, I couldn't be any prouder of you."

Madison's mouth went agape.

This isn't happening. You're hallucinating again.

She froze, warily peeking out of the corner of her eye.

Elizabeth sat beside her, grinning like a shy adolescent girl. "I never saw the signs in you as you grew up. Yes, at times you were unruly, but that's to be expected during the teen years. But you hold something extraordinary inside. Your Aunt Emily had it, and of course, I have it, too."

Madison found the nerve to speak. "Mother, I'm baffled. What are you talking about? What are you saying?"

"Your Aunt Emily called it, 'The Purpose.' She first shared our family's history with me when I was a young girl in high school. She saw the signs in me and helped me to understand. She became my guide. But it's my fault for not recognizing that same gift inside of you. I accept complete responsibility."

Madison's eyes darted around the room as the voices inside her mind split asunder, becoming distinct entities. The missing piece to Madison Sanders's puzzle was found, completing the picture of her life. She now knew that the divergent identity was not newly born. It was merely revealed and vigorously declaring it's right to exist.

This cannot be happening. It can't be. No!

But it is happening. You know that everything is true. Stop fighting. You're home. Doesn't it all make sense now?

Madison was afraid to look at her, but she needed more answers. "Have you done the same thing? Killed someone?"

Elizabeth laughed. "Yes, of course. My first was in high school. My second and third were during college. The rest?" She smirked, "That's a discussion for another day." Elizabeth patted her back. "Go to sleep and get some rest. You've had a long night. We'll finish talking about this tomorrow." She leaned close. "We have our entire lives to talk about it. That's even more of a reason for you to stay here, with me. You need stability and guidance. I can assure you, from now on, our relationship will be much fuller, closer, and intimate." She smiled. "As it should have always been."

At that moment, Madison yearned for her father's presence, unlike any time before.

Elizabeth stood and moved the chair away from the door when she heard Madison's cries from behind.

Madison looked up with tears streaming. "Daddy. I wish you were here. I'm sorry. Don't hate me for what I did. I love you."

Elizabeth stood in the doorway, returning to her frigid demeanor. "Your father wasn't the man that you remember as a child. You don't know what he did. He broke his vows to me and before God."

Madison shook her head.

No, no, don't tell me!

"It's time for you to know what happened to him. I chose him, and he served 'The Purpose.' Goodnight."

The door closed, and Madison released a deep, primordial moan of pain heard throughout the house. Elizabeth casually strolled into her room, closed the door, and got into bed. She couldn't sleep. The excitement of the night and her plans for Madison would keep her awake for hours, but she didn't mind.

She was unaware during that moment that Madison was having a seizure, a bi-product of her inability to escape the madness which was now her life. Regardless, Elizabeth was filled with gratitude to regain control over her prodigal daughter once again. She offered sincere recognition to the source of her psychopathy. 'The Purpose.'

CHAPTER 17

The following morning, Elizabeth stood at the kitchen counter, washing potatoes and sipping her coffee, while basking in the bright rays of the morning sun through the window. The window faced East, allowing the kitchen to become fully illuminated until noon. The natural luminance of the kitchen was a sharp contrast to the rest of the dimly lit house. Madison wandered in, wearing a t-shirt and wrinkled shorts. She sat at the kitchen table, squinting and shielding her eyes.

Elizabeth glanced. "Good morning." She looked at the clock. "You should feel refreshed after sleeping most of the morning away."

Madison leaned against the wall, occupied with her phone. "Good morning."

"I've made coffee and have already eaten breakfast. You'll have to fend for yourself," she said while placing the potatoes onto a cutting board.

"Yes, mother. I'm not hungry. I feel sick."

Elizabeth looked. "I agree. You don't look well. I need you to do something for me. Peel these potatoes while I cut them. I'm making potato salad for dinner."

Madison sighed, leaned her phone on the table napkin holder, and moped over to the counter. Elizabeth handed her the potato peeler, and they began. The scene was reminiscent of past years when they cooked together in silence. But this time, the silence was not only uncomfortable, but it was also intolerable, and Madison could not keep quiet.

"Mother, I have to tell you something. You were honest with me last night, and I want to be honest with you."

Elizabeth glanced over at her but continued cutting. "Confession is good for your soul. By all means, do tell."

Madison continued peeling, rinsing, and placing the potatoes next to the cutting board. "When I was in college, I snooped a lot. Once, when you left the house, I looked on your computer and read your emails. You called yourself Lauren and used a fake email address. I knew that you were dating a lot of men, but that…"

Elizabeth turned and pointed the knife at Madison. "You had no right to do that! No right!"

Madison backed away. "I know, I know! I should have never done that. I'm sorry!"

Elizabeth glared, still pointed the knife and huffing. A few moments later, she calmly returned to cutting, as if nothing were ever mentioned. Madison eased beside her without saying a word. The simmering pot of eggs on the stove began to boil. The bubbling resonances, interrupted by the thud of the butcher knife, became rhythmic and melodic.

Elizabeth continued to cut. "I never dated any of those men in the traditional sense. I am not a whore. Do you understand me?"

"Yes, mother, I know."

"I chose those men because they were all married, and each one was a whoremonger."

Madison handed her a potato. "How did they die?"

Elizabeth smirked, gloating. "Oh, by various means. Men are strong until they are disabled in some form or fashion. I prefer to use a particular sedative, although I've tried many other home recipes over the decades. Once incapacitated, I merely suffocate them with a plastic bag. The key is to gently seal the bag around their neck and be careful not to leave any marks. The autopsy finding will be non-specific. The chemical sedative will show up as an unknown substance but not warrant a test for specificity. That goes for white and black men, too."

"Black men?"

"There's no need to discriminate. Men are men, regardless of any other factor. They are all the same. You should have learned that by now."

"Yes, you're right about that. They are all the same. So, what did you do with the bodies?"

"Leave them where they lay or sat. It didn't matter. In the future, you must be very careful not to leave any evidence behind. Your presence must be untraceable. There are a lot of aspects to consider, and precise planning is required. From now on, you are to follow my instructions exactly to the letter."

Madison's stomach was in knots, fearful of broaching the subject of her father. "What happened to daddy? The last time that I saw him alive, he was wearing..."

"A Halloween mask?" Elizabeth cackled. "No, Madison. I'm the one who told you that. You were only six years old when I killed him.

He came home one night, drunk, smelling like a whore, so I knew that he had been with one. It had been going on for years, but I could never catch him in the act. I didn't need to anyway. I chose him, and when he asked me to make him a drink, I did and added something extra. Within a few minutes, he was in a deep sleep, unconscious, and that's when you walked out. You went up to him and called his name."

Madison finally remembered the full details of that fateful night.

"Why won't daddy answer me?"

"Madison! Go back to bed."

"Why does daddy have a plastic bag over his head?"

"That's not a plastic bag. It's a Halloween mask. Your father is sleeping. Now go back to bed before I give you a spanking!"

Tears fell from Madison's eyes as she peeled the potatoes. She held her breath to silence the sniffles.

Elizabeth peeked over. "It's been very irritating over the years to hear you ignorantly praise the man as if he were some kind of saint. Now that you know the truth, there shouldn't be any more mention of him."

The eggs had boiled long enough. Elizabeth put down the knife, washed her hands, and went to the stove to turn it off. She noticed something at the kitchen table. It was Madison's cell phone, leaning upright against the napkin holder.

"Madison."

"Yes?"

"There's a tiny white light shining from your phone. What's that for?"

Madison turned to look, then went back to peeling. "I must have turned on the flashlight."

Elizabeth looked closely, and her forehead wrinkled. "Have you been video recording our conversation?"

"No, mother. Why would I do that?"

Madison skinned faster but unsteadily as Elizabeth dissected her reaction and witnessed her quiver.

"Liar! Why would you do that to me? I'm your mother! After everything that I've done for you. Is this the way you thank me? You're nothing but an ingrate!"

Petrified, Madison glanced back just in time to see Elizabeth hurl the pot's scalding contents at her; she ducked it and slipped, catching the countertop edge. "Don't!"

Elizabeth flailed the empty pot at her, barely missing. "I'm going to kill you!" Elizabeth rushed over to the cutting board and grabbed the knife. Madison tried to run but slid and fell on her stomach. She rolled over on her back as Elizabeth came down with the blade, but she kicked at her feverishly, striking her once in the shin. It did not affect Elizabeth as she fought to break through Madison's defenses and targeted her chest, thrusting relentlessly.

Madison screamed in pain as the blade sliced her calf, and moments later, her thigh. Elizabeth saw a clear path to her heart and collapsed onto her, blade first. Madison jerked sideways, avoiding the thrust to her chest, and the knife cut through her t-shirt, drawing more blood. Madison grabbed the knife handle and her mother's wrist, and they struggled for control, rolling around the floor.

Elizabeth was near twice her size, and Madison's petite frame slowly buckled under her mother's weight. No words were uttered by either, only the animalistic grunts of survival. Their faces were inches apart during the frenzy, and Madison witnessed her mother's demonic expression for the first time and began to fade. She couldn't win this fight and knew that death was imminent. Nearly exhausted, with her eyes shut, Madison prepared herself for death. She didn't want to see it or her mother's deranged grin of satisfaction and began to withdraw.

Elijah? Mommy is coming to be with you now. I'll be with you forever!

She found a tranquil moment of peace and exhaled. Then she heard a small but familiar voice. It was Elijah.

No! Don't let her kill you, mommy! I don't want you to die! Fight! Fight for me!

Madison's eyes exploded open. Her strength, body, and mind, reinvigorated. She bit down on Elizabeth's hand holding the knife, disregarding Elizabeth's screams as the warm blood trickled into her mouth. Elizabeth dropped the knife and tried to push her away, but Madison bit down harder, causing her to squeal even louder before climbing on top of her chest.

Elizabeth clutched her bloody hand while Madison savagely pounded down on her forehead, unchallenged, until her wailing stopped. Madison wheezed and looked around the bloody kitchen, locating the knife on the floor. She staggered to her feet, stumbled over to pick it up, and set it on the counter. Elizabeth began moaning, and Madison looked at her cell phone. The camera light was on, and it was still recording, causing her to wonder how it wasn't knocked over during the violent brawl. She focused on Elizabeth.

I want you to feel what daddy felt.

Madison opened a drawer, took out a roll of plastic wrap, and stretched it out. "He didn't deserve to die. He didn't deserve to die!"

She dropped to her knees and began wrapping Elizabeth's entire head. When Elizabeth fully awoke and realized that she was being suffocated, Madison was on her third, fourth, fifth pass. Elizabeth clawed at the plastic around her mouth, but Madison grabbed both of her wrists and pinned them against the floor. As Elizabeth's head gyrated back and forth, her muffled screams sealed within as Madison loomed over her, gloating. Her appetite for revenge was insatiable.

Madison's weight on Elizabeth's chest, combined with the lack of oxygen, quickened her mother's leap into unconsciousness. The rising pulsations from her breaths were made visible by the plastic covering her mouth, and the movements slowed to a halt. Her mouth gradually opened wide, and her body remained motionless as Madison let go of her arms and sat upright. She touched the plastic that covered Elizabeth's mouth with her index finger, poked a hole through, and waited.

Madison looked down at her. "I might be like you, mother. But I'm my father's daughter, too."

There was silence. A few seconds later, Elizabeth inhaled violently, instinctively tearing at the small opening until her mouth and nose were exposed. Madison crawled to her feet, picked up the knife from off the counter, and limped toward the kitchen table. She picked up her phone and collapsed into the chair.

She stopped recording and eyed Elizabeth. "Mother, stay down. If you try to stand, I promise to bury this knife in your heart."

She dialed 911. The operator answered.

"Hello, my name is Madison Sanders. I need the police and an ambulance immediately. My mother just tried to kill me."

***

By 10:00 a.m., the house was swarming with law enforcement and medical personnel. Arriving on the scene were, Lead Detective Lopez, and Detective Harrison, from the Seattle Major Crimes Unit, Criminal Investigations Division. They exited the sedan and met the responding officers standing in the driveway. After exchanging handshakes, an officer handed Madison's cell phone to Lopez.

"This phone belongs to the victim, Madison Sanders. The video is self-explanatory from start to finish. The older, taller female is Elizabeth Sanders, and the other is her daughter, Madison, who recorded the assault and gave it to us when we arrived. It's assault with a deadly weapon, with the intent to kill, but it's what the mother said that caused us to ring the alarm. There's something big here. You need to check this out."

The four men crowded around Madison's phone as Lopez pressed play, and the five-minute-long video began. After it finished, the two detectives glanced at each other.

"Good job, guys. What's their status?" Harrison asked.

"They're both being receiving medical attention in the ambulances, each of them accompanied by two officers. We haven't read Elizabeth Sanders her rights yet, but they both need stitches at the hospital. The paramedics are itching to go, and everyone is waiting for you guys."

Lopez popped a handful of Skittles into his mouth and looked at Harrison. "I'll interview the daughter. You get the mom."

Harrison gave a thumbs up, and they separated. This was a change of pace for Lopez, having seen thousands of violent scenarios over his 25-year career, and he delighted in these unique allusions. He went over to the closest ambulance and looked inside.

"Hello, I'm Detective Lopez from the SPD, Major Crimes Unit, Criminal Investigation Division. How are you feeling?"

Madison sat on the edge of the gurney, probing her freshly wrapped thigh. "Hello. I'm okay, I guess. They said that I need stitches in my calf and thigh."

Lopez cleared his throat. "I would say you're very fortunate to be alive after that scuffle. I just watched the video recording that you made. You did make the recording, correct?"

"Yes."

"Are you aware that in the state of Washington, it is illegal to record a two-person conversation without permission or a declaration?"

"No. I had no idea."

"I can understand. But, what exactly led you to record that conversation or interaction? I'm curious."

Madison huffed. "My mother woke me up from sleep last night around midnight, ranting and raving like a maniac. I've only been back home visiting for a week, but she's acted out like this ever since I can remember. But it was different this time, and she got physical with me when I tried to calm her down. That's when she assaulted me. She punched me in the face three times, calling me a liar. But she finally left me alone. This morning I woke up and wanted to record how she treats me and show it to her later. That way, she could see her disturbing behavior firsthand. I started with a token of honesty and confessed to snooping on her computer years ago. As you saw, she flipped out, and that's when it all started. I couldn't believe the things that she was saying. Detective, my mother has serious mental health issues, but she refuses to take the necessary steps to seek treatment." She covered her face. "My God. I had no idea that was doing something illegal." She frowned at him. "Am I in trouble?"

He opened his notepad and began scribbling. "In this instance, I don't think so. The law that I mentioned does have a revision that allows recording without consent. You won't remember this, but it's the Revised Code of Washington 9.73.020. The revised code vindicates you because of the criminal statements that she made to you before the assault. Besides her unsubstantiated confessions, she told you to 'follow her instructions,' and it appeared as though she was eliciting you and or conspiring to commit future murders. What else can you tell me about the things she mentioned? If you have any prior knowledge, no matter how insignificant you believe it to be, please share it with me. Now is the time."

Madison dropped her head. "If she was telling the truth, then I can only suspect that the men whom she met on dating sites would be the people to call. My mom has been living a double life since my father died, and it's seriously creepy. You should look at her computer. It's over ten years old. There's probably tons of evidence on there."

He smirked while scribbling. "You should have been a detective." He looked up. "That's all for now. I'll find out which hospital they take you to and pick you up. If you don't mind, we want to properly interview you and get your official statement at the precinct. Okay?"

"Yes, sir."

He got his camera and walked through the house to the kitchen. There, he began taking photos. Harrison peeked inside the ambulance that transported Elizabeth. She was lying down on the gurney with her wrist wound bandaged.

"Hello, I'm Detective Harrison with the Seattle Police, Major Crimes Unit. Are you Elizabeth Sanders?"

Elizabeth raised her head. "Yes, I am."

He stepped into the back of the ambulance, holding his clipboard, and sat across from her.

"Ma'am. What exactly went on here this morning between you and your daughter?"

"My daughter is mentally unstable. Excuse my language, but she's crazy. She asked to visit me for a few days because she missed me, but she came for money in reality. She's broke. Last night, I caught her sneaking in the window to her room and confronted her. She went ballistic and got physical with me, crying about her son's father and saying that she killed him! His name is Tony Putnam. He's black. She said they were together at Green Lake. I would begin a search there."

She paused, waiting for his reaction.

"You would begin a search at Green Lake. Okay, I've noted that. Please continue."

"Thank you! She also confessed to killing her fiancé in Minnesota. She even told me how she did it. You need to write this down correctly. With both men, she claimed to have used the chemicals Hydroxy-Methaburate and Tricozomine. The synergistic effects of both can incapacitate an individual and also be lethal."

He paused, raising his eyebrows. "Ma'am. How do you know so much about these chemicals? How would you know about the combined effects?"

"Detective, you can trust me. I'm an authority on the subject. I'm a retired chemistry professor and hold a Ph.D. in Chemistry."

"Oh, I understand now." He continued writing. Then he signaled a deputy.

Elizabeth appeared confused. "Detective. Have you arrested my Madison yet? I've been troubled by all..."

"No, ma'am. We have no reason to arrest her. After watching the video recording that she provided, we are placing you under arrest for assault and battery, with the intent to kill or do great bodily harm to your daughter. This officer will read you your rights and accompany you inside the ambulance to the hospital. You'll be needing that hand looked at first, and then you'll be taken down to the precinct to be processed."

Elizabeth sat up. "That's unacceptable! She tried to kill me!"

"That's not what the video evidence shows," he replied, nodding to the officer standing by. "Cuff her good hand to the gurney and be careful with the other."

Harrison hopped down as the officer stepped inside.

"I want to call my lawyer! Young man, don't touch me!"

He produced his handcuffs.

Harrison pursed his lips. "Yes, ma'am, noted. Elizabeth Sanders, you have the right to remain silent..."

Her protests and outrage drowned out his words. Unwilling to be placed under the control of another, she rolled over, attempting to cover her wrists.

Harrison finished reading her rights and rubbed his temples. "The sooner that you comply, the sooner we can get that hand properly treated."

She panicked as he signaled another officer for assistance. Her worst fears and phobias were coming to fruition. The feeling of helplessness, and loss of control, combined with her claustrophobia, sparked her 'fight or flight' instincts. She knew that resistance was futile, and there was nowhere to run. They carefully but forcefully cuffed her hand to the gurney, closed the doors, and drove off. The unimaginable began to smother her as she found herself in dire straits.

***

Two hours later, both women were treated, receiving stitches and antibiotics. Elizabeth was taken into the precinct for processing, while Madison rode with Detective Lopez back to the station to be interviewed. It was noon, and Madison was depleted. She closed her eyes and reclined, hoping to gain a brief respite along the way.

Lopez peeked at her. "So, how do you like Minneapolis? I've never been."

"It's nice. There's too much snow in the winter, but it's still beautiful," she said, looking out of her window.

"I've heard that. Where do you work?"

"Traxtonite. I transferred from the Seattle branch two years ago. I started working there after college. My son and I moved there for a new start. It wasn't the new beginning that I wished for."

"Where is he now?"

She paused. "He died three months after we moved there."

Lopez turned suddenly. "That's terrible, Madison. I'm sorry for your loss."

"Yes, it is. Thanks."

The following silence was uncomfortable for Lopez but appreciated by Madison.

"Ms. Sanders. Do you mind if I ask how he passed? I apologize. It's the detective in me."

Madison winced from her wounds. "Some guys at work thought that it would be funny to fill my tailpipe with snow, so my car wouldn't start. It ended up killing my son. His name was Elijah. One man is awaiting trial. The other man was killed in jail."

Lopez dipped his head, clearly upset by the news. "I pray that justice will be served. And now, you have to deal with this disturbing situation. You must be a powerful person." He glanced over at her. "Hang in there the best way you can. Don't give up."

They arrived at the station, and Lopez seated her inside an interview room, where he gave her time to complete an official statement. He left, coming back thirty minutes later to inspect it.

He sat across the table from her. "Ms. Sanders. May I call you Madison?"

"Yes. That's fine. Calling me Miss makes me feel old for some reason."

Lopez chuckled, then appeared serious. "I want to ask you a few questions that have come to light since the assault. The attack by your mother is not in question. We have enough video evidence before and after the incident to be confident in the arrest and charge her with felony assault with the intent to kill. That part is clear-cut. But your mother made some startling allegations against you, and that's what I want to discuss."

Madison sat up straight, crossing her arms. "Fine. What do you want to know?"

"Your mother stated that last night, she caught you sneaking into the house near midnight. After confronting you, she said that you confessed to killing a man named Tony Putnam at Green Lake. She claims that you poisoned him with chemicals." He looked at his notepad. "Hydroxy-Methaburate and Tricozomine. She also stated that he is the father of your son. My apologies, Madison, I meant to say, your dearly departed son." He bowed his head. "You should be aware that when I am told a crime has been committed, it is incumbent upon me to inquire as to the validity of those claims. To our knowledge, there's no evidence of any crime. I'd like you to confirm or deny these allegations, and please feel free to share whatever you will."

Madison's eyebrows raised in bewilderment. "Sir, the last time I saw Tony was seven years ago. As for him being my son's father, I don't know that to be true. There were others, and back then, I wasn't sure who his father was. My mother knows this and knows that Elijah's birth certificate lists the father as unknown. I don't know why she would say that I did something to Tony, anyway. He didn't do anything wrong to me. She's the one who hated him because he's black. My mother has serious issues, as you can tell. Those things that you mentioned, the Hyd...whatever you said. I have no idea what that is."

Lopez was attentive, scrutinizing her body language, and gleaning any possible inferences, then jotting them down. "Okay. She also mentioned that you used the same chemicals to kill your fiancé. Would you care to comment on that?"

Madison leaned on the table and covered her face but was unable to force her tears. So she used the tone of her voice to express pretension. She breathed faster. "It hasn't even been a full month since he drowned," she whimpered. "I still can't accept that he's gone—first my only child, then the man I loved. I've cried so much that I feel dead inside." She glared at him. "Have you ever felt like that? The feeling of being adrift. Empty. Have you ever lost one of your children? Your wife? Partner? Have you?"

He tossed the pen on the desk and leaned back, dropping his head. "I'm sorry, Madison. I'm sorry for everything that's happened to you." He looked up. "It may take a while, but just know that life will get better. I can tell that you're a survivor."

She sat upright with her hands on her lap. "Thank you, Mr. Lopez. I've had a hard time coping with my pain, and I've missed too much time from work because of it. That's why I reached out to my mother. I needed a loan, not much, just enough to get me through the month until I could get back on my feet. I asked her to wire the money, but she insisted that I drive across the damn country and visit her first. After a few days back home, she insisted that I move back and live with her. I couldn't do that. My mother has always been abusive. I'm not naïve, either. Look at my face."

"Yeah, she must have worked you over. She also said that you have had mental issues and required hospitalization. Is there any truth to that?"

"Yes, that is true. Growing up with an abusive mother like her is one thing, but add the pressure of getting pregnant in college and receiving no emotional or financial support from the father. Even though that's my fault for making bad decisions, I still had a nervous breakdown. I crumbled. But the woman who I call mother caused the most damage. There is no doubt in my mind."

"I understand completely. It appears that your mother may have some psychological issues herself. Those statements that she made to you before the physical altercation was troubling, however that part of the video may be inadmissible should we decide to request a search warrant for her premises. Judges are very particular. The recording was made without consent. But you are a firsthand witness of her confession, and you also mentioned the existence of possible corroborating evidence within the home, of which you have firsthand knowledge. Your signed statement regarding the events is the first step in expanding our investigation."

"Yes, everything is inside the house. I can let you inside to search around. You can come over tonight."

"Believe me, we appreciate your cooperation, but we can't do that. You're a guest in the home and can't authorize us to come inside to search the premises. Don't be too concerned. If we find a justification and a need, then we'll get a warrant. That won't be an issue. By the way, what was your fiancé's name?"

"Conor Gregory."

Lopez wrote it down and stood up. "Thank you, that'll be all for now." He looked at the clock. "Your mother should be getting arraigned later today, but the backlog has been heavy this week, so my guess is it will be in the morning."

"Then I need to get out of the house tonight?" she asked.

"That's up to you. If you do, then let us know where you will be staying. It depends on the bail amount determined by the Magistrate, but regardless, he'll issue an order of protection for you. It is her house, so I would plan on leaving by the morning. We'll make sure that you're not still there before she is released. Okay?"

"I guess. I don't have anywhere else to go." She picked at her short hair. "I have no family or friends here."

"You don't have anybody to help you? No one?"

"I'll think of something. Please let me know if she is released on bail before she comes home. I'm afraid to be in the same room with her."

Why did you run Brittany off? You deserve to be stranded. It's not her problem.

"We will, Madison. Trust me. I'll have an officer give you a ride to the house. Try and get some rest." He smiled and left.

Rest? Are you kidding me?

Lopez walked down the hall and met Harrison at the drink machine.

"What's it look like, buddy?" Lopez asked.

"Her attorney claims that she blacked out. She doesn't remember a thing."

They both laughed.

Harrison picked his teeth. "I'm not sure that her attorney explained his next course of action to her. When he requested an immediate psychological evaluation, she flew off the handle, shouting, "I'm not crazy!

I am mentally fit and quite stable." Man, she's nuts. I mean, she's refined and well-spoken, but coo-coo."

They left the building, got into their car, and Lopez drove out of the parking lot.

"Hey, let's try that new Mexican place. I heard it's pretty good," Harrison said.

"Alright. I'm curious. What else did our loving mother have to say? Any more cloak and dagger talk?"

"She kept insisting that we check for a body at Green Lake. She says his name is Tony. The last name starts with a P, Pullem, Portney?"

"Putnam," Lopez chimed.

"Yeah, that's it. I told her that we would keep our eyes open, and thanks for the tip. I'm betting that you want to request a search warrant for her daughter."

"For what? We don't have any reason. Momma's word doesn't mean squat. Her daughter nearly had me in tears in that room. The shit that she has endured is mindboggling. If she killed two grown men, then I'm Michael Jordan in disguise. Give me a fricking break."

Harrison laughed. "Like I said, coo-coo. Let's forget all that shit for a moment. Are you buying? It's your turn."

"I got it. Today, it's on me."

***

At 3 p.m., Elizabeth was moved from the city jail to the courthouse's basement to await her arraignment hearing, tentatively scheduled for 4 o'clock. Livid and out of sorts, she nervously rocked back and forth in the central holding cell, plotting. She knew that incriminating information inside her house had to be disposed of as soon as possible and was desperate to escape her confinement.

I don't belong here with these animals. They all need to be euthanized.

Her hatred for Madison was unfathomable, and the betrayal unforgivable.

How could she have done this to me? How? I should have done away with her long ago. My life would have been much easier. She's just like her father, weak and defiled.

At 3:10 p.m., correctional officers escorted her from the dank, drab, holding cell to the brightly lit courtroom. There she sat, along with a small group of offenders, each awaiting their bail orders.

***

At 3:18 p.m., Lopez and Harrison sat at their desks, participating in office banter with their coworkers, when the Deputy Chief walked over to them.

"Lopez, Harrison, contact dispatch and get over to Green Lake. We've got a D.O.A. Black male, mid-thirties. It looks like drowning. A fisherman called it in."

They glanced at each other and hustled out of the office.

They were met by the responding officers at 3:42 p.m. and led over to the corpse, pulled onto the shore.

"Can you believe this shit?" Harrison said as he turned the body over, searching for identification. He checked the stiff, waterlogged body for a wallet, finding it in the back pocket. He opened the tattered and saturated billfold and handed it to Lopez. "It's our man. It's Tony Putnam. Hot damn."

Lopez looked at his watch. "Shit! Let me make the call. We might be too late."

***

Elizabeth Sanders stood before the Magistrate Judge with her attorney as he formally informed her of the charges in the indictment and reviewed her bail conditions.

She looked at Elizabeth, then her attorney. "Does your client wish to enter a plea at this time as to the charges in the indictment?

"Yes. She will plead not guilty to each count," he replied.

"All right. A plea of not guilty is entered as to all counts of the indictment."

A clerk hurried into the courtroom and approached the lead prosecutor, whispering in his ear. His eyebrows raised.

The Judge looked at the prosecutor, perturbed. "Is there discovery?"

"There is discovery, which will be going to the defense shortly. Your Honor, there is another pressing matter relating to this defendant, which causes the prosecution to request a change to our bail petition formally. The prosecution has recently become aware of new information in a related investigation involving a potential homicide. The defendant, Elizabeth Sanders, claimed to have specific knowledge about and shared specific details with law enforcement of the alleged crime, such as the location and the identity of the deceased. Due to the nature of these recent events, the Assistant District Attorney is now seeking a search warrant for her premises to acquire additional information. The prosecution now requests that bail be denied and that the defendant be remanded into custody until the search warrant on her domicile is executed. The defense may petition the Court at a later date or appeal the decision per their prerogative. The alleged victim of the charges perpetrated within this current indictment, the defendant's daughter, Madison Sanders, was invited as a guest and currently resides in the home. Subsequently, we maintain our request for the no-contact order and ask that the daughter be granted ample time to leave the premises if needed. If it so pleases the Court."

The Judge listened to the defense counter-arguments while Elizabeth stood awestruck. Her hopes for freedom were rapidly deteriorating. The Magistrate decreed her order to deny bail and remanded her into custody with a trial date pending.

"Do something! Please? I can't go back there," Elizabeth whimpered to her attorney as they led her away. She was deflated, and her weakened legs nearly collapsed under the weight of her despair and the impending doom to follow.

***

Two hours later, Madison woke up from her nap. The officer dropped her off earlier at noon, and although she knew Elizabeth was in police custody, she was hesitant to enter the house. Earlier, she nervously stepped into the kitchen, but the sight of the smeared blood, and scattered eggs covering the floor, caused her stomach to erupt, and she vomited in the sink. Panting and spitting, she wiped her mouth and looked at the raw potatoes, which now turned brown. She hung her head and rinsed out the sink. Madison was starving but too exhausted to eat and stumbled into her room, collapsing on the bed.

After waking from her two-hour nap, she was still groggy and crawled out of bed to change clothes. Unable to shower due to her nerves, she used the bathroom, and while on the commode, she motivated herself to clean up the mess in the kitchen.

You've got to eat something, so get it over with. The sooner, the better.

She finished, and washed her hands, then headed to the kitchen.

The doorbell rang. It startled her, and she froze. It rang again, and she went to the door and looked out the peephole.

Oh my God! No!

What's wrong? Don't cry now, little girl. You knew this time would come. You could never get away with what you did.

She leaned against the front door as the bell rang for the third time before she opened it. It was Detectives Lopez and Harrison, accompanied by several others.

Lopez handed her the search warrant. "Madison, we apologize for disturbing you this late in the evening, but we have a warrant to search the premises. We will be here until late tonight, but I'm not sure exactly how long. If you don't mind stepping aside, we need to get started."

She had been lost in time, forgetting about their earlier discussion, and was relieved. She moved aside to let them pass and handed the warrant back. "I didn't realize that you would be here today. You surprised me."

"I see. We were also surprised today after discovering a body. Let's sit and talk for a minute. I need to share something with you."

They went into the living room, and she sat on the couch while Lopez sat in the recliner.

"No. Please don't sit there. I'm sorry, but that's my father's chair. If you don't mind."

Lopez jumped up and went over to the couch. "I apologize. We are here tonight because Tony Putnam's body was recovered this afternoon from Green Lake. Your mother had specific knowledge in advance of his discovery, and so an emergency search warrant was issued."

Madison's eyes bulged. "Tony Putnam is dead?"

"Yes, he appears to have drowned, but we don't believe that is the case. His autopsy and full toxicology are being expedited as we speak. We're interested to see if the particular chemicals that your mother mentioned are present. By tomorrow, we'll be certain of the cause of death and any contributing factors."

She hung her head. "Why is everybody in my life dying?" She looked at him. "Why?"

"We don't know yet. But where there's smoke, there's usually fire. We'll find the answers. I've never been directly involved with a case before that has such far-reaching implications as this one."

"I'd like to have answers too," she added.

"We are going to have your bedroom processed first, so you can close the door and have some privacy while we move throughout the residence."

"My room? Why do you need to search in there? Am I a suspect?"

Lopez held onto her last sentence. It was a red flag. Previously captivated by her sincerity and painful experiences, he empathized with her but now dreaded that he might be playing the fool. He knew that a victim or an innocent person never asks if they are a suspect. On a hunch, he redirected and chose another path.

"No, of course not. Our search warrant includes the entire premises which belong to Elizabeth Sanders. That includes every room and entire property. You are a guest and also a victim. She could have evidence hidden in your room, but you needn't worry."

"Oh, I wasn't worried. I was only asking a question, and now I understand."

"Good." He smiled. "Oh, there is something that you can do for me, which will help our investigation.'

"Yes, I'll do anything."

"Would you mind if we look at your phone? The timestamps, GPS positioning, yada, yada, and other data could help us in the case against your mother. We have the video, but you can never have enough evidence. These defense attorneys can be very slick."

Her neck muscles tightened, and the color drained from her face.

Now what, dummy? Yes, you'll do anything. You can't turn back now. Silly girl.

"Alright." She handed her phone to him. "When will I get it back. I need it."

He stood, signaled a forensics technician, and handed over the phone. "Do me a favor. Take this out to the van and clone it for me, please. She's going to need this back ASAP." He looked down at her. "He should bring it back within the hour. I need to get cracking. If you need me, just pull my coat tail."

"Okay."

He left, and she sat there, observing bustling house traffic while scouring the depths of her memory.

What's on your phone? Do you even remember?

You know they can track your location history. Silly girl.

I know! I made sure to leave my phone home last night.

Where?

Under my pillow!

Ha! Are you sure, dummy? Are you sure of anything anymore?

***

During the same time, back in Minneapolis, Detective Schultz finished his third beer while sitting on his couch, going through Don Carson's hard drives. There was nothing of interest to be gleaned besides a mix mash of pornography, client interviews, and junk. He connected the last hard disk, which appeared to be the newest of the lot. The data was partially corrupted, but there were a few remaining files to sort through. He checked the time. It was getting close to eight O'clock, and he needed to wrap up his unofficial assignment.

I'm not getting paid for this shit. Screw it! I'm off duty.

He clicked through the files, opening, assessing, and closing each one. He debated whether to drink another beer now or wait until he was finished and then shutting down for the night. Then he saw a folder with a name that teased his curiosity.

He clicked on a folder named Solex Vid backdoor 01 and explored the video footage.

Where is this? It looks vaguely familiar.

He got another beer and continued his probe. He reclined and chugged, searching his brain for the pesky recollection. He yawned, and stretched, then sat his beer and laptop on the coffee table. After looking at the dated folder, he arbitrarily played one of the videos. Within the first sixty seconds, a car pulls into the driveway across the street from the camera, and a woman steps out.

He enlarged the video.

Madison Sanders? Yeah! Now, I remember. That's her house. Wait. Hold on. That is her house!"

He thought about the case, remembering that no video footage had been available. He was convinced, recalling that he had done the canvassing and interviewed the neighbors. He placed the date of the initial investigation and searched for a video file that matched. He found it and pressed play. He forwarded past the midnight timestamp and resumed. He saw a figure walking up the driveway to the rear of the car. Gritting his teeth, he paused, rewound the segment, and zoomed in.

Schultz's eyes were fixated on the culprit with the video now enlarged, waiting for him to turn around and show his face.

Come on, Ron, smile for the camera. You piece of shit.

He reached for his beer as the figure turned around and knocked the bottle over.

"No way! Holy shit!"

He grabbed his head, staring at the screen, as he witnessed Conor creep down the driveway and into his truck. Schultz was in disbelief, stunned. Moments later, he realized the spilled mess that he had made.

He brought the laptop and hard drive to the kitchen table and replayed the clip several times.

He closed his eyes and slowed his breathing as he searched for links and answers to the torrent of questions that now flooded his mind. "Think Schultz, think. Put it together. Relax."

How the hell did Carson get this video? How could I have missed it?

He racked his brain about those past events and the principals involved.

Conor Gregory, Elijah Sanders, Terrance Roberts are all dead, and Ron Tatum is in jail. What's the common link?

He grabbed another beer from the fridge.

Is there a link between their deaths? No. There's no known link. The manner of death was unique to each victim.

He sipped.

The only initial link between all parties would be Madison Sanders, also victimized.

"Damn it! Come on, Alex!"

He was frustrated, knowing that there were more implications to this video footage, but could not pin anything down. He had hit the wall. Now, he had the burden of deciding what exactly to do with the footage. If divulged, the video posed a devastating threat for the prosecution in Ron Tatum's trial. But there was another problem. Since the hard drives were illegally confiscated, they couldn't be used as valid evidence in court. Any complicity admission would be foolish and cost him his job, with a felony conviction to follow. He wondered if this was only a copy and if the original still existed. He calculated the direction of the viewing angle and figured out where the house the camera was located.

Stop off there tomorrow morning before going to work and check it out. Talk to the homeowners and find out what's shaking. And don't break your ethics again! Not even for your partner.

Due to the unforgiving turn of events, he foresaw two outcomes. The homeowners would have the original video, which would go to the prosecution, and destroy their case, setting an innocent, although despicable, man free. That outcome would leave a smear on the department's reputation. All because of two bungling detectives who couldn't find their way out of a paper bag. Or the other conclusion would be that the homeowners wouldn't have a copy. In that case, Schultz would be in sole possession of the truth, illegally, and forced to live with his disgraceful and dishonorable secret while an innocent man rotted in prison. Honor and ethics were important to him. He wasn't perfect, but he strove to maintain his integrity at all costs. This time, he screwed up.

He finished his beer, copied the hard drive to his personal computer, and went to bed, knowing that tomorrow would be a critical day for him.

CHAPTER 18

The following morning in Seattle, the customarily subdued Criminal Investigations Division office had transformed into a bustling operations center overnight. The results of Tony Putnam's complete autopsy and comprehensive toxicology reports had returned, signifying the presence of Hydroxy-Methaburate and Tricozomine. The Underlying cause of death was poisoning, and the immediate cause of death was by drowning. The findings were a bombshell, and despite Elizabeth's attempt to incriminate Madison, she was now considered the primary suspect in his death.

Lopez and his team worked all night, uncovering mountains of incriminating evidence, including Elizabeth's supply of Hydroxy-Methaburate and Tricozomine. They quickly discovered her secret life through communications from several bogus email accounts and fake dating site profiles. Together with the discovery of several pre-paid cell phones, the horrific imagery of her crimes began to take shape. Lopez and Harrison recorded the names of the men who Elizabeth had first met online and subsequently communicated with her by phone before arranging dates. They became suspicious that there was never any more contact or communication between both parties after each initial meeting. These men needed to be contacted and interviewed.

Harrison began his online search on his laptop to locate the first individual's physical address and soon learned that he was deceased. He moved on to the next name and checked. Also, deceased. Harrison postured, scratching his head, thinking that he must have made a mistake. He picked another name. Then another. That's when he knew what Elizabeth was, and he called over Lopez to share his findings. The entire team left the house near midnight, and per investigative procedures, they did not disclose any evidence to Madison. She had neither the right nor the need to know.

Back at the precinct, the Chief called Lopez and Harrison to his office for the latest investigation update. They walked in and sat in front of his desk.

"I hope that your overtime hours yielded something spectacular. I've heard rumors since I stepped in the door. What exactly do you have?" The Chief asked bluntly, tapping his pen.

Lopez handed him a folder. "We found the identical chemicals inside the home, which are listed in Tony Putnam's toxicology report. Elizabeth Sanders had prior knowledge of the crime, citing the victim's name, location, and cause of death. She accuses her daughter of committing the murder. We've scoured cell phone data on every device located, and their GPS location history shows Elizabeth, and Madison, at home during the window of opportunity. That alone means nothing. The phones could have been left at the residence while the crime was being committed. However thin, the mother had more motive than the daughter, but both had equal opportunity. The mother may have never gotten over the alleged fact that her daughter was knocked up by a black guy, then deserted. As I said, the motive is thin."

The Chief stopped tapping. "So, both of them had access to these chemicals. Why choose the mother as a suspect over a scorned young woman?"

"I'm not one hundred percent at this point, but noting the mother's assault on her daughter and her professional knowledge of chemistry, I have to lean that way."

"True. I see your point."

Harrison was squirming in his seat, eager to be heard. "That's just the tip of the iceberg, Chief." He looked at Lopez, grinning. "Tell him."

Lopez frowned at the unnecessary prodding.

He dipped his head at Harrison. "Chief, we've found emails, four pre-paid cell phones, records, and texts between Elizabeth Sanders and seventeen middle-aged men, all married. The records show that each one agreed to meet with her. She made her initial contact through dating websites using fake profiles."

"So, what? The woman has an active sex life. There's no law against being lonely. What else do you have?"

Lopez shook his head. "All seventeen men are deceased."

The room went silent as the Chief processed the news, trying to contain himself.

He cocked his head. "Are you saying that we have a serial killer in custody?"

The detectives glanced at each other.

"Unless you have another scenario to suggest, that is our belief," Lopez replied.

Harrison scooted forward. "Chief, I've checked half of their autopsy reports, and they all are listed as dying from natural causes due to either respiratory failure or cardiac arrest. But when I compared their toxicology reports, they all had one thing in common; each victim had three unknown substances in their system at the time of death. It's too late to test those samples again for specificity, but we still have a load of incriminating and circumstantial evidence to connect her."

The Chief leaned back in his chair and resumed tapping. "Here's the plan. First, I'll contact the Attorney General and get him up to speed on the situation. I'm positive now that he will file charges against the mother for the 1st-degree murder of Putnam. Stay the course, and give me a daily morning and afternoon briefing. I'm busy, but I'm tracking this. Keep an eye on the daughter, and don't let her get lost. We might need to interview her again before mommy's trial date. As always, I have your backs, but keep it tight. I commend you both for a job well done so far. Let's bring it all in for the big win. You copy?"

Lopez raised his finger. "One more thing, Chief. Elizabeth Sanders alleges that her daughter used the same chemicals found in Tony Putnam to kill her fiancé, Conor Gregory, back in Minneapolis this month. I verified his obituary, and he did drown. According to the news archives, Madison Sanders with him at the time, and his death was ruled accidental. Last night, she willingly volunteered her phone to me during the search. I had it cloned and looked through it. I read her past texts and noticed that she was expecting a package."

The Chief stopped tapping. "Can you take a shortcut and get to the point?"

"Yes, sir, Chief, I'm almost there. Now, two things stood out to me. Oddly, her coworker and friend received that package, and Madison

Sanders arranged to receive it in their employer's parking lot on her day off. She had called out sick that day. Secondly, that was the same day that her fiancé drowned. I'd like to contact the Seattle P.D. and see if we can't get some information on that case. What was in that package? What did Mr. Gregory's autopsy and toxicology reveal? Are there any unspecified substances in the report? Are they aware of any of this information? I know that there is more. Will you sign off on this?"

The Chief scratched his chin, contemplating his options. "You may be on to something, Lopez, and we need to be thorough. Let's determine the status of the daughter once and for all. Whether she's in play or she's out, it's a loose end that needs to be tied up. Get me the lead detective's contact info that worked the Gregory case, and I'll arrange a conference call with him and his boss. I'll need one of you to be here to facilitate. There's no need to tie you both up. So, Lopez, it's you. I'll send you word after receiving confirmation."

"Thanks, Chief."

The two detectives left the office, bumping fists, and went to their desks.

Harrison strutted, wearing a smile. "I feel a shiny new commendation pinned to my chest. Now, where's that promotion?"

"Good luck with that. Don't count your chickens too soon. We're still in the third quarter."

"We can't lose. The Chief has our backs on this one. We are anointed for all intents and purposes."

"Yeah, but I'm not taking any chances. I don't have faith in this conference call. That friend of Madison, Brittany, is the one who received the package. She might be our back door if the boys in Minneapolis decide to guard their sandbox and won't cooperate."

"How so?" Harrison asked.

"I'll call her before noon today and try to work her with a delicate touch. Let's see what comes out. If she's holding anything, she might spill it. Who knows what could happen? Any slip or implication gives us standing to get a search warrant for Madison Sander's electronic data and hardware. We need to take a hard look at her online transactions and bank history. I have a strong hunch that Madison Sanders might be spending time in prison next to her mother. I want you to keep track of her today until the conference call, then bring her in for questioning. Have her wait in a room until it's over. Make sure that she doesn't try to skip out of the state while we aren't watching. That would complicate things in a major way."

"I'll head over to the house now. But good luck with her friend. Most chicks stick together like glue, and these two are friends. You're wasting your time, pal. I don't see why you're spending extra energy to chase this. We already got the mom, and she's the grand prize."

Lopez patted Harrison's back and detoured into an interview room. "Friends, you say? You need to listen to a tune by the R&B group, The O'Jays. They made a song called, Backstabbers. It explains the reasons why you're wrong. Trust me. I'm not wasting my time." He winked and closed the door.

***

Madison woke up late, riddled with angst. The search warrant was somewhat expected, but the process, traumatizing. Although the focus was collecting evidence from Elizabeth, Madison regretted relinquishing her cell phone, which justifiably sparked her paranoia.

It's over. You're going to jail. You deserve it! Silly girl.

I'm guilty! I know, I know!

She curled up on her father's recliner, covered with a blanket and cradling a steak knife. She imagined the incriminating evidence that her phone would provide, and in an attempt to distance herself from the outside world, she turned it off. Her stomach rumbled with hunger pangs, but she was too nervous to eat.

What's that noise?

She sprung out of the chair, clutching the knife, and ran across the house and into her mother's room, halting in the doorway. The place was quiet. She listened intently, looking around the displaced room before running inside the closet, and turning on the light. She stood alone, waiting, listening over the sound of her thudding heartbeat for the imaginative intruder. There was no one. To make sure, she marched throughout the house, checking every closet and underneath the beds, before peeping through the window blinds. Feeling temporarily placated, she moved back to the recliner and covered herself.

I miss you, Brittany. I'm sorry. I'm sorry.

You complain but won't call her. How dumb.

No. I can't, not after what I did to her. She loved me, and I used her!

Yes, you did. That was stupid. You don't deserve to be her friend. Silly girl.

The minutes passed, and her agitation grew, compelling her to peep out of each window at fifteen-minute intervals. She wanted to catch any intruders before they were able to gain entry. Although aware of the irrationality of her behavior, the obsession was overpowering. However, when she noticed that Detective Harrison was parked across the street, she began to trust the dominant inner voice.

You were right. I am going to jail. You knew it. You seem to know everything.

Then listen to me, dummy, and do what I say.

***

It was five minutes until lunch, and Brittany put her computer to sleep as her cell phone rang. She answered the unrecognized caller.

"Hello?"

"Hello, may I speak with Mrs. Brittany Lewis-Daniels?"

"Yes, this is she."

"Ma'am, this is Detective Arturo Lopez from the Seattle Police Department. I work for the Major Crimes Unit, Criminal Investigations Division. If possible, I'd like to have a few minutes of your time and ask you few questions about an ongoing investigation here in Seattle. Is that alright with you?"

"Yes, I have a few minutes. Seattle, you say? What is this about?"

"Thank you. Mrs. Brittany Lewis-Daniels, do I have your consent to record our conversation?"

"Okay. Yes."

"Thank you. Do you know Madison Sanders?"

"Yes, I do."

"Did she contact you last month and ask you to receive a package for her?"

"Yes, she did."

"Did you ultimately receive that package last month and personally transfer it to her possession?"

"Yes."

"Do you know as to the contents of that package?"

"I don't know for sure, but I was told that it was cologne for her fiancé. A surprise present."

"Did Madison Sanders tell you that? Did she mention anything else?"

"Yes, that's what she told me. She didn't say anything else."

"Did you happen to keep the packaging invoice for that package? If not, do you remember who the sender was?"

"No, I didn't keep the invoice, and I didn't look to see who shipped it. I received the package and gave it to her. I have no idea where it was purchased from either."

"Did Madison Sanders ever happen to mention the subject of chemicals at any time during your relationship?"

"No. What's this about? Is Madison alright? Is Madison back in Seattle?"

"Ms. Sanders is fine. This inquiry is part of an ongoing investigation, and I appreciate your cooperation. I have one more question, and we'll be finished. During your communications with Madison Sanders, has she said or done anything which you would consider to be out of the ordinary?"

"No, she didn't, now please tell me what's going on with Madison."

"Ma'am, do you consider Madison to be a good friend?"

"Yes, she's my best friend."

"Then I assume that since you two are best friends, you have recently spoken to her."

Brittany sighed.

"No, we haven't spoken in over a week."

"Why is that?"

"We just haven't. There's no particular reason, but I will be calling her shortly. I don't intend to be rude, but is that all? I have other obligations waiting, sir."

"Yes, ma'am, that's all I have for now. I thank you for your time."

Brittany's hands trembled, and she ended the call.

My God! Madison, what is going on with you?

Her relationship with Madison had been fractured, but it wasn't broken. The anger once harbored was now replaced with a deep concern for her best friend's wellbeing. She grabbed her lunch belongings and stopped in the doorway to send a text message.

Hey Madison, I hope all is well. I miss you. I'm here for you anytime, so please call me when you get a chance. You know that I love you. XO.

Send.

***

The color left Elizabeth's face as she hung up the phone with her attorney, and the correctional officer led her away. The new charges filed against her by the prosecution for Tony Putnam's death, and the discovery of evidence showing her complicity in the deaths of multiple men, was damning. She saw no recourse, or avenue, leading to exoneration, and resigned herself to defeat.

Handcuffed, the officer escorted her to the assigned pod, where she was released, and walked into her cell. Sitting on her shabby six-inch mattress, she closed her eyes, marinating in the darkness of her mind, but was unable to escape the constant racket from her new community. It was futile. Even the night before, intermittent uproars kept her from sleeping only a few hours. Her greatest torment was the prison protocol of asking the guards for everything that she wanted or needed to do. She could not tolerate nor accept being relegated to child status. It was an unbearable living hell, with no escape, and her pride fizzled with each passing moment. She felt publicly and professionally humiliated.

Without notice, three unknown females entered her cell. Elizabeth looked straight ahead without making eye contact.

The most formidable of the three loomed over her. "Look at me. I said, look at me bitch!"

Elizabeth peeked.

"We know who you are, rich bitch. This is what's gonna happen." The big-boned woman dropped a piece of paper onto Elizabeth's lap. "The first of every month, you're gonna have your people deposit $400 into the commissary account number written on that paper. The money pays your protection for that month. If you don't pay, everyone in this pod will whip your ass daily, including us three. That's every day, all day. If you try to be smart and tell the staff, then you're gonna still get the daily ass beatings and something else to go with them. You can sit there and look dignified if you want to. But in the end, you'll just be looking stupid. Do you understand me, bitch?"

Elizabeth nodded. "Yes, I understand." She looked at the paper and folded it. "I'll call my attorney tomorrow and tell him to make the necessary deposits. But I need some things today."

The woman crossed her arms. "Alright, but we better see that deposit tomorrow, or that's your ass. What do you want?"

"I need everything needed to write a letter and the stamps to mail it. I also need a small razor blade or some sort of cutting instrument."

"Cutting instrument? What the hell? The letter shit, we got that. You don't need any kind of blade. We'll be protecting you."

Elizabeth pursed her lips. "I told you what I want. If you don't give it to me, then I'll ask the others around here. Whoever gives me what I want gets the privilege of protecting me."

The woman drew back to slap her, and Elizabeth shrunk back, causing the group to laugh.

One of them jeered. "Look at her scary ass! You don't need to beat her yet. She's gonna pay. Give her what she wants."

The woman looked around, grinning, and then back to Elizabeth. "Alright, we'll get the shit. But that's extra. Tell your attorney to make the first deposit of $550. Anything else you want?"

"No, thank you. The deposit will be made tomorrow."

"It damn sure better be."

They left the cell, and Elizabeth tossed the paper aside, shivering with her arms crossed.

Madison, you dummy. One day there will be a reckoning. I promise you, even from beyond my grave. Silly girl.

***

At 2:15 p.m., the Chief sent word to Lopez, informing him that the conference call was scheduled for 3:00 p.m. with Assistant Attorney General Joseph Angelletti and homicide Detectives Olson and Schultz. Lopez phoned Harrison, telling him to bring Madison into the precinct, and hold her for questioning. For Lopez, this was now the pivotal moment of truth. Disappointed that Brittany's loyalty held fast, he knew that the prospective door of entry was currently closed and locked. Although frustrated, he remained optimistic.

***

Alex Schultz worked at his desk near the end of his shift when he got word from Olson. There was a special conference call scheduled in Angelletti's office at 5:00 p.m., and his presence was requested.

Great. Something always comes up when it's time to leave work.

He hustled over to the Assistant Attorney General's office and met Olson inside. Angelletti was on another phone call, so Olson patiently waited.

Schultz tapped Olson on the shoulder and whispered, "What's this about? I had plans tonight. How long will it take?"

"Our girl, Madison Sanders, really gets around. She was back in her hometown of Seattle visiting family when her mother attempted to kill her. Go figure that one out. Anyway, her mother swears that Madison killed Conor Gregory."

"What? How?"

"I'm not positive, but by some sort of chemical poisoning. Angelletti said they want information about his toxicology. They want to verify if he had any unspecified substances in his system at the time of death."

Schultz shook his head. "No way. I do not believe this."

Olson smirked and leaned closer. "I know. They are chasing their tales. Why would she kill her fiancé? She had no motive. We've decided to shut them out. Our prosecutors don't need any more surprises or more complications than they already have."

Schultz ran his fingers through his hair. "I need to speak to you outside, Roger."

"They'll be calling any minute. Just hold off."

"No, Roger, right now."

Schultz stepped out of the office, followed by Olson.

"Hurry up, Alex. Damn."

"Roger, we screwed up. I was debating when to tell you this, man, but Ron Tatum is innocent."

Olson's face was twisted. "What the hell did you say?"

"I found video surveillance footage last night showing Conor Gregory committing the crime. It's all there, packing the fricking tailpipe and everything. The footage was from the neighbor's camera across the street, mounted in their backyard. I went there this morning and interviewed one of the homeowners. She told me that any footage from that camera was stored on her laptop. She sold that laptop to Madison Sanders not too long ago."

Olson pulled him to the side of the door. "Listen to me. I don't know where you're planning on going with this, but I'm telling you to stand down. We're about to have this conference call, and Angelletti has already decided our course of action, so keep your mouth shut."

Schultz pulled away. "Stand down, my ass. We need to take responsibility for this mess. From the beginning, we were slack with everything. We fumbled the processing of her car. We missed the backyard camera. We didn't dig deeper with his toxicology and didn't have the unknown substances tested either. It's no coincidence that they are asking about the same thing. Roger. Partner. Let's do the right thing."

Olson pointed his finger. "No, Detective Schultz. You need to take responsibility for your failures and your crimes."

"Crimes? What the F...?"

"How did you gain access to this alleged video surveillance?"

Schultz's nostrils flared. "You know exactly how. You told me to make a copy and..."

"That's a lie. I never told you any such thing nor advised you to break any procedure and commit a crime. You did that by your own volition, and yes, you fumbled the processing of her car. That's right, and you also failed to detect the location of that camera. Shit, Alex, you're even the one who conducted the neighbors' interview. This is all on you." Olson took a breather and looked around. "Alex. I'm not the enemy here, but if you want to go in there and embarrass the Assistant Attorney General, the department, and destroy the prosecution's case against Ron Tatum, then go for it. Just understand that your career will be over, and you'll also incriminate yourself. And for what? That video would be inadmissible as evidence anyway, and you know that. We can't give Seattle PD an inch, and I'm not going to let your screwup keep me from making Lieutenant."

Schultz's eyes glazed over, knowing that his senior partner spoke the truth. Whether he agreed with Olson or not, the die was cast. He raised his head, buttoned his jacket, and faced the door.

Olson stood beside him, patting his back. "I like you, Alex. We like you. What you do here today, whether wise or stupid, won't ever be forgotten. Remember that."

They walked inside as Angelletti answered the call, and the conference began. After the introductions and formalities, Lopez discussed the appeal's scope and reasons before summarily presenting his request.

"Mr. Angelletti, in light of the recent allegations, at a minimum, would you consider petitioning the Court for an electronic search warrant of Madison Sanders banking transactions, purchases, and online browsing history?"

Olson looked at Angelletti, who winked. "I will defer to the experience of the Lead Detective on the case. If he feels that the potential for evidence has standing, or can provide additional evidence, or findings that warrant such measures, then I will concede."

Olson stood up, pocketing his hands. "Hello, Detective Lopez, Detective Olson here. I'm going to be honest with you. I think the current direction of your investigation is skewed. You're missing motive right out of the gate. The allegations you cite come from a woman charged with the attempted murder of her daughter and the murder of another man. It seems unreasonable to pursue this course of investigation. My recommendation to the Assistant Attorney General is not to proceed. I don't intend to sound disrespectful, but I can't believe that you guys are making this request."

Schultz rolled his eyes, and Angelletti noticed. "Detective Schultz, is there anything that you would like to add?"

"No, sir. Detective Olson and I share the same sentiments."

Olson turned to him and smiled.

Lopez made one last attempt. "We respect your decision. Are you willing to at least tell us if there were any unspecified substances within Conor Gregory's toxicology report? That information could provide us a path to seek a search warrant on our end. We would certainly be grateful."

Angelletti raised his eyebrows and glanced at Olson, who squinted in return.

Angelletti leaned toward the intercom. "Sure, we can share that. He had two unspecified substances in his bloodstream at the time of death. They were deemed a non-contributory factor in his autopsy report. I'm not sure how that helps you. There are no blood samples to be tested, having expired weeks ago, and I'm sure that they have been disposed of properly. Well, if that's all, gentlemen, we have investigations to conduct. We're glad to have been of some help to you." He ended the call and stood up. "Thanks for coming down here, guys. Good job."

"Anytime, Joe," Olson replied as the two walked away.

"Roger, stay behind. I've got some exciting news to share with you about the future."

Schultz left Olson behind, closed the door, and headed to his car.

His professional pride was injured, and he felt the sting along with resentment of marginalization. But the deepest wound was to his shattered courage, and it bled profusely. Regardless of the consequences, he still had a clear choice to make to receive redemption. He chose the easy route—the path of the coward.

Alex, you're not hot shit! You're just another punk ass, crooked cop!

He taunted himself, allowing his conscience to exercise its form of psychological self-deprecation while still being appreciative that he had any conscience at all. He pounded the steering wheel in repentance and drove home.

***

An uneasy calm followed the end call as Lopez looked at the Chief.

"Chief, that confirms our suspicions about the toxicology. That should be enough to petition for a warrant and get at those records. I have Madison Sanders on hold for questioning. Do you want me to make the call?"

"There won't be any call. Consider this loose end to be tied up. Disengage from the Sanders girl and continue with the mother."

"But Chief, I think..."

"I don't care what you think, Lopez. Why are you so damn greedy? There's no promotion coming up. You already have enough food on your plate. You should be thanking that young lady, and actually, the mayor should give her a key to the city. She led us to the capture of a serial killer! But wait, she did that without getting paid, which is more than I can say for you. She turned in her mother! No, the department and the people owe her a debt of gratitude. Let's start by releasing her immediately and apologizing to her for any inconvenience. There won't be any more discussion about Madison Sanders. End of story."

He motioned toward the door, and Lopez left, discouraged.

Game over, Lopez. Suck it up and move on.

Harrison was leaning against the wall in the hallway, wearing a smirk. "You don't look thrilled."

"Cut her loose. Seattle shut us down. Tell her that we made a mistake. It was a misunderstanding. Let her know that she's not a person of interest."

Harrison frowned, crossing his arms. "So, I have to apologize for you?" He laughed. "You're something else, amigo."

"Just do it, please, and give her a ride home, if you don't mind. The Chief jumped ship and then talked shit. I need to get some fresh air."

"Wow. You did get your ass chapped, buddy. Don't let it get you down. I'll take care of her."

"Thanks, Rick." Lopez sauntered off, and Harrison went to inform Madison of the good news.

***

Madison sat quietly in the interview room. She resigned herself to the inevitable fate of life in prison. Her paranoia had come to fruition, depleting any fear and bringing her into the stark reality of the present. She was weak and spent, her mind adrift.

Why else would they have you here? I told you. I told you!

I deserve it. I'm guilty.

That's true. You are!

The door opened, and Harrison walked inside.

"Ms. Sanders, I apologize. There was a misunderstanding, and you should have never been brought in for questioning. I'll give you a ride home now. I'm sorry to have ruined your day."

She stared at him.

"Ms. Sanders, are you alright? I understand that you're upset. Again, we apologize for the mistake."

She stood up and walked past him, and he followed her out.

During the ride home, Harrison kept quiet, deciding against small talk. He saw the shell of a once vibrant young woman sitting next to him and understood the emotional trauma that had been inflicted on her. He encountered the same scenario daily, and as with any other victim, held reverent sympathy for them all. He dropped her off, and she went inside, heading for the bathroom. She stripped off her clothes and show-ered without any apprehension as the certainty of her freedom became apparent. As the steaming water inflamed her skin, turning it red, there was no excitement. She felt numb.

Don't get your hopes up, dummy. They'll be back. You'll see. They're playing games with you!

She changed clothes and went into the dining room where Elizabeth kept her liquor reserved for those rare guests who indulged. She looked through the cellarette, grabbed a bottle of Cognac, and went into her room. Sitting in silence, she broke the seal and swigged on the bottle. The sweet liquor burned, causing her to cough, but she kept on gulping anyway.

Give it up. Stop fighting! There's no reason to live! You have nothing to prove. Look. Go and see what Mother has left in the lab. The police didn't take everything. I'm sure you can find something to end your pain.

Within ten minutes, the bottle was half empty, and without any food in her stomach, she quickly began to fade. She guzzled again and began to waver as alcohol dripped from her chin. Within thirty minutes, the bottle slipped from her hand, and she passed out on her bed.

***

That night, a few minutes before lights out, Elizabeth dropped a letter into the outgoing mail slot and hobbled back to her cell. The issued footwear aggravated her plantar fasciitis, and the concrete floors only added to her discomfort. She eased past her cellmate, who was reading a magazine on the bottom bunk, and prepared for the climb to the top.

"Watch your goddamn feet," she snapped as Elizabeth groaned, pulling herself up and over. She rolled onto her back and gazed up.

At once, all the individual cell lights flickered off, signaling night chatter throughout the pod. Elizabeth waited for her cellmate to fall asleep, and, within the hour, she heard her snoring.

She rolled onto her side, lifted the pillow, removed the razor blade beneath, and inspected it.

It's long enough. Sharp. It will do fine.

She rolled flat on her back and covered her entire body with a blanket. She turned her head to the right, probing the side of her throat with her fingers to find her pulse.

There you are. Now, take me home.

She mustered her strength, and with one quick motion, drove the blade through the tissue, partially severing her Carotid artery. Reflexively, she retracted her hand as the spurting blood beat against the wool blanket covering her. The clamor within the pod became faint, and the rhythmic snoring of her cellmate ceased. Within minutes, Elizabeth Sanders was no more.

***

11:30 a.m. the following day, Madison woke to the sound of the doorbell. Hungover, dehydrated and hungry, she rubbed her eyes and sat on the edge of the bed. The bell rang again, so she went to the door and looked through the peephole. The man standing outside wore a suit and carried a briefcase. She opened the door.

"Hello, Madison. My name is William Devall. We were never formally introduced, but I was your mother's attorney. First, please accept my condolences on the loss of your mother. This was a shock to all of us. If there is..."

"What are you talking about?"

He appeared puzzled. "Oh my." He exhaled. "I assumed that you had been informed. I'm very sorry."

"Is my mother dead?"

He sighed. "Yes, I'm afraid that she is. She died last night, and they discovered her this morning inside her cell."

"I don't believe it. What's this really about? Are you trying to play mind games with me?"

"Absolutely not, Ms. Sanders. Your mother is deceased."

"How? Tell me."

"It wouldn't be proper for me to elaborate. I shouldn't have assumed that..."

"Tell me how she died. Please."

"I'm not certain, but I believe it was by suicide. The prison chaplain or Seattle homicide should have contacted you by now. Has anyone called you?"

"I just woke up. I don't know where my phone is." She squinted at him. "Are you sure? She's dead?"

He nodded. "Yes."

She struggled with her emotions, the new, the old, and the unfamiliar, then began to shut the door.

"Wait, Ms. Sanders," he exclaimed. "I need to inform you of something."

She stopped to listen.

"Your mother passed away without having a will, despite my advice to draft one." He handed her his business card. "This isn't the time for a detailed discussion about the matter. You need to grieve for your loss, but you should be aware that you are the next of kin. I don't anticipate that a third party will protest her estate, so when you are ready to proceed to probate, I want you to know that I am ready to assist you."

Madison was confused. Her mind was still foggy from the overload of mind-boggling information, but her feelings remained dormant.

"I don't understand what you want from me."

"Ms. Sanders, your mother's assets and estate are substantial. She was also a woman who did not believe in debt of any kind, and to my knowledge from our past conversations, she had no creditors. You are her only surviving child and next of kin. You are her only heir. I believe that we can have her entire case settled within seven months if we proceed directly."

"I don't care about her money."

He stepped forward. "I'm not sure that you understand the gravity of the situation. Conservatively speaking, I would estimate your mother's net worth to be upwards of $750,000, and that money belongs to you, not the government or the courts. You have my card, and whenever you're ready and feel comfortable, then please call me. Again, my sincere condolences for your loss."

He left, and she closed the door.

You should be happy she's dead. What's wrong with you?

I know, but I'm not. She was my mother. Why did she hate me? Why did she kill my daddy? I want to hate her! I thought I did. But I don't. I can't!

She wept, but not for Elizabeth. She cried for the mother that she never honestly had and for the fundamental love denied her as a daughter.

I don't deserve to be loved! That's why everybody left me. It's me!

I told you to look in Mother's lab. Your answer lies in one of those vials. You're right. Nobody loves you. Silly girl.

She covered her ears, screaming, and ran to her father's recliner.

Don't dare me, or I'll do it!

I don't believe you. You're all talk. No action. I know you. You're too dumb to carry it out.

She curled up beneath the blanket, fighting the destructive impulses within her mind.

Please, God, help me! I just want to be loved! That's all I ask.

She squirmed in the chair as a rigid object pressed against her ribs. She reached for it. It was her phone. She thought of Brittany, longing to see her image one last time. She pressed the power button.

She can't save you! You know what you need to do. Get to it!

Shut up! She's my friend. She loves me.

No, she was your friend until she found out that you were a murderer. She doesn't care about you. She's forgotten that you even exist. Looking at her photo won't change anything. Silly girl.

The phone screen brightened beneath the blanket, and she focused through her watery eyes. There was one new message.

Hey Madison, I hope all is well. I miss you. I'm here for you anytime, so please call me when you get a chance. You know that I love you. XO.

Madison wailed, "I love you too!"

Shaking and unable to contain herself, her unsteady fingers trembled as she called and waited.

"Madison."

Madison blubbered and was barely coherent. "Brittany, I need you. I need you so bad. I'm sorry. I'm so sorry for everything that I did. Please forgive me. I need your help."

"Madison, I'm here; it's alright. Calm down, and don't apologize. There's no need. All that mess is in the past. Tell me what you need me to do."

Madison sniffled and wiped her eyes. "Just talk to me and don't hang up. Please, don't hang up on me."

"Of course I won't. Are you in any legal trouble?"

"No. Not anymore."

Brittany exhaled. "Good. A detective called me yesterday from Seattle asking questions about the package that you had delivered. I didn't tell him anything that would get you into trouble. I want you to know that. I would never do that to you."

Madison fought back her tears. "You didn't have to do that, but you did. I love you, Britt. Thank you, thank you."

"Madison, I want you to know something. I understand. Do you hear me? I might disagree, but I understand. I'll always forgive you. Whatever you did in the past is between you and God."

"I know it is. I'm sorry for everything that I've done. But I couldn't stop myself, and I don't understand why."

"You need to get help. You can't avoid it anymore. When are you coming back? I had no idea that you had even left the state."

"I'm going to get help. You're right. I'll stop denying the truth. I can't hide what's inside anymore. I've got to get it out of me somehow."

"You can do it, and I'll be with you every step. How has your mother been treating you?"

Madison hesitated. "I found out just now that she committed suicide last night while in jail."

"Suicide? Jail? What in the world happened? Wait. I'm sorry. You don't have to tell me right now. You just found out about it, sweetie."

"Britt, so much has happened that you don't know. I wanted so badly to talk to you. I'll explain everything later when you can talk. I know that you're working. At the moment, I am flat broke and about to get fired if I don't get back home soon."

"We can fix that right now. Tell me how much money you need me to send."

"Oh my God, thank you! I won't need much. Let me figure it out, and I'll tell you when we talk later. I need to get out of here as fast as I can."

"Where are you staying now? At your mother's house?"

"Yes."

"I can wire the money to you tonight." Brittany paused. "I'm just curious. Did your mother leave a will?"

"No, she didn't. Her attorney came to the house earlier and told me. He gave me his card and said that he would represent me in probate court or something. I'm the next of kin. Honestly, I don't want anything from her. I'd like to keep a few things, my dad's belongings and some things from my room. But I don't need anything of hers. I don't want it."

"Be quiet. That's foolish talk, Madison. Everything belongs to you: any life insurance, money, property, or whatever. You can always sell what you decide not to keep. I know that you and your mother weren't close, but you deserve this. Everything that has happened is a tragedy, but this part of it is a blessing for you. Don't miss out. I want you to think about it. That's all, just take your time and think."

"I will." She stood up and dropped the blanket. "I feel so much better after talking to you. You have no idea. I feel like a new person."

"That's what I'm here for."

"I'll let you go for now. Call me when you get home. Okay?"

"Yep. Talk to you soon, bye."

The call ended, and Madison waited quietly, listening for the voice.

Silence.

You were wrong! Brittany does love me. Why are you so quiet now? Don't you have something mean to say?

Silence.

You wanted me to hurt myself. But I won't. What do you have to say about that?

Silence.

"Speak! Say something!" she screamed.

Silence.

"Then stay the hell out of my mind. You're not welcome ever again. I'm free. Do you hear me? I'm free!"

She marched throughout the house as tears streamed down her face, opening the curtains and raising every window blind, allowing the light to enter. Then she opened the front door.

This is a fresh beginning, Maddy. Focus on constructive thoughts and positive energy. You can do it. You can make it on your own. Live! Live and never kill again!

She stepped outside into the majestic sunlight, closed her eyes, and spread her arms wide. In her heart, she believed that Elijah was smiling down on her, and, with that conviction in mind, she inhaled the first breath of her new life.

EPILOGUE

One year and two months had passed since the funeral for Elizabeth Sanders. Although her obituary was published in the local newspaper, few mourners attended, including Madison. She refused to go and instead went back to her home in Minnesota, but not before retaining the services of her mother's former attorney, William Devall, Esq. He represented Madison's interests in Probate Court while she returned to work at Traxtonite and reassembled the broken pottery of her life. The process of rehabilitating herself from the trauma that she had incurred, and dispensed to others, became a daily journey of adjustment and self-introspection.

It took months to break herself free from the cloud of paranoia overshadowing her mind, but an announcement from Brittany breathed new life into her tortured soul when she announced that she was pregnant. Madison rejoiced with her best friend after hearing the news, and after the birth of a healthy 9 lb. baby boy, Brittany asked her to become his Godmother. Madison nearly collapsed in tears from the unexpected honor, believing herself unworthy and unfit to accept the obligation. Brittany convinced her otherwise and encouraged her to undertake the responsibility.

"Madison, I don't know anyone else outside of my immediate family who would treat my child as if he were their own, except for you. Now, you have one son in heaven and another son on earth. I trust you. We are family."

That moment propelled Madison over the threshold of despair and into a newfound psychological freedom. Within the same month, Madison received news of the Probate Court's decree from her mother's estate proceedings which awarded her money and assets totaling $763,300. Without hesitation, she decided to sell the family home in Seattle and purchased a small cottage within a few hundred yards of the Elk River and Orono Lake. She decided to set a new course for her life and resigned from Traxtonite, taking a year-long sabbatical.

She wanted everything old to pass away and intended to recreate herself into the person she wanted to become. She contemplated a new career field, but not vigorously. Instead, she took her time. Madison now had time to decompress, so she purchased a camera and completed two college courses on photography. While she perused her career options, she spent most of her time riding throughout the countryside, finding scenic reminders of how beautiful the natural world stood, alone, unapologetic. Majestic.

***

Ron Tatum was released from jail before his jury trial began. To his astonishment, a video was sent to a local news outlet by an anonymous source which severely compromised the prosecution's case against him. Rather than argue against the potential evidence against him, the District Attorney dropped all charges against him. Ron Tatum was freed. But it was too little and too late. The damage to his life and reputation had been done. His wife, Kathy, had divorced him, retaining the majority of their property and the sole custody of their children.

He moved back to Ohio and lived with his brother. Unable to fully support himself independently due to his alimony and child support obligations, he was fortunate to gain a management position at a local Express Oil Change shop in town. Ron spent most of his nights with his brother and friends in the front yard of their mobile home, drinking beer around a burning barrel and listening to 70's classic Rock and Roll. His daily struggle was to put his ordeal behind him and look toward the future. It was a futile struggle, and he always returned to his primary fantasy, strangling the person who caused it all. As time allowed, he silently stalked Madison on social media, remembering the time when she was absent from it all.

He looked at every new photograph that she posted online and despised every positive comment that she received.

Having a good time, eh? I see that life is treating you well. Cool. Enjoy it while it lasts, slut. Karma is a bitch. Just like you.

***

It was the day that 40-year-old Max Himmel had been waiting for; his release from the King County Jail in Washington state and sitting on his front porch. After serving fourteen months for an illegal weapons possession charge, he was ready to hit the streets and get back to earning his living. He didn't believe in Karma, or God, or anything that he couldn't see, touch or taste. He chalked up his last arrest as a 'fluke' which could have happened to anyone, and it just so happened to be him.

"Bring me the box," he said to his 20-year-old girlfriend sitting beside him. She sprung out of her chair and hustled inside, returning with a cardboard box.

His girlfriend sat nervously beside him. "I did just what you said. I put every letter in there and ain't opened nothing."

He grunted and opened the box, sorting the past years' worth of mail. He shuffled through the pile, dropping each letter to the floor of the porch beside him, then stopped, holding one letter up to read. He grinned, opened it, and read.

Dear Nephew,

I am not long for this world, but I want to thank you for your tears of loyalty. You are the son that I never had, regretfully so. You now know that I am confined and pending charges of a most severe nature by the return address. You know me and understand that I cannot and will not allow myself to be subjected to this cruel and heartless future. So, with my most profound sympathies, I bid you farewell. I've done everything humanly possible to care for you since your mother's death, and I'm sure that sweet Emily is looking down from heaven with satisfaction.

My daughter has betrayed me and is the solitary source of my demise. I discovered recently that she has 'The Purpose.' I hoped that in time I would be able to develop this gift within her, and at the correct time, we all would be able to come together and exercise our gifts together. I enter my eternal rest, assured, knowing, expecting, that you will honor my memory and do what needs to be done. Goodbye.

Love, Aunt Elizabeth.

He stood up slowly and leaned over the porch railing in disbelief. He grieved profoundly but was unable to shed a tear. Instead, he searched his memories about the night he was arrested. He was on one of his many 'missions' with Aunt Elizabeth, parked only fifty yards from their next victim's vehicle when a police cruiser pulled up beside him. It didn't take long before they rousted him, found his unlicensed .38 caliber revolver, and placed him under arrest. That had never happened before while he maintained his post as the Vanguard for his beloved aunt. He shadowed her while she dispatched her victims and was an insurance policy if they overpowered her instead or tried to escape. This scenario rarely occurred throughout the years, but she compensated him regardless. Now that a large portion of his cash flow was gone, evaporating into thin air, he was left to survive off of his small-scale methamphetamine distribution and whatever else came down the pike.

That's why Auntie didn't bail me out. She must have been locked up, too. What the fuck! She wouldn't have done this to you, Aunt Elizabeth, if you had let me meet her again as I asked! I hadn't seen her since before I was sent off to Juvenile Corrections. You should have listened to me, Auntie! Goddammit!

He stormed into the house and sat down at his computer, searching for his dear aunt's obituary. He read it and then covered his face, trying to restrain the fury growing inside. He searched for Madison Sanders and found her social media results, enlarging the most recent posted photo. He turned red, stood, and flung the chair across the room, and stared at Madison's smiling photo.

Madison. Cousin. I'm going to find you and peel your skin like a fucking onion. For my momma and yours. I promise.

The End

I thank you for reading **Can't Hide What's Inside**, the first book of the Madison Sanders Trilogy. I hope that you enjoyed this novel! If you would like to leave an honest review, please take a minute of your time to review the book on Amazon. The following link will take you directly to the **Can't Hide What's Inside** product page where you can leave your review: Can't Hide What's Inside - Amazon Review

Other novels by C.J. Heigelmann: **Crooked Fences** (Contemporary Fiction). You can view the product and description here on Amazon/ Kindle: Crooked Fences

Other novels by C.J. Heigelmann: **An Uncommon Folk Rhapsody** (Historical Fiction). You can view the product and description here on Amazon/Kindle: An Uncommon Folk Rhapsody

If you would like to sign up for my email list (we never spam) to receive news on other novels by C.J. Heigelmann, free book giveaways, book signings and new releases sign up here:MustReadCJ.com

Made in United States
Troutdale, OR
03/15/2024

18483191R00226